W9-BGJ-108

INSPIRED BY A TRUE STORY

A Novel

Fearless

PAULA DÁIL

ISBN: 978-1-957723-39-6 (hard cover)
978-1-957723-40-2 (soft cover)

Edited by: Karli Jackson and Amy Ashby

Published by Warren Publishing
Charlotte, NC
www.warrenpublishing.net
Printed in the United States

To my treadmill and to our dog, Stanley Horace Archie Geronimo George, AKA SHAGG, with enormous thanks for all the useful ideas that have emerged during the thousands of hours we have walked together. And to the baltimore oriole who suddenly began pecking at my office window and singing to me as I was completing this manuscript. In return for his encouragement, I fed him several jars of grape jelly. He hung around until the day the manuscript was finished, then flew away, never to return.

A Note to the Reader

Full disclosure: I am a cradle Catholic who spent several years in Catholic girls' boarding school. Later, beginning in graduate school at the University of Wisconsin—Madison and onward through my career as an academic poverty researcher, I came to know many selfless, dedicated, tough-as-nails nuns who toiled tirelessly, day in and day out, in the trenches of the everlasting war on poverty as they sought justice for the marginalized. As a result, I am quite familiar with both the Roman Catholic Church and the sisterhood of "vowed women religious" who stand firm on the front lines of the fight to bend the arc of the patriarchal Catholic Church toward fairness and equality toward women, and all other groups it willfully ostracizes. This familiarity allows me to reflect on the largest, wealthiest, most influential religious institution in the world with a deep awareness of its culture, majesty, goodness, faults, and failings that combined to make room for the true story that inspired this book.

Like Sister Maggie Corrigan, I want the Catholic Church—which despite its many flaws, I still respect for all the social welfare good it does in the world—to get over its patriarchal self and view women through the clear eyes of justice, especially in the areas of women's reproductive rights and women's ordination to the ministerial priesthood. Yet I remain horrified, deeply disappointed, and profoundly saddened by the Church's ongoing failures, corruptions, abuses, and persistent subjugation of women and other disenfranchised groups. These moral failings encourage the wider society to follow by bad example and, for many, make being an observant Catholic in today's world possible only on one's own terms.

For those of you who seek greater justice for women and all others who deserve it, I hope you find this story informative, thought-provoking, upsetting, and inspirational, because all are necessary to fulfill the responsibility each of us has to repair that which is broken in the world.

Chicago

by Carl Sandburg

Hog Butcher for the World,
Tool maker, Stacker of Wheat,
Player with Railroads and the Nation's Freight Handler;
Stormy, husky, brawling,
City of the Big Shoulders:
They tell me you are wicked and I believe them, for I have seen your painted women under the gas lamps luring the farm boys.
And they tell me you are crooked and I answer: Yes, it is true I have seen the gunman kill and go free to kill again.
And they tell me you are brutal and my reply is: On the faces of women and children I have seen the marks of wanton hunger.
And having answered so I turn once more to those who sneer at this my city, and I give them back the sneer and say to them:
Come and show me another city with lifted head singing so proud to be alive and coarse and strong and cunning.
Flinging magnetic curses amid the toil of piling job on job, here is a tall bold slugger set vivid against the little soft cities;
Fierce as a dog with tongue lapping for action, cunning as a savage pitted against the wilderness,
Bareheaded,
Shoveling,
Wrecking,
Planning,
Building, breaking, rebuilding,
Under the smoke, dust all over his mouth, laughing with white teeth,
Under the terrible burden of destiny laughing as a young man laughs,
Laughing even as an ignorant fighter laughs who has never lost a battle,
Bragging and laughing that under his wrist is the pulse, and under his ribs the heart of the people,
Laughing!
Laughing the stormy, husky, brawling laughter of Youth, half-naked, sweating, proud to be Hog Butcher, Tool Maker, Stacker of Wheat, Player with Railroads and Freight Handler to the Nation.

Prologue

October 1995

Fear the Lord, your God, and serve Him.
Swear oaths with His name.
Deuteronomy 6:13 (*New Catholic Bible*)

On a warm Chicago afternoon in fall, two middle-aged men—expensively dressed in custom-tailored black suits, bright white Roman collars, ornate pectoral crosses, and twenty-four-carat gold episcopal rings bearing precious stones that the faithful kneel to kiss—arrive at the Roman Catholic Cardinal Archbishop of Chicago's opulent private residence. They have come for a luncheon meeting with the mansion's current resident, His Eminence George Michael "Mick" Sullivan.

The twenty-one-thousand-square-foot redstone mansion, one block from the Lake Michigan shoreline, occupies one acre of prime real estate on Chicago's Gold Coast. Inside, original oil paintings depicting Christ's suffering, encased in heavy gold frames and insured for several hundred thousand dollars each, hang on the walls; thick Persian rugs grace the heavily waxed, wooden floors; and small, bronze crucifixes hang over the doors. The majestic structure demands one move about reverently and, more importantly, with respect for the power contained within its walls.

"I'm not looking forward to this. I'd rather have food poisoning than a conversation with that pompous kraut, Werner," Cardinal Sullivan remarks to his secretary, Monsignor Gerry O'Meara, as the two exit the second-floor elevator, slowly walking toward the dining room where the other two men wait.

Sullivan, who is one of only five cardinal princes of the Roman Catholic Church in the United States, outranks his other two luncheon companions, who are among the two hundred middle managers—otherwise known as bishops—that the Catholic Church relies upon to keep the seventy-four million American Catholic faithful in line. Bishops Joseph Santora, leader of the Peoria, Illinois Diocese, and Karl-Heinz Werner, who leads an obscure western Indiana diocese bordering eastern Illinois, have come to the meeting to discuss a personnel problem concerning a Catholic nun, Sister Maggie Corrigan, that threatens to plunge them, and the institution they represent, into a public relations nightmare. The cardinal and Bishop Santora both prefer ignoring the problem in hopes it will eventually disappear on its own. Bishop Werner insists they cannot remain silent and must "do something" about it.

Each place setting on the richly polished mahogany table includes fine bone china, carefully ironed linens, and heavy silver utensils. The cardinal occupies the armed chair at the table's head, facing the windows; one bishop sits on each side of him, and Monsignor O'Meara sits unobtrusively several seats away, preparing to take notes. After a perfunctory prayer before their meal, the cardinal rings the small, silver bell beside his plate, signaling to the kitchen staff that they are ready to be served lunch.

"Rather than risk ruining a good meal by engaging in a controversial discussion, I prefer to delay serious consideration of the issue that has brought us together until after we have finished eating," Cardinal Sullivan instructs the others, while a young nun carries serving dishes that offer a choice of salmon flown in from the Pacific Northwest, accompanied by a creamy dill sauce and fresh, green vegetables, or lamb stew prepared with a variety of root vegetables, simmered in thick, brown gravy to the table. Freshly baked bread, sliced beefsteak tomatoes from the mansion's hothouse garden, and a choice of wines complete the main course. Lunch concludes with French-press coffee made from imported, freshly ground Panamanian coffee beans, complimented by a selection of homemade pastries.

"Thank you, Sister," the cardinal tells the nun who has been serving them. "Please tell Sister Hildegard she prepared a fine meal."

The serving nun bows slightly, remaining silent as she backs through the swinging door into the kitchen, carrying an armload of dishes. After she leaves the room, the cardinal suggests they all remain at the table to finish their coffee and carry out their discussion, because he has another engagement in an hour.

Two months ago, Cardinal Sullivan and Bishops Santora and Werner finally agreed, at Werner's insistence, to meet in person to discuss the "Sister Maggie Corrigan problem." Only one of the three men is looking forward to this discussion.

Several weeks earlier, the largest Chicago newspaper presented photographic and other evidence that Sister Maggie Corrigan, a member of the worldwide, three-hundred-year-old Pax Christi Sisters of Charity and Justice, has been, for at least the past two years, working as a patient advocate in a remote, central Illinois abortion clinic. The front-page article labeled the nun "the patron saint of abortion."

These actions run afoul of the Catholic Church's expectations for vowed women religious' public behavior, its Code of Canon Law, and its moral opposition to abortion, which it contends is murder of the unborn. Bishop Werner strongly believes they, as Church leaders, are called upon to intervene and discipline Sister Maggie Corrigan; Cardinal Sullivan and Bishop Santora both strongly prefer looking the other way.

Cardinal Sullivan, who inherited the Maggie Corrigan problem from both of his predecessors, is a ruddy-faced, back-slapping, jovial native son of Chicago. With abundant white hair, sky-blue eyes, and deep connections to the Irish-Catholic mafia that runs Chicago City Hall, he is one of the most powerful men in the city. Each year the cardinal, smiling broadly despite suffering from achingly painful flat feet that require prescription orthotics in his custom-made shoes, marches down Michigan Avenue alongside Mayor Pat Callahan at the head of the city's Saint Patrick's Day parade. Sullivan likes nothing better than hoisting a few and promising to die for Ireland at the annual Hibernian Society dinner held at the elegant Palmer House Hotel. He claims it is his favorite night of the year.

Fond of a good joke, a generous bourbon or two every evening, and a Guinness for lunch on the days when his afternoons are free, Sullivan advanced through the ranks of Chicago clergy to become an auxiliary bishop and, eventually, Archbishop of Chicago, a position he has enjoyed for nearly twelve years. Slowly, he has fallen more in love with the external trappings of his office, including the adoration Chicago Catholics heap on him. The most well-known of the three church officials, his abundant Irish charm has served him well throughout his life.

"You can trust me on this because I know Chicago better than I knew my sainted mother, God rest her soul," Sullivan responds on the rare occasions when his decisions or motives are questioned publicly. He is nearing seventy-five, the mandatory retirement age for priests of all ranks except the pope, who serves until he either dies or resigns. In anticipation of gaining elder statesman status in the Church and in Chicago politics, Sullivan has adopted a "live and let live" path of least resistance approach to governing the archdiocese. He abhors controversy and negative publicity, which he avoids by all means possible including, when necessary, unequivocal denial and outright manipulation of verifiable facts.

Like all good Irishmen, Sullivan believes the Church's primary purpose is to offer hope and solace to the suffering people of the world, which in his view is nearly everyone. His priests consider him a weak leader and generally ignore him, but like him personally and never refuse an invitation to his weekly poker game—that involved plenty of cigar smoking and bourbon drinking—in a basement room at his residence reserved solely for this purpose.

Bishop Werner, the only child of German immigrants who relocated to Milwaukee after World War II, could not be more unlike Sullivan in personality, popularity, and leadership style. Humorless, authoritarian, and generally irritable, his excesses include heavy, dark beer, sauerkraut, fried potatoes, and fat, greasy bratwurst, which his priests claim he resembles during fits of anger. He suffers from chronic gout, obesity, bunions, and the troublesome side effects of his high-dose cholesterol medication.

A rheumy-eyed, self-absorbed pseudo-intellectual who publicly admits to the ancient monastic practice of self-flagellation, Werner is an ultraconservative who is not predisposed toward flexibility in interpreting the Code of Canon Law governing the Church. As a result, he is unpopular among both the people and the priests in his diocese. He doesn't hesitate to unapologetically remind his many critics that the Church is not a democracy; it is a dictatorship, and he is one of the dictators, so nothing compels him to listen to parishioners or priests' concerns, honor their wishes, or grant their requests. He finds himself making this pronouncement so frequently that he no longer bothers to couch the message in less inflammatory language.

The bishop enjoys traveling around his diocese offering theatrical, high-drama Masses designed to resemble those in Saint Peter's Basilica in

Rome. However, because of his weight, his priests refuse to carry him into church on the ceremonial throne he commissioned for himself, forcing him to waddle down the long aisle on feet too small to support his bulk.

While Werner preaches love of neighbor, as long as that neighbor does not include women, Jews, gays, lesbians, or anyone else who isn't a white male and Catholic, the faith that sustains him rests solidly on his own ambitions. These have led him to establish himself as a rule enforcer with a strong tendency toward pompous intellectualism. Often his directives sound like obtuse gobbledygook that makes no sense to the average Catholic.

Werner erroneously views the obscure Indiana diocese he leads, which includes less than one hundred thousand Catholics in three counties southwest of the industrial steel hub of Gary, as having "a high comfort level with an absence of public morality." No one is sure what the bishop means by this. Nevertheless, he has made it his mission to exorcise the devil in their midst, thereby saving his flock from grave sin. However, life in this industrial, rust-belt region, often referred to as the armpit of the nation, is difficult enough without an unpopular bishop adding to its woes, so his flock generally ignores him.

Aware of his shrinking influence, Werner grasps at any straw that permits him to exercise his episcopal power. Accordingly, the single item on his agenda for today's meeting is to convince the other two prelates that invoking his powers of excommunication to expel Sister Maggie Corrigan from the Roman Catholic Church, and consequently from her religious community, is appropriate.

"The teaching of the Catholic Church regarding the grave evil of abortion and formal cooperation with any act of abortion is clear," he said at the press conference he called to announce his intentions, which two people attended. He made these same points to Sullivan and Santora when he requested the meeting with them.

Santora, a native of New York City's Little Italy is the youngest, least experienced of the three Church leaders. He walked into the Sister Maggie Corrigan problem when he arrived in the Peoria diocese six months ago, following an assignment in Little Rock, Arkansas. The assignment was, for the son of a populous, Italian-speaking enclave in a city of over eight million people, a three-year sentence to the outer ring of hell.

"I lost twenty pounds in Little Rock, where neither a decent plate of homemade pasta, nor a decent bottle of chianti could be found anywhere," he complained as he left Arkansas. This was not necessarily a bad thing for the slightly overweight, squarely built Italian who, in his youth, had been a starting lineman on one of Notre Dame's championship football teams. Because of this achievement, Joey Santora spends most of his free time in a recliner, watching old tapes of his Notre Dame games, and reliving his glory days on the gridiron, while crunching beer cans and consuming thick salami and provolone cheese sandwiches lovingly prepared by his devoted housekeeper, Mrs. Maria Colluci.

The bishop thanks God every day for Mrs. Colluci, who speaks little English, makes a cannoli to die for, and lets out his trousers as his waistline expands on her daily diet of carbohydrate-rich, lovingly prepared food. He teases her with Italian love songs in the kitchen every morning and whistles "Drop-kick me, Jesus, through the Goal Posts of Life" while walking his dog, a nameless mutt who showed up at the back door of the rectory the week Santora arrived in Peoria and, despite Mrs. Colluci's objections, has been sleeping in his bedroom ever since.

By the time Santora took over the Peoria diocese, which includes just over a half-million Catholics spread across seven counties, Sister Maggie's activities were well known and well established. Young enough to have higher ambitions within the Church, assuming his arteries hold out, he is very reluctant to become involved in this emerging drama that involves three men who live entirely apart from the realities of women's lives, and under the protection of the most powerful religious institution in the world, acting as judge, jury, and executioner of a vowed woman religious he has never met.

"I have to be honest with you, I think pursuing this is a bad idea. I grew up with six sisters and am very hesitant to cross a determined woman. I find the best approach is to stay out of their way, let them do whatever they want, and hope for the best," Bishop Santora told Cardinal Sullivan when the cardinal telephoned to discuss the upcoming meeting.

"I don't disagree with you, Joe, but Werner's a stubborn old fart, and he's not going to let this go. It's best we let him get whatever is bugging him off his chest and then ignore him...and I think an Irishman and an Italian can handle an overinflated German, don't you?"

Laughing, Santora said he was looking forward to doing just that.

Santora and Sullivan are both aware of several previously unsuccessful attempts to curtail Sister Maggie's passionate pursuit of justice, and both realize that whether or not they agree with her actions is, in Sister Maggie's mind, irrelevant and therefore unlikely, in practical terms, to dissuade her. As a result, they are very reluctant to pick a fight they believe they are likely to lose.

"It's pretty clear Sister Maggie Corrigan strongly believes in what she is doing and has the courage of her convictions, which I admire and respect. I don't think she'll be easily deterred," Santora told the cardinal.

"You know what happened when I called her superior a year or two ago?" Sullivan asked. "She told me they don't tell their sisters what to do, and if I didn't like what Sister Maggie was doing, I should call her myself, and she gave me her phone number."

Santora asked the cardinal whether he followed through.

"Do I sound that stupid to you? Hell no, I didn't follow through. The last thing I am ever interested in is a testy conversation with a pissed-off Irish woman. I don't need that shit."

Complicating Bishop Santora's feelings about this problem is that having listened to his own sisters' endless complaints, he is well aware of the negative effects of the Church's position on women in general, and on birth control in particular, and sympathizes with their arguments. Despite the cardinal's assurances they can handle this, he much prefers avoiding any discussion of the issue. He ends the conversation by asking to put off the meeting for as long as possible.

•••

Six weeks later, Bishop Werner arrives in Chicago for the pre-arranged luncheon meeting between Cardinal Sullivan, Bishop Santora, and himself, well prepared to remind the others that the Catholic Church is an authoritarian patriarchy and that they, as bishops, have the ultimate authority regarding any potential actions involving both faith and morals. Additionally, canon law does not guarantee due-process rights for the accused. Any consideration of excommunication presumes guilt, which is his excuse for not inviting either Sister Maggie, a five-foot-tall spitfire with flaming red hair and an unfiltered mouth, or her religious superiors, to the meeting to explain themselves.

"You must not have any sisters," Santora remarks, after hearing Werner declare that Catholic women are expected to submit to male authority, especially theirs, as church leaders.

"You really are a dumb shit," Cardinal Sullivan mumbles, looking directly at Bishop Werner.

Before Bishop Werner can request an explanation, Santora adds that the bishop is "obviously very uncomfortable with women."

"More likely afraid of them," Cardinal Sullivan, who has three sisters of his own, adds under his breath.

Werner bristles but holds his tongue.

"Before we can consider any action against Sister Corrigan, including excommunication, which I strongly oppose, we first must settle the thorny question of jurisdiction, which determines who among us would execute whatever plan of action we may, or may not, decide upon," Cardinal Sullivan points out. "I remind Bishop Werner that he can commence excommunication proceedings against Catholics in his own diocese, but he has no jurisdiction or authority over Catholics in other dioceses. The difficult question, in this case, is which of us has jurisdiction over Sister Maggie?"

The Midwest Province headquarters and motherhouse for the Pax Christi Sisters of Charity and Justice, generally referred to as the Sisters of Charity and Justice—SCJ—or Pax Christi Sisters with which Sister Maggie is affiliated, is located in Bishop Werner's diocese. However, she lives in Chicago, which falls under Cardinal Sullivan's ecclesiastical responsibility, and is performing her abortion activities near Peoria, which is within Bishop Santora's purview.

"Further complicating the jurisdiction question," Cardinal Sullivan continues, "is that even though they are located within his diocese, Bishop Werner has no formal authority over the Pax Christi Sisters, who answer first to a local provincial prioress and leadership council elected by the sisters themselves, and second to the mother general who presides over the worldwide Order. The current mother general, who has served for fifteen years and resides in Spain is a rebel herself. As a young nun, she participated in the underground political resistance movement protesting the regime of Spanish dictator Francisco Franco. I expect she understands the courage it takes to resist authority and is unlikely to look favorably upon any effort to sanction or excommunicate one of her nuns, regardless of the reason."

"Are you saying that while the provincial motherhouse leadership prefers to have a cordial relationship with Bishop Werner, they also have the upper hand in any dealings with him because they are autonomous and operate independently of the diocese he leads?" Bishop Santora asks.

"That's exactly what I'm saying. Nothing in their covenants obligates them to obey him or to go along with any ideas he proposes. No matter how strongly Bishop Werner believes Sister Maggie has gravely sinned, he cannot force the Order to bend to his will, impose a punishment, or follow through on any sanctions he might try to impose. As the ranking prelate among us, I want to be perfectly clear that I strongly oppose taking any action. If we try to do anything to her, we'll get trouble we didn't bargain for, and if that occurs, I might as well shoot myself, because if I don't, somebody else will," the cardinal proclaims.

Turning red in the face, Bishop Werner nevertheless remains silent.

"Very rarely has any Catholic been excommunicated in modern times. To take such draconian action against a well-known, popular nun who has committed her entire religious life to a fight for greater equality for women in the Church would create an epic public relations debacle the Church, and especially the Chicago Archdiocese, would not survive undamaged. The general public believes that after never having begun excommunication proceedings against a single one of its pedophile priests or enabling bishops, because pedophilia is not a crime under canon law, the Church has little credibility when it comes to claiming the moral high ground on anything," Bishop Santora points out.

"My impression is that Sister Maggie enjoys a large, enthusiastic following among progressive Catholics, and they are unlikely to stand by quietly while the three prelates attempt to discipline or excommunicate her. I believe any attempt to silence her will backfire," Santora continues.

As the spiritual shepherd for Chicago's 2.3 million mostly Irish and Italian Catholics (roughly 40 percent of the entire population of 1,400-square-mile metropolitan Chicago), CEO of the largest diocese in the world-wide Roman Catholic Church, and manager of an over one-billion-dollar budget, Sullivan has been well aware of Sister Maggie Corrigan's various activities, including her reproductive choice activism, for a long time. She is a rough-cut, South Side Chicago native who had been speaking out in favor of women's equality for several years before the pope appointed the cardinal to lead the archdiocese. Over time, he has grown quite comfortable ignoring her.

Every day he faces pressing issues that weigh heavily upon him, and one nun—whose actions are making a sociopolitical statement on women's rights—is not a big enough problem for him to take seriously. He is old, tired, and still mopping up the after-effects of the scandals enveloping the Church, including those brought about by his predecessor, James Cardinal O'Grady's "memorable" leadership, which ended in accusations of tax fraud, misappropriation of diocesan funds to support a woman with whom he'd had a long-term relationship, and an FBI investigation—all of which was widely believed to have been leaked to the press by one of O'Grady's own priests. Worry over what will happen next is causing Sullivan to eat too much, drink too much, and sleep poorly at night.

After listening to the others, Werner says he has consulted a canon lawyer whose considered opinion is that canon law provides for dismissal from a religious community, and excommunication from the Church, for any nun who has been an accomplice to abortion or has given grave scandal arising from culpable behavior. He insists this is the basis of his argument for pursuing the Sister Maggie Corrigan case.

"Canon 695 calls for the mandatory dismissal of a religious guilty of the delict of abortion described in Canon 1398," he explains. "The argument is that Sister Corrigan is an accomplice to abortion under Canon 1329, which would then make Canon 695 applicable."

"The novelty of nuns serving as murder mistresses in abortion clinics means there is not much prior case law," Sullivan, who is a canon lawyer himself, counters. "What you're claiming is a stretch."

"It may be a stretch, Your Eminence, but it is still a theory worth exploring," Werner insists.

"Bullshit," Sullivan responds, standing up to signal their lunch and discussion are both over.

"Pursuing this is fucking stupid," Cardinal Sullivan adds as a parting shot. "Any fool knows nuns stick together like crusaders for Christ, and we get on the wrong side of any one of them, every goddamned other one will be riding our asses all the way to Rome. I don't need this shit, and the archdiocese doesn't need it either."

"I beg to differ, Eminence. What Sister Corrigan is doing goes against everything the Church stands for. We can't ignore her," Werner counters

"Like hell we can't. If anybody asks, we say we're weighing our options. Back off and shut up, and I guarantee it'll go away on its own."

Having no concern about being tried and convicted of abuse of power in the court of public opinion, as he leaves the mansion, Bishop Werner clamps down on the Sister Maggie Corrigan problem like a dog chewing on a bone and refusing to let go.

PART ONE

2017

The seeds of every story are planted somewhere...

I.

When your only regret is that anyone thinks you regret anything
—that is the definition of conviction.

CRISS JAMI

The handwriting on the envelope, addressing me as Professor Dr. Gillian Spencer, PhD is barely legible, and the address is incomplete, making it a perfect candidate for a dead letter box. It happened to find me because it is addressed to my office, and the university mailroom knows me. Opening it, I find a brief note: "Call me." It is signed Maggie Corrigan, followed by a telephone number.

Maggie isn't one to keep in touch, so we haven't seen or spoken to each other in several years. I have no idea what she wants but am sure she wants something. Past experience with her has taught me she always has an agenda—and ways of getting what she wants, which isn't necessarily what I want to become involved with.

After several days, curiosity overtakes me, and I dial her number. She answers on the second ring.

"I want you to come to see me," Maggie says after I identify myself.

"Where are you?" I ask.

"In the middle of a goddamned Indiana cornfield."

"How'd you end up there? If I recall correctly, you vowed never to leave Chicago."

"I got old."

"Everybody who gets old doesn't end up in a cornfield."

"Don't be a smartass. It's the equivalent of putting Grandma on a downriver raft because she's old and cranky and nobody knows what else to do with her."

"That's a little harsh."

"The truth usually is. I can't manage on my own any longer, and there was no place for me to go except back to the motherhouse, and they put me in a care facility surrounded by miles of cornfields."

"Where, exactly, is your cornfield?"

"I'm not sure—someplace on the banks of the Wabash River."

"The Wabash is a big river, Maggie. If you want me to come to see you, you'll have to do better."

"We can figure it out later. When can you come?"

"I haven't said I will. Why do you want to see me?"

"We have things to discuss."

"What things?"

"I'll explain when you get here."

"It's a long trip from Virginia to the middle of Indiana, Maggie. You'll have to tell me what this is about before I agree to come."

"I'll tell you when I see you. Let me know when you can make it." She hangs up.

She may be old, but she makes the Three Stooges sound like amateurs at carrying on a circular conversation, I think as I replace the phone receiver.

Two weeks pass before I decide to decide to fly from Virginia—where I direct the Hanover Poverty Research Institute at Virginia Southern University near Richmond—into Chicago, which is the closest major airport to my eventual destination in the middle of a cornfield somewhere in North Central Indiana, on the banks of the Wabash River. When I call Maggie to tell her I've decided to come, she doesn't sound at all surprised, doesn't thank me for making the effort, and says she'll have someone send me specific directions.

"It's a three-hour drive from Chicago. Get here for lunch. Everybody will be shocked I'm having a visitor. It'll be the most excitement they've had since our last fire drill."

•••

On a hazy morning two weeks later, as I navigate my rental car through traffic on the perpetually congested, potholed Dan Ryan Expressway out of Chicago toward Interstate 65 South into Indiana's endless miles of cornfields, I begin wishing Maggie's letter had ended up in a dead letter box. My thoughts turn to the first time I heard her name. I've forgotten the exact date, but I've never forgotten the riveting conversation on a snowy Sunday evening, near the end of my graduate school days at the University of Wisconsin.

Three of my friends and I were sitting in front of a fireplace, drinking cheap wine and indulging in a lively, late-night discussion about the sorry state of the Catholic Church we were all born into. The consensus was that the Church was morally, intellectually, and spiritually bankrupt and it was up to our generation to right the ship. The promise of post-Vatican II reforms loomed large, and nearly all Catholics believed serious change was on the horizon and within our grasp.

That evening, I was the only one among us who had not formally committed myself to vowed religious life. But I had spent ten years in Catholic girls' boarding school with tightly braided hair and long-sleeved black uniform with a white collar, which was, in my mind, basically no different from life in the convent. Nine years later, a lot had changed. My go-to uniform was faded Levi's and a black cashmere turtleneck sweater, my thick, dark auburn hair hung loose at my shoulders, and I was Monsignor Sam Kennedy's serious girlfriend.

A dark-haired, dark-eyed, naturally charismatic, deep-voiced Irishman with a hearty laugh, sentimental nature, and laconic humor, Sam Kennedy was a charming, attractive man, and none of his acquaintances expected him to remain in the Catholic priesthood forever. Most believed that if the rumors of relaxing the celibacy rule and allowing a married priesthood proved true, he wouldn't last much longer. Those things mattered surprisingly little to me because I knew we were a handsome, well-suited couple, and I was proud of it.

That evening's rant centered around the Church's refusal to allow Catholic women the freedom to make their own reproductive choices—in other words, the Church's insistence that women not practice any form of artificial birth control. Since all of us were of childbearing age, and to varying extents still locked into the Catholic culture, this issue was personal.

"I think your interpretation of the Church's issues is bullshit!" my friend Julia said. "Vatican II ended years ago, and the supposedly modernized, twentieth-century Church is still sitting on its fat, patriarchal ass, keeping its priests officially chained to celibacy and viewing women as 'near occasions' of men's sins, servant wives and baby machines unable to exert any control over the deepest, most personal aspects of their lives. Supposedly celibate men who know nothing about male-female relationships thinking they have a right to any opinion about what is acceptable in any aspect of women's lives is obscene and just doesn't play well with us," Julia pointed out with such vigor she stopped just short of slamming her fist on the table. A robust woman who had worn the habit of vowed religious life for nine years before she fell in love, she still possessed the confident, no-nonsense, strongly opinionated demeanor common to most nuns.

Then the conversation turned to a recent report presenting solid evidence that most Catholic women ignored the Church's position that forbid artificial birth control and were no more reluctant to seek an abortion for an unwanted pregnancy than non-Catholic women. It also stated that between 30 and 40 percent of all abortions occur among Catholic women. This finding was not surprising in a religious group that opposed any means of controlling conception, but nevertheless sent shock waves through the Church.

"Without birth control, unwanted pregnancies will occur, and then be terminated. Preventing conception is the strongest, most effective means for avoiding an abortion, and the Church's attempt to have it both ways on this issue is profoundly unjust, manipulative, and denies Catholic women the right, and the freedom, to control their own lives," Julia added.

My contribution to the conversation was that the issue was particularly acute among women without access to economic and other resources. As a sociology graduate student currently writing my doctoral dissertation on women and poverty, I knew the strongest predictor of lifetime poverty for women was early and repeated childbearing and found this recent research both fascinating and informative.

The report had outraged James Seamus Cardinal O'Grady, head of the Catholic Archdiocese of Chicago. O'Grady labeled the report "hogwash" and forbade Chicago Catholics to read it. However, O'Grady was currently drowning in controversy involving a woman, misuse of diocesan funds, the FBI, and Chicago priest Jack Brody. O'Grady accused Brody of leaking the report to the press to embarrass the Church and divert attention away from their very public feud over archdiocesan leadership. In the fine Irish tradition of never backing down from a fight—especially with another Irishman—Brody's response included calling O'Grady "a tyrannical maniac" and vowing to "get him, one way or another." Most found this claim visually amusing, given that O'Grady, standing over six feet tall and carrying around more than three hundred fifty pounds, dwarfed Brody, an elfin man barely more than one third of O'Grady's weight. At best, Brody might have been able to kick the cardinal in the shins.

"The Brody-O'Grady grudge match will go on forever, or until Brody finally runs O'Grady out of town," Monsignor Kennedy remarked that evening, pouring us all more wine. Originally from Chicago, Sam intuitively understood Chicago Irish-Catholic politics and found them more entertaining than most movies.

"One thing you have to understand about the Irish, Gillian, is that they love a good fight, especially with each other, and there are none better than those that occur on the verbal battlefield where Chicago's Irish-Catholics find their most worthy opponents."

I found this fact amusing but had never taken it too seriously until that evening, when I began to fully grasp how powerful the Catholic Church is.

"People forget that the Catholic Church is foremost a political institution," Sam explained. "It functions as a religious institution, but it's also a nation-state. No one sends ambassadors to the protestants—"

"Because they're not centrally organized like the Catholics," I interjected.

Sam nodded his agreement and continued.

"Nearly one hundred countries, including our own, send ambassadors to the Vatican, and the Vatican sends papal *nuncios*—diplomats—to hundreds of nations and organizations. The nuncio, or apostolic delegate, assigned to the United States has a fancy house on Embassy Row in Washington, DC. And the pope routinely meets with heads of state around the world because the Vatican state maintains diplomatic, political, financial, and cultural relationships with nearly every world nation. All of this occurs with the clear intention of exerting political influence—and seriously messes with the uniquely American concept of the separation of church and state. The relationship between the Chicago Archdiocese and City Hall is no different."

Fair point, and not one I'd thought about before.

"It's more complicated than that," Julia's husband, Jim, interjected. "Technically, the more than one billion Catholics in the world, who are about one-seventh of the global population, hold dual citizenship in their home countries—and in the Vatican. Theoretically, this creates divided loyalties, which was the core issue Jack Kennedy faced when he ran for president. Voters questioned where his loyalties lay—with America or with the pope."

"Playing political games is the most interesting way for celibate men, who are cretins at relationships anyway, to spend their time. It's not like they have anything else to do," Julia added. "Plus, success in the political arena is key to the Church's survival—both locally and on the world stage. Otherwise, the institution risks becoming irrelevant."

Another good point.

Sam believed O'Grady was correct that Brody had purposely shifted their argument over to the explosive report on women and birth control, but not for the reasons O'Grady claimed. "I've known Jack since our seminary days, and he truly loves the Church, and honestly believes women are getting a raw deal. My guess is his motives are pure this time, because he has to know about the uprising some nun in Chicago is spearheading and probably wants to help her out."

"What uprising?" Julia asked.

"A fire-breathing feminist nun in Chicago is making a lot of noise about changing the Church to make it more equitable for women, and she's leading with the women's reproductive rights issue—not something anyone would expect a vowed nun to take on. Sister Maggie Corrigan, I think her name is—a feisty Irish girl with a big vocabulary. She doesn't hesitate to speak out and is building quite a following."

Believing that real change had to come from within the patriarchy itself, and not from outside pressure, Julia expressed serious doubts about how successful one smart-mouth nun's efforts might be.

"Hell hath no fury like an Irish woman scorned, and she apparently feels scorned by a Church run entirely by men, so I wouldn't bet against her," Sam responded, grinning broadly.

"How is she getting away with running headlong into the Church hierarchy, and why isn't O'Grady doing anything about it?" I asked.

"He's got more pressing problems, so her timing is perfect," Sam replied. "She's gutsy and passionate. Whether or not you agree with her, she's becoming a force to be reckoned with, and there isn't much O'Grady can do about it."

"Plus, she's in Chicago where the Irish fight among themselves for sport. It's their favorite pastime. If you think about it, there's no better place to stage such a rebellion. It'll be a good ol' barroom brawl, and while everybody's swinging their verbal fists, she'll march right through the middle and tackle O'Grady from behind," Jim chuckled.

"You're right," Sam laughed. "It'll be fun to watch."

I remember doubting whether Sister Maggie Corrigan would describe what she was trying to do as fun, but it would be a good many years before our paths would cross and I would have the opportunity to find out.

Now we are about to meet for the second time.

Walking up to the entrance of the address Maggie provided, I find her waiting by the front door of the large building situated on the periphery of a vast complex of older ones. Sitting in a wheelchair, she is wearing oversized 1970s-style black cat-eye glasses, an ill-fitting orange-brown wig she must've found at an after-Halloween sale in a costume shop, a grey Chicago White Sox sweatshirt, ankle-length red pants that fail to cover her white support stockings and tan sneakers.

"It's wonderful to see you again, Sister Maggie," I say, offering my hand.

"Apparently you've forgotten I don't like being called Sister. It's a divisive term. We're all sisters," she reminds me as a greeting, ignoring my outstretched hand. "Do you refer to yourself as Doctor Spencer or Professor Spencer?"

"Sometimes...generally in reference to my academic work. It reminds the male egos in the room that we're on an equal plane and cuts through a lot of—"

"Bullshit," she interrupts to finish my sentence.

"Well, yes, that is what I was referring to, but I try not to swear in front of a nun."

I ask whether she wants me to wheel her wherever we are going and she declines, then manages to wheel herself about twenty feet before motioning to me to push her, while giving explicit instructions about how to do it. Finally arriving at the dining room, I see a large calendar hanging on the wall outside the entrance, indicating the religious and other activities for the month.

"Looks like you have plenty to do around here," I comment.

"If you're brain dead and can stand being around people," Maggie replies while signaling me to take her to a table in the far south corner of the large room, near a wall of windows looking out over a wide expanse of cropland.

"Pretty view," I remark.

"The Chicago skyline is a pretty view. This is crap," she answers as she directs me to park her wheelchair precisely in line with the table setting. It takes me three tries to satisfy her. I offer to pour her some water.

"Forget water. I like beer for lunch and three fingers of bourbon, neat, before dinner, but they won't allow me to have either. I don't suppose you thought to bring me a bottle."

"Sorry—that didn't occur to me. I'm sure you would've enjoyed it."

"Not as much as cigarettes, which I can't have either."

"Living here must be difficult."

"It's a death sentence. I'm hoarding my blood pressure pills in case Dr. Kevorkian doesn't show up when I call him."

"If you're referring to the assisted-suicide doctor, I think he's dead."

"My point exactly."

"I don't think storing up pills is a good idea."

"And I care about what you think because...?"

"You probably don't."

"Correct."

Looking for a way to shift the conversation, I turn toward the entrance and see about thirty other, variously mobile sisters entering the dining room, chatting among themselves. Four, including two with walkers, sit down at the table next to ours.

"They're wondering who you are and why you're visiting me," Maggie says. "Otherwise, they wouldn't bother coming over here."

I ask whether I should introduce myself, and she shakes her head no.

"You should do something with your hair," she says instead.

"What's wrong with my hair?" I ask, wondering why, considering her own style choices, she can possibly care about mine.

"Cut it shorter and get rid of the gray," she tells me.

"I like it the way it is," My shoulder-length hair isn't quite the deep auburn it once was, but it's still dark. I like it slightly threaded with gray and think it looks fine.

"Do you always dress up for lunch?" she asks. I'm wearing a navy-blue cotton sweater and tan linen pants, which seem suitable for visiting a convent nursing home, so I'm not sure whether she's being sarcastic or asking an honest question.

"What did you expect?" I answer.

"You don't look like a poverty researcher and women's rights advocate, is what I'm saying."

"I'm not sure what a women's rights advocate or a poverty researcher looks like. But it's the work, not what I look like, that matters, don't you think?" She ignores the question, and I conclude she's testing me, although I'm not sure why.

Our lunch, which looks good considering its origins, arrives. Maggie sends hers back to the kitchen three times: once because there is a pickle on her plate, and she hates pickles. Then the portions are too large and waste food. The third problem is she doesn't like the mixed vegetables. This back-and-forth with the dining room staff takes up the first fifteen minutes of our meal.

"Would you mind getting off the subject of my hair and clothes so we can talk about why you want to see me?" I ask as we finally begin to eat.

"I want you to write my story," she says.

"Your story?"

"Yes. You write about women's struggles in society, and I think I have something to say about that."

I ask her to tell me more.

"The fight for women's equality isn't over, and whoever takes it up next might learn something from what I have to say. Don't you agree?"

The longer I remain silent, the longer she stares at me, slowly chewing her food.

"Do you want the truth or the answer you're looking for?" I finally ask.

"What answer do you think I'm looking for?" she replies.

"The one that says I'm awe-struck by all your efforts to bring the Catholic Church into the twenty-first century of women's rights and want to write a book about you because I've written several books about strong women, and you fit into my publication goals."

"Would you consider writing a book about me?" she asks, setting down her fork.

"Probably not," I answer.

"Why?" She frowns.

"Because you're too hard to get along with," I smile.

"Then I guess you better give me the truth."

"I deeply admire what you've tried to do for women's reproductive rights and agree that the next generation of women activists in the Church who want to carry on where you left off will benefit tremendously from knowing your story. Your life and efforts are definitely book-worthy—and I'd love to be the one who writes that book. But you're a control freak, and no writer in her right mind, including me, willingly gets involved in that kind of situation."

Silence sits heavy between us for a long time before Maggie speaks again. "I raised a lot of hell because I honestly believed I was doing the right thing—fighting the good fight for the right reasons—and I paid a high price."

I ask her to explain.

"My fellow sisters disagreed with what I was doing and wanted me kicked out of the Order and excommunicated from the Church. They accused me of everything from being possessed by the devil, to outright heresy. Now they blame me for bringing on the downfall of the Order.

They think the reason so few aspirants come to us anymore is because they don't want to be associated with me. They claim I've plunged us into such perilous circumstances that we are on the brink of financial ruin. They resent that it's costing the Order fifty thousand dollars a year to take care of me when all I've ever done is cause trouble and embarrass them. Very few bother speaking to me."

"You must be lonely," I remark, after another long silence.

"I've been lonely all my life. But this is different. I watch television all day and rarely leave my room, even for meals. A few friends from Chicago phone occasionally but don't visit. Everybody else is dead. Worst of all, other than being unable to walk, there's nothing wrong with me. This could go on for years and cost the Order, which is already in deep financial trouble, hundreds of thousands of dollars."

"Would the Order want a book written about you?"

"Probably not."

"Then why do it? Your Order has already stood by you through so much angst, and a book about you will resurrect memories they would prefer to remain at rest. Doesn't that concern you?"

"Not really. The Order is all about 'hate the sin, love the sinner' Christianity, and I've provided them with the perfect opportunity to put that belief into action. They ought to be thanking me."

"That's a little convoluted—and selfish."

"You aren't the first person to call me selfish, and you sure as hell won't be the last."

"I respect your Order a great deal and am not particularly interested in helping you pick another fight with them."

"What, you're not brave enough to take them on?"

"I didn't say that."

"Look, Gillian, I'm pushing eighty-six years old, and there's nothing left for them to do to me that they haven't already done. Kicking me to the curb would create a public relations nightmare, and they've got enough problems without that.... You remember what Janis Joplin said about freedom being just another word for nothing left to lose?"

I nod.

"She was talking about me. I'm free as a bird because I don't have anything left to lose."

Just then, two of the sisters sitting at the next table turn toward Maggie and ask if she is coming to Mass later that afternoon. She waves them off without responding.

"She doesn't want any friends," one of them remarks. Another offers that Maggie holds lifetime grudges and is still upset that not everybody agrees with her.

"She's never been remorseful or asked for forgiveness for all the hurt she caused," a third sister points out. "You'd think she'd be grateful we're taking care of her anyway."

Maggie doesn't indicate that she has overheard any of this, though it's been spoken loudly enough it would be hard to miss.

"You know my real problem?" she asks.

I admit I don't.

"If I had it to do over again, I'd do the same damned thing and wouldn't change one single minute of any of it. I only have one regret. Most people have a lot more."

"And what is that regret?" I ask, and she shakes her head.

"It's personal," she says, falling silent for a moment.

"I took on the Catholic Church I loved enough to put up one hell of a fight to try to make it better," she finally continues. "And I'm damned proud of that. It's more than anybody else around here can claim. I didn't succeed in changing things as much as they need changing, but they've changed some. I came closer to smashing the patriarchy than anyone has ever come, and I might've succeeded if I'd had more time. Nothing, and nobody, can take that away from me." A lone tear runs down her cheek.

"Apparently not everybody thinks smashing the patriarchy is a good idea," I say.

"Then they're not Christians."

Surprised at this assertion, I ask for more.

"True Christians don't believe anybody is better than anybody else. Gender doesn't come with rights over other people, so men aren't entitled to dominion over women. 'There is neither Jew nor Greek, slave nor free, male nor female, for you are all one in Christ Jesus'...or something like that. I forget the exact words, but it's in Galatians."

I nod in agreement.

"Here's what I don't get," she finally continues. "If you really believe in gender equality and a woman's right to control her own life, why aren't you willing to help me keep my story alive so that fight doesn't die out? Surely you understand there's still a long way to go and nothing is more important than not giving up."

Because she has challenged me, and because I agree with what she is saying about the fight for women's rights not being over, this is the moment I decide to tell Maggie's story.

II.

One became aware of the butchery long before stepping off
the streetcar near the great stone and iron gate of the
Chicago Union Stockyards. The unique Yards smell—a mixture of
decaying blood, hair, and organic tissue; fertilizer dust; smoke;
and other ingredients—permeated everything....

James Barrett

"Here's the situation, Gillian: I've heard from a couple of generally credible people that the area surrounding the stockyards, and especially the Back of the Yards neighborhood, is someplace you would be wise not to wander into if they don't know you. With a little luck, all you'll get are dirty looks and cat calls; but more likely, somebody'll either not so playfully bust your chops or seriously insult you, especially if you go into a local bar," Sam's boyhood friend, Joey Noonan, tells me over lunch at Vito's, a tiny, cash-only, red-checkered-tablecloth, Chicago spaghetti joint.

Four months after deciding to accept Maggie's challenge to bring her story to life, I am in the Windy City on sabbatical from my faculty position to begin work on the project. I find Joey's concern for my welfare amusing, and I reassure him that if anyone bothers me, I can handle it.

"They'll bother you worse than poison ivy on a hot summer day if they think you're an undercover cop, honey—and let's face it, there's absolutely nothing about you that suggests you're a tough-as-nails South Sider, so why the hell else would you be snooping around their neighborhood?" Joey chuckles.

"First, I don't believe I look like a Chicago cop. Second, last I heard it's still a free country, and people can wander wherever they want to. Third, I'm not planning on hitting the local bars, at least not on this trip. I'm sure I'll be fine."

A handsome, red-haired, brown-eyed charmer, Joey left the Catholic priesthood for the Episcopalians after he fell in love with an advertising executive at the *Chicago Sun-Times* he met in an upscale gay bar. Years later, he reached out to me following Sam's death, and we have remained in touch. As a native, he is a great source of information about the emerald jewel of the Midwest—otherwise known as Chicago, Illinois.

"The thing about Chicago," Joey continues, "is that being born here is like being vaccinated—or ordained a priest—it marks you for life, and you always know who your people are."

I ask for more.

"It's something you feel—a survival instinct," Joey insists, twirling his spaghetti around his fork. "Outsiders think Chicago is a melting pot, but it really isn't. Every neighborhood is its own ethnic community with its own language and customs, and the locals don't mix well with outsiders."

"Sounds like cross-city chaos," I comment.

"Think of it this way: the entire European continent, Ireland, Africa, and the Mediterranean shoreline are all squeezed into just over two-hundred square miles that are the Chicago city limits. Germans, Poles, Italians, Jews, Czechs, Lithuanians, and two kinds of Irish—lace curtain Irish on the North Side and shanty Irish on the South Side, neither of which speaks to the other. You know where you are by the smells drifting out the kitchen window where Ma is cooking, what language you hear on the streets, the signs on the stores, and whether Germans or Poles stomp on you; Italians or Irish pelt you with rocks, bricks, and bottles; or Jews, Czechs, or Lithuanians yell at you while hurling tin cans and garbage to discourage you from trespassing. They're reminding you that you don't belong and better never come back."

"You're basically describing gang warfare," I point out.

"Not really. It's more subtle than that."

"The North Side lace curtain Irish wouldn't be caught dead associating with the South Side shanty Irish, because North Siders think South Siders are crude, foul-mouthed hooligans who talk with their fists, are too fond of the drink, can't hold down a job, and live off the dole. So, for a variety of reasons nobody ever admits to, folks tend to stay in their own neighborhoods, generation upon generation. I suppose it's the comfortable familiarity—the devil you know is better than the one you don't sort of thing. But it's pretty amazing, if you think about it," Joey reflects.

"Amazing and miraculous. With all this ethnic tribalism, what holds a huge city like this together?"

"The Catholic Church. Square mile for square mile, Chicago's an Irish-Catholic, meat-and-potatoes, corned beef-and-cabbage, Guinness-on-tap town, and nearly everyone is connected to the Church in some way or another. It's a lot to unpack for a book."

"And a fascinating challenge," I counter.

Joey repeats his reluctance for me to venture alone into the rough, South Side Irish neighborhood where Maggie Corrigan was born and grew up, but he is not enthusiastic about accompanying me either.

"The only way I can get a feel for a place is to wander its streets, best done alone...and I'm not going in blind. Sociologists have been documenting the squalid, dangerous working conditions in the bloody killing fields that were the South Side Chicago Union Stock Yards for years. The yards were the beating heart of Maggie's childhood world, and I'm looking forward to seeing it all for myself."

"Fine." Joey sighs, and then, unable help himself, he asks, "You're sure you know what you're doing?"

"Never been more sure of anything in my life," I tease. "First I'm going to the Chicago Public Library to look up back issues of the *Chicago Tribune* from the years when Maggie Corrigan was making headlines. That will tell me a lot."

"As long as nobody flashes you in the stacks, you should be fine in the library," Joey reassures me.

•••

Later that afternoon, with assistance from Mary Ann, an eager librarian who vaguely remembers hearing about an abortion activist nun when she was a teenager, I learn a few things about Maggie's activism, her background, and a little more about Chicago. Mary Ann stays after her shift ends to help me, and suggests asking Maggie's home parish, which we determine is Holy Family, for permission to spend some time in their archives.

"Sometimes they consider their records confidential; other times, access depends on the good will of the pastor and parish secretary. They might not want to cooperate on a story about Sister Maggie since she was so controversial, but it won't hurt to ask...and you don't have to tell them exactly why you're interested," Mary Ann says, smiling like the coconspirator she becomes after I promise her a signed copy of the book when it is finished.

As we are leaving, she says my best bet for getting to the South Side is to take the L, Chicago's rickety elevated commuter train system, south to 47th and catch a crosstown bus west to Back of the Yards. "The entire area is pretty rough, even in daylight. Taking your car probably isn't a good idea—if you want to hang onto it, that is."

The next morning, in Levi's, dirty sneakers, the faded sweatshirt I usually wear to mow my lawn, and my hair tied back in a ponytail, I set out for South Side Chicago. My hope for blending into the surroundings shatters as soon as I board the southbound Red Line L.

"Whattaya want to go there for?" the ruddy-faced conductor asks me when I buy the ticket to the South 47th Street station. "It ain't no tourist destination."

I catch a few glimpses of the area as the L pulls into the station and agree with the conductor. The run-down, densely populated area, with no shortage of young men loitering in the streets, would never be mistaken for a tourist destination. I assume there has been some improvement since the stock yards closed, but judging by what I see around me, not a lot. The two-block walk to the crosstown bus stop is through a neighborhood of rundown houses with dirty windows framing torn window shades and broken Venetian blinds. Cracked asbestos siding is missing pieces and weeds fill the tiny front yards, sometimes enclosed by waist-high chain-link fences. Empty oil drums collecting the household garbage sit on front stoops, no more than ten feet from buckled concrete sidewalks and broken curbs. Upended bathtubs sheltering statues of the Blessed Virgin Mary are everywhere, erasing any doubts about how Catholic the community is.

Dark bars where, I assume, locals go to drink their meals outnumber the empty storefronts. These are not cocktail lounges where someone takes a Saturday night date; they are cheap, straight-up whisky joints where bartenders serve beer on tap because handing out bottles is supplying drunk customers with deadly weapons when the inevitable fights break out. The windows are too dirty to see inside, but most have their lights on, suggesting that regulars begin showing up well before noon.

After a twenty-minute bus ride, I discover that the Back of the Yards—home to the meatpacking industry that employed thousands of European, mostly Irish, immigrants from the nineteenth through much of the twentieth century, working in the stock yards for slave wages—is even more rundown than I expected. Looking around, it seems to me the immigrants living here might have been better off back in the old country where they would have been short on money, but at least had land under their feet, which is much more valuable than endless black asphalt.

This is where Maggie Corrigan was born in 1932 to young, Irish immigrant parents three years after the 1929 stock market crash plunged the nation into the most devastating economic depression in American history, rendering millions jobless, homeless, and hopeless for the foreseeable future. Maggie and her twin brother, Tommy, the first two of Paddy and Maureen Corrigan's seven children, were born during an era when starting a family could not have been more difficult. They went on to have five more children over the next nine years, until Maureen died in childbirth at age twenty-seven, eleven days after the Japanese attacked Pearl Harbor. Her death left her oldest daughter, barely nine years old and still a child herself, responsible for a newborn infant brother and four younger sisters.

Paddy's obituary, which Mary Ann had located in the newspaper archives, indicated he died from yellow jaundice, had worked in the stock yards his entire life, and never remarried. Two daughters entered the convent, and his eldest son went to the priesthood. Three other daughters were married, and between them, produced nineteen grandchildren. The obituary does not mention Paddy and Maureen's youngest son, Frankie.

The address for the Corrigan family, mentioned in Maureen's obituary, turns out to be a walk-up apartment above a small bar with a neon beer sign in the window. It is directly across the street from McClanahan's Funeral Home, which has been serving the community at this location since 1889 and is the funeral home of record for both Corrigan deaths. It is impossible to know whether the bar was downstairs when Maggie was living upstairs, but the building, with two small windows and a narrow door, is not suitable for much else, and would be a handy place to drown one's sorrows after the visitation and rosary for the repose of the souls of the deceased resting in McClanahan's.

The window shades in the former Corrigan apartment are torn, and a noisy air conditioner hangs out of one of the upstairs windows, dripping water onto the sidewalk. It's not a warm day, so a running air conditioner probably indicates the apartment is occupied and its windows are painted shut, and the unit is the only source of fresh air.

Standing in the shade of a dying linden tree, looking up at the apartment, I try to imagine daily life for a family with seven children crowded together into what cannot possibly be more than a two-bedroom living space. With loud bar noise below them night after night, how did anyone sleep? Where did the children play, do their homework, eat their meals? How did Paddy explain their mother's death to her children, at least three of whom were still in diapers? Who changed those diapers in an era before disposable ones? After their mother died, who washed the children's clothes, cooked their meals, changed their bedding? Did they have a washing machine, or did they wash everything in a tub and hang their wet laundry to dry on lines strung around the apartment? Was there any joy in the Corrigan household, especially after Maureen died?

These are all questions I may never know the answer to because chances are good that breaking into a locked bank vault would be easier than convincing Maggie to talk about her childhood in great detail. Nevertheless, standing in this rundown neighborhood, staring up at the apartment's dirty windows, speculating isn't difficult.

After wandering the streets for another hour, I discover a small café next to a Saint Vincent de Paul thrift store, one of many Catholic Charity initiatives throughout the city, located in the Back of the Yards' sparse business district. The area is currently comprised mostly of abandoned storefronts with broken-out windows and missing doors. The sign in the dusty window says The Greasy Spoon, and a brief look inside suggests the name fits. Lacking other options for lunch, I decide to go in. The café is nearly empty, and thinking the lunch counter is more likely than the tables to be wiped down regularly, I claim one of the round metal counter stools covered in cracked red plastic.

"You ain't from 'round here," a grizzly old-timer with jaundiced eyes, dirty fingernails chewed bloody, brown-stained, broken teeth, sitting three stools down from mine, says. His face has not seen a razor in recent memory, his clothes are filthy, and he emits the sour odor of someone who habitually consumes large amounts of alcohol. Yet he is still alert enough to recognize a stranger when he sees one. My effort to blend in has clearly failed, and his attempt to point this out causes the other two men and one women in the café to stop eating and stare at me.

"Nobody comes 'round here without a reason, so you gotta be an undercover cop or somethin'," he continues. Despite validating Joey's prediction about how I would be received in a neighborhood where I did not belong, the old guy apparently wants to talk, and I'm eager to find out how chatty he might be.

"I'm not a cop. I'm a writer, and I'm thinking about writing a book about this area. What do you know about the yards?" I ask him.

"Them yards—that was butt-ugly work, I gotta tell ya," he begins, staring at the counter. "The slaughterhouse turned the streets blood red... and the stink—there's no describing the god-awful sweet smell of clotting blood, especially in summer...gags me just thinkin' about it. We hated it real bad, and there weren't much else we could do to stand it besides gettin' drunk and fightin'. We lived in shacks and weren't gettin' paid shit. Our women and kids were goin' hungry, and every day somebody got hurt bad... or killed, which didn't matter none because a hundred others was waitin' outside the gates to step up and take the poor bastard's place."

After letting loose with what may have been the most words he has uttered in a long time, the old guy hunches over to release a deep, consumptive cough. I push his glass of water toward him, which he reaches for without looking at me.

"How many of the locals worked in the stock yards during the thirties and forties?" I ask.

"Everybody did. The yards were the only job there was for somebody who couldn't read or write, and that was just about everybody. Us poor suckers, we came to this country thinking our life was gonna get better, and it got better all right—for everybody else. This city got built on the backs of us piss-poor Irish," he says, pounding the red Formica countertop.

Hearing this, a waitress comes over and cautions the man she calls Brownie to take it easy, then disappears again.

"Do you know any Corrigans from around here?" I ask him.

"Tougher 'n rail spikes, the lot a 'em. Most people watch out for 'em."

"Have you ever heard of Sister Maggie Corrigan?"

"Yea, I heard of her. Feisty, that one. Only reason she didn't get excommunicated is her brother was a priest who played poker with old Cardinal Sullivan since before he was a cardinal. Otherwise, she'd been run outta town straight into hell doin' what she was doin."

"What else do you know about Sister Maggie's family?"

"The old man—Paddy Corrigan—poor sod didn't have two nickels to rub together. With all them motherless kids, it weren't no wonder he was so fonda the drink."

"Sounds like you might've known some of his children."

"I knew his boy, Frankie...don't know much about the others. I think Maggie and another one went to the convent. I mighta heard someplace another girl had ten kids."

"Would you like some more coffee—maybe a piece of pie?" I ask.

"The peach pie with a little ice cream—maybe."

Overhearing this, a blond, stiff-haired waitress whose nametag says Betty reappears. I order a slice of peach pie with vanilla ice cream and coffee for my informant and a grilled cheese sandwich and hot tea for myself—a choice that seems the least likely to give me food poisoning.

"That's not much lunch," Betty says.

"I'm not that hungry." I smile, then turn to my new friend and ask him what else he remembers about Paddy Corrigan.

"Like all the rest of us poor suckers, Paddy done come off the boat fulla hope and promise of a better life and didn't know nothing 'bout what was waitin' for us. Didn't have nothin' but the clothes on our backs, and the only jobs was in the yards. Nobody survived for long; you either got hurt, or killed, or couldn't take it no longer and left. Didn't even bother to quit—just walked out. It was worse in summers with all that hot, sopping-wet heat hanging all over everything. Air stunk so bad you couldn't breathe."

As Brownie is describing this, my lunch and his pie arrive. Betty refills his coffee.

"One of the worst riots we ever had was when I'd only worked there two, maybe three days," the old guy says. "Back then, iron gates closed off more than a square mile of blood, guts, dirt, and cryin' animals. Rumor was a couple hundred thousand more was waitin' to get their throats slit to make the other people rich," he continued, diving into the homemade pie. This seems like a terrible conversation to have while eating and takes away what little appetite I have, but if it bothers Brownie, he doesn't let on.

"We slaughtered animals in plants fulla rats chewing on rotten meat. Rot was spread out over everything, and finally somebody couldn't take it anymore and a fight broke out. The fire wagons came, and for hours, firemen, under police order, shot us with water. It's not something I like remembering, I can tell you that. The yards were a real lousy way to try making a living, and fact was, we didn't."

What he was describing to me were fights among the men working in the jungle squalor of bloody killing fields, amidst squealing hogs and lowing cattle awaiting violent, gruesome deaths. Conflicts were constant, but most frequent in summer when, in one hundred ten-degree heat the raw, bacteria-laden meat coming off the animal bones nearly cooked itself. Often it rotted within hours, emitting a suffocating odor that gagged everyone within smelling distance. All it took to send everyone into an irrepressible, blind rage was one worker accidentally slipping on the blood-soaked floor, knocking into the man next to him, and the only way the men knew to respond to the deep, guttural anger always lurking just beneath the surface of their lives was with their fists.

This was the world Maggie Corrigan's father came to when he left his native Ireland, longing for a better life. It's no wonder he, and so many Irish like him, sought relief from their disappointment and unfulfilled dreams in alcohol.

"Tell me about Frankie," I ask, referring to the son who wasn't mentioned in Paddy's obituary, and the old guy suddenly goes silent, concentrating on his pie. I wait a few minutes and ask again.

"He went bad," he says quietly. "Eventually got sent to prison as a lifer, and the family disowned him."

"That's really sad," I reply. "Must've been hard on you, as his friend."

"I weren't Frankie's friend," he answers, slamming his hand on the counter.

"I'm sorry. Since you said you knew him, I assumed..."

Before I've finished the sentence, the old guy gets up and walks out, leaving a half cup of lukewarm coffee and an unfinished piece of peach pie, covered with melting ice cream, sitting on the counter.

"Guess I touched a nerve," I say to Betty.

She nods.

"Do you think he knew Frankie Corrigan?"

"They were either in the same gang or in rival gangs, but they all knew each other, and none of them came to any good. The ones who survived don't like a lot a questions and aren't interested in no trips down memory lane."

"Where does he live?" I ask, feeling bad for upsetting him so much he left before finishing the pie he was so enthusiastically enjoying.

"Most of the time he sleeps at the old Shannon Hotel over on west 49th. Used to be the only hotel in the area, but it's a flophouse now," Betty answers. "He's on the dole and splits his money between the bars and hotel. If he runs short at the end of the month, he sleeps in a doorway someplace. He stops in here a few times a week—knows I'll give him leftovers. Best you leave him alone and don't go botherin' him none. No tellin' what he'll do if he feels cornered by a lot of questions about a past he's tryin' hard to forget."

"Thanks for filling me in," I say, handing her a generous tip as I prepare to leave.

"Can you point me in the general direction of Holy Family Church?"

"What you want to go there for?" she asks.

"I'm hoping to find out more about the Corrigan family."

"The school's closed now, and they got some young guy as the pastor, and he ain't around much, so don't know what kind of help he'd be. But if you want to find out, it's about six blocks from here, going toward the lake."

I decide to take my chances and walk over to Holy Family. In the church office, I find a pleasant-faced, well-fed woman whose desk nameplate identifies her as Mrs. Murphy. She's not too busy to visit with me for a few minutes while she waits for her nephew, Father Murphy, to return from his hospital rounds. She asks me what I want.

"I'm doing background research for a book and want to learn about the people and the area in general. Some of the history and so on..."

"People around here aren't real keen on outsiders coming around asking questions, and don't want no books written about them neither," she says dismissively.

Changing the subject, I ask whether I can see the inside of the majestic greystone church while I'm waiting.

"Sorry, but it's locked, and I don't have a key. People wandering in off the street steal anything that isn't nailed down, including the offertory boxes payin' for the vigil candles. It's a pity, really, because churches are supposed to be open, but you can't trust nobody anymore. If somebody thought I had a key, they'd beat me bloody to get it."

"The neighborhood's that rough?" I ask.

"We got a serious gang problem."

"How serious?"

"The gangs got worse when the stock yards hit the skids, making what was already bad even worse. With no jobs, young boys figured out they didn't have futures and started forming gangs—greaser gangs, they were called—and their gang was more important to those kids than their families."

"Greaser gangs?"

"Kids with steel-toed boots who rolled cigarette packs in their T-shirt sleeves and rode around on their motorcycles, terrorizing the neighborhood. When Blacks moved into the area looking to work in the stock yards, racial tensions increased, gangs got bigger, and violence became even worse. The yards got known as home to the most violent greaser gangs in Chicago. We still have a reputation as one of Chicago's toughest, most dangerous neighborhoods."

"Holy Family Parish must've played an important role in the community back then...trying to keep things under control."

"Our parish is the social hub of the neighborhood with a proud history dating back to the 1880s," she beams.

Then the phone rings. Before answering it, she points to a pamphlet on the rack in the corner that contains a brief history of the church. Her lengthy conversation concerning available dates for premarriage instructions gives me time to read a brief summary of the parish history and learn that the founding pastor, Father Seamus Mooney, was native-born Irish and heavily involved in community life. Several years before prohibition—the federal ban on the production and sale of alcoholic beverages was enacted—he became intensely focused on the sober well-being of his parishioners. This evolved into a personal crusade for temperance—an unusual cause for an Irishman in an Irish community where no one ever missed a baptism, wake, wedding, or Saturday night dance, none of which have ever been known to be temperate occasions. Nevertheless, the priest fought to halt the proliferation of saloons throughout the parish. He did not live to see prohibition enacted, or to observe Chicago bars transformed into speakeasies thanks to wildly clever, highly successful Chicago gangster Al Capone's thriving 1920s bootlegging enterprise.

According to the pamphlet, under Father Mooney's guidance, Holy Family embraced the opportunity to attend to the spiritual lives of those living in the South Side squalor surrounding the stock yards and went about creating a parish life that was wide "sacred space," extending outward from the resplendent church into the homes of the faithful, most of whom were domestic workers, day laborers, and meatpackers. Sacramental occasions like baptism—particularly of the first-born son—or the oldest child's First Holy Communion, were monumental social events similar to weddings or funerals, and celebrated by the entire parish. According to the pamphlet, the parish filled the community's social as well as spiritual needs as the place where the Catholic faithful could offer the trials and tribulations of their hardscrabble lives up to God. My guess is little has changed since then.

After Mrs. Murphy hangs up the phone, I ask where the money to build such an elaborate church in such a poor area came from.

"Father Mooney was a good businessman," she explains. "He got the land donated, and the city made some kind of deal with the archdiocese to fund the rest. It was in everybody's best interest that the parishes, no matter where they were located, thrive—especially in the poor neighborhoods. Back then, the Church provided the only beautiful thing in the people's otherwise miserable existence, and they wouldn't miss Mass for anything. It was a quiet, peaceful hour in lives filled with the daily struggles of dirt-poor poverty. The Church gave them hope they couldn't find anywhere else. It still tries to do that."

Her explanation makes sense, although I still feel the money might have been better spent on providing food and decent shelter for the poor, including the Corrigan family, who struggled mightily for both.

III.

Chicago is not the most corrupt of cities...Chicago, though, it is the Big Daddy. Not more corrupt, just more theatrical, more colorful in its shadiness.

Studs Terkel

"I love Chicago. I was born here, and I loved being an Irish-Catholic priest here," Joey Noonan tells me on the evening after my day spent in the Back of the Yards. We are sitting in Berghoff's, Chicago's historic restaurant in the downtown Loop, drinking from ornate ceramic mugs filled with rich German beer while discussing the extraordinary, far-reaching influence the Catholic Church has in Chicago.

"It was a lot to give up—the priesthood. Just being Irish-Catholic means you own this town, and if you're Irish-Catholic and a priest, you're sitting at the right hand of the pope. Nobody and no other religion can claim that kind of power."

I know Joey is right, because what he is saying echoes what Sam always remarked upon whenever he talked about Chicago.

"The Irish saw to it that being Irish and Catholic in Chicago was not much different from being Irish and Catholic back in the old country," I recall Sam telling me when we were sitting in O' Reilly's bar, crunching peanuts and drinking Guinness on tap after one of the many Chicago Cubs baseball games we attended.

"At least the Jews give a baby boy eight days before claiming him for the faith by applying a potato peeler to his penis. The Catholics lock a Roman collar around the neck of the first-born son right out of the womb, before the umbilical cord is cut, which it never really is. It doesn't make a damned bit of difference what that kid wants; he will become a Catholic priest because his Irish mother, and the archbishop, won't have it any other way!"

In the last two days, I have learned a lot about Chicago, and understand better why native Chicagoans, Maggie included, love their city so much. I am beginning to grasp how deeply Chicago and Maggie are intertwined and how the city made her into who she became. I realize I need to further explore its influence on her and then arrange to visit her again.

Meanwhile, for nearly all of the next two days, I sit in a large reading room in the stately Chicago Historical Society building, plowing through the fascinating history of the politically corrupt, tough as nails, don't mess with me, blue collar town. A study in ethnic and economic contrasts, The Windy City's colorful history has dominated America's heartland since early in the nineteenth century.

From the beginning, the political and social influence the Irish exerted was far out of proportion to other ethnicities for one, very valid reason: it was never a "no Irish need apply" town. But most impressive of all, Chicago is home to a well-greased, smoothly running Democratic political machine no other American city has ever come close to rivaling and is something local, state, and national politicians have depended upon and benefited from again and again.

For most of Chicago's storied history, the Irish maintained solid control over both City Hall and the archdiocese, which is the first thing I ask Maggie about when we meet again several weeks later. Upon arriving, I find her sitting in her small room that contains a bed, a dresser, a straight-back chair, and a small television set. She looks exactly as she did the last time we met. Having declined my suggestion for lunch together, she is just finishing eating.

"How was your meal?" I ask.

"Barely fit for human consumption," she says, handing me her tray.

"Do the aides a favor and take this back to the kitchen," she instructs, without a "please" or a "thank you."

"When you get back, close the door all but six inches and move the chair over so I can look straight at you."

Feeling that I'm about to be interrogated, I follow Maggie's orders, hoping she won't go off on my hair or what I'm wearing again. A few minutes later, after everything is finally arranged to her satisfaction, I ask her to tell me about Chicago, then watch her face light up as she begins describing a city she seems to love as much as life itself.

"We Irish own Chicago. For most of my life, the mayor was Irish, and even if the archbishop's surname wasn't Irish, you can bet your pension he had an Irish mother," she tells me, driving home my impression that the troika the Irish, the Catholic Church, and city government form is unbreakable, even though nobody openly admits it.

"Let's start with the politics," I suggest.

"You're hilarious," Maggie responds. "Chicago is the undisputed Queen Mother of political corruption, but we sure as hell don't talk about it. There might be other corrupt cities, but none of them hold a candle to Chicago in terms of political theatrics, kickbacks, patronage, bribery, and general entertainment. City Hall is the best show in town—makes Shakespeare's dramas seem like preschool playground arguments. If they're registered Democrats, even dead people vote in Chicago. It's tradition."

"You're not the first person who's told me that. I had a friend from Chicago who thought Chicago politics were more entertaining than a first-run movie."

"Whoever said that was right. A world without Chicago politics would be so dull all of Illinois would drop dead from boredom."

"Which mayor do you know the most about?" I ask

"Pat Callahan, of course," she replies, referring to Patrick Daniel Callahan. Known as 'Paddy' to his closest confidants, but not to anyone outside his inner circle who wished to see the next day's sunrise. Callahan was notorious for his political influence over Chicago for his entire life, and most of what he put into place still endures.

Because it is difficult to imagine living in Chicago and not absorbing, either by osmosis or direct experience, Callahan's legendary political style, I ask Maggie to tell me more about the city's infamous mayor. She begins with a geography lesson.

"Callahan was one of us—a South Sider. He grew up around street gangs, so establishing his powerful political machine and keeping it running came naturally to him. If you can lead a gang, you can lead anything."

"Was Callahan an actual gang member?"

"There are lots of kinds of gangs, and it depends on whether you believe the Irish Mafia is one of them. He's never admitted it, but he was too good at what he did not to have learned how to get his own way early in life. The South Side neighborhoods were, and still are, beer-pail, lunch-bucket communities that revolve around their ward bosses whose job it is to get out the Democratic vote, and Catholic parishes, where the parochial school enrollment always outnumbers the public schools, and their sports rivalries make the pros look like neighborhood pick-up games. That all plays a big part in all this. Relationships in those communities are forged early, intensely loyal, and last a lifetime. That was Callahan's style—he never forgot where he came from."

"What else can you tell me about him?"

"He was the only child of Irish immigrants, was born, lived his entire life, and is buried within about a six-square-block area. He only left the Chicago city limits once each year, on June first, for his annual one-month pilgrimage back to his ancestral homeland in Shannon, County Clare, to visit his extended family, which I heard included sixty-eight first cousins on the O'Meara side of the family and an additional forty-seven cousins bearing the Callahan surname."

"Seriously? That's a huge kinship group."

"Irish have gigantic families, and we believe we're all related somehow. The bigger the family, the more people to defend you when trouble comes, which, especially for the piss-poor Irish, it always does. Callahan used this to his advantage. But he also began every day by attending early morning Mass at Queen of Heaven Catholic Church, where he was baptized, confirmed, married, and buried following a heart attack during an explosive city council meeting. I think it was in his eighth term."

"That's nearly thirty-two years!" I exclaim.

"That's right, and what short, fat, bald Pat Callahan lacked in height and public displays of Irish good humor, he made up for with his booming voice, temper tantrums, and generally sour disposition. He always reminded me of some weird combination of Russian Premier Nikita Khrushchev and the Irish Mafia mob boss he actually was. But I'll never forget how he wept openly when President Kennedy was shot. Claimed he loved him like a son and personally helped elect him—probably by nefarious means."

"I've heard that everybody in Chicago pays close attention to local politics. Is that true?"

"Is the pope a Catholic?" Maggie shoots back. "Keeping up was harder when I was at the motherhouse. But I had my ways."

"Can you elaborate?"

"Hell no," she replies, shutting me off. "What's important is that Callahan's legacy lives large after him. He took himself very seriously and ran City Hall like a private family business. He was the head of the family, and they never washed their dirty laundry in public laundromats—or hung it to dry on an outdoor clothesline—so nobody knew what was going on.

But one thing we were certain of is that eventually, one way or another, it would affect us. That's strong motivation to pay attention. Whenever his City Hall family was fighting among themselves, which was all the time, Callahan did not accept the criticism gracefully and took refuge in scripture. Once he claimed that not even Jesus could create perfection because the apostles constantly caused him trouble, so Chicagoans could not expect him, as mayor, to run a perfect city government. I thought that was pretty clever."

"What about his infamous political machine?"

"For starters, it was the most powerful political organization in American history. During his tenure as mayor, Callahan reminded every Democratic candidate for president of the United States that without his blessing and his political machine, they were destined to lose. Furthermore, if they failed to win, don't dare blame him. His connections got the money that enabled him to build the world's largest airport, tallest office building, a massive lakefront convention center, a Chicago campus for the state university, an intricate network of expressways that log nearly 50 million vehicle miles in any given year, and a giant web of mass transit lines. The list of his accomplishments is endless, because he knew how to get things done, and because he loved Chicago."

Concerned that this conversation is wearing her out, I ask Maggie if she wants to take a break.

"That's like asking me whether I noticed when hell froze over. I'll tell you when I need a break. Nothing else in my life is nearly as interesting as Chicago politics, and nobody around here has enough brains left to carry on a conversation anyway."

Clearly, enough brains are not Maggie's problem.

"What impresses you the most about Chicago politics?"

"Callahan was one of Chicago's most colorful mayors and he managed to stay out of jail, which by no means suggests he wasn't corrupt; it just means he never got caught—and that's definitely impressive. His administration was widely viewed as a fertile training ground for future crooks."

Paging through my notes, I find several other questions I want to ask.

"Did you know that Illinois ranks first in the nation in terms of elected officials serving prison time after convictions for state and federal crimes committed during their time in office?"

"Of course. Everybody knows that. It adds to Chicago's notoriety. Those're the kinds of accomplishments people tend not to forget, or not to care much about unless they are directly affected."

"Tell me how you think the Irish fit into all this?"

"From the very beginning, the Irish influence was far out of proportion to the general population, which gave Callahan a tremendous political advantage over everyone else. He became one of the most powerful men in the nation and ruled over an empire that was never prejudiced against the Irish in the ways other early twentieth-century American cities were. It's not much more complicated than that."

"My impression is that a good deal of Chicago's more recent growth is directly attributable to Callahan's leadership, which continued the tradition of weaving ethnicity, politics, and religion into a knot so tight, and so strong, even today it remains impossible to untie. It seems like the Irish maintained solid control over both City Hall and the archdiocese for much of Chicago's storied history, and during the Callahan era, neither the mayor nor the archbishop made major decisions without consulting the other. This extraordinary working relationship created a legendary political patronage system that spilled over into every aspect of the city's life and inner workings of the archdiocese, and neither made any effort to hide it. Am I correct?"

Maggie nods.

"During Callahan's reign, the sanitation workers who picked up the city's trash and cleaned the city streets, the men and women who collected money in the expressway toll booths, ran the elevators in Cook County Hospital, drove the Chicago Transit Authority trains and buses, and mopped the floors in City Hall all were foot soldiers in the army that protected and defended Callahan's far-reaching political machine. In return, these people were guaranteed jobs. In situations where there were two candidates for the same job, by default the Irish-Catholic won out over everybody else; however, if the other applicant was a good Catholic and faithful party member who consistently delivered the votes in his ward, he was offered a different job. It might not have been his first choice, but it was still a job, and a working Catholic was a financially solvent Catholic who could throw an envelope into the collection plate every Sunday."

"This payback system guaranteed Callahan got what he wanted, and my guess is the political machine he built from the ground up continued running smoothly, even after his death," I say.

"That's right. Ask any Irish-Catholic Chicagoan about Callahan, and they beam with pride, forgetting his notorious political corruption and claiming the robust Irishman is Chicago's patron saint."

"Do you agree?"

"Of course. It doesn't really matter that City Hall is one big patronage system, trash-hauling is sporadic, the streets aren't plowed for days after a crippling snowstorm, or that the complex system of interstate highways into and out of the downtown Loop are in a perpetual state of disrepair that creates chronic traffic jams. Chicago is a great city, thanks in large part to Pat Callahan—and don't you let anybody tell you differently."

"Your loyalty is pretty fierce. Tell me why?"

"Years ago, I pretended to be a newspaper woman and snuck into Cardinal Sullivan's first Annual Knights of Columbus dinner shortly after his appointment to lead the archdiocese. I wanted to hear what kind of bullshit he'd sling—sort of a 'know your enemy' move. He claimed he had walked down some of the most famous streets in the world and would take a back alley in Chicago over any of them. 'I was born here, will die here, and go to my rest in eternal life with our almighty and forgiving God right here in Chicago,' the cardinal proclaimed, which I've obviously never forgotten, because I couldn't help agreeing with him. It's not a boring town, and even with its arctic cold winters, steaming hot summers, perpetual traffic jams, and a river that runs green on Saint Patrick's Day, and flows backward the rest of the time, it is the toughest, liveliest, most politically corrupt, and most entertaining city in America. It's hard not to love a city with such a big heart overflowing with Irish sentimentality, never-ending, robust enthusiasm for life—and always spoiling for a good fight," Maggie says, tears forming in her eyes as she reaches for the roll of toilet paper she uses to blow her nose.

I wait a minute before continuing.

"I sort of know what you mean," I acknowledge. "Whenever I'm out of the country, I always return through Chicago, because I love the moment when I walk down the transit corridor into the international terminal and see a burly Chicago cop standing under an American flag call out 'all travelers holding passports from the United States of America bear to the left—and welcome home!' I know he really means it, and want to hug him."

Maggie nods while still dabbing at her eyes and wiping her nose.

"Explain how Chicago politics influenced you," I ask, after waiting a minute for her to compose herself.

"How didn't they?" she shoots back. "Politics is all about who gets what, and how they get it—and anybody can do anything they damned well please as long as they know the right people, have a strong coalition behind them, and maintain the courage of their convictions. If you know what you want, and know you're right to want it, nothing else, including what other people think, matters. And if you need dead people's votes to win, dig 'em up and get them to the polls."

It takes me a minute to realize she is actually serious about the attitude that doing whatever it takes to get what you want is fine—that the end nearly always justifies the means.

"Let's end this on a happy note: tell me what you love about Chicago."

"You don't have enough time, and you wouldn't understand anyway, because you weren't born there and didn't grow up there," she answers thoughtfully.

I wait to see if she'll say more.

"You know that song that Frank Sinatra sings about Chicago being his kind of town?"

I nod.

"I want it at my funeral."

PART TWO

1949 – 1959

...to eventually emerge and begin the journey to coming alive...

IV.

Hearken, O daughter, and consider, and incline thine ear; forget also thine own people, and thy father's house; so shall the King greatly desire thy beauty: for He is thy Lord; and worship thou Him.

PSALM 45: 10-11 (*DOUAY-RHEIMS CATHOLIC BIBLE*)

"Tell me, my child, why do you want to enter religious life?" a tired-sounding Mother Michael Joan, Superior of the Midwestern Province of the Catholic religious Order of the Pax Christi Sisters of Charity and Justice, asks bright-eyed, fiery red-haired, nearly seventeen-year-old Maggie Corrigan. The older nun and young aspirant to religious life are sitting across from one another on heavy wooden chairs placed in a stuffy, windowless room off the reception area in Holy Family convent, adjacent to Maggie's home parish. The rundown structure, badly in need of repair, smells of incense, dusty furniture, and floor wax.

Maggie's inquisitor is a grim-faced, large-framed woman who has worn the dark grey habit of religious life for thirty-three years, since the end of World War I. She has been interviewing teenagers aspiring to religious life for nearly twenty of those years and has grown weary of what she considers her most important duty as Superior: recruiting new members to her religious Order. Holy Family Parish is one stop on a month-long trip through Illinois, Michigan, and Indiana to interview high school senior girls who have expressed a desire to commit their lives to God by joining the Pax Christi Sisters of Charity and Justice.

Maggie is a member of Holy Family High School's 1949 graduating class and the last of its scheduled interviewees. Each has been recommended by the parish priest or the sisters teaching at Holy Family

High School, and has expressed an interest in pursuing vowed life as a nun—the Church's highest religious calling available to a Catholic girl. Although knowing almost nothing about the rigors of religious life, each interviewee believes she fits well with the SCJ mission. Mother Michael Joan's job is to determine whether she agrees.

The superior is keenly aware that many Catholic girls who express an interest in religious life come from struggling, generationally poor families. With further education far out of reach, their only other options are marriage or minimum-wage employment, most often as domestic workers, waitresses, store clerks, or factory workers.

Yet marriage under the conditions set forth by the Catholic Church, which regards any attempt to control conception and childbirth as a mortal sin, is not appealing to all Catholic girls. This is especially true of those who, like Maggie, come from impoverished, devoutly Catholic homes where there are more hungry mouths to feed than money to feed them. These young women have had front-row seats to their mothers' suffering and struggles with the responsibilities of raising more children than they could emotionally or physically care for, and thoughts of taking on that life for themselves repulse them.

The third choice is vowed religious life, which historically has provided the Church with a large workforce that willingly labors in the Lord's vineyards for almost nothing, which is only a problem for nuns. Parish priests receive salaries, free housing, health insurance, and a retirement fund, as well as special favors from parishioners and additional income from stipends for weddings, funerals, special blessings, and other religious occasions. Their Roman collar opens the door to cultivating the rich and powerful on a regular basis, while the much more restrictive sisterhood enjoys none of these benefits.

When Maggie fails to answer the question about why she is interested in religious life, Mother Michael Joan asks again.

"I'd really like to be a priest, but since women aren't allowed to do that, which isn't fair because women would be just as good at the priesthood as men are, being a nun is the only option I have," Maggie finally replies, staring back at the mother superior, whose deep-set eyes are boring into her own. With her hands folded in her lap, Maggie is successfully hiding any nervousness she is experiencing as she tries to secure the future she seeks.

"Surely by now you understand that life isn't always fair, my dear, and you do have other options," Mother Michael Joan points out, shifting her bulk around in her wooden chair and rearranging her heavy habit. "You could marry and have children."

"My mother died two weeks after I turned nine years old, and I've already spent years taking care of little kids, which I didn't choose and hated every minute of. I've changed enough smelly diapers and wiped enough snotty noses to do penance for every sin I could possibly commit in two lifetimes. I'm not interested in spending the rest of my life beholden to some man telling me what to do and having babies for the pope." Saying this, Maggie's eyes widen but remain locked with her interviewer.

"Do you think religious life is what God wants for you, Margaret?" the mother superior asks with a deep sigh while deciding to keep the interview formal by using Maggie's baptismal name. Taken aback by Maggie's forthright demeanor, she is watching Maggie's reactions to her questions carefully while unconsciously fingering the large wooden rosary beads hanging from her leather belt. In her experience, most girls who pursue religious vocations claim God is at the center of their lives and are more submissive and eager to please than Maggie appears to be, and her failure to exhibit these traits gives the mother superior pause. She finds Maggie's honesty disconcerting and realizes the young girl is quick-witted, exceptionally bright, and wise beyond her years, which is making this an unusually trying interview.

"If God wanted me to be a mother, I'd know it—and I don't. What I do know from raising my sisters and younger brother is that I am unfit for motherhood, and that it was only by God's grace that I finished high school, because being responsible for a bunch of little kids left no time for anything. I only managed to graduate because I'm smart and didn't need to be in class every day to pass the exams. The only hope for my future is within the Church...it means more to me than anything, or anyone, in my life," Maggie continues defiantly, resenting the challenge to her desire to enter religious life. What she does not say aloud is that she has seen what bearing more children than a woman can manage has done to her female relatives and wants no part of repeating that misery.

"The Church and the Order both require those who aspire to religious life to take vows of poverty, chastity, and unquestioning obedience to their superior, Margaret, and my information is that you have difficulty with obedience. This causes me to seriously wonder how well you are suited to vowed religious life."

"I grew up shanty Irish in the shadow of Chicago Union Stock Yards, Mother—I've been poor all my life. I figured out a long time ago that unless I want to have babies, which I don't, men are a bad idea, so chastity isn't a problem either. I admit obedience is harder, but I'm not afraid of hard work. If I was, I'd have run away from home a long time ago," Maggie tells the woman who will decide her future.

"The commitment to the vows is much deeper than mere superficial behavior, Margaret. They ask much more of us, and we must recommit ourselves to them each day—sometimes each hour and each minute. Fidelity to vows is the most rigorous and demanding aspect of religious life."

"It can't be more rigorous or demanding than motherhood, and I survived that for the last several years."

"You have also made it very clear that motherhood is not a challenge you care to repeat, and religious life has many repeated challenges," Mother Michael Joan reminds her.

"I'm only trying to say that facing difficulties is not an insurmountable problem for me—it's the story of my life, which should be obvious by now."

"There are hundreds of religious Orders in the Church. Why are you drawn to the Pax Christi Sisters of Charity and Justice?"

"I don't want to teach, and I don't want to be a nurse, which are the two main choices for women in religious life. I am personally familiar with the miseries social justice seeks to fix, which are no picnic. I completely understand living hand-to-mouth, having a baby every year, and I can plead the case of the suffering women who find themselves in that situation. SCJ's mission includes that kind of work. I'm also smart and can think fast on my feet—and I'm not afraid of a fight. Seems to me this will help me advocate for women who can't advocate for themselves."

"Where do you intend to take this campaign for justice for women?" Mother Michael Joan asks, feeling more and more exasperated by Maggie's answers.

"Wherever it leads me, I guess. I haven't thought that far ahead."

"Most of our sisters are more interested in hands-on charity work. They believe this is sufficient advocacy, and don't see themselves becoming involved in public pursuits that distract them from their real focus, which is on loving God and living out His will for their lives. We pray for justice but don't waste time trying to change the world, because that is up to God, and serving Him is our primary commitment."

"I can't see how charity does much good if it doesn't include a fight for justice," Maggie counters.

"Perhaps that is not for you to understand," the worn-down mother superior responds, looking around the stuffy room that she feels closing in on her as the interview continues. She has met her match with this brash young aspirant and is both impressed and alarmed by Maggie's articulate answers to her questions.

"You are very outspoken and appear to lack the humility required to fully surrender your life to God, causing me to question whether religious life will be enough for you, Margaret."

"I don't know whether it will be enough either, Mother, and the only way either of us will find out is if you give me a chance to try," Maggie challenges.

•••

Like many aspirants to religious life she has interviewed over the years, Mother Michael Joan left a childhood in poverty to enter religious life directly out of high school. She understands the burning desire for a better life and wants to do all that she can to provide this opportunity to young girls seeking it. She does not hesitate to accept four of Holy Family Parish's seven applicants immediately. Two others are judged poor matches for the SCJ mission and gently encouraged to look for other religious communities whose focus is more suitable to their interests.

She remains undecided about Maggie Corrigan.

"The girl is far too smart for her own good and isn't lacking in ego, which is not a particularly desirable quality becoming a woman religious, but she has a compelling aura of sincerity and intensity about her that could make her a strong leader, and we need good leadership," the superior tells Sister Marie William, the Order's novice mistress whose job it is to mold the young girls Mother Michael Joan sends her into committed women religious.

"I can't help wondering whether she has a true vocation or merely an overabundance of enthusiasm for the pursuit of social justice. She has a mind like a steel trap and is probably best suited to becoming a lawyer," the older nun notes with a frown while looking out her cramped office window in the main building on the motherhouse grounds. Heavily burdened by her management responsibilities, she often spends long periods staring out across the acres of grazing fields and cropland, hoping to hear the voice of God.

"And who do you suppose would pay for her to attend college and law school?" Sister Marie William, now in her tenth year as a solemnly vowed member of the religious community, counters. "There's no money for those pursuits in her family, and even if there was it would all go to her brothers."

"She'll be a handful, Sister. She might be more than you can handle," the superior warns.

"If she wants to come, I think we should accept her, and let me worry about the rest," Sister Marie William answers. At half Mother Michael Joan's age, the novice mistress has the energy and patience to deal with a strong-willed, high-spirited young aspirant to religious life that the older superior lacks.

Mother Michael Joan prays over the decision to admit Maggie Corrigan for another month before, reluctantly and against her better judgment, surrendering to the wishes of the novice mistress and sending an acceptance letter. In it, she requests the three hundred fifty-dollar dowry required of all postulants be sent by return mail, along with a certificate of good physical and dental health.

•••

"Where the hell am I gonna get three hundred and fifty bucks to send you to the convent?" Paddy Corrigan rants at his daughter when Maggie tells him of her acceptance and the dowry requirement. "I can't even scrape together a dollar for the Sunday collection plate, for Christ's sake."

"You could if you'd stop with the drink," Maggie yells back, seeing her dream of religious life evaporate as quickly as the alcohol on Paddy Corrigan's breath. Despondent and in tears, she runs down the apartment's back stairs into the alley, past overflowing garbage cans, all the way to her Aunt Molly's apartment, where she explains what has happened. Her mother's ever-resourceful and only surviving sister says she will pass the hat among the family and suggests Maggie ask Monsignor Doyle, Holy Family Parish pastor, for the rest.

"He baptized you and has known you all your life. I'm sure he has the money," she tells her niece. "If the parishes didn't pony up, no kids from poor families could go to religious life, and they're the only ones who are even interested. Everybody else has other opportunities."

"I'd be begging him, and I'd rather die," Maggie tells her aunt.

"Sometimes the choice between begging and dying makes begging look pretty good, Maggie. There are lots of ways to die, and they don't all end with being put in the ground."

"What about the health certificates?" Maggie wails. "My teeth are crammed into my mouth and the only doctor I've ever seen is the one who comes to school to give vaccinations."

"I'll call the free health clinic. I think a dentist volunteers there every week or two. If you don't have any toothaches, that should work. Same with a doctor. Several volunteer every week and all you have to do is show up and wait your turn."

Maggie's extended family eventually comes up with twenty-six dollars toward her future, which means she must either forego religious life or ask the parish priest for the remaining three hundred twenty-four dollars. She dreads explaining all this to Monsignor Doyle.

•••

When Maggie arrives at the well-furnished rectory, the housekeeper, Mrs. McMurray, escorts her into the priest's large office, where he sits behind his desk, waiting for her. Even though he knows precisely why she is there, Monsignor Doyle, who was recently promoted up one level from plain Father Doyle, signifying that he is now a ceremonial chaplain in the papal household, tells her to sit down and explain why she has come.

"I have been admitted to the Pax Christi Sisters of Charity and Justice and my family can't afford the dowry," Maggie begins through clenched teeth, seething at the indignity of her situation.

"How much money can your family afford?"

"Twenty-six dollars."

"How much do you need?"

"Three hundred and fifty, total."

"And you want me to make up the difference?"

"Not you, Monsignor, the parish."

"This is not a wealthy parish, Margaret. Where do you think this money will come from?"

"The annual collection for vocations—where else?" Maggie answers. "Aren't situations like this exactly what that money is for?"

"Families who send several children to religious life receive priority when the funds are distributed. Remind me how many vocations have come from the Corrigan family?"

"My brother's going to the seminary. He got a full scholarship, which won't cost the parish anything."

"Any others?"

"Not that I know about," Maggie continues, staring at the priest's smooth, carefully shaved face and neatly trimmed hair.

"That's unfortunate. I feel it only fair to wait and see what requests come in from priority families before giving you the money. I am aware there will be several." He pauses for nearly a minute before continuing.

"There's another issue. The parish has subsidized and is still subsidizing every one of Paddy Corrigan's children, including you, to enable you all to receive a Catholic education in the parish school. That is a lot of charity directed to one family."

"I'm supposed to send the money immediately," Maggie points out, staring at the floor and clenching her jaw.

"You want me to give you three hundred and twenty-four dollars today, is that it?"

"Yes, Monsignor."

"Usually, families are given time to find the money themselves, and I'm a little surprised at the urgency. May I please see your acceptance letter?"

Maggie hands it over.

"I see this is dated just last week. Yours was a decision that seemed to take a long time and required much thought on the part of the Order leadership. How can I be sure you are serious about your vocation when they are obviously wondering the same thing?"

"You think I'd be sitting here begging for money if I wasn't serious?" Maggie blurts out. "One way or another, I intend to walk through the motherhouse door on July first. I've begged from my family, and am begging you, and it's humiliating. If you won't help me, you'll have to explain it to the Order and to my family who, by the way, are faithful parish members. They don't give much money, but they always show up when it counts and help out however they can."

"I don't have to explain my decisions to anyone," Monsignor Doyle points out, then waits several seconds for the full effect of this proclamation to sink in before continuing.

"Your entrance date is in less than two weeks. If I give you the money now, you will have to sign a promissory note indicating that if you ever leave religious life, you must repay the money, with interest, just as if it were a loan."

"Does everyone have to do that?" Maggie asks.

"No, not everyone," the monsignor acknowledges. "We only give money to those we are quite sure won't fail in their religious calling, so there's not usually any need for a guarantee that the money is a good investment."

"Then why do I have to do it?" Maggie asks.

When the silence, and Maggie's unrelenting gaze, become unbearable, Monsignor Doyle finally answers her. "In your case, it seems prudent."

Rather than risk him changing his mind, Maggie tells the priest she will sign the note and wait while the document is typed up. He leaves her sitting alone for nearly an hour before returning and handing her a piece of paper and a pen, showing her where her signature is required. She signs the note without reading it, reaches for the check he has placed on the table, and walks out the front door of the rectory, neither thanking him nor saying goodbye.

"There's no way in hell he'll ever collect that money from me. First, he'd have to find me, and then he'd have to figure out how to get blood out of a rock," Maggie chuckles as she skips down the street toward home.

•••

A few days later, while sitting on the fire escape dangling down from the back of apartment, Maggie recounts this to her best friend, Mary Pat Donovan, who in addition to being the prettiest, most popular girl in their high school, is also her brother's perky, boy-crazy former girlfriend. Maggie has never understood why Mary Pat was so in love with Tommy, or how Tommy, who Maggie views as a thoroughly disgusting human being, ever convinced Mary Pat to be his girlfriend. And Mary Pat refused to talk about it, especially after they broke up and she started dating Joe Finnegan, the captain of the football team. Too overwhelmed with family responsibilities and school, Maggie has never had time to make friends, and even though she suspects Mary Pat comes around mostly because of Tommy, she is always happy to see her.

"Are you really sure you want to go to the convent?" Mary Pat asks. "Think about all you're giving up: love, getting married, kids...sex," she giggles.

"I don't believe in love, marriage, or motherhood, so I'm not giving up much," Maggie points out.

"I don't believe you. You're just saying that because you haven't ever had a boyfriend."

"I've learned all I want to know about boyfriends from a drunken father and a bully brother who have problems with personal boundaries—namely mine—and I will be plenty happy when there are a lot of miles between me and them. I'm not interested in having any men in my life."

"What are you saying, Maggie?"

"More than I should. I don't want to talk about it anymore."

"Tommy didn't do bad stuff to you, did he?"

"I said I don't want to talk about it anymore. You should be glad he's going to the priesthood and will be out of your life for good. Trust me, he's not worth thinking about ever again."

•••

Later that evening, while Maggie is checking off items she is required to bring with her when she enters the convent in a few days, her sister, Fiona, sits down on the bed next to the open suitcase. Dark-haired and blue-eyed, with her mother's delicate looks, Fiona is the beauty of the family.

"I think you're being really selfish going off and leaving us," Fiona tells her sister.

"You're just mad because it means you'll have to pick up the slack," Maggie answers.

"You're needed at home, Maggie. Mary says she's going to the convent next year, which leaves me responsible for Colleen, Annie, and Frankie, and he's such a terror I'm afraid of him. And Pa's never sober enough to help out; he's just another kid to take care of. It's not right, you turning your back on us and leaving me to deal with everything—especially Frankie. He's headed for no good, and with Tommy gone and Pa drunk all the time, nobody's going to be able to stop him."

"You've no right to ask me to stay, Fiona. I gave up the last eight years of my life because I never had a choice. You and the others got everything I had to give—all day, every day—and now it's my turn to do something I want with my life. Asking me to stay when I finally have a chance to get out of here isn't fair. Besides, you'll get your chance eventually."

"I'm not as smart as you, Maggie. I won't have choices."

"Everyone has choices, Fiona. And I've made mine."

"I'm only fifteen years old, Maggie…this is too much for me."

"You'll be sixteen by the time Mary leaves—I'm sure you can manage. And Tommy's going to the seminary in a couple months, which will be one problem off your hands."

"I kicked Tommy in the balls when he tried messing with me, and he never tried again," Fiona tells her sister. "It's Pa I'm more worried about. He'll hit me."

"Put a chair under the door handle when you go to bed. That way he can't open the door without waking everybody up."

"I never thought of that."

"I wish I'd thought of it sooner."

"I still hate you for leaving, Maggie. It makes you seem better than us...like we're not good enough for you...like you don't care about us enough to stay."

"I'm sorry you feel that way, Fiona. But I'm going anyway, and there's nothing you can do about it."

•••

On Maggie's last Sunday at home, Monsignor Doyle preaches vehemently against women's rights, particularly advances in birth control becoming more widely available, which will revolutionize women's lives.

"This discovery goes against the laws of nature and of God, and the Church rightly declares that any woman who uses any form of birth control, including this pill, is committing a mortal sin against God and family life," he shouts from the pulpit, his purple face emphasizing his point. Simultaneously, his fire-breathing rhetoric fuels Maggie's commitment to fighting for Catholic women to gain agency over their own lives and independence from authoritarian tyrants like the priest who baptized her into the Church and is now yelling from the pulpit.

Walking back to the family apartment after Mass, Maggie's thoughts turn to her mother. She's old enough to understand that her mother's death was preventable, if only she had been able to avoid a pregnancy every year of her marriage. Increasingly, Maggie blames the Church for robbing her of a loving mother she finds harder and harder to remember, and of the childhood she never had. Each day, her resolve to somehow help other women who want to avoid pregnancy succeed in doing so, grows stronger, despite resenting being the last of Holy Family's applicants to receive an SCJ acceptance letter and finding Monsignor Doyle's homily profoundly disturbing. With these thoughts swirling in her head, she is not beginning religious life with a peaceful, open heart.

Despite her misgivings, forty-eight hours later, Margaret Ann Corrigan, having relinquished all her worldly possessions, prepares to leave home to present herself to the motherhouse of the Pax Christi Sisters of Charity and Justice in Saint Xavier, Indiana. As the majestic Chicago skyline fades from view, the several-hour drive toward her new life breeds even more trepidation. Used to tall buildings, asphalt streets, and cement sidewalks, all she can see ahead are miles and miles of cornfields reaching toward the mid-summer sun.

Looks like a hard place to escape from and live to tell about it, she thinks, as the solitary, walled-in motherhouse comes into view. She takes a deep breath and prepares to walk through the iron-gated portal into the unknown, bringing with her a small cardboard suitcase containing a one-week supply of underwear, two nightgowns, black leggings, a black cardigan sweater, and black Oxford shoes. The thoughts in her head are her only mementos of home.

Dry-eyed, Maggie tells her father, her twin-brother Tommy, and her two youngest sisters goodbye without a hug, a kiss, or any other sign of affection. Resolutely, she walks through the entrance to the motherhouse without turning around.

"A buck says she won't last a month," Tommy says confidently, as he drives his father and sisters back toward Chicago.

Maggie is among the last to arrive and joins the other eager young girls standing around in a reception area. Five minutes later, Sister Marie William walks in to welcome them and asks about their journey.

"I didn't know I was coming someplace a hundred miles past nowhere," Maggie answers.

"Coming here is an adjustment for those from large cities," the kind-faced novice mistress explains patiently. "However, with fewer distractions, you will find it easier to remain focused on God and your preparation for dedicating your life to serving Him."

"Well, there's certainly nothing distracting about miles and miles of cornfields and the occasional cow," Maggie whispers to herself while walking toward a room where she and the others surrender their secular clothes and receive the postulant's black dress and wide black headband.

While two resident sisters fold the discarded clothing and place it in boxes, Sister Marie William instructs Maggie to twist her unruly hair into a braid and then into a tight knot at the base of her neck. Maggie explains that she does not have the tools to follow this order, which sends the other sisters scrambling in search of rubber bands. When everyone is suitably dressed in the postulant's uniform, Sister Marie William leads them into the gathering room for a brief orientation.

Postulancy is the boot camp, goodness-of-fit phase of vowed religious life, and generally lasts six months. It offers a low-investment opportunity for the young aspirant to experience religious life and begin the process of developing the virtues required of her if she is to succeed in her chosen vocation. It is also an opportunity for her superiors to assess her commitment and suitability for membership in their Order.

"Your postulancy begins a rigorous period in your religious life that requires you to give up everything in the material world, including family relationships, friendships you cherish, and your sense of who you are to fully surrender yourself to God," Mother Marie William tells them.

"You will never look into a mirror again and will become emotionally detached from everything and everyone, including yourself, so that God can remake you anew, in His image for you. This is your invitation to form a deep emotional relationship with Christ, and only with Christ. Some of you will find this too difficult and will leave. Others will persevere to eventually wed yourselves to Jesus Christ by becoming solemnly vowed members of the Order."

Hearing this, the postulants look at each other, wondering who among them will succeed in overcoming their loneliness, homesickness, and personal failings to become worthy Brides of Christ and who will succumb to their human faults and failings and suddenly disappear without explanation.

"You are forbidden personal friendships," Mother Marie William continues. "You confide in God, in me, or in Mother Michael Joan. To avoid the temptation to confide in one another, maintaining silence while doing your assigned work is strictly enforced. You are also required to maintain custody of your eyes, meaning you are not to make eye contact with others or use your eyes to communicate your private thoughts. Failing any of these constitutes a fault that must be confessed to the community, on your knees, each Friday before morning Mass."

Coming from a loud, boisterous family that says whatever enters their heads at the moment the thought occurs, this requirement appalls Maggie. Although not accustomed to sharing her interior, emotional life, which she has never had the luxury of nurturing, she still cannot imagine not being allowed to speak with the other postulants. *Guess I'll be doing a lot of talking to myself,* she thinks, finally understanding why so many nuns she has known over the years walked around mumbling to themselves.

"From this moment until your fifth month here, you will have no contact with your family. Beginning in the fifth month, you will be permitted one communication with family each month, by letter. I will read both the letters you receive and the ones you write, which will assist me in determining how well you are adjusting to religious life and enable me to identify, and hopefully correct, potential problems before they become insurmountable," the novice mistress explains.

Maggie realizes there is no one in her family she has any desire to remain in touch with, and decides Mary Pat is the person she will write to. *I'll just say she's my older, married sister,* she decides. *They'll never know whether this is true.*

"You will rise at five o'clock each morning, line up for the bathroom, dress, and be in the chapel by six-thirty for meditation and reading the Divine Office of the Day, silently and in Latin," Sister Marie William tells them. "Celebration of the Mass follows the Divine Office, then breakfast, after which you are allowed to break the solemn silence that has been in place since nine o'clock the previous night. However, breaking this silence is not for idle chitchat; it is only to allow necessary conversations, which must be quiet, respectful, and reverent." The novice mistress pauses for effect before continuing.

"Between breakfast and lunch, you will perform your assigned duties, which include laundry, kitchen chores, general cleaning, and outside work during the spring, summer, and fall months." At this point, she pauses again, then reads each postulant's name and assignment. This is when Maggie learns that, for the next two months, she will be scrubbing the convent floors.

"Meals are in the refectory, where you will sit at long tables, eating in silence while one of the sisters stands behind the lectern at the front of the room, reading from a spiritual text, sacred scripture, or the lives of the saints. You are to listen without comment or questions," the novice mistress explains, looking directly at Maggie.

"After the noon prayer, you may begin eating, and when the sister finishes reading, you may clear your lunch dishes and wait for me at the entrance. Now, please follow me."

After lunch, the postulants process single file to a classroom to receive further orientation. They will later return to the same classroom for instructional classes devoted to their spiritual formation and indoctrination into the Order's specific rules and regulations. The hour before dinner is spent recreationally walking as a group around the inside perimeter of the wall enclosing the motherhouse grounds. "You are not permitted to walk outside alone or with just one other postulant. During your daily walk with the others, your conversation is limited to what you are learning, not what you are feeling or experiencing, and certainly not commenting on the behavior of others that you may have overheard or observed," the novice mistress emphasizes.

"To maintain your devotion to Mary, the mother of our Lord Jesus, at precisely five o'clock each afternoon, you will gather again in the chapel to read the Office of the Order and pray the rosary, led by Mother Michael Joan or one of the professed sisters," Sister Marie William instructs.

"Supper follows, after which you will return to the classrooms to complete your study assignments. When the tower bell rings, signaling the end of the day and the beginning of the solemn silence, you will return to your cell to prepare for bed."

"Six months of this crap is a damned long time," Maggie whispers to the postulant seated next to her.

"Did you say something, Margaret?" Sister Marie William asks.

"No, Sister, I was just clearing my throat."

Following the verbal introduction to their new life, Sister Marie William invites the postulants on a walking tour of their new surroundings. For Maggie, whose first trip outside the Chicago city limits was the drive to the motherhouse, the silence of the rural landscape is deafening. There is not a siren, honking horn, belching bus, or clanging L train anywhere. *I'll never be able to sleep,* Maggie silently laments. *It's like a tomb in here.*

The surrounding area, inside and outside the walled motherhouse, includes more than four hundred acres of woods, pasture, and tillable cropland belonging to the Order. Giant burr oak, maple, ash, and birch trees provided a canopy over the buildings and, in the fall of the year, create a panorama of color so stunning it forces any onlooker, no matter how doubtful, to believe in God, at least for that moment. Fourteen Stations of the Cross, depicting Jesus' journey to his death, are scattered around the landscape. Each station includes a bench to sit down and meditate on Jesus' suffering, and a kneeler to pray. Resting against the thick trunk of a giant oak tree is a stone and wood grotto dedicated to the Blessed Virgin Mary. Another bench for those who wish to sit and pray the rosary faces the weathered wood and plaster statue, creating a serene, peaceful, and prayerful setting. *This is a great place to live if all you want to do every day is eat, pray, and sleep,* Maggie silently observes.

The buildings include two stately, interconnected stone structures, both more than one hundred years old. All are named for saints Maggie has never heard of, and she raises her hand to ask about them. The novice mistress ignores her.

The first floor of the largest building contains a kitchen; laundry, dining room, reception areas; and a chapel named for Saint Vincent de Paul, a seventeenth-century French priest whose generosity and humility inspired the SCJ founders more than three hundred years ago. Classrooms occupy the entire second floor, and the top level contains large dormitory rooms providing sleeping space for the postulants. Cells, measuring seven feet by seven feet each and surrounded by six-foot long curtains, line the walls of the three rooms. The center aisle of each room leads from the bathroom at one end to the only window in the room at the opposite end. Each cell includes a large crucifix affixed to the wall above the bed, a kneeler, and a small table with one drawer. A single hook against the back wall holds one change of clothing and sleepwear. With no soundproofing between the cells, everyone hears every cough, sneeze, hiccup, giggle, burp, moan, and tearful sob a postulant releases during the night. With only one window in the room, air circulation is poor, suffocating the occupants in the summer heat. If anyone dares complain, she is told religious life is not intended to be comfortable and to offer her suffering up to God with gratitude and joy.

Attached to the west side of the main building is a four-story convent and novitiate where the vowed sisters live in small, individual cells similar to those in the dormitory, except plaster walls instead of curtains separate them. A much smaller, single-story building attached to the convent's east side contains offices and conference rooms.

Separately, there is an ornate, minor basilica that seats over eight hundred people and honors Saint Martin de Porres, the patron saint of social justice. That both the chapel and main church are named for male saints, which outnumber female saints by about ten-to-one, doesn't escape Maggie's notice. *Male saints are another way for the Church to hold power over women,* she thinks, tempted to ask why, since this is a community of women, the church and chapel are not named for women saints.

The Order maintains an agricultural operation that includes chickens, goats, a few pigs, a working dairy farm, and a very large garden that produces large quantities of vegetables and fruit. This effort provides some income as well as food for the postulants, novices, and professed members of the congregation living at the motherhouse at any given time.

"We are a self-sustaining community, and you will be expected to do your share to keep us this way," Sister Marie William tells the new postulants. "For those of you who do not come from a rural setting, this will include learning the importance of farm and garden chores."

I don't know the back end of a cow from the front end of a goat. How the hell am I supposed to tend farm animals? Maggie silently wonders. *This is not why I came here and doesn't have a damned thing to do with religious life. They're using us as slave labor to keep this place going, so the old nuns will have a roof over their heads until they die.*

The tour ends at Saint Vincent de Paul chapel, where the vowed sisters are gathering in the long, wooden pews to kneel to read the Office of the Order—a collection of daily prayers focused on imploring God and the saints to guide them in their mission of providing charity to those in need, followed by the rosary. At the chapel entrance Mother Michael Joan hands each postulant a leather-bound prayerbook that is theirs to keep and tells them to follow along with the others. The late afternoon sun shining through the small stained-glass windows casts an eerie, green-tinged light over everyone and everything in the otherwise dark, austere space containing several rows of pews, a plain altar, a life-sized crucifix, six boxed confessionals, and fourteen Stations of the Cross, depicting Christ's suffering and death, and a small pipe organ. A tall, slender statue of the Virgin Mary stands to the left of the altar. A wooden kneeler has been placed before Jesus' Blessed Mother, making it easier for the brides of Christ to ask her to intervene with her son on their behalf, if they feel the need. By the time the entire ritual is completed, Maggie has been kneeling for ninety minutes and can barely stand up afterwards.

Because the postulant on the other side of the curtain closest to her bed sobs for hours, which the lack of outside noise amplifies, Maggie sleeps little during her first night in the convent. Consequently, she begins her first full day of religious life barely able to keep her eyes open. She nods off during a brief ceremony in the chapel admitting the young aspirants into the postulancy, followed by the celebration of the Mass. This ritual marks the formal beginning of her religious formation process and, hopefully, her eventual acceptance into the religious Order of Pax Christi Sisters of Charity and Justice, which currently numbers four provinces and nearly five thousand nuns across the Americas.

During his morning homily, the priest explains that the postulancy orients a young woman to the requirements for religious life in community. She is expected to gain a firm grasp on the vows of poverty, chastity, and obedience that she will, if she goes on to become a Bride of Christ, take and be expected to live by for the rest of her life. He blesses each postulant individually, then sprinkles them all with holy water and bids them to go forth and give thanks for this opportunity to abandon their temptation-filled secular lives, and serve their glorious redeemer, God.

Even here another man is telling me what to do, Maggie bristles as holy water rains down on her.

After the blessing, the priest invites each postulant who wishes to do so, to go to confession so that she can begin religious life with a pure soul and sin-free heart. Maggie is among those who do not accept this invitation and gives no thought to whether her superiors notice her dismissal of this important aspect of sacramental life.

After breakfast, Maggie reports to the convent to begin work assignment. Her mind struggles to pay attention to the verbal instructions an older nun gives her regarding how to properly scrub a floor. "This is an important assignment you are fortunate to receive," the sister tells her. "It toughens your knees so you can kneel in prayer for longer periods than you might be able to do otherwise."

Bullshit, Maggie thinks as she positions her skinny legs on the hard, wooden floor. Three hours later, her knees are throbbing, her back aches, and she can barely walk. Noting this, her supervisor tells her to gratefully offer her pain up to the glory of God as penance for her sins, both real and imagined.

After lunch, the postulants gather in the largest of the second-floor classrooms to begin their formal instruction. Blackboards cover the space on either side of the crucifix and the wall opposite the windows. Each young woman faces forward, hands in her lap and both feet resting flat on the floor, silently watching their novice mistress pace back and forth across the front of the room. The long wooden rosary beads hanging from her waist click together, creating the only sound in the room.

When the one o'clock bell tolls, the three-hour lecture on religious life begins with a prayer imploring the Holy Spirit's guidance, followed by Sister Marie William explaining the solemn vows each will take if the Order admits her into lifetime membership. Looking over the tall novice mistress's shoulder from above is the large, crucified Christ, who died for humankind's sins, which has always puzzled Maggie. *I don't understand how Jesus can die for my sins when I wasn't born until nearly two thousand years later and, obviously, hadn't done anything yet,* she asks herself yet again. *He had no way of knowing what I might, or might not, ever do.* Other than falling back on the original sin argument, which claims everyone is born with the stain of sin on their soul that baptism magically removes, none of her high school religion instructors were able to satisfactorily answer this question. She has not decided whether to raise it again during her formation process, but it has always bothered her that a graphic, outsized image of a man who was brutally murdered nearly two thousand years ago is the centerpiece of her religious life.

"The vow of poverty leads us to reject the material world in favor of seeking to know God through simplicity, and carefully avoiding the distractions material wealth imposes. We strive to imitate Jesus, who lived in poverty his entire life, showing us by example that the poor are the most blessed among us, for they shall inherit those things that really matter. Jesus was telling us that living in poverty is living in holiness," Sister Marie William begins.

Bullshit, Maggie thinks for the second time on her first full day in religious life, which is only half over. *There's nothing holy or blessed about rats, goddamned cockroaches, and going to bed hungry every night.*

"Poverty means surrendering any interest in, and claim to, material things, freeing ourselves from responsibilities that interfere with our commitment to live in God's service and, through God, serving others. This allows us to discover, through our personal relationship with Jesus, far greater wealth than we can possibly imagine. Achieving this requires us to give up all rights to personal property and surrender ourselves to living interdependently within our community," the novice mistress explains, pausing to walk up and down the aisles and allow what she has just said to take hold.

Seated near the front of the third row from the windows, Maggie raises her hand, hoping to point out that she believes the explanation of poverty she has just heard is missing some important points, the main one being that it's nearly impossible to focus on God and any promise of inheriting the earth when someone is so materially poor they don't know where their next meal is coming from. After a few minutes, the novice mistress resumes speaking without inviting questions and continuing to ignore Maggie's raised hand.

"The vow of chastity," the nun continues, "is a promise to remain physically and emotionally pure, thereby imitating Jesus, who lived a chaste life. This frees us from the demands of exclusive human relationships so we can give all our love to God, and through God to all people equally. We promise not to marry or to engage in romantic or sexual behaviors that interfere with our commitment as Brides of Christ. Like all who marry, we avoid anything that detracts us from our most important relationship, which is with our beloved spouse, Jesus. We promise to avoid near occasions of sin in thought, word, or deed that might tempt this vow. We strive to remain sin-free and pure in Jesus' eyes, making ourselves worthy to be his loving bride forever."

Again, Maggie has several questions about this explanation of purity, which focuses on sex rather than striving to live in truth and honesty. *Any idiot knows pregnancy is a good reason to avoid sex. It's something men think they are entitled to do and that women should submit to, whether they want to or not. Only a fool would go along with that,* she thinks, intending to never repeat the sexual experiences she has already had, which began when she was too young to understand, and were never consensual. *I'm too confused about all this to even think about temptation with either men or women,* she admits to herself. This sudden realization surprises her so much, she decides against raising the question of how anyone knows Jesus lived a chaste life when most men don't.

Sister Marie William pauses for several minutes before turning to the blackboard and printing the word OBEDIENCE in large letters, underlining it twice.

"The vow of obedience directs us to imitate Jesus' obedience to God the Father. This requires a continuous effort to seek, discern, and then surrender to God's will, and to obey our religious superiors as well as the doctrines of Holy Mother Church." Again, she pauses before continuing.

"As members of a religious community, we continually, every minute of every hour of every day, endeavor to discern what God is calling us to do through prayerful reflection, careful attention to the gospels and sacred scripture, and reading about the lives of the saints. Formation in religious life is an ongoing, never-ending process of seeking God and listening for God, always in a state of gratitude to Him for the opportunity to follow His will for us as our superior directs us to do."

Again, Maggie raises her hand. "What if our view of the will of God and our superior's view of the will of God are different?" she blurts out without being called upon.

The novice mistress glares at Maggie and reminds her that she is only to speak when called upon to do so, then takes a deep breath and attempts an answer. "We humbly accept that we may not always know God's will and take it on faith that God is speaking to us through our superior. Then, willingly and with a glad heart, we obey her. If our spiritual life is healthy, this is not difficult; if it is faltering, obedience can become very problematic," she acknowledges.

"You don't know the half of it," Maggie whispers to herself, remembering the few times she was forced to do something she didn't want to do. Having grown up in a motherless home with a psychologically absent father, she rarely answered to an adult. For as long as she can remember, she has made her own decisions and is not accustomed to routinely obeying anyone other than the nuns who taught her in school. At a very early age, she quickly figured out that sneaking around them was not difficult. She has always willfully disobeyed any order she didn't want to follow and rarely suffered the consequences, making the vow of obedience of little concern to her.

V.

The vowed religious life is very difficult. You give up all material possessions, surrender control over everything, including your own life and body, to God and the Order, and promise to live in total obedience to someone else forever.

JULE WOODSON, FORMERLY SISTER ANGELA JEROME

After six months of hard physical labor and rigorous mental work, during which time Maggie and the other postulants are continually observed and evaluated to determine whether their vocation to religious life is developing as expected, and whether they are a good fit with the SCJ religious community, the moment of reckoning finally arrives. If the answer to these two questions is "yes," the postulant is declared a Bride of Christ and accepted into the novitiate—an important rite of passage on their journey toward fully committed religious life.

On January 11, the day after Jesus' baptism, which marks the end of the Christmas season, fifty of the postulants who entered the SCJ motherhouse six months earlier enter the novitiate. Of the remaining thirty-three, ten decided religious life was not for them and returned home. Fourteen others, deemed unsuitable either for religious life or for permanent membership in the SCJ community, or both, were asked to leave. Nine, including Maggie, are held back for an extended postulancy.

"I'm fine with this, Mother," Maggie lies when Mother Michael Joan informs her of the decision. "I admit religious life does not come naturally to me, but I am not afraid of the hard work it takes to overcome these faults, and intend to keep trying, no matter how long it takes."

Even though pride is a sin, and humility remains a foreign concept, the decision to hold her back, which she perceives as an embarrassing personal failure, disappoints and deeply angers Maggie. She decides against informing her family that she will not be entering the novitiate as scheduled. She doubts her progress in religious life ever crosses their minds and does not want to give them the satisfaction of thinking she has failed. *They won't show up the day I enter the novitiate regardless of when it happens*, she consoles herself.

The ceremony takes place in the ornate, cavernous Saint Martin de Porres minor basilica used only for occasions large numbers of people are expected to attend. The one-hundred-year-old stone church, which took nearly five years to build, includes a raised altar and a one-hundred-foot tabernacle reaching upward into the dome. Sixteen massive stained-glass windows, eight confessionals, and nine statues of various saints line the side walls. A majestic pipe organ, capable of flooding the basilica with sacred sound, sits in the balcony above the entrance.

The ritual signifying acceptance into the novitiate closely parallels an actual marriage ceremony and is designed to emphasize the postulant's ongoing personal transformation, carrying her ever deeper into her lifetime partnership with Jesus. Wearing white bridal gowns and veils, the postulants process into the church and kneel before the altar where their superior is seated beneath and slightly in front of a sixteen-foot crucified Christ. With their families and religious communities bearing witness, they recite their first solemn vows aloud:

> *To the honor of Almighty God, Father, Son, and Holy Spirit, and of the Blessed Virgin Mary, and our patron saints, Vincent de Paul and Martin de Porres, I [baptismal name] make my first religious vows, consecrating my life to God in complete submission and fidelity to the Pax Christi Sisters of Charity and Justice and to the Holy Roman Catholic Church. I place this ring upon my left hand, as a symbol of my promise to my savior, Jesus, to live in poverty, in chastity, and in obedience to Almighty God; to you, Mother Michael Joan, superior of the Order; and to your successors, until my death.*

After proclaiming their vows, Christ's young brides each receive a thin, gold wedding band which their superior places on the ring finger of their left hand, signifying they are now married women. One by one, they are led out of the church and down the basement stairs into a large empty room where professed community members prepare them for this next phase of religious life. Their hair is shorn off an inch from their scalp and each is clothed in a dark-gray, floor-length, leather-belted woolen dress reminiscent of poor women's clothing during the Middle Ages. Carved, wooden rosaries blessed by the current pope hang from their belts, and floor-length brown scapulars, signaling devotion to the Blessed Virgin and faithfulness to their spousal Christ, overlay their dresses. White caps cover the sisters' heads and necks, allowing only their faces to show. A permanently vowed sister wears a waist-length, black cotton veil pinned to the front of the head covering. If a sister has not taken the permanent vows that fully surrender her life to Christ in a marriage intended to last the rest of her life, she wears a white veil.

After having their white veils pinned onto their heads, the former postulants re-enter the church, receive their religious names, and publicly repeat their vows, using the name by which they will be known for the rest of their lives. Instead of facing the altar, where Mother Michael Joan remains seated, the new novices look outward toward their religious community and assembled family members, publicly signifying they are no longer of the world and are now formally committed to religious life.

For most aspirants, the novitiate lasts between three and five years, during which time they further discern whether religious life suits them as a lifetime commitment. At the same time, the community continues observing how well the novice fits into their way of being apart from the world. Most novices go on to receive full acceptance in religious life and make solemn vows.

After the ceremony, the new novices, accompanied by family members, walk to a reception area to celebrate their marriage to Jesus. Although the other postulants rush to congratulate the new novices, Maggie doesn't want to take part in this joyous occasion the ecstatically happy new novices are sharing with their proud, loving families, an experience she has never known. More downhearted than she anticipated, she returns to the convent and her floor-scrubbing assignment.

Down on her knees, pushing a scrub brush around in circles, the doubts that have been plaguing her, which she is fighting hard to resolve, resurface. *I don't know why my* reasons *for wanting to join the Order have little to do with loving God or even wondering whether God is calling me to religious life. I just want to continue trying, even if it isn't for the reasons Sister Marie William insists are the right ones. I'm not giving up.* But *if I tell the truth about what is bothering me, I'm sure I'll be sent home, so I have to keep acting the role they want me to play until they're satisfied with my performance.*

•••

Finally, on December 8, 1950, the feast of the Immaculate Conception of the Virgin Mary, and eighteen months after entering the postulancy, Maggie, and four of the nine others who were held back, are admitted into the novitiate. She is not yet nineteen years old.

Maggie's decision to take her first vows and continue pursuing religious life marks the beginning of a series of conflicts that will repeatedly try the patience of her superiors and her Church, beginning immediately. Shorter than average, she finds the long, heavy habit uncomfortable and is unhappy about her religious name. *I feel like a dwarf with a dumb name dragging around yards of sack cloth,* she tells herself.

"I don't like my name," Sister John Mary, formerly known as Margaret Corrigan, tells the novice mistress and the mother superior the day after she receives it. "Especially the John part. It doesn't fit me." *It's another man telling me what to do,* she thinks, but doesn't say aloud.

"Your name is chosen for you to honor the holy saints and blessed sisters who have come before you, bearing the same name," Sister Marie William explains. "It recognizes our beloved ancestors in the Order and signifies complete surrender to the religious life. Your name is not for you to choose; it is something you receive, with gratitude and resolve to learn all you can about the saints and the sister you are named for. Each day you should pray to them for help and guidance as you strive to imitate their holiness."

"You're telling me I've just been named after the Virgin Mary, a dead sister buried in that cemetery in the churchyard, and some man who lived nearly two thousand years ago?" Maggie asks, a little too loudly.

"That is correct, Sister. This is a time-honored tradition in our Order and questioning it is an act of disobedience that reflects a level of pride unbecoming in religious life and must be resisted," a weary Mother Michael Joan responds, sighing deeply.

This conversation further underscores the doubts Sister John Mary's superior still harbors about how well the young novice is suited to religious life and has been unable to put to rest. So far, her solution has been to pray about it and then turn the matter over to God, which she has not found helpful.

"As your penance, I want you to go into our archives and research the first Sister John Mary and write a one-thousand-word essay describing who she was and what examples from her holy life inspire those of us who have followed in her footsteps, and will inspire you, as her namesake."

Maggie frowns deeply, preparing to argue the point further. "My mother was a saint if there ever was one; why can't I be called Sister Maureen Ellen?"

"You renounce your family ties when you join the community. It would be inappropriate to name you after your mother. Accept your religious name with humility and return your focus to becoming worthy of being God's most humble servant. You are dismissed," Mother Michael Joan directs.

Hands hidden in the sleeves of her habit, Sister John Mary bows to her superior and backs out of the room.

Sainthood is the Church telling itself how great it is. Aunt Molly says the Church has declared some real jerks and nutcases as saints and it's all a bunch of crap, Maggie recalls, comforting herself as she walks toward the convent that is her new home. She knows her life as a novice won't be very different than it was when she was a postulant; she'll just be wearing different clothes and living in a cell with plaster walls rather than curtains. Otherwise her day, as before, is carefully structured to include prayer, work, meals, instruction, and one hour of recreation.

The young novice, who still thinks of herself as Maggie, continues to struggle daily with these requirements. Most of all, she hates her new work assignment, which is in the community's large garden in spring, summer, and fall, and doing farm chores during the winter months.

Maggie uses her one allowed letter per month to write to her pretend sister Mary Pat, who always writes back.

"This outdoor work is killing me, Maggie writes her best friend. I don't know a weed from a radish, and I'd give anything to stand on a cement sidewalk or walk across an asphalt parking lot, she laments. By the end of the day, I'm so exhausted, I fall asleep off during evening prayers. She signs the letter Love, Maggie."

The letter is returned to her with instructions not to complain about her religious life, and to use her religious name. As a penance for failing to follow the rules, it will be three months before she is allowed to write another letter. Because Maggie has not found a way to sneak letters out of the motherhouse, she has no choice but to obey this order, and never writes to Mary Pat again. She has no way of knowing whether her friend writes to her.

•••

When Sister John Mary isn't reading sacred scripture, praying, or engaging in the other formation activities required of novices, she is searching for some way to convince her superiors to change her name to Sister Ellen Clare—a name she chose because, for no particular reason, she's always liked the name Clare, and Saint Ellen, about whom little is known, is her mother's patron saint. Legend has it Saint Ellen died at age ninety-six, after roaming the world friendless and seeking a virtuous man. Finding none, she spent her life among goat men, who she supposedly described as "much better than humans because at least you know where you stand with them." Maggie admits to herself that, given a choice, she also prefers goats, with whom she has become well-acquainted during her farm assignment.

"I think we should petition the Order for flexibility in choosing our religious names," she tells her fellow novices and younger vowed sisters during their daily recreation hour.

While the centuries-old tradition of assigning religious names is not one that her immediate superiors can change themselves, Maggie convinces the leadership council to persuade Mother Michael Joan to take the idea to the bi-annual meeting of the Order's solemnly professed, duly elected mother superiors in Saint Louis in three months. This is an unprecedented step toward more democratic rule within a much larger institution that is decidedly and intentionally undemocratic.

Ultimately, the vote for offering novices the option of choosing their own religious names, if they wish to do so, is the majority view of the mother superiors attending the Saint Louis meeting. Those who are against the move, including Mother Michael Joan, find letting go of the time-honored naming tradition deeply upsetting.

"I strongly oppose this change," Mother Michael Joan tells her community upon her return. "I do not favor allowing postulants to choose their religious names or allowing any others of you who wish to do so to change your professed name to a different one, but I am solemnly bound to accept this as the will of the Order and therefore obligated to honor it."

Hearing this, Maggie sits on her hands to keep from clapping. Within the hour, she submits her name change request to her superior.

Almost immediately, Sister John Mary becomes Sister Ellen Clare.

"We won the first round—maybe we can change other things," Maggie whispers to her fellow novices during daily recreation.

Meanwhile, Mother Michael Joan and Sister Marie William continue discussing their young novice's high-spirited approach to religious life, trying to determine whether she should be allowed to take permanent, solemn vows. "Eventually she will be a problem, if not for me, for my successor. I'm sure of it," Mother Michael Joan insists.

"Maybe," Sister Marie William counters, "but it probably won't happen for a while, and I don't think it is our job to break her spirit. Our job—my job—is to channel that energy into a force for good. I don't want to give up on her."

Meanwhile, Maggie's questions about her future continue plaguing her, until one day, sitting in her superior's office for their monthly conference, she experiences a Damascus moment when, with a deep, visceral sense of knowing, she becomes aware that her life is on the right trajectory. She realizes she may not agree with or ever understand everything about what is expected of her in religious life, but the burden of doubt about her future suddenly evaporates and a wave of profound relief sweeps over her, causing her to shiver uncontrollably. Seeing this, Mother Michael Joan asks if she is unwell.

"I'm fine, Mother. Just overcome by happy thoughts of what the future holds," the young novice smiles, wishing she could share this revelation. But never having confessed her doubts to her superior, she finds it impossible to begin the conversation.

•••

After nearly a year of working on the farm, Maggie receives a new assignment: preparing the chapel for daily Mass. This involves laundering, starching, and ironing the altar cloths, and placing fresh flowers each day, except during Lent and Advent, the periods in the Church calendar set aside for intense personal introspection to enhance one's worthiness to receive God's love and preparatory sacrifice as an offering to God in gratitude.

Because saying Mass requires a priest, this is one of the few times a man is allowed onto the motherhouse grounds. While her duties include answering the Mass prayers in Latin from a kneeler outside the altar rail, Maggie is forbidden from being an altar server or directly assisting "My Dear Father Don," as the priest is commonly referred to, during Mass.

Maggie doesn't like the middle-aged priest with foul breath and abundant, flaking dandruff who comes from the nearby parish each morning to say Mass. He smells bad, has food stains on the front of his cassock, shoelace problems, doesn't shave regularly, and overshares, claiming he suffers from chronically painful hemorrhoids, among other maladies most people keep to themselves. Nevertheless, he always accepts the sisters' invitation to stay for breakfast after Mass.

"He gives me the creeps," Sister Ellen Clare whispers to Sister Barbara Anne while they are cleaning up the kitchen after a particularly loathsome morning with the priest.

"He's the kind of guy who couldn't do anything else except be a priest, otherwise nobody would have anything to do with him," Maggie says. "I really don't get why the sisters fall all over themselves to serve his every wish. 'Yes, Father, dear; oh my, Father dear; you are so funny, Father dear.' It's enough to make you vomit. It's not like he's someone special; he's an ordinary person with bad hygiene and poorly managed health problems."

"It is pretty weird," Sister Barbara Anne agrees. "It's almost like they all have a crush on him, although a more unattractive man is hard to imagine."

"Other than the fact *His* Holiness won't allow it, there's no reason we can't be offering Mass ourselves," Maggie says. "Nowhere is it written that a penis is required for saying Mass or administering the sacraments, and we'd do a hell of a lot better than a priest who never brushes his teeth and farts until the entire sanctuary is a lethal gas chamber."

Sister Barbara Anne giggles and nods her head in vigorous agreement. "Do you think the reason the pope won't allow women priests is because they'd be better than men?"

"That's exactly what I think! Men are afraid of women because they're smarter and better than they are at lots of things, and men feel threatened by that," Maggie exclaims.

"Pity they're so insecure," her fellow sister adds, returning her attention to scrubbing the remnants of Father Don's scrambled eggs with fresh cream from the heavy iron skillet.

•••

Five years later, in the fall of 1955, six years after entering the Order, Sister Ellen Clare Corrigan, along with twenty-six other novices, process into Saint Martin de Porres Basilica for the second time since beginning religious life. One by one, each prostrates herself before the altar. With the light coming through the massive stained-glass windows on either side of the altar, casting large shadows across the pews, Maggie repeats her sacred vows, this time replacing the word "first" with the word "solemn" and thus permanently committing herself to God and her community. From this moment forward, only the Vatican, six thousand miles away in Rome, can release her from this sacred commitment. In return, she receives the black veil of a fully professed member of the SCJ religious community and is allowed to place the initials SCJ after her name.

Bishop William Francis Courtney, the liberal and popular first bishop of a small, newly formed central Indiana Catholic diocese, presides over the ceremony, which is heavy with ritual and lasts nearly three hours. The only member of Maggie's family in attendance is her brother, Tommy, who three months earlier, was ordained a priest for the Chicago Archdiocese. With his dark brown eyes, neatly trimmed sandy-red hair, black suit, and white collar, Maggie realizes he looks better than she has ever seen him.

"The priesthood obviously agrees with you," she tells her brother when they meet after the ceremony.

"It does. And I'm so proud of you, Maggie," Tommy Corrigan tearfully tells his sister as they walk from the church to the reception for family members. "I never thought you'd last, and now you've made us officially a good Catholic family—a priest and a nun. Mom would be so proud and happy, and so is Dad. He would've given anything to be here, but he's not well enough."

"Nothing wrong with him that laying off the sauce won't cure," Maggie points out. "But since he's never shown up for any other big day in my life, I didn't expect him to suddenly start caring enough to show up now." She doesn't bother asking about her other siblings, none of whom have acknowledged her important day.

"Just so you know, Tommy, I didn't do this to make anybody proud. I did it so I can change women's lives, and the Church is a good place to start." Maggie bristles. Ignoring the startled look on her brother's face, she continues. "Here's the thing: I'm in this for the justice part, and this Order is at least nominally committed to that cause. Nobody wants charity; they want dignity and respect, and that's what I want for women who, if the Church has its way with them, are nothing more than sex slaves forced to reproduce like rabbits."

"That's wrongheaded, Maggie. The Church does more charity work than any other institution in the world. A lot of really desperate people with no place else to turn depend upon that." newly ordained Father Corrigan replies, slowing their pace.

"Charity, by its very nature, robs those who are already struggling of whatever is left of their dignity and self-worth, and I don't want that for women. I want to help them gain the self-confidence and freedom to control their own futures, which begins by being able to control their reproductive lives. It means using birth control."

"What you're saying borders on heresy, Maggie. Where'd you get these weird ideas?"

They have stopped walking and are facing each other, oblivious to other guests who are walking around the two siblings standing in the middle of the sidewalk leading up to the motherhouse entrance. Each taking a deep breath, Father Tommy Corrigan and Sister Ellen Clare Corrigan prepare for another in their long history of standoffs.

"In our kitchen, where else? Watching Mom, pregnant with Frankie, struggle to get a meal on the table, despite constant headaches and feet so swollen she could barely stand up. Listening to Mom and Dad argue about her not wanting any more kids when she found out she was pregnant again. She cried and screamed at him about feeling like a cow, Tommy—when she wasn't throwing up or needing to lie down. How can you not remember that?"

"Sorry, Maggie. I just don't."

"I suppose you don't remember Aunt Molly ripping into Dad the night of Mom's funeral, telling him that if Mom hadn't kept on having babies he forced on her, she would still be alive and there wouldn't be seven motherless children she, as Mom's sister, now felt responsible for, on top of her own nine kids. That's sixteen kids, Tommy. You think that was easy?"

Her brother remains silent.

"Aunt Molly told Dad the goddamned Church saying no to birth control is what killed her sister—our mother. She was crying so hard, she was shaking, while Frankie screamed himself scarlet in his bassinette. I remember it like it was yesterday."

"What did Dad say?"

"He was drunk...kept mumbling that good Catholics do what the Church says, and he and Mom were good Catholics...said he didn't know which kid he wouldn't want to be born, and he never thought it would end with Mom dying...never thought God or the Church would let that happen."

"I don't know where you get these ideas, Maggie. I don't remember any of that."

"You just don't want to remember—and why would you? Men don't want to think about anything that controls their freedom to have sex any time they want it. Controlling women is what the patriarchal Church wants too: good Catholic women who submit to their husbands and make babies for the pope who, supposedly, isn't making them himself. That's what Mom did—until it killed her—leaving seven kids to grow up without a mother. You tell me how that's fair and just for anybody."

"It sounds like you became a nun to change the Church, not because you love God and want to dedicate your life to Him. If that's the case, you've been dishonest with everyone and are nothing more than one goddamned pissed-off woman, if you don't mind my saying so."

"I mind you saying so a lot. And I don't care if you are my brother—so to speak. Don't you dare ever talk to me that way again. I have every right to be pissed as hell, and you have no choice except to respect that. I have no intention of letting go of my anger and pretending all is forgiven, because it's not, and claiming otherwise is what would be dishonest. Instead, I'm going to nurture that anger and use it for good."

Tommy remains silent, looking at the ground.

"Another thing, just because you've been ordained doesn't mean you know God's a man, Tommy. You just want it to be that way because you're one and you like belonging to an exclusive club where no women are allowed. God might be a woman, and dedicating my life to Her means making other women's lives better—ever think of that?"

"No, Maggie, I haven't. And truthfully, I don't see how that's relevant to anything, or how these ideas of yours are going to come to any good." The frown between his eyes deepens.

"Maybe they will, and maybe they won't, but it's my Church just as much as it's yours. It gave me hope when I didn't have any, and in my own way, I love it deeply—maybe even more than you do—because I'm willing to try to make it better. I hope you'll pray I can do some good because I'm not backing away from this."

"No, I suppose you're not. But I don't agree with any of it. Your superiors are in for a wild ride, and they'll need my prayers a lot more than you do. And just for the record, I think you're way too hard on Pa. He's had it rough being left to raise seven kids on his own, and most of the time barely able to find work. He needs your compassion, not your anger."

"Pa didn't raise seven kids on his own, Tommy. I did. He barely noticed."

"Can I ask you something?" Maggie says, changing the subject.

Tommy nods.

"Did Dad, Fiona, Annie, and Colleen come to your ordination?"

"They were all there, including most of Aunt Molly's kids and their families. Fiona and Colleen brought their older kids, and all the husbands came. We were one of the largest family groups at the lunch afterward. It's too bad you and Mary couldn't be there." Tommy smiles.

"In case you forgot, or didn't notice, Mary's choice to join a religious community in Los Angeles enabled her to move as far away from the family as she possibly can. I wish I'd thought of that," Maggie says to her obviously puzzled brother.

"Did you write to Frankie and let him know you're a priest now?" Maggie asks, referring to their youngest brother who is currently serving a maximum sentence in a high-security juvenile detention facility in downstate Illinois.

Tommy shakes his head no. "I haven't been in touch with Frankie since he was sentenced. I pray for him, but I'm afraid he's a lost cause. He'll kill somebody else just as soon as he gets out and end up a lifer in the Illinois prison system."

"Frankie's a bad seed, and without a mother to love him, or a father who was sober long enough to care, he never had a chance. I didn't know how to handle him, but we all failed him...poor kid."

Tommy nods in agreement, then says he needs to be getting back to Chicago.

Maggie tells her brother goodbye without a smile or thanking him for coming. Deciding not to attend the reception for new novices and their families, she returns to her cell, resolved not to cry because, other than Tommy, none of her family made any effort to share this momentous occasion with her. What was supposed to be a joyous day in her life is, once again, a very lonely one, and she is frustrated with herself for thinking it would be any different. *I suppose wishing things to be different is only natural, even if it based on false hope*, she thinks.

•••

Following their solemn profession, the sisters receive various assignments. Whereas previously, they went wherever their superiors sent them without complaint, following the Saint Louis meeting, professed sisters now have input into their assignments. The final decision depends upon what and where the needs are, so a sister's choice isn't always honored, and Sister Ellen Clare's request to return to Chicago is denied. Instead, she will remain at the motherhouse as an administrative assistant to Mother Michael Joan and Sister Marie William. *Even though they let me take solemn vows, obviously they still don't trust me,* Maggie thinks when informed of the decision.

"I know this assignment is a disappointment, Sister, but our administrative needs have increased substantially," Mother Michael Joan explains.

"I'm not sure I understand," Maggie responds.

"The Order is expanding rapidly, bringing with it many challenges to our centuries-old traditions that we need to carefully consider as we move forward. Discussions about the various new possibilities have already begun, and we realize this will be a massive undertaking. Your job will be to assist with the correspondence involved. Long, carefully worded letters from myself and Sister Marie William will be exchanged with our sisters, with superiors in other provinces, and with the superior general."

"In other words, I will be your secretary," Maggie replies.

"I prefer to think of it as my assistant. You will also be responsible for the travel arrangements for my annual trip to interview aspirants and for soliciting money."

"Soliciting money?" Maggie asks.

"Yes. We have identified the wealthier parishes in our province, and various sisters visit them regularly to ask for money. You will make those arrangements, as well as making several visits yourself."

"I can't beg for money, Mother. I grew up living off the dole, and it's humiliating."

"Religious life is no different, Sister. Surely you have figured that out by now. We rely upon the kindness of strangers to support us and are deeply grateful to God for this opportunity to practice the virtue of humility."

"I'd not thought about it that way."

"Then you have an opportunity to learn a very valuable lesson."

•••

On a bright October day in 1958, at morning Mass, Father Don tearfully announces that His Holiness, Pope Pius XII, the two hundred sixty-third Vicar of Christ and Keeper of the Keys to the Holy, Catholic, and Apostolic Church, has died. The aloof and controversial pope ascended to the throne of Saint Peter when Maggie was seven years old and reigned over the Church for the next nineteen years. The only thing she recalls about him is that, speaking ex cathedra, the pope declared, as a matter of doctrine, that the Virgin Mary bodily ascended into heaven, and he named the day celebrating this impossibility the Feast of the Assumption, to be celebrated annually on August 15. As a reminder of the theological importance of his pronouncement, Pius XII then declared August 15 a Holy Day of Obligation. In practical terms, this meant that Catholics worldwide were required, under pain of mortal sin, to attend Mass each year on this day, which also obligated them to put an additional envelope in the collection plate.

This matters to me how? a young Maggie wondered when the new feast day was announced. But she couldn't stop thinking about it, partly because she knew it was physically impossible for a dead body to go anywhere, yet she was expected to believe it anyway. Over time she realized that what bothered her even more, especially since she had entered religious life, was the idea that some old man in Rome, elected to his position by a bunch of other old men, could make pronouncements every "good Catholic" was obliged to accept without question, regardless of their factual accuracy or provability. *Maybe I think too much, but just accepting something is true without questioning it is a bad idea. Women should have a say in their own lives, and in running the Church they are baptized into, and are obligated to submit to for the rest of their lives. It shouldn't be up to men to decide what women are supposed to do. Imagine what my mother's life would've been like if she'd had choices?* she wonders.

•••

Since taking her solemn vows, Maggie has lobbied for a new assignment at every opportunity. Finally, her wish is granted, and on January 25, 1959, the day Pius XII's successor, the newly elected Pope John XXIII, announces he is convening a second Vatican Council in three years to clean out the cobwebs in the church, Mother Michael Joan tells her she is going to Chicago.

"I don't know what this Vatican Council will do, but whatever it is will present many obstacles to religious life. The pope is calling it an *aggiornamento*—bringing the Church into the modern world. Bishops worldwide will be making changes with a view toward creating a more welcoming, pastoral Church. God only knows what they will decide, and I'm not looking forward to any of it," Mother Michael Joan sighs. She knows other Church conservatives like herself fear centuries of tradition will be swept away—and their liberal counterparts fear they won't be.

"I know it feels like an earthquake, Mother, but sometimes things have to fall apart before they can be rebuilt...and change is exciting," Maggie responds, trying not to sound too enthusiastic about the unknown just beyond the horizon.

Unfortunately, Maggie views her new assignment, which will begin on July 1, as far afield of her desire to work for social justice. Instead, she will be doing charity outreach at Holy Family and Saint Brendan's parish schools, serving the Back of the Yards and surrounding slums, where she grew up and likely still knows many of the families living there. Sisters who had this assignment previously usually requested a transfer within two years, but when Mother Michael Joan informs her of the position, she makes it clear that because the neighborhoods are familiar to Maggie, she expects her to remain longer.

This is exactly the kind of work I don't want to do, Maggie thinks but doesn't say aloud. Instead, she balks at the assignment in general terms. Mother Michael Joan repeatedly reminds her that she has taken a vow of obedience to her superiors and is expected to do as she is told.

"Charity work is what the Order does, and you will be doing charity work somewhere, Sister. When we discussed this, you said wanted to go back to Chicago and claimed a useful familiarity with the problems and the neighborhoods. But I could just as easily send you to another province. You could go to Kansas City or El Paso, for example. Perhaps you wish to pray about this," the mother superior smiles.

"I don't speak Spanish, so El Paso is out," Sister Ellen Clare responds. "And I don't even know where Kansas City is. Wanting to go back to Chicago is never going to change. I'd rather be doing different work, but that is not nearly as important to me as being in Chicago. If I had to choose between not going back there and cutting off my arm, I'd lose the arm in a heartbeat."

"I am concerned that your desire to return to Chicago overrides your reason for being there, which is to serve God. Do you honestly feel you can keep God's will and not your own at the forefront of your life in a place that you are so emotionally attached to?"

"I've never been able to see myself anywhere else. The smells and noise and scenery are all familiar to me, and this will work to my advantage—it's where I belong."

As Sister Ellen Clare prepares for her new assignment, Mother Michael Joan sends for her again. This is when Maggie learns she will be living in the convent adjacent to Saint Brendan's School, which is currently staffed by the School Sisters of Saint Dominic, who also teach at Holy Family, Maggie's parish school.

"You'll be responsible for helping Sister Agnes James become acclimated to the area and learn to find her way around."

This is the first Maggie has heard about the older nun accompanying her to Chicago, and immediately realizes it is because her superiors feel someone needs to keep an eye on her.

"Of course, Mother, I'll be glad to," Maggie replies through clenched teeth.

Sister Ellen Clare prevails upon her brother, Tommy, to drive her and Sister Agnes James to their new home in Chicago. Several times during the nearly four-hour trip, Sister Agnes James reminds them that this is the first time she has ridden in a car in more than thirty years, and she hopes she doesn't get carsick. Maggie says nothing in reply, but tears of joy and relief run down her cheeks when, through the rain-spattered windshield of her brother's standard-issue, priestly black sedan, she catches her first glimpse of the far distant Chicago skyline in nearly a decade.

PART THREE

1960 – 1983

...and change the world...

VI.

Living in a convent means there are so many things you can't do and don't have to worry about, that life is very simple.
Lorrie von Trier

When Sister Ellen Clare sees the convent adjacent to Saint Brendan's parish school in the Back of the Yards neighborhood where she was born and grew up, her first thought is that the parish has ignored the three-story building for a very long time. The brick needs tuckpointing, the windows need reglazing, the peeling trim needs scraping and repainting, and missing shingles on the roof guarantee leaks. The priests' rectory next door, with its flowers, neatly trimmed lawn, shiny front door, and sparkling windows, looks to be in much better condition.

"My goodness," Sister Agnes James exclaims, getting out of the car. "This yard is more weeds than grass—someone needs to tidy the place up. I hope they don't expect us to do it...my arthritis and all...."

Father Corrigan carries the two nuns' suitcases up to the front door while Maggie rings the bell. No one answers. She knocks loudly and still no answer. They try the door and then the gate into the back and find both locked.

"Are you sure they're expecting you today?" Tommy asks his sister as all three stand in the rain. They walk back around the convent and try the front door again. This time, still held by a chain lock, the door opens slightly.

"Who's there?" a voice calls out. "Step up and identify yourselves, keeping your hands where I can see them."

"Really, Sister? You think I've got a loaded gun hanging from my rosary beads?" Maggie responds. "We're the new sisters assigned to help with the parish. Do you suppose you could open the door and let us in? We're getting wet out here."

"We weren't planning on you arriving today."

"It doesn't sound like they're glad to see us," Sister Agnes James frets. "We'll have to pray for them."

"Please just let us in, Sister. We can settle the details of our arrival later," Maggie says.

"Very well, but we haven't prepared for dinner guests. We may not have enough."

"Please, just open the door."

The door closes, the chain drops, and the door opens again. An elderly nun in a brown and black habit, with a scowling face framed in a white wimple, motions them inside.

"I've not been well, and you disturbed my nap," she tells them. "Put your things in the hallway and wait over there." She motions toward a long bench along the far wall of a dark hallway. "I'll see if anyone else is here to attend to this situation."

"I have to get going," Father Corrigan, as he now prefers being called, tells his sister.

"Thanks for the lift," Maggie replies without looking at him.

As instructed, Sisters Ellen Clare and Agnes James sit down on a wooden bench placed against a section of wall watched over by a larger-than-life plaster statue of Saint Dominic, dressed in his colorfully elegant twelfth-century robes.

I wonder who scrubs these floors? Maggie asks herself, looking at the wood worn bare of finish in several places and remembering how many times that was her job.

"Guess they aren't too excited to have us," Maggie mumbles.

Sister Agnes James, fingering her rosary beads, does not respond.

Nearly an hour passes before brisk footsteps come down the dark hallway.

"I'm Sister Gertrude Veronica and you are Sisters Ellen Clare and Agnes James, I presume," the tall nun smiles, extending her hand. "I'm sorry for the confusion. We thought you were arriving next Saturday. All of our sisters are at our motherhouse on retreat. I stayed behind because Sister Josephine Ann wasn't up to traveling to Milwaukee. I didn't want to leave her alone, and I needed to catch up on the book work. Can I offer you some tea?" She opens one of the hallway doors and leads them into a sparsely furnished sitting room.

"Thank you, Sister, but I think we'd like to unpack first, if you have rooms for us," Maggie says.

"Of course," Sister Gertrude Veronica smiles. "Your rooms are at the south end of the third-floor hallway, next to each other on the back side of the building. The bathrooms are at the other end, and the sign-up sheet for showers is outside the door. When you're finished unpacking, come back downstairs, and I'll show you around."

"Oh dear," Sister Agnes James, mutters. "I'm not sure I can manage two flights of stairs."

"If you can try for a few days, Sister, I'll see what I can do about moving you down to the second floor after the sisters return. That is, if you don't mind being separated from each other," Sister Gertrude Veronica replies.

Suits me just fine, Maggie thinks, holding her enthusiasm for the idea in check.

Their rooms are only slightly larger than their cells at the motherhouse. Each contains a desk, chair, and a large crucifix hanging above the bed, on the outside wall next to a tiny window. A small closet holds two shelves and two clothes hangers. In both rooms, the damaged ceiling areas directly above the crucifix reveal that, in addition to hanging on a cross, Jesus frequently suffers from water dripping on his head.

After unpacking, both sisters return to the convent's first floor, where Sister Gertrude Veronica is waiting.

"The reception area, the gathering room, refectory, kitchen, and a small chapel are located on the ground floor," she says as they slowly walk from room to room.

"We're on our own for food this week, but you're welcome to join Sister Josephine Ann and me for a sandwich supper at five o'clock this evening. Otherwise, the first morning Mass is at 7 a.m. You can walk over to the church with me. Afterwards, I'll introduce you to whichever priest in the parish is saying the morning Mass. Later this week, I'll fill you in on the bare bones of what we're facing. The sisters you'll be working with, both here at Saint Brendan's and at Holy Family, can offer more after they return next Saturday. Between now and then, I'll see if I can't find someone to further acquaint you with the parish and the surrounding neighborhoods."

"Sister Agnes James might take you up on your offer to explore the neighborhood, but I grew up in the Back of the Yards and know the area pretty well already," Maggie responds.

"I'm sure you do, Sister, but you've been gone how long?" Sister Gertrude Veronica smiles.

"Nearly ten years. In some ways it seems like an eternity and in other ways, it seems like I never left. But it still feels comfortably familiar—like I was born here."

"I thought you *were* born here," Sister Agnes James interjects.

"I was making a joke, Sister," Maggie sighs, rolling her eyes.

"I'd venture to guess things are much is different now," Sister Gertrude Veronica says. "You might find yourself very surprised."

Maggie startles at this remark, not realizing until now that she hasn't given any thought whatever to how Chicago, or her old neighborhood, may have changed in the time since she left.

•••

Over the next few days, Sister Ellen Clare is surprised to discover how much living at the motherhouse, isolated and apart from the secular concerns of the outside world, has diluted her natural familiarity with her old neighborhood. It is still the ethnic enclave it always was, defined by the smells of the food and the cultural habits of the people living there. In this case, being mostly Irish, the community enjoys a lively tavern culture where the men spend most of their time drinking, playing cards, and generally ranting on endlessly over the pitiful state of their lives—until their wives, sisters, or daughters show up to drag them home. But the boundaries are cracking open now. African Americans, Puerto Ricans, and Mexicans are moving closer in and, finding themselves unwelcome, responding with their fists and whatever else they can find.

"I never really thought it could get any worse, but it looks like it has," she tells Sisters Gertrude Veronica and Agnes James over supper after an afternoon spent walking the familiar streets. Because Sister Josephine Ann is taking her meals in her room, the three of them are eating at a small table in the kitchen.

"Some areas have improved in the last ten years, but most have only gotten worse. I fear you're in for a lot of surprises in the coming weeks," Sister Gertrude Veronica tells Maggie while dishing up ice cream for dessert.

The convent routine is nothing like what Maggie expected. Instead of silence and prayer several times a day, the atmosphere is much more relaxed. She's never had the opportunity to watch television and, every evening after supper, finds herself glued to the one in the gathering room. She is astonished to learn that a handsome, charismatic Boston Irishman,

John Fitzgerald Kennedy, is running for president of the United States, and if he succeeds, will be the nation's first Irish-Catholic president. She brings this up while washing the supper dishes three days after her arrival.

"The other sisters are ecstatic and can't stop speculating on what this means for the Church and American Catholics," Sister Gertrude Veronica says.

"Kennedy's election doesn't mean anything. He's just another Irish Mick working the system to gain power—no different than all the others who do the same thing. I'm sure his old man bought all the votes his son needed to go forward—and Callahan will do the same thing for him here in Chicago," Maggie, politically astute and wise beyond her twenty-eight years, replies, scrubbing out a soup pot.

Maggie has also learned that a Southern Black preacher, Dr. Martin Luther King, Jr., is spearheading protests to gain civil and voting rights for Southern Blacks and that the United States Supreme Court has handed down a decision forcing public schools, including those in Chicago, to integrate.

"How are you handling the school integration issue?" Maggie asks Sister Gertrude Veronica the following evening over dinner.

"We aren't. We're private and as long we don't accept federal money, which we do not, we are under no obligation to comply and can do whatever we want to."

"These are poor schools in poor parishes. Wouldn't that money help?"

"It would, but it comes with too many strings attached, including being forced to accept students we might prefer not to enroll."

"So you don't want to integrate?"

"Both parishes have slowly divided themselves into two groups: the haves, meaning those with jobs, which aren't very many families, and the have-nots, who are on the dole and by far the majority. Neither is particularly accepting of the other. The Irish in both groups are a particularly clannish bunch and not known for being tolerant of differences. Father O' Donnell, Holy Family's assistant pastor—he's from here, you might know him, Finn O'Donnell—believes integration will create too many problems and has counseled against it. Monsignor Flanigan, St. Brendan's pastor, agrees."

"And you're okay with this decision?"

"I haven't really thought about it," the nun answers, standing to clear the dinner dishes from the table.

•••

Maggie's three sisters, Fiona, Colleen, and Annie, all married to locals they grew up with, who are known to drink up their paychecks on occasion, still live in the old neighborhood. Maggie has no idea how many kids they have, but knows they look out for Paddy, who lives in a rented room on the second floor of a single room occupancy hotel near the expressway that he rarely leaves. According to Tommy, they all get together regularly, and she is sure he told them she is back. When none of them reach out to her, she is confused, hurt, and angry.

*I gave up my childhood to raise them and this is the thanks I get? I know they were upset when I left for the convent, though I figured they'd get over it eventually. But if nobody bothered to attend my final vows, I guess I shouldn't expect them to welcome me home now. Still, I don't know what they're so pissed off about...unless it's that they're stuck in a shit life with too many kids, not enough money, and drunk husbands who only work when they sober up, which isn't my fault. Maybe they're jealous that I made a different choice for my life...*are all thoughts rolling around in Maggie's head.

Because the meatpacking industry has begun its slow exit from Chicago and the Stock Yards and continues laying off workers, the area is becoming increasingly economically depressed. Without other job options available, both unemployment and crime rates are high. Big Catholic families, which is nearly all of them, who were barely scraping by before, are leaning hard on Saint Brendan's and Holy Family for handouts. Maggie's several walks around the neighborhood tell her that everything looks at least as bad, if not worse, than when she left.

Most houses are either abandoned or badly abused. Gang rivalries that have plagued the area for years continue unchecked, and open warfare is a fact of life on the streets. Maggie can't help wondering how many of her nephews are gang members like their Uncle Frankie was. *Probably all of them,* she thinks.

•••

"There's just no money," Sister Gertrude Veronica explains when Maggie brings up the surrounding neighborhood decay over lunch. "Cardinal Stritch is sympathetic toward our problems, but he's not from Chicago, and so far, he hasn't stepped forward with financial assistance, so we're on our own."

Maggie expresses surprise at this, since the Irish, for all practical purposes, own the Chicago Catholic Church, and generally get what they want from it, and both Holy Family and Saint Brendan's are nearly 100 hundred percent Irish.

"I'm not sure the cardinal quite realizes that just yet," Sister Gertrude Veronica smiles. "Hopefully he will figure it out soon. In the meantime, we make do and pray a lot."

"What is the financial arrangement that brought Sister Agnes James and me here?" Maggie asks.

"I don't know the details, but Monsignor Flanagan grew up next door to Mayor Callahan, who, you probably know, is devoutly Catholic. I think he prevailed upon the mayor to divert city funds our way. I'm sure he pointed out that it's cheaper to bring in sisters to do the badly needed charity work than it is to lean ever harder on the already understaffed and underpaid city social services department. It might not be entirely on the up and up, but I'm sure you understand Chicago politics well enough to know how difficult it is to imagine anyone in the mayor's office ever questioning this expenditure."

"And it guarantees the mayor votes," Maggie adds.

"I wouldn't know about that," Sister Gertrude Veronica claims.

"Oh dear—you mean we're being supported with illegal money?" Sister Agnes James asks, her eyes widening behind her thick glasses.

"No, Sister, that's not what I mean at all. This is a situation where a good Catholic is doing what he can do to assist his Church in caring for the poor—nothing more. You mustn't think otherwise," Sister Gertrude Veronica answers evenly.

"Do you know why Monsignor Flanagan asked our Order to send sisters here?" Maggie asks.

"His cousin is your current novice mistress," Sister Gertrude Veronica answers, stacking their lunch plates to signal that the conversation is over.

•••

The nine other sisters living in Saint Brendan's convent return the following week. Sister Ellen Clare helps Sister Agnes James move her things down to a second-floor room after one of the resident sisters agrees to trade with her. She is just closing the door to the newly vacated room when a voice calls out to her.

"Don't close the door, Sister, I'm bringing my things in now." While unloading an armful of boxes, the sister introduces herself. "I'm Sister

Esther Mary, but since we're going to be neighbors, you can call me E.M.," she says, slowly turning around. "And you are...Maggie Corrigan. Holy Mother of God, that can't be you!"

Maggie looks up, dumbstruck to see the face of her childhood friend, Mary Pat Donovan, wearing the habit of the School Sisters of Saint Dominic, standing in the dimly lit hallway. Seeing Mary Pat, who had been both her best—and only—friend while they were growing up, and her brother Tommy's first love, is a major shock.

"Mary Pat...what the hell are you doing here?" Maggie finally exclaims.

"I could ask you the same question," the young nun answers. "You stopped writing to me, and I didn't know what happened.... My sister heard from Fiona that you took final vows. I can't believe I'm looking at you!" Mary Pat sputters.

"The novice mistress forbade me writing to you again—said I should be sharing my thoughts and complaints with her," Maggie explains. "I felt terrible, but there wasn't anything I could do about it...and I can't believe I'm looking at you either. I think I have to sit down." Maggie backs around the corner into her room and sits down hard on the bed.

"I still wrote to you," Mary Pat says, following her.

"I thought you might, but I never got the letters. Maybe I should've tried harder to get word to you, but I didn't know how. They read everything we wrote and every letter that came to us, and we weren't allowed visitors. Tommy was the only one who came to my vows, and I couldn't very well send word with him. I didn't know what to do."

"It's okay—I figured it was something like that. And now, here we are. I can't believe it! When we were told that two SCJ sisters were coming to live with us, it never crossed my mind one of them would be you."

"I can't believe it either!" Maggie answers.

"I'm one of the younger nuns here, so I agreed to move up to the third floor and let Sister Agnes James have my room. After lights out tonight, I'll knock on your door, and we can catch up—okay?"

"Sure," Maggie agrees, still trying to figure out how the most beautiful, most popular girl in her high school ended up a fully professed nun.

"You look surprised," Mary Pat adds.

"You have no idea," Maggie answers.

"The last I knew, you were thick with the high school football captain—Joe Finnegan, wasn't it? That probably broke Tommy's heart, you know."

"We were kids, Maggie. Our hearts never stayed broken for long."

"I was kidding. Tommy doesn't have a heart to break. And I had four sisters and a baby brother to look after while living in a hell-hole apartment with barely running water. I went to school in my spare time, mostly to get out of there and have a few hours to myself. I never had a chance to date in high school, much less think about anybody's crushed romances."

"My orders are to move myself up here before supper. We can talk about all this later, I promise," Mary Pat smiles, quickly hugging Maggie then walking toward the stairs.

"I wasn't supposed to do that—hug you—but I couldn't help it," she calls over her shoulder, leaving Maggie, dumbstruck at seeing her long-lost friend again.

•••

Later that evening, after optional prayers in the chapel and lights out, Maggie hears a firm knock on her door. Before she can get up to open it, Mary Pat, minus her habit's headgear, asks if she can come in. "I brought us a couple of beers," she says, passing her hand through her tragically chopped-off, coal-black hair. With her tall, slender frame, China-blue eyes, and long, thick curls, Mary Pat had been a high school beauty. Her good looks pushed her into the coveted head cheerleader spot, and she was prom queen an unprecedented three times. Despite a very bad haircut, she is still exceptionally pretty.

"Where did you get those?" Maggie asks, pulling off her own head covering to reveal two-inch long, randomly cut, curly red hair sticking out all over her head.

"Joe Finnegan. He stops in for a visit every so often to bring me a few bottles and collect the empties. There's no way I can just throw them in the trash," Mary Pat giggles as she pulls a bottle opener out of her habit pocket, opens the beers, and hands one to Maggie. She sits in the only chair in the room, facing the bed. Taking the beer, Maggie leans back against the wall, sitting cross-legged. Silence ensues.

"I probably have more to say than you do, so guess I should start," Mary Pat finally says.

Maggie nods, taking the first taste of beer she's had since leaving home for the convent, when she was still too young to legally drink.

"Obviously I didn't marry Joe Finnegan. I thought I was going to, but I got into trouble, and Joe wasn't interested in being a father right then, so he broke it off. He's been doing penance ever since," Mary Pat laughs.

"You got pregnant? What happened to the baby?" Maggie asks, wide-eyed.

"My folks insisted on an abortion. Unfortunately, there were complications."

For the second time in a few short hours, Maggie's jaw drops.

"The thing is," Mary Pat finally continues, "it wasn't my first one—pregnancy, that is."

Closing her eyes, Maggie isn't sure she wants to hear this. "The first one...it wasn't Tommy, was it?" she finally asks.

Mary Pat nods.

"Oh...my God...," Maggie exclaims, feeling the blood drain from her face. "Does Tommy know?"

"I think he probably knows, or at least suspects. Remember the summer before junior year when Tommy and I broke up and I left?"

"Sort of," Maggie nods.

"I didn't tell him why I was going—I just left. The baby, a boy, was stillborn. A problem with the cord, or something. It crushed me. I desperately wanted Tommy's baby...more than I've ever wanted anything in my life, before or since. But my parents insisted on sending me to a home for unwed mothers in Milwaukee that arranged for adoptions. They told everybody I got polio because the vaccine hadn't worked and I had to go away for treatment so I wouldn't be paralyzed, which was a pretty clever story because nobody asked me a lot of questions when I came back to school after Christmas vacation," the young nun says, reaching into her habit pocket for a handkerchief.

"I was secretly glad the baby died because I never could have given Tommy's baby up to someone else...it would've killed me. And since it ended up the way it did, I never told Tommy—not that I ever had that chance." Mary Pat takes another drink of her beer. "He avoided me whenever he saw me, so I figured he'd found someone else. And whenever I asked you about it, you played dumb and claimed you didn't know."

"I wasn't playing dumb, Mary Pat. I honestly didn't know. I had no clue about what Tommy did, or how he felt—about anything. He was rarely around and never would've confided in me anyway. We were barely on speaking terms. But as far as I know, not that I necessarily would, Tommy never dated anyone after you. He went straight to the seminary after high school, just a couple weeks after I went to the convent."

"Joe was a rebound situation," Mary Pat continues. "I still loved Tommy, but Joe was a good enough substitute...until I got pregnant the second time—with Joe's baby, probably the night of high school graduation. The shit really hit the fan a couple months later when I realized what had happened. I got an abortion, and the complications rendered me sterile, and I can't say I cared much. By then, Tommy was headed for the priesthood, and I knew marriage with anybody was unlikely because no good Catholic boy would marry a girl who couldn't have his babies, especially when the reason was a botched abortion."

"How does Joe figure into all this?" Maggie asks. "You're obviously still in touch."

"We're connected by good old Irish guilt. A few months later, my dad got drunk one night and went looking for Joe's father to tell him what his kid had done to me. Hearing this, Joe's old man beat the crap out of him. A couple of weeks later, Joe sent his sister Maura to give me a message about how sorry he was for the way it all turned out and promised he'd never abandon me again. By this time, he'd knocked some other girl up and was getting married. It was pretty obvious the convent was the only option left to me."

"Does...the Order know about all this?" Maggie asks, nearly speechless.

"They didn't ask, and I didn't volunteer the information. I was a model aspirant during the formation period and am an obedient, submissive member of the community now. Funny thing is it turns out I like religious life pretty well."

"You do?" Maggie asks. "I'm shocked. You're the last person I ever pictured taking the veil."

"I could say the same about you," Mary Pat laughs. "The truth is I didn't picture it, either, but it's worked out—except I'm getting tired of the kids. Teaching a bunch of squirming ankle-biters how to read isn't my idea of fun, and I wish the Order had something else to offer, but they don't. So I try to make peace with life among the rug rats and carry on."

Maggie doesn't comment, and the two friends sit in silence for several minutes, absorbing their conversation and nursing their beers.

"Come on, Maggie—your turn."

"Nothing as dramatic as your story. I entered to avoid the gruesome alternatives and want to do advocacy—working for justice for women. The Order supports this in theory, but in reality, they're focused almost entirely on charity work. This is my first assignment, and I'm not looking forward to it."

"What kind of justice?"

"Reproductive justice...women's freedom to make choices about how many kids they want and access to birth control that guarantees they stay in control of that choice. Women are morally capable of making their own decisions and entitled to do it. They deserve a voice in everything that affects any part of their lives. This is not the Middle Ages, and women should not be subjects of Holy Mother Church and forced to submit to the will of those graybeards over in Rome who think they get the last word on women's lives. The Church has got this so, so wrong." Maggie raises her voice.

"Shhh.... these walls are thin. We don't want anybody hearing us."

"Sometimes I don't care who hears me," Maggie retorts.

"Didn't your mother die in childbirth?" Mary Pat asks. "I remember Tommy saying something about that."

"She did, and I'm surprised Tommy mentioned it because now he claims he barely remembers—and maybe he doesn't. After she died, he went on with his life like nothing had changed, which, for him, it hadn't because he wasn't suddenly stuck home changing dirty diapers and feeding screaming babies."

"A lot of men have selective memories, Maggie. Joe never talks about what happened between us either. Sometimes I think he comes around because he's tired of his wife's nagging him about their six snot-nosed kids and no money, plus she's probably refusing him and he's still in love with me. We'd be having an affair if this habit didn't make that pretty difficult."

"Seriously, Mary Pat?"

"Serious as a mortal sin," Mary Pat smiles. "Changing the subject... I know we talked about it, but I never envisioned you taking the habit, either, and when you did, I doubted you'd stick with it. I kept expecting you to turn up back here."

"I wasn't interested in marriage, and I couldn't see living single without a decent way to earn money to support myself. I'd end up the maiden aunt to my sisters' kids, and being called upon to rescue the family every time there was a crisis. Except for its position on women, I really do love the Church. I'm not sure how devout or well-suited to religious life I am, but coming from my screwed-up family, where I've always felt like an outsider, I crave a sense of belonging—and I can't find that anywhere else. The way I see it, if I seriously want to advocate for change for women, I have to do it from within the Church. I'm not sure how, but that's my plan. In the meantime, I'm stuck doing something I'm not trained to do."

"Catch me up on everybody," Mary Pat asks.

"You know about Tommy. He's an assistant over by Fuller Park. Fiona, Colleen, and Annie are in what I imagine are lousy marriages and producing litters of kids. Mary joined a teaching Order out west and has stayed there. I never hear from her, and doubt the others do."

"What about Frankie?"

"He eventually got sent downstate as a lifer."

"You've not tried to reach out to him?"

"Frankie's got bad blood, and I was always a little afraid of him. We all were. Tommy's not in touch with him, and I doubt the others are. Maybe Mary is, but I have no way to know that. Best to not to disturb that sleeping dog."

"Since neither of us is thrilled about what we're doing, maybe we can help each other tolerate it," Mary Pat says, changing the subject again. "Word on the street is that Vatican II is going to change the Church in some pretty big ways. I'm anxious to see what happens."

"Would you ever consider leaving the Order?" Maggie asks.

"I don't know. I'd have to figure out how to support myself, which is a very big question without an obvious answer."

"Couldn't you get a teaching job someplace?"

"Probably not. None of us have valid teaching credentials. Everything we know comes from being in charge of a classroom, with no idea what we are doing, and being forced to figure it out on our own. Teaching is a much better fit for some than for others—and that's one of the problems. I know I'm not doing a great job because I don't care enough. I'm just one cog in the wheel that keeps Saint Brendan's school going, and I know what I don't teach the kids they will learn eventually from someone else, so I don't try very hard."

"I don't expect charity work to suit me either, to be honest," Maggie admits, rolling the neck of her beer bottle between her hands. "Watching people continually make bad decisions keeps me constantly upset, even though I know they're victims of circumstances they can't control and aren't their fault. And I think the Church is partly responsible for this. Men get frustrated not being able to support their families and drown their sorrows in alcohol. Women don't want all the kids they end up having and are angry about it. Tensions run high all the time, and when a laid-off worker comes home after a night of drinking at the local bar, he is just as likely as not to beat his wife, force her to have sex with him, or both. The babies keep coming even when the money doesn't—and I won't be able to fix any of it. Sooner or later, it'll get to me." Maggie takes the last swallow of her beer.

"It's getting pretty late, and prayer time comes early, so we better call it a night," Mary Pat says, reaching for the empty beer bottle as she drains her own.

"I'll take care of these. Be sure to drink a couple of big glasses of water tonight, so your breath doesn't smell like alcohol in the morning and get us both busted. It was good catching up, Maggie, it really was. But please don't ever say anything about what I've told you to Tommy. It can only come to no good," Mary Pat says, softly closing the door behind her.

•••

Eventually, Sister Ellen Clare settles into her new responsibilities as best she can, reaching out to families the teaching sisters refer to her. Most often, the situation involves a child who is chronically dirty, inadequately clothed, sickly, missing a lot of school, and acting out. Maggie makes home visits, attempting to determine where the problems are and then connecting the family with the resources that might help them. Most do not welcome what they view as interfering in their private lives, and very few are willing to follow her suggestions. She finds the work frustrating, thankless, and depressing, and can count on one hand the number of successes she has had.

And it seems like the world around her is unraveling. President Kennedy is assassinated, and the country's involvement in a civil war in Vietnam—a country Maggie has never heard of, located on a continent she would not, if asked, be able to locate—continues to escalate. Because conscription is still in effect, most of the young men the women in the Back of the Yards are involved with are being drafted into the military to fight in this unpopular war. Others volunteer, because without jobs, they don't have anything else to do. With so many men leaving women behind to figure out how to keep their families afloat, life begins to change. Rather than missing their husbands, the women in the mostly Catholic community welcome the reprieve from sex-on-demand and yearly pregnancies.

"I miss my husband, but I don't miss being pregnant all the time," are words Maggie hears often. Many are deciding to take the birth control pill when their husbands return, and some talk about getting tubal ligations, even though they need their husband's permission. A few have convinced a cousin or brother to sign their husband's name on the consent form.

"I know it's a sin, Sister, but the only thing I'm sorry about is my husband had to go off to war before I could get myself fixed—so no point in going to confession," a young mother of four children under age five defiantly tells Maggie.

"There's no sin in doing what's best for your family," Maggie assures her and the others.

•••

But the event destined to most directly affect Sister Ellen Clare occurred on October 11, 1962, in Saint Peter's Basilica in Rome, when His Holiness, the jovial, personally popular Pope John XXIII, finally convened the second Vatican Council. Its purpose was to pull the Church out of the Middle Ages and force it to adapt to changing social conditions in the modern world. The ambitious agenda was long, and excitement among all but the most conservative laity and religious was palpable, until the council bogged down in obscure details, causing many to lose interest.

The council closes at the end of 1965 having made some immediate changes, and most progressive Catholics hope more will be forthcoming. Meanwhile, the sisters teaching at Saint Brendan's and Holy Family are too busy managing overcrowded classes filled with hungry children whose families can't afford to feed them a decent breakfast to pay even scant attention to what is happening in Rome. They are scraping by with broken chalk, thread-bare rags as erasers, worn-out textbooks, used workbooks, and outdated teaching materials because the parish can't afford better. Several, including Mary Pat, worry that their students won't pass the required Illinois School Achievement Tests.

"I'm sure a lot of my kids will flunk the state tests, and I have no idea what to do about it. I doubt anybody else does either...but it's not like they can fire us," Mary Pat tells Maggie over a beer one night. "These kids have too many basic, unmet needs that are huge stumbling blocks to their learning, and even the best teaching in the world cannot overcome them. Even with your efforts, which are half what they could be if Sister Agnes James wasn't afraid to go into the neighborhood homes, most children from both Saint Brendan's and Holy Family lag far behind their public-school peers."

"It's not a solvable problem," Maggie admits. Meanwhile, she is paying careful attention to the news from Rome and sneaks away to the public library every chance she gets to read everything she can find about the Vatican II outcomes. *Here we go, it's finally coming,* she thinks after reading a particularly informative article about the Church's official language shifting from traditional Latin to the local vernacular, allowing the institutional Church to begin acting like an actual human community that talks to each other in their mother tongues. Restrictions on saying Mass are eased; eternal damnation is de-emphasized; fish on Friday becomes voluntary; and both purgatory for those who die in a state of sin, and limbo, where those who die unbaptized spend eternity, no longer exist.

I guess all that money school kids collected to save pagan babies from limbo was for nothing, Maggie chuckles to herself as she reads a final summary of the council proceedings. But the most dramatic changes release clergy and women religious from their historically restricted lives to be more and more among the people rather than aloof and apart from them. Ministry becomes about personal relationships.

"You watch—pretty soon priests will be allowed to marry," Maggie tells Mary Pat one evening over a beer.

"That's assuming anybody'd want to marry one," Mary Pat quips.

Maggie finds the changes to the sisterhood exciting. Nuns begin replacing their bulky, medieval habits with ordinary street clothes. Those who are willing to capture and run with their new freedoms pull away from restrictive convent life and move into local community settings that encourage fuller participation in public life, and have the option of reverting to their original baptismal names.

Upon hearing this news, Sister Ellen Clare notifies the Order that she is discarding both her habit and her religious name immediately and will be heretofore known as Sister Maggie Corrigan. The next day she calls Tommy, whom she hasn't spoken to since he drove her and Sister Agnes James to Chicago, and asks him to meet her Saturday morning.

"What do you want this time?" Tommy asks his sister.

"I'm shedding the habit and need a few bucks to go to Saint Vinnie's thrift store over on 49th for some clothes."

"I hope you know what you're doing, Maggie, because I think this whole modernization thing is a flash in the pan and won't last."

"Sorry, Tommy. Not everybody agrees with you on that. The changes in the Church will heavily impact the lives of Catholics everywhere, and this is a once-in-a-lifetime opportunity. Maybe not everyone will embrace everything, but women in particular are likely to enthusiastically welcome the shifts as a hopeful sign of things to come. I'm really excited to help shape how Catholic women are thinking about their futures as members of the most powerful religious institution in the world, which stubbornly adheres to the mistaken impression that it owns women's wombs."

"Are you done yet?" Tommy asks.

"No, I'm not. The doctrines needed to support the new changes will take years to develop, and even longer to be accepted. This leaves the faithful without a solid foundation upon which to build the new faith structures that are evolving and creates an opening that allows the Catholic faithful more freedom of choice than ever before, especially around big issues such as birth control. Time won't stand still while all this happens."

When her brother doesn't reply, she continues. "Here's the thing, Tommy. If saying Mass in English and eating meat on Friday are suddenly okay, then other requirements can be discarded just as easily."

Without commenting further, her brother agrees to meet her at the nearest neighborhood Morty's, one of several Chicago-franchised, day-old donut shops that sell cheap, weak coffee and a selection of yesterday's bakery items.

Maggie arrives wearing her habit without the headdress, because the long robe is the only clothing she currently owns. Her brother arrives a few minutes later wearing a Roman collar and when she acknowledges him, he reminds her again that he prefers to be called "Father Corrigan."

"You're my brother, for Christ's sake. I'll call you whatever I want to. Asking people to call you 'Father' is patronizing and disrespectful. You're lucky I don't call you something that isn't your name."

Not wanting to risk her brother deciding not to give her the money she needs, Maggie declines his invitation to further reveal her thoughts on the opportunities in the Church that she sees unfolding. They drink their lukewarm coffee mostly in silence, staring out a grimy window at the Dan Ryan Expressway. Maggie asks about her sisters and receives one- or two-word answers. In less than half an hour her brother hands her a twenty-dollar bill and leaves.

Later that evening, Maggie shows Mary Pat her new clothes, which include two plaid skirts, one green and one brown; two blouses, one a red-and-black print and the other multicolored stripes; and a purple sweater, several sizes too large. Grimacing at the combinations, Mary Pat asks Maggie what happened to her hair, which is sticking out unevenly all over her head.

"I ran out of money, so cut it myself."

"Next time, let me help," her friend says before asking about the plain, slender gold ring given to her when she took her solemn vows as a Bride of Christ.

"You going to ditch the ring?" Mary Pat asks.

"I don't think so," Maggie answers, twisting it on the ring finger of her left hand.

"How about the SCJ initials behind your name?"

"Not sure, but probably going to keep them too."

Changing the subject, Maggie invites Mary Pat to a talk by Chicago native and Catholic feminist scholar Millicent Delavan, who is on the faculty at Chicago Union Theological Seminary. "I saw the flyer posted in the library. The talk is at a large, women's domestic violence shelter located between Little Italy and Greektown—a rough neighborhood about two miles southwest of the downtown Loop. I haven't been out at night alone in years, and I'd appreciate the company," Maggie tells Mary Pat. "Besides, you'll have better luck than I will swiping a key so we can get back in after hours."

VII.

In every generation, women have to be taught their place one more time. The subordination of women is never accomplished for once and for all, and this pattern must stop.

Rosemary Radford Reuther

"The way things are now in the Catholic Church, women are handmaidens—both within the Church itself and within the privacy of their own homes. Men hold complete dominion over women, who have no agency regarding their personal lives, and this situation has been going on since Jesus was in diapers," Professor Millicent Delavan explains to about sixty women sitting on metal folding chairs arranged in two semicircular rows around a tabletop podium. A short, stocky woman whose brainpower far surpasses her sense of style, the remarkably plain woman whose reading glasses hang unevenly from a chain around her neck, paces as she speaks without notes.

The group is gathered in the far corner of a makeshift meeting room in one of the largest women's domestic violence shelters in metropolitan Chicago. Formerly a parish school in a formerly Italian Catholic parish that was relocated because warehouses and other storage facilities were displacing parishioners, the Sisters of God's Mercy of Omaha bought the abandoned brick building from the archdiocese for a song ten years ago. On a wing and a prayer, they have managed to raise enough money to deal with the leaking roof, rotting rafters, rusted pipes, and potentially explosive boilers. Eventually, a very generous benefactor provided sufficient funds to convert the classrooms into bed space to temporarily house one hundred women domestic violence victims and their children, after which the city building inspector granted an occupancy permit.

Sister Bridget Mary Murphy, a squarely built, business-like woman with a slight Irish twang, a black eye patch, and a style sense nearly identical to Maggie's, is the founding director of Holy Mother of Consolation Women's Domestic Violence Shelter. The organization—bearing one of the more than one thousand names the Church has given Mary, the mother of Jesus—stays afloat primarily through generous volunteer help. Nuns from around the city who work day jobs and spend their evenings and weekends mentoring the shelter residents in practical, social, and parenting skills necessary to rebuilding their lives are vital to the operation.

"These dear sisters offer emotional support and a nonjudgmental ear to the broken women who come through our door, and it makes all the difference in the world regarding their ability to recover from truly heinous experiences and move forward," Sister Bridget Mary routinely tells the potential donors she habitually squeezes for money. "As a crisis intervention organization, we're always flying by the seat of our pants, and every nickel helps."

The shelter director treads lightly over the reality that although Catholic nuns administer the shelter initiative, the archdiocese does not provide financial support, because the shelter's mission is to assist women in gaining control over their lives, including leaving their abusers, often their husbands.

"Our mission flies in the face of the Church's pro-family message, which steadfastly opposes divorce, no matter the circumstances," Sister Bridget Mary admits when asked directly, adding that in addition to providing a safe, albeit temporary place for abused women and their children to lay their heads at night, the shelter houses an on-site legal clinic to assist with filing restraining orders and addressing other legal concerns, a women's health clinic that provides family-planning services and referrals, and listings for subsidized housing.

"Direct programming includes tutoring for the high school equivalency certificate, social skill building, Illinois state employment services enrollment applications, applying for indigent health-care coverage and welfare assistance, counseling, anger management, and addiction recovery programs. Retired teaching nuns assist with temporary schooling for the children, and generally supply us with a tremendous amount of free labor," the nun proudly brags, whenever a donor asks for more details about how their contribution will be spent.

Sister Bridget Mary has organized this evening's meeting. The idea came to her after reading *The Second Sex* by French feminist Simone de Beauvoir and finding she couldn't let go of de Beauvoir's claim that "one is not born a woman—she becomes one." Realizing how strongly she disagrees with the Church's position on women, Sister Bridget Mary is ready to fight back. She believes that what the Church, and men generally, think about women is irrelevant, but how women think about themselves is vitally important, and began sharing these thoughts with other Chicago shelter directors, who enthusiastically agreed with her. Eventually, she decided to get organized.

"This program is the first step in an effort to organize a Catholic women's group to take up their own cause," she explained as she made several phone calls to invite others to attend tonight's meeting. Word of mouth publicity has resulted in more than sixty women, and a few men, crowded into the room, listening very carefully to the speaker, a dispirited Catholic herself, who agreed to appear for free.

"The only possible way women will achieve equal status in the Catholic Church, and in the wider society, is when they have a seat at the table where decisions that affect them directly are made. As regards the Church, this means two things: women becoming ordained priests equal to male priests, and getting rid of the ban on artificial birth control. Because until women have control over their reproductive lives, they'll never have any control over their lives at all. Until women achieve reproductive autonomy—the right to make their own reproductive choices—they will always be trapped in the web of control an unjust Church exercises over them, will always be constrained by men's expectations for them, and will never become all they can be," Professor Delavan concludes, forty-five minutes after she began.

Hearing this, the women, including Maggie and Mary Pat, applaud and cheer loudly. When things quiet, Sister Bridget Mary invites everyone to stay for refreshments and asks that anyone interested in working with her on pushing the Catholic patriarchy in directions that will improve Catholic women's lives, an effort she calls Catholic Women Demanding Change, or CWDC, to please add their names to the sign-up sheet on the refreshments table. Both Maggie and Mary Pat sign up. As they are leaving, Maggie tells Sister Bridget Mary that she would also like to volunteer to work with the women, doing anything that would be useful.

"Why did you volunteer for the shelter?" Mary Pat asks Maggie as they are walking toward the L stop. "Isn't what you're already doing enough sorrow and misery? Do you seriously think you need any more?"

Maggie shrugs. "The misery I see now I can't do anything about. The women won't leave their abusive husbands or try to make life better for themselves and their kids—they just wallow in their suffering and ask me to pray for them, like that'll do one damned bit of good. Women in the shelter have at least taken the first step to help themselves; otherwise, they wouldn't be there."

Mary Pat agrees this is a good point.

"Working with the school families is so frustrating—you know what I'm saying?" Maggie asks.

"Of course I do. I see those women's hungry, vacant-eyed kids in my classroom every day and wonder what awaits the little girls in a few years, after Dad or Uncle Harry or their big brother, or all three, have had their way with them and robbed them of any sense of who they are as women or even as human beings," Mary Pat reminds her. "The boys—they'll probably do something that will land them in the slammer at some point. But it's the girls who break my heart—they'll end up reliving their mothers' miserable lives and never understanding why."

"It sounds like Bridget Mary's group wants to do something positive and concrete to help women to help themselves. That would be a welcome change for me, and when I know more about what's out there in terms of lifelines, I might be able to help others make different choices," Maggie reflects.

"Or not," Mary Pat cautions. "I used to think I could fix people's lives too, but nobody can do that. In the end, it's their lives, and their misery, and they have the right to do with both as they wish. Sometimes we end up being asked to support a decision to do nothing, even when we know it's a bad one...but their lives are not our lives, and their decisions are theirs, not ours."

"Yeah, that simple reality really does drive you to drink," Maggie admits.

They remain silent until the commuter train stops at the end of the line, three long blocks from Saint Brendan's convent. To be sure no one is lurking in a doorway of an abandoned building or staggering out of a bar toward them, one or the other looks over her shoulder every five or six steps along their walk back to the convent, lit only by the neon beer signs in the dirty windows of the single-door bars along their way. Finally arriving, they see a light on in the kitchen and, upon unlocking the back door, are surprised to find Sister Gertrude Veronica in the kitchen, dressed in a robe and without her head covering, making herself a cup of tea.

"Good evening," she says. "I assume you are out after curfew because of something so important you couldn't wait until tomorrow, in broad daylight, to deal with it." She opens her hand, expecting to receive the door key.

Maggie waits for Mary Pat to answer, and when her friend hands over the key without a word, Maggie decides to speak up.

"We were at a talk at Holy Mother of Consolation women's shelter," Maggie explains, opting for the truth over an unprepared, flimsy excuse for being out alone after dark.

"What sort of talk?" Sister Gertrude Veronica asks evenly.

"About how women need to take control of their own lives, especially as regards their relationship with the Church."

"Who was giving this talk?" the superior interrupts.

"Millicent Donovan, a professor at Chicago Theological," Maggie replies, deciding she will not apologize for breaking curfew.

"Pity you didn't let me know about it. I read Millicent's book *God Our Mother* and found it fascinating. I would've enjoyed going with you." She places her teacup in the sink and prepares to leave.

"By the way, Sister Ellen Clare, Sister Agnes James was looking for you earlier. I told her I didn't know where you were. She was quite distressed. You might want to speak with her first thing in the morning, which according to my watch, is about five hours from now."

"Shit," Maggie whispers, rolling her eyes in Mary Pat's general direction and deciding against, once again, reminding Sister Gertrude Veronica that she has forgone her religious name for her baptismal one.

Maggie oversleeps the next morning and is late for the hour set aside for reading sacred scripture before six-thirty Mass. As the sisters are preparing to walk over to the church, Sister Agnes James taps her on the shoulder.

"I looked everywhere for you last night. Where were you?"

Hoping to distract her, Maggie answers the question with one of her own. "What did you need, Sister?" she asks the older nun, who has rejected the baptismal name and secular clothing options in favor of continuing to wear her religious habit and keeping her religious name.

"I'm preparing our monthly report for the motherhouse and need a list of your expenses. This is past due, so please get it to me today. It must be in tomorrow's mail."

This the first Maggie has heard of needing to file a monthly report that includes her expenses and asks when this practice began.

"After I sent last month's report, Mother Michael Joan wrote back and suggested I include your itemized expenses. She might be wondering where you're finding the means to purchase clothes and other incidentals and wants to be sure you're meeting your other obligations," Sister Agnes James smiles.

"I'm under surveillance?" Maggie frowns.

"I wouldn't say that, exactly. It's more a matter of accounting for your time and expenditures, which I'm sure she realizes are few, since we only receive fifty dollars per month for necessities."

"It's surveillance, Sister, and you damned well know it! Please tell Mother Michael Joan I will be sending my own reports, so she needn't worry you with this responsibility any longer."

The older nun blanches at Maggie's outburst.

During Mass a few minutes later, Maggie realizes that as soon as she can figure out the finances, she needs to move out of the restrictive convent environment into a place of her own, which she knows a few of the other Order sisters have already done. Otherwise, she will never be able to pursue her desire to volunteer at the women's shelter or to work with Sister Bridget Mary and the social justice initiative she seeks to establish. The key is figuring out a plausible story so compelling that Mother Michael Joan cannot refuse her.

As soon as she returns to the convent after Mass, Maggie places a call to Sister Bridget Mary, requesting an appointment.

Two days later, she is sitting in the Holy Mother of Consolation shelter director's office, which was the janitor's closet when the building was still a school.

"Let's begin by you calling me Bridget Mary, and me calling you Maggie," the director says. "I feel all women are sisters and we either name them all as sisters or don't name any of them sisters—otherwise we are just creating a barrier that divides rather than unites us."

Maggie nods her agreement and begins explaining that she wants to become involved with the work of the shelter and the fledgling CWDC initiative if she can find a way to manage the financials.

Listening carefully while periodically adjusting her eye patch, Bridget Mary asks her what she needs to move forward toward her goal.

"For starters, I need to move out of the convent, so I'll need a job where I earn enough money for my living expenses."

"Where would you live?" Bridget Mary frowns.

"Three of our sisters are doing outreach and sharing an apartment on the near South Side. I might be able to stay there, but I'll need to contribute to the household expenses and have at least a little spending money for myself. I don't need much, but I won't have any if I give up my current work. I need a paying job."

"I can't offer you a job, but I have another thought," Bridget Mary smiles. "You can live here with Sister Catherine Theresa and me at no cost. You obviously don't eat much, so one additional mouth to feed is no problem, and I'm sure we can find a place in our private living quarters to put an extra bed. This will take care of your basic living expenses. In return, you will rotate night duty in the shelter with us and work on funding applications to keep the shelter afloat. We're desperate for money and need a full-time grant writer to chase after available funding but can't pay even a part-time one. The applications we do manage to put together are all done by volunteers in their spare time, which is not a sustainable business plan. Neither Catherine nor I have the time to devote to writing grants, but if you work on it, you can write a position for yourself into the applications—and create a paying job for yourself."

"This sounds perfect, but honestly, I have no grant-writing experience and no idea where to begin with something like this. I wish I did, but I don't."

"The hard part is finding funding sources that match our interests, which involves a lot of tedious library research and asking around. The actual writing is straightforward. There are forms to fill out, open-ended questions to answer, and then figuring out how much to safely pad the budget. The goal is to convince potential funders that we are a cause worthy of their interest, and their money. I'm sure it's something you can handle, once you're familiar with our operation. After the first two or three applications, you'll get comfortable with the process."

Offering a rare smile, Maggie says they have a deal and asks how soon she can begin.

"As soon as you're ready," Bridget Mary says, just as a loud argument between two women living in the shelter breaks out in the hallway outside her office, followed by the sound of one slapping the other.

"See yourself out—I have to deal with this," Bridget Mary instructs, walking toward the door. "Call me with your start date."

Maggie can barely contain her excitement as she rides the L back to St. Brendan's. Her only remaining problem is getting permission from her superior to make the move, and she isn't sure whether this is best done in writing or by telephone.

She is still thinking about it later that evening when Sister Agnes James sits down next to her at supper and whispers that they need to talk immediately. Maggie puts a finger to her lips and says whatever it is can wait until they have finished eating. Sister Agnes James insists it can't wait and motions Maggie to follow her, which everyone in the dining room notices.

"What's so important it can't wait half an hour?" Maggie grouses.

"Mother Michael Joan has resigned," Sister Agnes James gasps, wringing her hands.

"How do you know that?" Maggie asks.

"We received a letter addressed to us both in today's mail. It doesn't say why she resigned, it just says Sister Marie William is in charge, effective immediately, until a new superior is chosen, and asks for our prayers during this transition. I don't like change, Sister. It's very distressing."

Maggie has never feared change and immediately realizes this is the opportunity she needs to make her move. Believing it is easier to beg forgiveness than to ask permission, she decides to put off writing to Sister Marie William, who tends to be more progressive than her predecessor. She is betting her new superior will be too overwhelmed with the unfamiliar responsibilities suddenly thrust upon her to bother about something as mundane as one of the sisters moving out of a convent. If she waits a while before informing her superior, she will be well-established in her new position and better able to defend herself.

Later that evening, Mary Pat, beer in hand, knocks on her door. Maggie is too excited to keep her plans a secret, so tells her friend of this new opportunity.

"This sounds great, Maggie, except for one problem. As soon as you tell Sister Gertrude Veronica you're leaving, which you have to do, she could pull an end-run on you and call your superior."

"Do you think she'd do that?" Maggie asks. "It's not like I'm leaving the Order. I'm just changing addresses."

"I'm sure she'd do it. And what about Sister Agnes James? She'll get hysterical when she learns you're moving out."

"I could just sneak away after hours."

"And have the cops looking for you by noon the next day? Won't work."

"I'm not that concerned about it. For one thing, Marie William will have more pressing things on her mind than one of her nuns moving somewhere. If anybody gets upset, I'll claim Mother Michael Joan gave me permission to take on different responsibilities and forgot to mention it. I'll tell Sisters Agnes James and Gertrude Veronica that I have a new assignment and, hopefully, the Order will send someone to replace me as soon as things settle down after Mother Michael Joan's abrupt departure, which is mostly the truth. Worst case scenario is a dustup I claim is all a big misunderstanding, and by then it'll be a done deal."

"That's pretty devious, Maggie, but it might work," Mary Pat smiles, raising her beer in a toast.

"Even if the shit does hit the fan, I'm not giving this up. I'm not looking for trouble, but I won't back down from it either."

"How'd you become so tough, Maggie?"

"Trying to survive my family—how do you think?"

"Well, just so you know, I'm very jealous. I'd love to be doing the same thing, but I'm still stuck back in the Middle Ages. We haven't even settled on habit options yet, and I'm still dragging around five yards of heavy material and a stiff wimple that rubs my forehead raw. Changing the subject, what are you going to tell Tommy?"

"I don't plan to tell him anything. He only hears from me when I call asking for money, which has been only once. Otherwise, we're never in touch."

"He was here looking for you the other day."

"He was? Why didn't you say something?"

"It got weird. He kept staring at me, and I think he recognized me—or thought he did. He said he'd stop back in a couple of days, then was back the next day. It shook me up, Maggie...he looked like the same handsome Tommy I was so damned in love with...probably still am in love with."

"I don't think you have anything to worry about. He's in love with being a priest now. He won't do anything to jeopardize that."

"What will you tell him if he ever asks about who else lives here?"

"What do you want me to tell him?"

"Lie to him, please. I can't risk a conversation with him. After seeing him again, I don't think I'm strong enough to not spill the beans about everything, and that won't do anybody any good, especially Tommy. He is the love of my life, Maggie, and I'm far from over him. I know that now." Mary Pat stares at the floor, unable to make eye contact with her best friend.

"It took nine years in the convent for you to figure this out, Mary Pat?"

"Probably not. But it took me that long to admit it."

"What difference does it make now?"

"None that I can think of, but if Tommy comes back into my life, I don't trust myself not to break my vows. This isn't like Joe, who's much easier to resist."

"Tommy has vows too."

"Priests break their vows all the time, and for them it's different. They're in charge of the Church, so they write the rules and can bend them however they want. That's not true for us. Please, Maggie, you've got to help me through this."

"If you want me to lie, I will, but you won't be able to run away from this forever."

"Tell him you're leaving here, so he won't come back. Please, Maggie. He'll find out sooner or later, so why not tell him now?"

"The best I can do is promise I won't wait too long before telling him," Maggie says, sighing. "In the meantime, if he comes back again, don't answer the door."

The next morning, for the third time in four days, Father Tommy Corrigan, wearing his Roman collar, knocks on the convent door, asking for his sister. Sister Agnes James invites him in and says she'll look for Maggie. When she finds her, Maggie asks her to say she's already left for the day.

"I won't lie to a priest," Sister Agnes James says indignantly. "He's waiting for you in the front parlor."

Fifteen minutes pass before Maggie enters the parlor, where she finds her brother standing at the window, looking toward the old church.

"I'm pretty busy, Tommy. Can't whatever it is wait a few days?"

"No, Maggie, it can't wait. Is there somewhere we can talk privately?"

Nervous that Mary Pat will walk by the parlor doorway at any moment, Maggie suggests they go for a cup of coffee at their usual Morty's by the expressway.

They arrive just as the morning rush is thinning out, and grab a table near the back, next to a grimy window looking out onto the Dan Ryan Expressway underpass where homeless people camp out. After purchasing two weak, lukewarm coffees and two stale chocolate donuts, Tommy sits down across from his sister.

"I might as well get right to the point, Maggie," he says, dipping his donut in the watery coffee.

Maggie, sitting across from him, remains stone-faced.

"I heard you're moving into Holy Mother of Consolation Women's Shelter to help them find operating funds and work with their programs."

"Where did you hear that?" Maggie asks, incredulous that her brother knows this when she only worked out the details less than twenty-four hours ago.

"Bridget Mary Murphy's second cousin, Liam, is our new assistant pastor. She told him about it when he stopped by there last night, and he mentioned it at breakfast this morning."

"For such a huge city, this can be a damned small town," Maggie replies.

"Is it true?"

"Yes."

"You do know how controversial that operation is? The archdiocese has serious misgivings about what they're doing there."

"It's controversial because they strive to give women a voice in their own lives, and the archdiocese doesn't like that because it flies smack in the face of total patriarchal control over women. Women collectively speaking up for themselves risks a power shift, and nobody gives up power willingly. That's no news, Tommy."

"Is it true that Bridget Mary is trying to get Catholic women organized to fight for their reproductive rights?"

"That's my impression."

"You do know how embarrassing this will be for me? I'm in tight with the archdiocesan hierarchy, and they'll frown on my sister getting involved in anything the Church doesn't approve of. I'll be expected to put a stop to it."

"Honestly, Tommy, I haven't given any thought at all to whether what I do might embarrass you, and I can assure you I don't care. If it comes up, you can explain to the cardinal's underlings, or to the cardinal himself, that you have no influence or control over me, aren't consulted regarding what I do or don't do, and don't know anything about my activities. All three statements are true, and to keep them that way, the less said, the better. I'm through discussing this and need to get back, so let's get going."

"One more thing, Maggie..." he says, his tone softening. "Is Mary Pat Donovan one of the nuns living in your convent?"

"Why do you ask?"

"I thought I saw her there when I stopped by the other day to drop off some paint we don't need and thought the convent could use."

Maggie doesn't answer.

When it's obvious his sister isn't giving up any information, Father Corrigan continues. "There was a lot unsettled between us that I still think about, and I'd like the chance to set some things straight with her. I heard she entered the convent, but no one I asked seemed to know much more than that."

Maggie doesn't say anything.

"So that was her."

"You're on your own with this, Tommy. I'm not getting involved. Sometimes it's better to leave things alone. If Mary Pat wanted to be in touch with you, it would not be difficult for her to find you."

Without another word, Father Corrigan stands up, fishes his car keys out of his pocket, and begins walking toward the door.

"Instead of going back to the convent, please drop me at the shelter," Maggie instructs as she follows her brother out of the dingy coffee shop.

VIII.

Thank you to all women who are wives. You irrevocably join your future to that of your husband.

Pope John Paul II

Maggie is on her first night-duty shift at the shelter when the phone rings at two-thirty on the morning after Christmas. A weary-sounding woman, identifying herself as Hanna Mae Morgan from Saint Joseph's Charity Hospital's social work department, asks whether the shelter has any space available for a twenty-six-year-old mother with four sons. Maggie is aware a lot of requests come from Saint Joe's, which is only six blocks away, and the shelter tries to accommodate them whenever possible.

"The mom was brought to the emergency room several hours ago, after a Christmas night domestic violence incident. She wouldn't agree to come to the hospital unless the kids came with her, so I've got four little boys sleeping on blankets on the floor of my office," Hanna Mae explains. "We're holding the mother for observation because of a concussion. She got knocked around pretty good, and is missing a few teeth, but should be okay. From what I understand, the two oldest boys, ages eight and six, tried to stop the father's drunken rage and got hit a few times, but they're basically okay too—physically, that is. What I need to do is send the boys now, and the mother will come later today or tomorrow," the social worker explains.

"I'm sorry, but we're full. And we can't take unaccompanied children in any case," Maggie sighs.

"You are my last resort. If you can't take them, I'll have to split the boys up and arrange for emergency foster care placement, which piles on their trauma. If they're placed, the mother will have to figure out the rest when she's released and, hopefully, reunited with her children, but once you get social services involved, there's no telling what might happen. They're sweet kids, and this is a damned lousy Christmas they'll never forget...you sure you can't make room somewhere?"

Maggie asks about the father who did this to his family.

"He took off when he saw the police cruiser's flashing lights. I doubt they'll bother looking for him. Domestics aren't a priority in a city with multiple murders every night," Hanna Mae answers.

"Bring the boys over. We'll figure something out," Maggie says, knowing that she's risking the shelter's operating permit by allowing more residents than they are licensed to accommodate, and is asking to get fired after just one week.

After several thank yous and God bless yous, the social worker tells Maggie she'll be bringing Stevie, Mikey, Johnny, and Casey Dolan in about an hour. Hanging up the phone, Maggie debates whether to wake Bridget Mary and tell her what she's done, then decides finding cots, blankets, a crib for the two-year-old, and someplace to put the boys for the night is more pressing. After searching both floors of the old building, the best she can do is jam the boys into an empty coat room outside what used to be classroom three. The space is in the cross traffic between two busy bathrooms with several sinks, stalls, and one makeshift shower, and offers the four little boys and their injured mother neither quiet nor privacy.

Accordion-style room dividers create individual spaces for mothers with children in the three classrooms on the first floor. The other two classrooms are filled with cots to accommodate single women without children, dormitory-style. Three more upstairs classrooms are separated into units to accommodate mothers and children, all of whom share one bathroom. A combination meeting and storage room takes up the remaining space, commonly used for Alcoholics Anonymous, Narcotics Anonymous, and anger management counseling. A section of the third-floor attic storage area has been converted into an apartment where Sisters Catherine Theresa, Bridget Mary, and now Maggie live. It is drywalled but needs taping and painting. The rest of the space is junk storage and a cleared-out area that's being used for the CWDC meetings.

To avoid blocking the door, the mother will have to be placed in the hallway beside the coat room, which is against the fire code, but being

Christmas week, Maggie doubts the fire inspector will show up and discover this violation. She is more worried about what Bridget Mary will say when she finds out Maggie has jeopardized their occupancy permit. An hour later, Hanna Mae Morgan, exhausted and frazzled, arrives with four frightened children. The two older boys, with significant bruising on their faces, stare at the floor. With eyes radiating fear, four-year-old Johnny is holding Hanna Mae's hand, and Casey, the baby, is asleep on her shoulder. Before handing him over, Hanna Mae gives Maggie a plastic bag and manila envelope containing paperwork.

"Johnny has soiled himself twice. I was able to find something for him to wear in our emergency closet, and these are his dirty clothes. Unless you can convince him to wear a diaper, expect him to wet the bed." Maggie nods and says they have a lot of diapers and extras for situations when women flee with nothing but the clothes on their backs, so they can handle this. Hanna Mae thanks her again, pats each boy on the head and assures them that they'll be safe with Maggie and that their mother will be arriving later.

"I hate fuckin' Christmas," she mumbles as she turns to leave. "I been doing this for coming on thirty-six years, and Christmas is always the worst. There's more domestic shit on Christmas Eve and Christmas Day than we normally have in a month, and it's some of the worst we ever see. Don't you ever wonder what the hell is wrong with people?"

Maggie pats her on the arm and thanks her for doing God's work.

"Honey, I'm sorry to be the one to tell you, but there ain't no God lets this crap happen," Hanna Mae says, shaking her head. "I figured that out a long time ago. The only reason I go to church is to see my friends and get a dose of positive once in a while...otherwise, I'd really hate the world." She pulls her hat down over her gray-streaked afro and lets the door slam as she walks out to the waiting cab.

Agreeing with Hanna Mae, Maggie sees that it has begun to snow.

The next morning, holding two-year-old Casey Dolan on her hip, Maggie confesses breaking the shelter admission rules to Bridget Mary. Speaking over the toddler's whining, the shelter director explains that the hardest part of their job is turning away cases like Maggie just admitted. She agrees that now that the boys have come, they can stay, as long as Maggie agrees to babysit them until their mother arrives and, hopefully, can care for them herself.

"Just don't put us in this position again," Bridget Mary admonishes, as the two-year-old leans over to grab at her eye patch. "We can't help everybody, and if we lose our license, we won't be able to help anybody."

As Maggie turns to walk away, Bridget Mary calls her back. "One other thing. As soon as the mother arrives, convince her to take out a restraining order against her husband immediately. We can't have that bastard showing up here threatening God knows what if we don't let him in. Tell her if she doesn't agree to the order, she can't stay. Once she signs it, which hopefully she will, take it to the police station over on Cermak Road yourself and give it to the desk sergeant. Tell him I said to send it over to family court ASAP. He'll know what to do."

With one eye swollen shut, several missing teeth, a broken nose, and a large bandage over a cut across her forehead, a still-dazed Mary Beth Dolan arrives at Holy Mother of Consolation Shelter late that afternoon, in a cab paid for with Saint Joseph's charity care funds. Maggie guesses Mary Beth had been a pretty young woman before her husband's fists rearranged her face, transforming her into a badly bruised, sadly defeated one.

Seeing how severely Mary Beth has been beaten, Maggie assumes getting her to agree to a restraining order won't be a problem and presents the request to her during the intake interview. The young mother's reluctance to take this step flabbergasts her.

"This is all my fault. If I'd saved more money, we would've had a decent Christmas dinner, and Jimmy wouldn't have gotten upset and started drinking. The boys need their father, and I can't keep him from them—or them from him, either...it wouldn't be right. This will all blow over," Mary Beth lisps through missing teeth, tears streaming down her face.

"Mary Beth—I want you to answer me honestly. Do you really believe that a husband who hurts his wife as badly as you've been hurt is a good father and role model for his sons?"

"I know my husband loves his family, and that's all that matters," she replies. "I'll try harder to please him, and everything will be fine. I'm sure of it."

"How can you be so sure?" Maggie asks.

"It only happens—him hitting me—when I upset him. And he's always sorry afterward and promises not to do it again. A good wife believes what her husband tells her, and I try to be a good wife."

"How often do these beatings happen?"

"I'm not sure, but it's not usually as bad as this...honestly."

Maggie notices Mary Beth's slightly crooked forearm and knows she isn't telling the truth. "And you believe him when he says he's sorry and won't do it again?" Maggie frowns.

"He begs me to forgive him, and the Church says to forgive those who hurt us, so I try to do that, to show my boys how important loving forgiveness is. If I do what you're asking—sign this order—it means I don't forgive him, and that'll be tearing our family apart forever. If I do that, God will show me no mercy."

"Who gave you that idea—that God expects you to just take this abuse over and over again?" Maggie asks.

"Father Corrigan. I went to talk to him when Jimmy first started getting so upset with me, right after Stevie was born. The baby was screaming all one night and Jimmy balled up his fist and told me to shut the kid up or he'd do it himself. It scared me. Father said marriage isn't easy and that a good wife submits to her husband and does all she can to make him happy...and for the sake of keeping the family together, forgives him, no matter what he does. It's what makes a good, strong Catholic family—a holy family like God wants and expects from us. He said when things get rough, saying a rosary or praying to the Blessed Mother always helps."

"Which Father Corrigan said this?" Maggie asks, hoping it's not her brother.

"Father Tom Corrigan I think was his name—the assistant pastor of Queen of Heaven, the parish we were living in at the time. Do you know him?"

Maggie's heart starts pounding and her face flushes bright, angry red. "Well, Father Corrigan is wrong."

"He preached the same thing from the pulpit," Mary Beth says, "and whenever things got to be too much and I went to him, he repeated the importance of keeping the family together. But no matter, Sister. I could never support the boys by myself anyway. I barely graduated high school before I got married, and I was already pregnant. I can't hold down a job, even if I could get one, and raise four boys on my own."

Maggie knows she has a point but doesn't want to discourage her from getting out of a dangerously abusive marriage. "We have ways we can help you, Mary Beth. We have job skill programs, and we'll help you find a safe place to live and connect you with the resources you'll need. But in the meantime, we must be sure Jimmy doesn't come here and cause trouble while we're helping you get on your feet again. For us to help you,

you'll have to agree to a restraining order. Otherwise, you're endangering others as well as yourself, and we'll have to ask you to leave...and I really don't want to do that."

"I'm sorry, Sister, I can't do what you're asking. If it means I have to leave, then that's what I'll do. I'll call my sister to pick the boys and me up. I can talk to Jimmy, and he'll promise me it won't happen again. But if I take legal action against him, it's admitting that keeping the family together isn't important to me. That's not true. It's the most important thing in the world to me."

Frowning, Maggie says she'll have to discuss this with Sister Bridget Mary and suggests Mary Beth rest while volunteers care for the boys. She takes her to the cot set aside for her and assures her she'll be back soon to check on her.

When Maggie returns, Mary Beth and her boys are gone. One of the volunteers tells her Mary Beth asked to make a phone call, and shortly afterwards took the boys and left. Heartbroken at this outcome and seething over what Mary Beth has told her, Maggie calls her brother, demanding to see him.

"I'm busy right now, Maggie. It'll have to wait," he tells her.

Hearing this, she slams down the phone, grabs her coat, and walks to the L station. Queen of Heaven parish is located six blocks from the Fuller Park stop, and today it's a long walk on slippery sidewalks, against a biting wind, but Maggie is too angry to care. Arriving at the well-maintained rectory, she bangs on the door for several minutes until the housekeeper finally answers.

"I want to speak with Father Corrigan," Maggie tells the older woman, shoving her way through the door.

"Do you have an appointment?" the startled housekeeper asks.

"I'm his sister. I don't need a goddamn appointment," Maggie barks, looking around the clean, well-appointed parlor with shining, recently waxed floors. The windows sparkle, and the entire area, smelling of lemon furniture polish, reflects hours of loving attention.

Having heard the commotion, Father Corrigan opens his office door.

"I told you I'm too busy to visit right now, Maggie," he calls out.

"This isn't a social visit, Tommy, and I promise you'll regret it if you don't listen to what I have to say."

Her brother motions the housekeeper to leave and walks toward a large, recently reupholstered wing chair in the reception area, where a life-sized statue of the Blessed Virgin Mary, also known as the Queen of Heaven, is prayerfully watching them from the corner of the room, listening carefully.

Maggie takes off her coat and slams the hallway door.

"What the hell is wrong with you?" her brother asks.

"Does the name Mary Beth Dolan mean anything to you?" she asks, standing directly in front of her seated brother.

"Should it?"

"You gave her marriage counseling a few times after her husband knocked her around and she came to you for help."

"I hear too many of those stories to remember each one. Pretty soon they all run together." He crosses his legs and rests his hands on the chair's overstuffed arms, looking straight ahead.

"She said you advise women not to leave the SOBs who are beating the shit out of them. You tell them to stay with these bastards and not break up their families, no matter what. She said that's what you told her to do when she came to you and what you preach from the pulpit. Did she understand you correctly?"

"Yes...that is the Church's position, and it's one I support, but I don't see how this is any of your business."

"Mary Beth Dolan's four boys ended up in our shelter in the middle of last night. She arrived several hours later, after being released from the hospital where she was held for observation after her husband rearranged her face and gave her a concussion. She refused to take out a restraining order against him because she said you told her God would never forgive her for breaking up her family. Did you tell her that?"

"Probably. Most of these things blow over by themselves, and the less fuss made over them the better."

"If you believe that, you're a bigger asshole than I thought you were, Tommy. Telling women to just take it when their husbands start pounding on them in a drunken rage is criminal. Would you tell our sisters to do that?

"I already have—told Fiona and Colleen—several times."

"Jesus Christ, Tommy. You're sentencing these women to death—and in the name of God, no less."

"That's a little dramatic, Maggie. It never goes that far. Imagine the trouble I'd be in if I started advising women to leave their husbands every time they got drunk and hit them...I'd have the cardinal and every man in the parish down my throat. I might even be disciplined for something like that."

"Tell me the truth, Tommy: do you believe what you're telling these women, or are you just saying it to save your own neck?"

"I've never thought about it. But what's it to you? You're not married, so this isn't your problem."

"What it is to me is that it's wrong to treat women this way—as some man's property to do with as he pleases, including beating the crap out of her whenever he feels like it. What it is to me is that my brother is too cowardly to do anything other than go along with the party line so he won't get in trouble. I foolishly hoped you were better than that. If you keep up with this shit-for-brains advice, someday you're going to have blood on your hands."

"I'm sorry you're disappointed, Maggie. Now, if you're finished, I need to get back to work."

Maggie grabs her coat and hat and walks out the door without saying anything further. On her way down the sidewalk, she pitches a large snowball at the rectory door, hitting its mark dead center with a loud thud.

•••

With every inch of useable space assigned to the shelter residents, there is no place for Maggie to do her grant work undisturbed. Bridget Mary suggests creating an office in the back corner of the attic storage area filled with musty odors, dust mites, and stale air.

"That end is an icehouse in the winter and hotter than a Southern barbeque in the summer, but we have a couple of fans and a space heater, which is a fired hazard, so you need to remember to turn it off when you leave. I'm sure we can find you a desk and a couple of chairs, so decide where you want to set up, and I'll get someone to help do it."

Maggie looks around the space that, like the small apartment, has been drywalled but never taped or painted. Lighting comes from bare lightbulbs screwed into sockets in the water-stained ceiling, several ventilation pipes run up through the middle of the room toward the roof, and discarded furniture is haphazardly shoved into various piles. A thick film of dust covers the floors. She decides the area near a small window, which allows the sun to illuminate the airborne dust particles, works best.

The next day, a desk with a peeling laminate top is sitting under the window, with two chairs stacked on top. Rummaging through the discarded furniture, Maggie locates a bookcase and an empty metal file cabinet to add to her workspace. After washing everything—including the floor—with soap and water, she is satisfied it is a workable arrangement, and sits down in her desk chair. Opening the second desk drawer on the left, she is surprised to find a half-full bottle of cheap bourbon. She smiles and decides to keep it, regardless of how it got there.

•••

Three weeks later, while Maggie is in her makeshift office reading a grant proposal, she hears a knock on the wall. She looks up to see Hanna Mae Morgan, out of breath from hefting herself up the two long flights of stairs, standing beside the file cabinet.

"Do you have a minute?" she asks. Maggie motions her to sit down on the metal folding chair beside her desk.

"Do you remember Mary Beth Dolan?" Hanna Mae begins, taking a deep breath.

Maggie nods. "She was my first failure, and I've never forgotten about her because I really wish I could've somehow convinced her to stay."

"So do I, because she was brought in three nights ago after what her husband claimed was a fall down the basement stairs. Her neck was broken, and she was completely paralyzed. She died early this morning."

"Goddammit!" Maggie exclaims, hitting her desk with her fist.

"Look, Maggie, this was a tough case, and I know you tried your best to help her. I wanted to tell you what happened myself, rather than have you find out some other way."

Hearing this, Maggie closes her eyes. Tears run down her face as she rummages through her desk looking for something to wipe them away. "I guess I'm not surprised."

"I wasn't surprised either, but that doesn't make it any easier...maybe it makes it all harder. Still, I truly don't think there was anything you could've done differently. She did ask me to deliver a message to you."

Maggie looks at the wizened social worker whose kind eyes have seen more sorrow than good in her nearly forty years trying to help people after life—or an angry husband—has dealt them a near-fatal blow.

"Mary Beth said to tell you that you were right, and Father Corrigan was wrong...that if she'd listened to you, her boys wouldn't have ended up motherless. Do you know what she meant?"

"Unfortunately, I do," Maggie sighs, mindlessly shredding a paper napkin left over from lunch eaten at her desk. "Her parish priest advised her to remain in the marriage regardless of what was going on, because that's what God wants, and if she leaves, God will never forgive her. What she didn't know was that the priest who told her this is my brother, and

I can assure you he doesn't have any better idea about what God wants than the rest of us do."

"Lord Jesus save us," Hanna Mae exclaims, lifting her glasses and wiping her face.

"For what it's worth, I ripped him a new asshole over it, and we haven't spoken since."

The two women sit in silence for a few minutes. Maggie finally asks about the boys and learns they are in four different foster care homes scattered throughout the city.

"Eventually, we may be able to find a placement that will accept all four, but in an emergency, that's impossible, and we have to take what we can get. After I leave here, I'm going to pick them all up and take them for ice cream while I tell them about their mother...try to reassure them that we're doing all we can to get them back together under one roof as soon as possible."

"How about relatives?"

"I'm looking into that, but I doubt there are any who can afford to feed four extra mouths and are also willing to do it."

"And her no-good bastard husband? What was his name?"

"Jimmy. The police got him this time. The way it went down is the argument started in the upstairs bedroom. Hearing the commotion, Stevie took his brothers downstairs and hid them under the kitchen sink. He called the police from the kitchen telephone, then climbed under the sink with others. He heard his mother scream, followed by thumps as she fell down the stairs. He thinks she got up and Jimmy went at her again, this time pushing her down the basement stairs, where she landed on the cement floor. Jimmy was so drunk, it took him a while to figure out what he'd done, and the police got there before he could take off. Due to past domestic incidents, he's looking at second-degree murder, or first, depending."

"Depending on what?" Maggie asks.

"What the district attorney thinks will stick, and how invested he is in the case, which I wouldn't bet is a lot. Thousands of domestics come across his desk every year, and they all start to sound the same after a while."

"Surely not all of them end up like this one, with four motherless kids, and a father looking at murder charges...that has to mean something."

Hanna Mae shrugs, then wipes her eyes again. "God only knows how this will turn out, or how it will affect those kids' lives...seeing their father abuse their mother until she dies from her injuries. There's no way they won't be screwed up...maybe become abusers themselves."

"Come to the funeral with me," Maggie says.

"You're going to go?"

"Yes, I'm going to go. And I'm also going to make sure my brother knows he's complicit in a murder."

Hearing the anger in Maggie's voice, Hanna Mae's eyes grow wide. "How in the name of all that is holy are you going to do that?"

"I'm heading over to his rectory as soon as we're finished here. You're welcome to come along—actually, I'd appreciate it if you would."

"I ain't gettin' in the middle of no red-hot family argument that's startin' to make the feud between the Hatfields and McCoys sound like a kindergarten playground spat—even if I do agree with every word you're saying. But I would like to go to the funeral with you. I don't go to the funeral every time a case ends this way, but this one...it's tuggin' at me real bad...like it's trying to tell me something...."

"Keep thinking like that, and I'll let you know what the arrangements are," Maggie says, anxious to talk to her brother and unwilling to wait any longer. "In the meantime, I'm on my way to have a meaningful conversation with Father Tommy Corrigan."

•••

When Maggie arrives at Queen of Heaven rectory a second time, she doesn't bother knocking at the front door. Instead, she follows the neatly shoveled sidewalk around the side yard to the kitchen door, opens it, and walks right past the startled housekeeper standing in the newly renovated kitchen. She remembers her brother's ground floor office is four doors down a recently painted hallway, with new carpet and a vase of fresh flowers on a side table. The rectory is remarkably elegant for a parish located in the heart of a blue-collar, working-class neighborhood in South Side Chicago. She wonders whether Mary Beth's funeral will be here and whether Tommy will be saying the funeral Mass.

"I think Father Corrigan is busy," the distressed housekeeper calls out.

Maggie ignores her and opens her brother's office door without knocking.

"I have someone with me," a startled Father Corrigan says, looking up from his neatly arranged desk and seeing his sister.

"Then tell them to leave," Maggie says. "What I have to say is a hell of a lot more important than whatever conversation you're having right now."

"Please excuse me for a moment. It seems my sister needs to speak with me," Father Corrigan says to the surprised young couple sitting across from him.

"What the hell is wrong with you?" he whispers, taking Maggie's arm and firmly guiding her out of his office. She begins speaking before he tries closing the door, which she has blocked with her foot. Tommy huffs and starts walking down the immaculate hallway away from his office. Leaving the door ajar, Maggie follows him.

"Remember Mary Beth Dolan? She died this morning from a broken neck that SOB husband you counseled her to forgive and stay with, no matter what, inflicted on her," Maggie says in a voice loud enough to be heard throughout the rectory.

"I just learned of the death a few hours ago, and I'm very saddened by what has occurred," Father Corrigan says.

"Not half as sad as you're going to be when I tell the police you're an accomplice in her murder."

"Calm down, Maggie, you're sounding a little crazy. I didn't have anything to do with what happened to her."

"Like hell you didn't, you pompous bastard," Maggie yells. "You knew Jimmy Dolan was beating her bloody and told her to stay with him anyway, and she did what you told her to do, because you're a priest who thinks he has a direct connection to the will of God. Sorry to disappoint you, Tommy, but you're wrong, and your shitty advice has deprived four little boys of a mother and cost an innocent woman her life."

"I didn't think things were that bad for her."

"Because you don't think at all—ever...because you don't want anything like a nasty dose of reality to disturb how Holy Mother Church thinks things should be," Maggie sputters, red-faced and so angry she is barely able to speak.

"Here's what's going to happen, Tommy," Maggie continues after taking a deep breath. Her brown eyes are riveted on her twin brother's matching ones, and she speaks in a voice so cold it could freeze water.

"I'm going to tell the police that Mary Beth Dolan went to you for help, and you counseled her to remain in a dangerously abusive marriage, which makes you an accessory to murder, even if they can't charge you with a crime. What you did will be in the criminal record and evidence to support changing the law to make the kind of advice you gave her so illegal that you, and others like you, will spend the rest of your lives wearing striped vestments, courtesy of the Illinois state prison system. Maybe Frankie can be your cellmate," Maggie fumes, taking another deep breath before continuing.

"This didn't have to happen. That it did happen is on your conscience for the rest of your life, and I hope you rot in hell for causing that beautiful young woman to die and her innocent children to lose their mother. There's no forgiveness for the likes of you, Tommy Corrigan."

Hearing his sister's words, the priest goes pale and looks for a place to sit down. "There isn't a cop in the city who will listen to you, Maggie," he finally says.

"Not every cop is an Irish mick. I'll find one who isn't—no matter how hard I have to look, or how long it takes me. This isn't going away, Tommy. I promise you."

As she is leaving, Maggie sticks her head into Father Corrigan's brightly lit, well-furnished office and tells the flabbergasted young couple waiting for him that if they're seeking marital counseling, they better go somewhere else because Father Corrigan has his head so far up his ass, he is unable to speak wisely on the subject. This is information she knows—and knows her brother knows—will be the talk of every bar within five miles by nightfall.

IX.

The priesthood is the love of the heart of Jesus.
When you see a priest, think of our Lord Jesus Christ.
SAINT JOHN VIANNEY

It is not yet six o'clock in the morning when Maggie hears the shelter's downstairs phone ringing. Let the games begin, she thinks, knowing Sister Bridget Mary is on night duty and will have to answer it. A moment later, Bridget Mary is knocking at her door.

"Phone for you, Maggie. She says it's urgent, and I believe her."

Maggie groans and picks up the extension next to her bed.

"You promised you wouldn't tell him," a panicked voice on the other end says.

Maggie asks who she promised not to tell what?

"It's me, Maggie—Mary Pat. Tommy's here, crying, drunk, and saying I'm the only one he can talk to. His pounding on the door woke up Sister Gertrude Veronica. He insists on talking to me, and she's standing in the hallway, waiting for an explanation."

"I didn't tell him anything, Mary Pat. He guessed, and I neither confirmed nor denied."

"That's the same as telling him, Maggie."

"There wasn't anything else I could do, but it doesn't sound like that's your biggest problem at the moment. What's he upset about?"

"He says he has to do a funeral later this morning for a woman you accused him of murdering. Do you know what he's talking about?"

"Unfortunately, I do, and it's a little complicated to explain right now."

"What should I do? He's half hysterical and won't give me the flask he's pulling from."

"Call one of the priests over at his parish and tell them to come and get him."

"That'll be a horrible embarrassment for him, Maggie."

"Not your problem. Just don't let him drive anywhere."

"Will you come over here?"

"I don't think I'm the person Tommy wants to see right now. Try to get some coffee in him and call his parish."

"He says he's never stopped loving me, Maggie...in front of Sister Gertrude Veronica. She's going to demand an explanation," Father Tommy Corrigan's former girlfriend whispers into the telephone.

"I wouldn't believe anything he says when he's drunk and scared shitless. You can have that conversation some other time. I'm sorry he's put you in this position, but sad to say, I'm not too surprised. He's turned into an even bigger jerk than you remember—not a brother I want to be related to, if he ever was, and definitely not someone you can possibly still care about."

"Seeing him again, and talking to him face-to-face, I know I still love him, Maggie. If Gertrude Veronica asks me, I doubt I'll be able to convince her otherwise."

"If I were you, I'd shelve any ideas about how you feel toward Tommy for the time being. Right now, you need to get him out of your convent. Everything else can wait. If Sister Gertrude Veronica wants to talk to me about all this, tell her to give me a call...and I'm really sorry this has happened."

Maggie hangs up the phone and sits on the side of her bed for several minutes, not sure what to make of what she's just heard. Eventually, she decides to get up. She has several things to do before Hanna Mae picks her up shortly after ten o'clock to go to Mary Beth Dolan's funeral. From what she's just heard, she doubts her brother will be saying the funeral Mass.

In the car on the way to the church, Maggie fills Hanna Mae in on what has transpired in the last few days, including this morning's phone call.

"I'd love to have been a fly on the wall for those conversations," she says when Maggie describes her rampages at the rectory, including the direct hit with the snowball. "I agree with everything you told your brother, but he ain't never gonna speak to you again—you okay with that?"

"I am, actually. We don't speak that often anyway. What he told Mary Beth was wrong, and he should pay for it. I can see how he may not think having me out of his life is any sort of punishment, especially since I seriously embarrassed him. The whole thing makes me so angry I could spit...and I wish I could do something about it."

"I've been thinking about that, Maggie. Remember how I said I feel Mary Beth is trying to tell us something?"

Maggie nods, admitting that she's been thinking about that too. "The only answer I've been able to come up with is to transform Mary Beth's life and death into the fuel we need to find some way to protect women from priests and other clergy who tell them that abusive husbands are their cross to bear, and bear graciously."

"That's a tall order," Hanna Mae responds as she drives into the nearly empty church lot.

Both women get out of the car and begin walking toward the large brownstone church.

"Are you surprised there aren't more people? In my church, everybody shows up for a funeral," Hanna Mae says as they make their way.

"Not too surprised. The Dolans weren't prominent in the community and were too poor to contribute much to the parish...and the circumstances are awful. It probably doesn't help that my outburst at the rectory is all over town by now and my accused brother's off somewhere on a drunken bender."

With a half-smile, Hanna Mae rolls her eyes.

They enter the church just as the closed, metal casket at the back of the church is being positioned for the procession up the aisle toward the altar. A small group of surprisingly stoic family members and four vacant-eyed little boys are gathered behind a plain, gunmetal gray box holding the remains of their deceased daughter, sister, and mother. About twenty-five people are scattered around the church that holds at least nine hundred. Maggie and Hanna Mae introduce themselves to the family, and Mary Beth's sister begins sobbing when she learns that Maggie was at the shelter where Mary Beth and the boys went after the Christmas incident.

"This is all my fault," she keeps saying, shredding a wad of paper towel she is using to wipe her eyes. "If I'd made Mary Beth stay at the shelter, this wouldn't have happened...I'm sure of it. Father Corrigan said I did the right thing to bring her back home, but I feel so awful."

Maggie stiffens at the mention of her brother, then tries to reassure Mary Beth's grieving sister that there was no way to know what was going to happen. At the same time, she is thinking about how the Church encourages women to automatically assume guilt, even in situations that aren't their fault and over which they have no control.

At that moment, a priest steps onto the altar and invites the funeral director and family members to push the cheap coffin up the aisle. "Please join me in the opening hymn to begin the Requiem Mass for the repose of the soul of Mrs. Jimmy Dolan," he says.

Maggie seethes hearing the priest identify Mary Beth as her abusive husband's possession. He can't even be bothered to show her the respect of calling her by her own, given name, she thinks.

Still holding Maggie's hand, Mary Beth's sister thanks her for coming and, as she walks away, whispers that there was no money for flowers or music but she hopes everyone will sing loudly anyway. Maggie and Hanna Mae find a seat close to the front and sing louder than anyone else.

"I threatened my brother that I would report what he said to the authorities, and I mean to make good on that threat," Maggie tells Hanna Mae as they slowly drive out of the cemetery after Mary Beth is laid to rest. Devoid of trees or other landscaping that would increase ambience and the cost of the burial plot, the young mother's final resting place is one small step above a potter's field.

"How you gonna make good on any threat? Comin' from you, it's just hearsay, and ain't nobody gonna listen to your opinion."

"It's not hearsay if she said it to you too," Maggie answers.

"Fine, but how you gonna do it? There ain't a cop in Chicago who'll listen to you rat out an Irish-Catholic priest, even if you are a nun."

"Then I'll have to find a cop who isn't Irish-Catholic."

Several minutes of silence follow.

"I might know one," Hanna Mae offers.

"Who?" Maggie asks.

"My son, Henry. He's a beat cop in Niggertown. They can't send any White guys there without 'em gettin' shot, so the city finally hired a few Black brothers to patrol the area. He might be willing to discuss this if I ask him. You up for some soul food some night?"

Maggie smiles and nods.

•••

A month passes before Hanna Mae calls Maggie and explains that dinner will be hard to work out but Henry has agreed to stop by her office at Saint Joseph's before his shift begins the day after tomorrow to listen to what Maggie has to say—if she can make it on such short notice.

"God Himself—or Herself—couldn't keep me away," Maggie says, thanking her profusely.

The interior of Saint Joseph's Charity Hospital is desperate for some charity of its own. The plaster is cracked, the metal waiting room chairs are bent, and bags are taped over the drinking fountains, where signs say the water is undrinkable due to rusty lead pipes. Hanna Mae's office is in the social services wing adjacent to the emergency entrance. As she walks in that direction, Maggie hears loud sirens and sees flashing lights from an ambulance and two police cars pulling into the dock outside. She also sees a handsome Black man proudly wearing the dark blue uniform of the Chicago Police Department turn down a side hallway and decides to follow him.

"Hey, Mama," the policeman calls from the hallway, smiling broadly as he enters an office.

Hanna Mae's ten-by-ten office is one of four similar-sized, windowless rooms arranged around a slightly larger, currently empty waiting area. File cabinets and other detritus of a dedicated, overburdened social worker fill the space. The only thing decorating Hanna Mae's office is a yellowed diploma from the Department of Social Work at Chicago City College hanging above her desk. Sitting on a shelf full of files is one family photo that includes a girl and a boy, a man resembling Henry, and a much younger Hanna Mae. More case files sit atop all three metal file cabinets. There isn't enough room for Maggie and Henry to sit down, so Hanna Mae suggests going to the basement cafeteria for a cup of coffee that she claims will make you stronger if it doesn't kill you first. She invites them to follow her down the back stairway around the corner from her office.

"My mother filled me in on the situation with the Mary Beth Dolan case. How do you think I can help?" Henry asks, once the three have paid for coffee and are settled into a Formica-topped table at the far end of the busy cafeteria filled with the sounds and smells of institutional food service.

"I want to report what Father Corrigan told Mary Beth to the authorities as a contributing factor in her death."

Henry stirs his dark, stale coffee for several minutes before speaking. "I can take your statement and file it as part of the record, but there are two problems," he finally says. "First, this is not my case, and precincts frown on interference from other precincts. I'd have to have a good reason for doing this...like information that comes out as part of an arrest I've made for something else. Even then, a Black cop pursuing anything to do with a case a white Irish cop is involved with is not likely to lead anywhere, and chances are an Irish cop is investigating Mary Beth's case."

"You think I don't know that?" Maggie snaps.

"I'm sure you do, and I know situations like this are frustrating, especially when you care as much as folks like you and my mother do." He pauses to take a drink of his coffee. "The other issue is more a question for you. Do you really want to rat out your own brother, who's protected by the most powerful institution in this city?"

Maggie nods her head yes. "It doesn't matter that he's my brother. What he did was wrong, and he, and others like him, will keep doing it until someone, or something, stops them."

"How involved are you willing to become?" Henry asks.

"Whatever it takes," Maggie responds immediately.

"These are always he said/she said situations that are nearly impossible to prove or introduce as evidence at a trial, especially a murder trial."

"Difficult, but not impossible," Maggie says. "In this case, Hanna Mae can support my claim that Mary Beth received bad advice that led to her death."

"That's true, but there's no law against giving bad advice, even in a professional capacity. In the end, it's up to the individual whether they want to follow the advice, and that's what Mary Beth decided to do. It was her right to make that choice."

All three sit, staring at their coffee, saying nothing.

"I understand what you're saying, but it's blaming the victim. I'm not giving up on this," Maggie finally says, folding her paper napkin.

"My mother told me that's what you'd say," Henry smiles. "And just so you know, I agree with what you're trying to do and am not blaming the victim—I'm playing devil's advocate because you need to clearly understand the law enforcement perspective on a case like this."

"So what can I do?" Maggie asks.

"A lot depends on who prosecutes the case. The Dolans are not politically connected or otherwise influential, so it'll fall to a rookie assistant in the district attorney's office to pursue the matter and file charges, if the evidence warrants. There's probably something there because the judge set bail too high for Jimmy Dolan to make it, which isn't always the case."

Except for the sounds of individuals bussing their dishes, there is silence, until Hanna Mae speaks up. "I know this is a challenge, Henry, but I didn't raise you to back away from a challenge, so think of something to move this off dead center."

"I know someone in the district attorney's office who might be interested in this case. I could get in touch with her and see what she thinks—and get her take on whether a Catholic nun testifying against her own brother the priest would be helpful or harmful."

"That would be wonderful." Maggie almost smiles. "But what if it all falls on deaf ears?"

"There's more than one way to skin a cat." Hanna Mae winks at her son, who laughs in response.

"There's no doubt in my mind you and my mother will think of some way to accomplish your goal." Henry laughs. "I'll call Marcia in the DA's office and let my mother know what she says." Standing up, he kisses his mother on the cheek and offers his hand to Maggie.

"He's a very nice young man," Maggie says as they walk back to Hanna Mae's office after finishing their second cup of coffee.

Two weeks later, Hanna Mae calls Maggie and instructs her to call Marcia Morgan in the Cook County District Attorney's office.

"Any relation to you?" Maggie asks.

"My daughter-in-law," Hanna Mae answers.

X.

Leaving an abusive relationship is very difficult. When women put their own welfare above their partner, no matter what he has done, they're called selfish, and a whole lot of other things...and accused of destroying their families. No woman wants that.

LALLI SMITH

For two hours each Tuesday and Thursday morning, Maggie meets with Eulalia Banks, a twenty-eight-year-old mother of six girls between four and twelve years old. With an outsized afro, Eulalia resembles members of the new generation of radical Black activists.

For nearly a year, Maggie has been tutoring Eulalia for the Illinois high school equivalency examination that will earn her a high school diploma and dramatically increase her chances of finding a job. During this time, Eulalia and Maggie have bonded, and for the first time in her life, the earnest young mother believes she has someone in her life she can trust. Eulalia's determination and strong personality encourage Maggie to hope that she will be one of their success stories. The young woman is bright and has a future that, if she makes good choices, won't include another violent husband and another extended stay in a homeless women's shelter. But on this day, Eulalia is distressed and unfocused.

"What's with you, Eulalia? You're all jittery and aren't concentrating," Maggie asks.

"My sister, she visited me yesterday and delivered a letter," Eulalia begins, staring at the marked-up table where they are sitting, surrounded by workbooks.

Maggie motions her to continue.

"The letter...it was from Jamal Jones, the daddy of some-a my girls. He says he's getting out of Joliet and wants to see us—the girls and me. Says he changed and misses us somethin' awful."

Aware of Jamal's long rap sheet, Maggie winces at this news. "What are you going to do?"

"Jamal...he's the love of my life. I ain't never been able to say no to him."

"Eulalia, he got sent up for armed robbery, which he committed while he was on parole after serving time for multiple assaults, including beating you until you were nearly dead—more than once. He's no good for you, and you know it."

"He say he changed—found Jesus and been saved, repented all his sins—and is begging me for forgiveness. And I wanna believe him real bad, because I still love him."

Distressed to see tears in Eulalia's eyes, Maggie's frustration begins to build. She wishes she'd never heard the word forgiveness because as far as she can tell, it always comes to no good for the women who are compelled, again and again, to grant it to the bad men in their lives.

"You need to think about this very carefully, Eulalia. You've worked so hard and come such a long way since you've been here. You're right on the verge of success if you stick with it just a little longer. Your life is changing for the better in so many ways. And the girls are caught up with their schoolwork. You don't need Jamal coming around and messing everything up."

"But he wants to see his girls. He deserves that much, and they deserve to know their daddy. And Jesus—he say to forgive a hundred times a hundred, or somethin' like that. I forget how many."

"There's a big difference between forgiving somebody and letting them back into your life, Eulalia, especially when they've hurt you as bad as Jamal has. He nearly killed you several times—and he stole money from you to buy drugs. The list is endless. He's seriously bad news, especially for you and the girls."

"But he say he changed."

"Prison doesn't change people for the better, Eulalia. It might make them wish they hadn't done whatever it was that sent them there, but it doesn't fix their lives. All the ways they were before, they still are. Once he's released, nothing is stopping Jamal from getting drunk and hurting you again."

Eulalia continues staring at the table. "But I love him, and love is all that matters...it fixes everything. Ain't that what the Bible say?"

This is another cliché Maggie hates. "Loving him doesn't mean letting him back in your life is a good idea, and it sure as hell doesn't put food on the table, Eulalia. You have to think about that."

"You don't understand," Eulalia finally says defiantly. "You ain't never loved a man, or had a man love you. You don't know how that feels. You can't know what I'm tryin' to say. You got no idea, no damned idea at all."

Hearing this, Maggie winces. Seeing the fire in Eulalia's eyes, she fights hard against the urge to say something hurtful in return.

Eulalia begins gathering up her workbooks and pencils. Placing them in a neat row on the table, she stands up and leaves. Maggie decides to let her go for now and talk to her again when they meet for their Thursday tutoring session. She hopes that, by then, Eulalia will have thought things through a little more carefully.

Thursday comes and Eulalia never shows up. When Maggie learns she has left the shelter, she feels overwhelming defeat and leaves to take a long walk around the rundown neighborhood, staring at broken-out windows in abandoned buildings and dodging stray dogs.

I tried so hard with her, and we were almost there...but it's just like with Mary Beth Dolan. My hardest isn't good enough, and eventually I fail...and I don't know why. It's not like I don't understand what these women are going through, because I do. But it's not enough. No matter how hard I try, I can't convince them to turn their lives around and start making better decisions...and there's nothing I can do about it she thinks to herself.

After more than an hour of struggling over Eulalia's decision to leave despite Maggie's best efforts to try to convince her to stay, Maggie's frustration has only gotten worse. She decides she is not cut out for working with abused women and the honorable thing is to resign her position immediately, before she fails again. She is surprised to find Bridget Mary waiting for her just inside the shelter door when she returns. The shelter director motions her into her office and shuts the door.

"I heard about Eulalia Banks, and I hope you aren't blaming yourself. If I had a nickel for every time a woman leaves here because a bad man reenters her life, I'd be relaxing in a condominium on a beach in the south of France," Bridget Mary begins.

"Of course I blame myself," Maggie answers. "I didn't try hard enough to talk her out of it."

"You can't talk someone out of something they want to do, or into something they don't want to do, Maggie. You should know that by now. These women make their own choices regardless of what we say, or how many opportunities we hand them. Some turn their lives around, but most don't. That's the nature of the work we do, and of the effect repeated abuse has on women. The pain it inflicts is chronic—it hurts all the time, but it's all they know. Offering them a different life confuses them. It's an invitation to walk through the looking glass into a totally unfamiliar world, and for many, taking that step is just too much. They don't have the self-confidence to try something different because the devil you know is better than the devil you don't know, and as long as they are feeling pain, they know they're still alive—even if they don't believe they deserve to be. Getting past all this requires enormous emotional support over a very long time, often years, and there just aren't resources, either public or private, to provide it. Long-term success is rare, but that's not a reason to stop trying, because for these women, even short-term help is better than no help at all...and every so often, we actually succeed."

"How?" Maggie asks.

"Usually, it's when someone develops a close relationship with one of our volunteer sisters, and their mentoring relationship continues after the woman leaves the shelter. You were well on your way to something like that with Eulalia if Jamal hadn't reentered the picture."

"I understand what you're saying, Bridget Mary, but I'm not cut out for this," Maggie says, clearing her throat and biting her quivering bottom lip. She blows her nose to divert attention from the tears in her eyes. The intensity of her emotional response to a situation she has so little control over has taken her by surprise.

"I'm sorry, and very surprised, to hear you say this, Maggie—I never saw you as a quitter."

"I'm just so damned tired of the love and forgiveness shit religion—and not just the Catholics—proclaim. All it does is make ending bad relationships more complicated. And Eulalia is right that I don't know anything about loving a man or having one love me...and after what I've seen, I'm damned sure I don't want to find out."

"Is this a crisis of faith? Because if it is, welcome to my world," Bridget Mary says.

"I'm not sure I have any faith...Catholic is just my cultural identity," Maggie continues. "I don't believe hardly anything the Church says anymore, and working with these women has reinforced that. The Church is a very powerful good ol' boys club that does more harm than good where women are concerned. It keeps them enslaved to men. I don't know where the hell God is in all this...I really don't, and I can't understand any of it."

"You have to keep this in perspective, Maggie," Bridget Mary says, absently readjusting her eye patch and bending down to tie her shoe. "We need the Church for what it does for us. Besides, how can you be Irish and not be Catholic?" she laughs. "Otherwise, I pretty much blow it off...and don't look so surprised...most nuns I know do the same thing, at least to some degree, until they are staring death in the face. They won't admit this publicly because their religious identity opens a lot of doors for them. They are dedicated women who go about their work in our harsh world simply trying to do good for others. Some think a lot about God and the Church, and others just don't. Most love the Church for its comforting rituals and all the positive things it does for people, including offering the hope that comforts the suffering and keeps them going. They've learned to turn a blind eye to everything else."

"The women we see here take what the Church—or at least what religion in general says—literally, without questioning any of it," Maggie observes.

"Of course they do. It helps them make sense of their suffering and gives them something to grab onto, and there's nothing wrong with that. Most of them aren't interested in taking a hard look at religion and trying to figure out how to take what is good from it and ignore everything else. We can try to nudge them in that direction, but it's much easier to be a follower than it is to make your own decisions and take responsibility for the outcomes that result. They're not used to doing that, and probably wouldn't have any idea how to take control over their own lives if they ever did get the chance."

"Yesterday I wanted to smack some sense into Eulalia when she started in on Jesus and forgiveness, but I was afraid that if I really let go, I'd say some things I couldn't take back and are better left unsaid."

"That's pretty unusual for you, Maggie, but probably a wise decision," Bridget Mary teases. "My advice is you need to take a break from working with the women directly. Focus on the grants and getting CWDC moving forward."

"I won't be earning my keep with that arrangement.," Maggie responds.

"We can be flexible. I want the CWDC activism to get going, and you have the fire in your belly to do that. You can turn all that anger and frustration into action that will change things—make them better. There's great potential there, Maggie. Please don't let us down. I'm afraid you'll hate yourself if you do, and I can guarantee I won't be kindly disposed toward that decision either. A lot of Chicago Catholic women seeking change are coming back here for another meeting in two weeks, and if you don't show up, they will be very disappointed in you."

Maggie doesn't respond.

"Sleep on it and talk to me again in the morning. I'll need an answer then because if you're going to leave, I'll have to start looking for another grant writer immediately."

"I'll stay," Maggie says, taking a deep breath.

"Good decision," Bridget Mary smiles.

On her way up to her office, Maggie stops at her mailbox and finds a message that Marcia Morgan returned her call. Someone has also left her a used copy of Chicago Catholic, the archdiocesan newspaper. Unfolding it, she sees why. Boxed off on the bottom right corner of the front page is an announcement that Monsignor Michael Keane, long-time pastor of Queen of Heaven parish, is retiring early for health reasons. Father Thomas Corrigan, the parish's long-time assistant, has been appointed the new pastor, effective immediately. Father Corrigan's installation, which Cardinal O'Grady will preside over, is scheduled for the following Sunday afternoon.

That's one way to deal with an asshole...promote him so he can do even more damage, Maggie thinks to herself.

That evening, Maggie goes to bed late and tosses and turns, unable to get comfortable. She can't get Eulalia or Mary Beth out of her mind long enough to fall into a sound sleep. Finally, she puts on her robe and walks into the kitchen, looking for something to drink. Bridget Mary, having heard her wandering around, joins her.

"Want to tell me what's bothering you?" the older nun asks. Her hair is wildly askew, and she is missing her eye patch.

"Not really."

"Tell me anyway."

"I can't get Eulalia or Mary Beth out of my mind."

"You don't understand why they went back to the men who were abusing them because you've never been in their situation...right?"

"That's not exactly true...."

"Really?" Bridget Mary exclaims, trying not to sound too surprised.

"A few years after my mother died, my father, and eventually my brother, decided I was theirs to do with as they wished. I knew what they were doing to me was wrong and I hated it—and them—but I never did anything about it or told anyone. Instead, I rationalized it away by thinking they were drunk and didn't know what they were doing and would never do anything like that sober. But the reality is that Tommy wasn't always drunk, and he did know what he was doing. I didn't know who to tell and doubted anyone would believe me if I did rat out either one of them. Plus if I squealed, it would've ripped the family apart, and I had four little sisters and a baby brother to look after. God only knows what would've happened to them if I wasn't there...."

"So you went along to get along and got out as soon as you could?"

"Basically, yes. I was scared shitless I'd get pregnant and still don't understand why I didn't."

"God's grace?" Bridget Mary offers, raising her eyebrows.

"Yea, right. The same God who was letting this happen to me. I don't think God gave a shit. It was pure luck."

"I'm sure your sisters and brother are very grateful to you for what you did for them, Maggie."

"Think again. Frankie is downstate wearing a striped suit for the rest of his life, and my younger sisters are never in touch. We're strangers who don't like each other very much—probably never have, if any of us was truthful enough to admit it. They don't give a rat's ass what I tried my hardest to do for them." For the second time within a few hours, Maggie's eyes again fill with tears.

"But your conscience is clear because you tried your hardest—and at great personal sacrifice. Doesn't that comfort you?"

"I didn't expect buckets of everlasting gratitude for raising them as best I could, but I didn't expect they'd stay mad at me for leaving home either. They've held onto this grudge since I entered the convent, so for nearly twenty-five years now...probably longer. I've lost count."

"Maybe they know more than you think they do and feel guilty for how hard things were for you."

"I doubt it. It's more likely they think they deserved better, and of course they did. It wasn't their fault their mother died and they ended up with a drunk father and an angry nine-year-old in charge of their lives. It was a no-good-answers situation they'll always be angry about...and I don't know why we're talking about it."

"Because it might help you to understand why the Mary Beth Dolans and Eulalia Banks of the world keep going back to their situations. They're trying to do what they believe is best, even if we don't see it that way. They deserve our compassion, not our anger because they don't do what we think they should do. We're not saviors, Maggie. All we are obligated to do is our best to help them—hold their hands while they find their own way, just like raising kids."

"I know."

"I don't think you do know, at least not yet...but you're trying. And working to change the things that encourage bad decision-making is a good start—it really is. I'm very glad you're going to keep on with that."

"What is so confusing to me," Maggie confesses for the first time in her life, "is that it's the Church that saved me. Not my faith, but the Church itself. It offered me another option for my life. If it wasn't for the Church, I'd be Mary Beth or Eulalia, or any one of the hundreds of thousands of other women just like them. The Church that rescued me from a life like theirs is the same Church that created the misery in their lives. I try and try, but it just doesn't make sense to me."

"Life is full of questions for which there are no answers, Maggie. But now that you're in your early forties, you should be close to done struggling with this and be ready to accept that not everything always adds up or is within our ability to understand, but we carry on as best we can anyway. That's all God, or anybody else, ever expects from us."

"Can I ask you a question?"

"Of course—anything."

"What happened to your eye?"

Bridget Mary takes a deep breath and waits nearly a minute before replying. "When I was twelve, my father came into my bedroom and tried to assault me...and as I was trying to escape, he slammed my face down on my bedpost...shattered my eye socket. It wasn't fixable. He made me promise not to tell what happened—to say I'd tripped on the rug beside my bed. Afterwards, he told me I had a face only God could love."

"And that's why you understand these women so well."

"Perhaps...I guess you could say that by going into this kind of work, I've tried to make the best of a bad situation."

"And I should do the same thing...."

"Your words, not mine. But yes, that's what I think. Life is much easier that way." Bridget Mary smiles and turns to leave.

Maggie returns to her room without saying more.

XI.

The Roman Catholic Church carries the immense power of very directly affecting women's lives everywhere by its stand against birth control and abortion.

ROBIN MORAN

"Saint Brendan's Convent. Who is calling and to whom do you wish to speak?" a firm voice says, finally answering the convent telephone after it rings several times.

"This is Sister Maggie Corrigan, and I'm calling to speak with Mary Pat Donovan."

"Who? I'm afraid there's no one here by that name."

"Sister Esther Mary."

"Oh. One moment please."

Several minutes pass before a voice identifying herself as Sister Gertrude Veronica comes to the phone. Maggie identifies herself again and repeats her request.

"I'm sorry, but Sister Esther Mary is no longer living here."

"Where is she?"

"This is all I can say, Sister. I'm only telling you this much, which is more than I should, because I am aware that you are friends. I'm sorry."

Maggie starts to ask how she can reach Mary Pat, but before the sentence is out of her mouth, the phone goes dead. Maggie leans back in her rickety chair and places her feet on the old desk in her cramped, makeshift office as she tries to figure out where to start looking for her best friend. She soon realizes that if Mary Pat wants to be in touch, she knows how to reach her, and decides to let the matter drop—for now. As she is preparing to leave her office, Bridget Mary appears, arms outstretched with a big smile on her face.

"That grant application you submitted two months ago—it was successful. We've got a year's worth of operating dollars, and you've got yourself a salary! Congratulations, Maggie. Great work!"

"I guess. I'm so used to living on nothing, I'm not sure what I'll do with the money. One option is to start paying room and board here...and admittedly, a little pocket money would be nice."

"I have another idea, if you're not too busy to hear it," Bridget Mary says, moving a pile of papers off the only other chair in Maggie's cluttered office and sitting down. "Keep some money for yourself, but instead of paying us room and board out of your salary, continue with the current arrangement. You earn your keep by chasing after grants, and we'll use the rest of your salary as seed money to support the CWDC, which is gaining momentum if the large number of women who signed up after the last meeting is any indication. But it needs leadership—and some cash."

"That's not a bad idea, but I'm not sure how that works with the grant specifications," Maggie replies.

"It works fine as long as we pay you the full amount. After that, what you do with your salary is entirely up to you, and if you donate it—minus spending money—to CWDC, it works out fine," Bridget Mary explains. "But there's a catch..."

"There always is." Maggie shrugs.

"You coordinate the effort."

"I already write a lot of grants and fill in here when there's an emergency. Where am I going to find the time to coordinate an activist group?"

"We can figure that out as we go along. Other concerns?"

"Explaining this to the Order. I'm required to report my income and expenses every month, and they are expecting me to have a paying job at some point. After meeting my expenses, I'm required to send whatever is left to the motherhouse."

"That's an easy fix. We'll create a balance sheet that indicates you are drawing a salary and are paying us room and board, and after your other expenses, there is nothing left to send."

"I suppose that could work—at least for a while. I'd rather the money go to CWDC anyway."

"Then we have a deal we can drink to?" Bridget Mary smiles, walking around Maggie's desk and taking the bottle of cheap bourbon and two plastic glasses out of the bottom desk drawer. She pours one finger in each glass.

"How'd you know I had this in here?" Maggie asks.

"Honey, in this line of work, if you don't drink, you're doomed!" Sister Bridget Mary laughs.

"So you're the one who put it in my desk?"

"You'll never know, my dear. Now, may I make one suggestion about how you could spend your extra money?"

Maggie nods.

"Your fashion sense could use some help. If you're going to coordinate a city-wide women's activism initiative, it wouldn't hurt to wear clothes that at least match. You don't have to aim for a magazine cover, just try to pay a little more attention to things like matching colors and not mixing stripes and plaids."

Maggie has never cared about how she looks and doesn't know whether to laugh, frown, or pretend she never heard the remark from someone whose own fashion choices lean heavily toward chaotic.

•••

The next CWDC meeting occurs on a bitterly cold, snowy Chicago evening. Earlier in the afternoon, Maggie and Bridget Mary agreed it would be lucky if twenty people showed up, and they are astonished to find what they estimate are ninety women, and perhaps a dozen men, milling about in the corner of the shelter's makeshift meeting space. Coffee and donated cookies sit on a back table.

Bridget Mary calls the meeting to order and introduces Maggie as the person who will lead the effort going forward. "It's time to stop talking and start taking action, and Sister Maggie is the one to lead the charge," she says.

Several in the audience applaud.

Maggie begins by explaining that the only item on the evening's agenda is setting priorities and her job is to guide the group in determining where they want to focus their energy. She has just begun speaking when out of the corner of her eye, she sees someone strongly resembling what Mary Pat might look like in street clothes enter the room, take a folding chair from the rack in the corner, and sit down in the back row.

Maggie continues, summarizing their last meeting, when it appeared that women's ordination and women's reproductive rights were the two most pressing issues facing Catholic women. An elegantly dressed woman identifying herself as Elaine Andrews, a former nun and superior of her religious Order, uses her experience in religious life to offer a well-thought-out argument in favor of making women's ordination the group's primary focus.

"There are so many committed women—inside and outside religious life—who are capable of ministerial equality with men," Elaine says. "This is a matter of justice and opportunity, of diversity, empowerment, and collective decision-making. It's a fight for suffrage for Catholic women, who don't have a seat at the table where decisions about their lives are made, and we won't have one until we have equal status with ordained priests," Elaine says in a strong, clear voice. "Gender should not be the deciding factor in who becomes a Catholic priest, and as the number of priests continues to decline, it won't be long until the Church will be forced to accept women clergy anyway. I'd like us to be proactive on achieving this."

After a loud round of applause, one of the few men in the room expresses doubt that the Church will be open to even discussing this issue because in the end, ordaining women is a matter of granting women power, and there is no compelling reason for a patriarchal Church to willingly give up any of its power.

"There's also the matter of Jesus being male and selecting twelve male apostles to succeed him. The Church claims the priesthood is only open to men because Jesus and the apostles were men. If God intended there be women priests, half the apostles would have been women. We'd have to come up with something to refute that claim," Bridget Mary points out.

"There is one way women can force this issue, and do it quickly," Elaine says and smiles.

The room falls silent, waiting for her answer. Maggie waves the tall, well-spoken former mother superior to the front of the room.

"Women comprise the largest group of individual donors to parishes," Elaine continues. "If they withhold their financial support and make it clear why they are doing it, it wouldn't be long before the Church hierarchy would be forced to negotiate with them."

"Sort of like withholding sex from your husband until he bends to your will," someone comments out loud, causing others to laugh.

Elaine smiles and agrees the strategy is fundamentally the same principle, adding that holding onto something someone wants from you until they give you what you want in return has been a proven strategy for success since the dawn of time, in a variety of circumstances.

"As a general rule, money and sex are the only two things that get men's attention, and in this situation, sex is less applicable—at least in theory," she explains, to chuckles from her audience. "What I want you to consider is what a Church that is not run entirely by men might look like, and whether that vision is worth fighting for."

When there are no further comments, Maggie says she will present the case for focusing on women's reproductive rights. She starts by acknowledging that this is not an entirely separate issue from the women's ordination concern in that achieving a policy change regarding the use of birth control won't happen without women being part of the discussion and decision-making process. But, in her view, the issue goes much deeper because the only way women will gain control over their personal lives is through the practical and emotional freedom to make reproductive choices.

"Think about it this way," she says, walking back and forth across the front of the room, speaking without notes.

"The strongest predictor of lifetime poverty for a woman is early and repeated childbearing. That one single factor will define a woman's entire life." Many women in the audience nod their heads in agreement.

"Just as concerning is that so many Catholic, as well as other, women are trapped in abusive marriages they can't leave because they have too many children—a pattern that began when they married right out of high school, usually because they were already pregnant and had decided their futures before they'd had a chance to consider other options. Fast forward a few years, and these women have so many children their health is impaired, and their husbands—angry when their wives refuse them and angry when their wives keep getting pregnant with babies they can't afford—drink too much and beat them. Even if these women could leave their violent husbands, they could never get jobs that pay enough to support themselves and seven or eight kids."

She pauses, then says she's going to give an example of what she is referring to and tells Mary Beth Dolan's story. When she finishes, the room is deathly silent. Maggie takes a deep breath and waits a moment before continuing.

"Imagine how different Mary Beth's life might've been if she had only one or two children and was able to acquire job skills to enable her to earn a living wage. Perhaps her marriage would not have been so stressed; perhaps the additional money she brought in would've kept the family afloat financially; or perhaps her husband would still have been violent and abusive, but if that was the situation, she would have had the ability to leave him and earn enough money to financially support herself and her children. She would have lived to see her sons finish high school, maybe graduate college, and later she might've sung lullabies to her grandchildren."

Maggie's audience remains riveted on her words.

"As I see it, there are two approaches to this problem: one is to empower women to make their own choices regardless of what the Church tells them, and the other is to shift the minds and hearts of the Catholic patriarchy toward a greater respect for women that includes allowing them to make their own reproductive decisions. The first approach is, by far, the easiest to achieve, but there is no reason we can't work on both at the same time."

Maggie stops speaking and looks around the room. She is surprised when no one raises their hand to comment or ask questions.

Finally, Elaine stands. "I agree with Maggie that the reproductive rights issue is the most immediate and pressing one for women, and suggest we begin by focusing our activism there. Women's ordination is very important, but it doesn't directly affect millions of women's lives every single day in the same way the birth control issue does. Women aren't dying because of not being ordained Catholic priests, but they are definitely dying because of a lack of reproductive autonomy. I hope the rest of you will agree with me."

She sits down and waits for further comments. When there are none, Maggie asks whether there is agreement that the focus should be on reproductive choice, and nearly every hand shoots up. She thanks everyone and says the next meeting, scheduled for two weeks, will focus on crafting an action plan.

"Anyone who isn't already on our list, please sign up, and remember that if everyone brings a friend, we'll have the critical mass needed to hit the ground running with some direct action," Maggie instructs, smiling.

As the meeting breaks up and people start leaving, she thanks Elaine for her gracious support, then hangs back, waiting to see if the woman she is fairly certain is Mary Pat approaches her. When nearly everyone has left, she does.

"I thought that was you," Maggie says, noting how pale her friend looks, then remembering it has been more than two years since she has seen her.

"Do you have a few minutes?" Mary Pat asks.

"I'm glad to see you," Maggie says, motioning her friend to follow her into her office. She clears a pile of loose papers off the extra chair and invites Mary Pat to sit down.

"You look good," Maggie says, not mentioning how tired the former nun's face appears.

"Thanks. One of my sisters gave me some of her old clothes and even cut my hair for me."

"I tried to call you and was told you were no longer at Saint Brendan's," Maggie says.

"Nice to see you wearing something that matches," Mary Pat responds.

"You didn't come here to compliment me on my wardrobe choices. Tell me what happened."

Mary Pat takes a deep breath, then continues. "As I suspected, Sister Gertrude Veronica overheard Tommy's drunken declaration, and right after Monsignor Keane came to pick him up, she confronted me."

"What did you tell her?"

"The truth—the whole truth. I didn't intend to, but it all just came out...how we'd known each other since high school, I'd gotten pregnant with his child, and later aborted someone else's child. I named names."

"Did she pass out from shock?"

"No, she was quite calm...said I couldn't stay at Saint Brendan's under the circumstances, and she would be sending me back to the motherhouse immediately. I said I didn't want that, and she said my only other choice was to leave the Order, which she hoped I wouldn't do. She said to think about it and give her my answer by the next evening after dinner.What she said next really surprised me."

"What did she say?" Maggie asks.

"She advised me to tell Tommy everything...said the entire situation was troubling me deeply and the only way to get it resolved was to deal with it, which meant talking to Tommy. I explained that I doubted he'd want to talk to me when he was sober, and I wasn't sure I wanted to talk with him either. She told me to spend the rest of the day composing a letter to him and then see how I felt. I took her advice...and it was surprisingly easy. I sealed the letter and mailed it that afternoon."

Hearing this, Maggie's eyes go wide. "Seriously, Mary Pat—you told Tommy everything, and then you mailed the letter?"

"I did. And later that evening I told Sister Gertrude Veronica I had been doubting my vocation for a while and had decided to leave. She said she understood and would give me a week to make other arrangements.

As I was leaving her office, she cautioned me that Tommy might not ever respond to my letter, or if he did, might not respond in the way I was hoping. It turned out she was right." Tears come to her eyes, and Maggie doesn't push her to continue until she is ready.

"A letter arrived the day I left. Tommy denied ever having any kind of relationship with me in high school. He said I was obviously mentally disturbed, and he hoped I would get the help I needed, and not endanger his position in the Church by spreading false rumors that could cause scandal. It wasn't even half a page—typewritten. He signed it Father Thomas P. Corrigan."

"What did you think?"

"I cried for about an hour, then threw up, tore the letter to shreds, and flushed it. After that, I apologized to our baby for having such a shithead for a father...said he deserved better."

Maggie remains silent for several minutes, waiting for anything else Mary Pat might want to say. When nothing is forthcoming, she continues.

"Here's the thing to remember about Tommy, Mary Pat. He's made a good life for himself in the priesthood—much better than anything he could've had otherwise, coming from a dirt-poor, illiterate family like ours. For him, it was the priesthood or the Yards, and he made the better choice. There's no way in hell he's going to let anything, or anybody, screw that up...regardless of any feelings he has for you. Without the Church, he's nothing. And he knows it."

"I suppose I realized that but couldn't admit it. Subconsciously, I was hoping Tommy would say he loved me and wanted us to be together. The next morning, while I was still thinking about that, Sister Gertrude Veronica brought me some street clothes and handed me twenty-five dollars. She told me to get dressed and leave by the back door, assuring me she would pray for me. I'd been awake most of the night, having second thoughts about leaving, but at that point I didn't see a way to back out. So I put on the clothes and left."

"Where did you go?"

"Remember my sister, Sheilah?

"Not really..."

"She married one of the Farley boys, had seven kids in seven or eight years. By that time, Billy was drunk all the time and had lost more jobs than he had kids."

"What'd he do?"

"Sanitation worker for the city. Didn't earn much, but it was something. The problem was some drunk guy driving a trash truck was a liability, and eventually, he hit some kid on a bike and went to jail—manslaughter or something. Anyway, Sheilah saw this coming and had started skimming money off the grocery budget and taking in ironing. She had a little saved, and after spreading the kids out among our sisters and a couple of weeks in a shelter, ended up at Cabrini."

"As city housing projects go, that's an especially dangerous place."

"No more dangerous than a drunken husband. She got a second-shift job in housekeeping at a nursing home. It's minimum wage, but you can stretch a dime pretty far in the projects, and the older kids watch the little ones. She said if I moved in to help with the kids, she could pick up extra shifts, so that's what I've done. It's worked out for us both."

"So nine people are living in a two-bedroom in Cabrini?" Maggie asks, astonished.

"The kids have the bedrooms. Sheilah and I share the couch—opens into a bed. She works days and some nights now that I'm there. And I got a job as a teacher's aide in the nearby public school, so I'm home when the kids are. The biggest worry right now is that welfare might get wise to the added income and start cutting her benefits."

"What about the little kids?" Maggie asks.

"The ones who aren't in school go to daycare where I work. I said they're mine, so I can bring them with me. Cuts into my salary to pay for it, but we're still coming out ahead. What happened with Tommy was probably a blessing for everybody."

"That's one way to look at it," Maggie says. Then she points to the announcement on the front page of the diocesan newspaper.

"Any illusions that Tommy and I had a connection or shared anything meaningful are gone, Maggie. I honestly don't care what happens to him."

"Neither do I," Maggie admits. Her anger at her brother fuels her passion to seek justice for Mary Beth Dolan, and she has no intention of letting any of it go.

XII.

Poor women suffer a great deal in the criminal justice system.
RETIRED WISCONSIN SUPREME COURT JUSTICE, JANINE GESKE

Nearly two months after Maggie's conversation with Hanna Mae's son, she and Marcia Morgan finally meet in person in Marcia's office, located in the back corner of the second floor of City Hall. *This must be where the domestic violence cases that actually reach the Cook County District Attorney's office go to die*, Maggie thinks, realizing it has been over a year since Mary Beth Dolan's funeral.

Seeing Marcia's windowless office, she discovers it's remarkably like her own. Aside from a framed diploma from Northwestern University School of Law hanging on the wall. Everything else, including the beat-up, government-issued desk, the two chairs, the metal bookcase, and the dented file cabinet could've been scavenged from the same junk pile Maggie frequents. Other than the diploma, there is nothing about the tiny room that reveals anything about the occupant.

Marcia is on the phone and waves Maggie into the crowded office, pointing to the chair in the corner that is stacked high with files. Maggie continues standing and is reading the diploma when Marcia finishes the call.

"Thanks to equal-opportunity affirmative action and the fact I scored well on the Law School Admission Test, I got a full-ride scholarship, in case you're wondering. Otherwise, there's no way I could've gone to any law school. I only got into college because my grandmother sat on my head after school every day making me study, and because I shot hoops in high school and was a great rebounder...something I learned during pick-up games with the boys in the projects that actually did me some good. But

I'll be paying my student loans off until the second coming of Christ—no offense," Marcia chuckles. As she is introducing herself, she stands to extend her hand, and Maggie sees that the informally, yet stylishly dressed woman behind the beautiful smile towers over her by several inches more than a foot. She is also considerably taller than her police officer husband.

"You must be Sister Maggie Corrigan. I'm so pleased to meet you."

Maggie returns the handshake and thanks Marcia for making time to see her.

"Sorry about my office, but the truth is, I never trust people with tidy offices—makes me think their focus is on the wrong things and they never get any actual work done. As a crime victim advocate, I need people to be comfortable with me, and having a messy office helps," Marcia says, moving to clear the stack of papers off a chair onto the floor.

"You're here to discuss the Mary Beth Dolan case," the young lawyer says, closing the door. "My husband and Hanna Mae filled me in on your concerns, and I admire you for wanting to push this as far as we can get it to go. Anything else you want me to know before we dig into the legalities?"

"Only that I would not be pursuing this if I didn't know, in the core of my being, that the Church advising women to remain in abusive relationships is bowing to the devil. Shining a light on this practice is vitally important, and if I didn't honestly believe we can find some way to stop it, I wouldn't waste your time."

"There's no question in my mind you're committed to seeing this through, Sister—"

"Please, just call me Maggie. I hope we don't need formal titles to work together."

"All right, Maggie. Suppose we start with me telling you what I know about where the case stands."

Maggie nods.

"Our office intends to prosecute the case, but unfortunately, it's not a slam-dunk conviction. The assistant district attorney taking the lead told me it would've been easier for him to argue the overthrow of the federal government than to convince the grand jury to return a murder one indictment against Jimmy Dolan based what he describes as 'fairly weak proof.'"

"Mary Beth is dead—how much proof does he need?"

"Despite evidence that Jimmy was a chronic abuser, it isn't enough to prove Jimmy intentionally killed his wife. The other problem is that grand juries in general hate domestic violence cases, probably because most of the men on the jury rough up their wives on occasion, especially when they get drunk, and they don't want to set any legal precedents that might negatively impact their own bad behavior...but I digress."

Maggie nods her agreement with the assumption.

"Because Mary Beth died, the grand jury can't ignore this case either, so the assistant DA led off with a giant meatball that contained charges of first-degree, intentional homicide. He knew the grand jury wouldn't indict on that charge, but it opened the conversation. Ultimately, the grand jury handed down an indictment for second-degree, unintentional homicide. The problem is that Jimmy plans to plead innocent and claim his wife tripped and fell down the stairs on her own—in other words, he had nothing to do with it."

Hearing this Maggie clenches her jaw. "Jimmy is a fucking liar!" she blurts out, immediately apologizing for the poor choice of words.

"Think nothing of it. There isn't a foul word in English, Spanish, Italian, or Greek I haven't already heard." Marcia smiles. "My understanding is Jimmy admits they were fighting and that he was drunk, but claims he doesn't remember anything else about the incident. Mary Beth never regained consciousness long enough for the police to interview her, so there's no statement from her to work with. The good news is he hasn't made bail, so he's still enjoying the county's generous hospitality while a public defender works on his case. Unfortunately, even an inexperienced PD just out of law school last week could introduce enough reasonable doubt to get Jimmy off. Practically speaking, the best we can hope for is a reduced-charge manslaughter conviction, based on circumstantial evidence and his history of domestic violence—and this is where you come in."

"I'm still not sure I understand," Maggie replies.

"And I'm not explaining it very well...I'm a rape and domestic violence victim advocate, not a prosecutor. The folks I work with are alive, and I'm not usually involved when a situation escalates to homicide. Don't get me wrong, I hear a lot of horror stories where some religious zealot advises a woman to return to an abusive spouse, and usually she can't do anything else anyway because she has no resources. Eventually, the husband ends up in jail and she ends up in my office, where I have to convince her to press charges, which is surprisingly difficult sometimes." Marcia stops to take a deep breath.

"I couldn't even get Mary Beth to take out a temporary restraining order against Jimmy the day after the Christmas incident, so I get what you're saying," Maggie offers.

"Just so you know, Maggie, I've been wanting to do what you're trying to do for a long, long time...to get at men, whether they're priests, psychiatrists, or anybody else who counsels women, and make it a crime for these folks to say what that priest said to Mary Beth. But currently there's no political will to pursue it. And, until Mary Beth, there's not been an opportunity to make it a relevant issue. This might be that chance, but doing it will be dicey."

"I'm listening," Maggie says.

"We share the same goal, which is that Mary Beth's sorry excuse for a husband doesn't walk free, and we have to figure out how to make that happen within the confines of existing law. This means you'll have to get involved and help us."

"That's why I'm here."

"Jimmy Dolan, bruiser though he is, has never been charged with domestic abuse. All there is to prove he is a habitual wife-beater are a few calls the neighbors made to police when they heard Mary Beth screaming. The strongest evidence of prior abuse is her Christmas-night ER visit, resulting in placement in a domestic violence shelter where you discovered she'd talked to her priest about the abuse several times. You can testify about her time in the shelter. Most of what you say will get overruled as hearsay, but the jury will have heard you say it, and even if the judge tells them to disregard your statements, unhearing something they've already heard is no different than trying to unring a bell—it's impossible."

"Can we get it into the record about the bad advice her parish priest gave her?" Maggie asks.

"You mean the part about advising her to go back to her husband and offering the effects of his fist in her face up to Jesus as penance for her sins?" Marcia replies.

"That's exactly what I mean," Maggie says.

"Technically, that's not relevant. People get bad advice all the time, and nothing forced Mary Beth to follow the priest's advice. It sounds convoluted, but it's not Jimmy's fault his wife did what the priest told her to do."

"If you're not Catholic, you can't possibly understand the grip the Catholic Church has on women. It's a full-blown cult situation. The priest represents God on Earth and has the last word on everything. If he tells a woman to forgive her husband after he's beat the shit out of her, or risk going to hell if she doesn't forgive him, she forgives him. If she dies as a result, too bad, but she must've done something to deserve it. And whatever that was, it sure as hell wasn't the husband's fault." Maggie's face reddens as her anger rises.

Both women fall silent.

"There's another issue," Marcia continues. "Chicago is an Irish-Catholic town and trying to hang any responsibility for Mary Beth's death on a Catholic priest would be political suicide for the DA, who has to win elections. It also risks alienating the jury, many of whom are very likely Catholic and Irish, Catholic and Italian, or Catholic and something else. In other words, it won't be possible to eliminate all the Catholics from the jury pool, and they could be so offended by any suggestion that a priest has any responsibility in this case, they'd exonerate Jimmy of all charges. Then he'd walk—free as a bird to do it all again to some other woman, or to his kids. And I'm sure the prosecutor doesn't want to begin his career by getting the reputation that he's out to get the Catholics, or the Irish." Marcia lets that idea sit for a moment.

"There has to be a way, because I'm not letting this go," Maggie finally exclaims, louder than she intended.

"There might one possibility, but it's a real stretch," Marcia offers. "There's a new reporting law that says anyone who learns of abuse regarding children is legally obligated to report it to the relevant authorities. Based on the assumption that an abusive husband is also likely to abuse his children, anyone who is aware of abusive behavior in a family with children would be obligated to report it. It's a law not everyone in the helping professions agrees with, for several reasons."

"In that case, I violated the law myself by not reporting the case to the authorities," Maggie points out.

"Technically, that's true, and you have to decide whether setting yourself up for possible prosecution for failure to report is a chance you're willing to take. If you do testify and then go down that road to get to the priest, the defense could nail you. You need to think very carefully about that."

"My defense is that since the cops and hospital staff were involved in the case, I assumed the proper authorities were notified."

"Works for me," Marcia smiles.

"What about putting the priest on the stand to bear witness to Mary Beth's devotion to her husband and children and then trapping him into admitting he knew of the abuse and did nothing further about it?" Maggie asks.

"Honey, you should've gone to law school—your mind's a steel trap. You'd make a great prosecutor." Marcia laughs, as she jots the idea down on a yellow legal pad.

Getting up a head of steam, Maggie continues. "It would accuse the priest by implication, but not directly, which would be less offensive to the jury and scare the shit out of him...or at least publicly embarrass him, and that's worth something, don't you think?"

"What I think doesn't matter. It's up to the prosecutor to decide how he wants to handle the case to give him the best chance for a conviction. If he pursues the priest involvement angle, he might decide it's better to let you bring it up and get the testimony thrown out," Marcia says, still scribbling on the yellow paper. When she is finished writing, she says she has a couple more questions.

"How will it play if a nun publicly accuses a priest of dereliction of duty, which is basically what this is? Would Catholics on the jury hear this as an angry, man-hating woman who, if she could just get a little, would settle down and get with the program, so to speak?"

"I don't know. They might think that, but in the Catholic culture, nuns are generally well-respected, considering they're women and thus automatically inferior to men."

"Aren't you, personally, taking a big chance accusing a priest of giving bad advice that, although technically could be argued violates the child abuse protection law, in reality, is common practice in the Catholic culture?"

"That's hard to say...I guess it depends upon how much it matters that the priest I'd be accusing is my own brother," Maggie answers.

"Sweet Jesus," Marcia exclaims, putting down her pencil. "You're willing to do that?"

Maggie nods her head.

"You're either really pissed off or involved in one hell of a family feud."

"I'm really pissed off. And I think the fact I'm willing to accuse my brother makes my testimony all the more powerful. It underscores how important I believe this issue is for women, how important it is to put priests on notice that the advice they habitually give has legal and life-threatening implications they've either never thought of or chosen to ignore. That counts for something...and it might save a woman's life in the future. I don't see any downside."

"I'll have to talk to the assistant DA in charge of the Dolan case about all this. One advantage is that Greg's a nice, White Anglo-Saxon Protestant who isn't controlled by the Catholic Church and is also a law school classmate—sharp guy, I like him. However, the DA, Tim O'Callahan, is a good Irish-Catholic boy whose fanny is in the pews several times a week, and he may pitch a hissy over the idea—or decide that his office getting involved in a case like this is worth the risk of alienating the cardinal and the mayor."

"O'Callahan any relation to Mayor Callahan?"

"I don't know. Probably. But as regards the case, it could go either way, and to be perfectly honest, I don't have any feel for how it might play out. What I can tell you is that the wheels of justice turn slowly, and especially in a city this size, it may be a year or more before there's any activity on this case. In the meantime, unless he makes bail—which, if he hasn't by now, he probably won't—Jimmy Dolan remains in jail."

Marcia stands and walks toward the door. "I have to run, but let me know what you decide about testifying as soon as you can. It will be the first question Greg asks me."

"I don't have to think about it. Of course I'll testify," Maggie says. "It's my chance to make Mary Beth Dolan's life mean something. Her sons, and women everywhere, deserve that."

•••

Sixteen months pass before Maggie receives a message to call Marcia Morgan. She has heard nothing about Mary Beth's case since Marcia arranged a meeting with the prosecutor, Greg Evans, to discuss her possible testimony and whether to name her brother. Holding the message, she takes the steps up to her not-very private office two at a time, glad she finally got a private office telephone last week.

Marcia picks up the phone on the first ring.

"Thanks for getting back to me, Maggie. I was hoping you'd call right away because I have news on the Dolan case and wanted you to hear it from me."

"I'm listening...."

"There won't be a trial. Jimmy agreed to serve time for manslaughter, which is seven-to-ten years, eligible for parole after six, including time already served. I know this isn't what either you or I wanted—"

"Son of a bitch! What happened?" Maggie interrupts, feeling anger heating up her face.

"I'm not sure. Greg told me the DA didn't want the case to go to trial and to force a deal."

"Did the DA explain why he didn't want a trial?"

"If he knew, Greg didn't tell me. He said he met with him and laid out the case and came away thinking everything was in place for second-degree, reckless homicide and willful disregard for life. He was very surprised to receive a call a few days later, telling him to cut a deal."

"Do you think the cardinal got involved?" Maggie asks, not sure she wants the answer.

"I have no way to know that, and no way to find out. I can say that if he did, it wouldn't be the first time. But why would this case matter to him?"

"The publicity—if even the hint that priests give bad advice surfaced it would embarrass the Church, and no question Cardinal O'Grady has many reasons to want to avoid that."

"Now that I think about it, you're probably right."

"You know what, Marcia? There's more than one way to win this fight—and I intend to win it. I'm volunteering to be charged under the mandatory reporting law. At trial, I can point out that priests telling women what to do has to stop."

"Hold on, Maggie. What you're offering is admirable, but as a general rule, only crazy people volunteer to be charged with a crime. When someone does that, it's always suspect."

"I have a solid defense, and I could get a trial, which is the opportunity I need to get the message out, because it would engender a lot of publicity."

"This would never go to trial. It's a misdemeanor offense, so you'd get a fine, and perhaps some other sanctions, and incur some legal bills. This said, the DA will never charge a nun with something so minor. He's swamped with serious crimes, and this issue just isn't worth his time."

Maggie remains silent for several seconds.

"I'm not willing to give up on this idea, Marcia."

"I hope you take some time to think it through very, very carefully before acting, Maggie. You could end up sorrier than you can possibly imagine that you opened that can of worms. Promise you'll talk to me before you do anything."

XIII.

[In Leviticus] God reveals that deliberate sterilization and any other methods which prevent conception are intrinsically evil.
Scripture Catholic

"Anyone who believes all sperm are sacred—which most men do believe, and most women do not—also views tampering with the natural course of the life of sperm as tantamount to murder. These individuals have a real problem with any form of birth control," Professor Millicent Delavan tells an audience nearly three times the size of the one she drew when she previously spoke at the first meeting of Catholic Women Demanding Change nearly two years ago. Enthusiasm for taking action has slowly grown, and tonight Maggie has invited her back to help formulate an action plan for the steadfast group of Catholic women, and several men, intent on changing the Church's opposition to any form of birth control. Once again, they are meeting at Holy Mother of Consolation Women's Shelter, and this time, it's a standing-room-only crowd. After brief announcements, Maggie quickly turns the meeting over to Professor Delavan.

With a haircut she undoubtedly gave herself, her glasses askew on top of her head and wearing a blouse she hasn't bothered to tuck in and pants that aren't long enough to entirely cover her white socks and brown orthopedic shoes, what Professor Delavan lacks in stature and concern for her appearance she makes up for in raw brainpower. Her ability to convey large amounts of information in a straightforward, easily understandable manner, coupled with her approachability—and, most importantly, her willingness to work with CWDC —make her the perfect partner for their efforts.

"Another issue with birth control is that, traditionally, it has been associated with pleasurable sex, and by implication, with adultery and promiscuity, an activity that is accepted but frowned upon for men and the worst possible behavior for women," Professor Delavan continues. She paces back and forth at the front of the room because she is too short to stand still and see over a podium.

"Pleasurable sex presents men with two problems and women with one big one. First, if women begin expecting to enjoy sex, men will have to provide them with pleasurable sex or risk being refused. If a man fails to do this, the woman in his life may leave him to seek pleasure elsewhere. This puts a lot of pressure on a man to perform, as well as forcing him to face the reality that sex is not just for his satisfaction, but also for the satisfaction of the woman involved."

Several in her audience laugh aloud.

"Adding to this conundrum, Saint Paul, the Church's pioneer misogynist, threw his hat into the theological ring and declared that women should be submissive to their husbands—an idea that has, unfortunately, endured. This perspective on marital life, coming from a life-long bachelor who has absolutely *no* credibility on the topic of marriage, puts women at a distinct disadvantage in both her relationship with her husband and in her ability to control her reproductive life."

A collective groan emerges from the audience. At the same time, Maggie tugs at Professor Delavan's sleeve. "Maybe a quick history lesson on sex and the Church would be helpful," she whispers.

Millicent nods and tells her audience that they are going to take a little detour. "Understanding a little more about the Church's views on sex would be useful because the better grasp you have on the Church's strange perspectives on this natural human instinct, the better you'll be able to counter their arguments against birth control."

Several in the audience applaud.

"I'd like to begin by emphasizing that the institutional Catholic Church is profoundly confused about sex—and I admit that I don't fully understand why. Sex is the most natural and the most powerful of human instincts, and it seems more prudent to recognize and accept this reality and work with it, rather than to keep fighting against it. Regardless, confusion is the name of the Catholic sex game, and isn't too surprising when you realize that a bunch of celibate men opining on something their vows forbid them from engaging in—and they supposedly have no experience with—is bound to result in some pretty bizarre ideas about a perfectly normal human behavior."

The professor's audience is enraptured.

"The other confounding variable in any discussion of sex and the Catholic Church is the supposed virginity of Mary. The Church not only wants us to believe that Mary was immaculately conceived, meaning she had a level of purity that did not include the original sin the Church says the rest of us are born with, she then went on to somehow conceive Jesus without ever having carnal knowledge of Joseph. Neither of these are possible, but the Church steadfastly maintains both are true and continues to celebrate the fact that Mary was conceived without original sin and one day an angel appeared to tell her she was pregnant, which is a rather frightening thought, as well as a minor feast day celebrated every March twenty-fifth.

"It's not difficult to see how both of these uniquely Catholic beliefs have contributed to a great deal of misinformation and misunderstanding around sex and procreation, and it's no wonder that children raised in this belief system will grow into adults who are deeply confused and guilt-ridden over this very important aspect of their human nature."

The audience collectively nods in agreement.

"Historically, two of the biggest names in the early sex discussions were Augustine and Jerome, who were fourth-century contemporaries with reputations for chasing after women with reckless abandon and apparently loved sex—until they hated it," Professor Delavan continues. "As far as we know, neither married, although each had mistresses, and a child out of wedlock. Eventually, for reasons that remain unclear, both concluded that sex is a highly problematic human trait that must be suppressed at any cost.

"Augustine graphically describes his struggles with this issue in his lengthy 'Confessions,' which he began writing in 397 C.E. He claims he prayed for chastity, but not too soon—in other words, 'I want to become chaste, but not before I've enjoyed myself as much as possible.' It doesn't take a mental giant to recognize that this is the desire of a deeply tormented, psychologically disintegrated man. Unfortunately, he also became a very influential one.

"Jerome's influence arises from supposedly having written the Bible, which gave him considerable influence over Church doctrine. Believing that sexual desire was the highest moral failing imaginable, his views of sex were at least as warped as Augustine's. As an early promoter of the virginity of Mary, Jerome strongly favored sexual purity, which his mistress, Paula, must've found quite baffling, since they had a child together. But we are not privy to those conversations."

Maggie can't help smiling at this.

"Of the two, I would say Augustine's views of sex were the ones that caught on the most. He concluded we are all born flawed, which is the foundation of the doctrine of original sin, and that seeking pleasure or sensual delights is selfish and sinful. In this way, one mortal man laid down the foundation of the Christian faith's view of sex with back-up from Jerome, another equally uptight, deeply conflicted personality."

Millicent stops to take a drink of water.

"Running a close third, in terms of influence, is Benedict, best known for defining seventy-six rules for monastic life around the notion of *ora et labora*—work and prayer—that still defines cloistered life today. At its core, *ora et labora* isn't a bad idea, and across the centuries, hundreds of thousands of men and women seeking a life of holiness have followed the Rule of Benedict. But Benedict also had serious issues with sex and feared it so much he claimed whenever he felt the urge, he threw himself naked into stinging nettles or thorn bushes to discourage an erection, which was probably a pretty effective remedy to fight off this near occasion of sin, especially in a monastery."

The men in the audience let out a collective gasp while the women chuckle.

"Before moving on to modern times, it's important to note two things: First is that these three guys influenced Pope Gregory the Great so much, he decided to trash Jesus' companion Mary Magdalene's reputation in order to use her as an example of what women should not be. Insofar as we know, Gregory gave little thought to how this declaration reflected on Jesus' choice of friends and, by implication, on Jesus himself. Until the late 500s, when Gregory got it into his head that she was a promiscuous whore, Mary Magdalene was generally considered a benign figure who cared for Christ in his suffering. But Gregory decided that because sex was bad, the only good Mary was a virginal Mary, and since there was no evidence that Mary Magdalene fit that criteria, Gregory declared her unworthy of admiration or respect. Basically, this view categorized all nonvirginal women as whores, which when carried to its natural conclusion, meant that once a woman consummated her marriage, she no longer deserved her husband's respect. It's hard to know whether this demented view of women is a factor in domestic abuse situations, but it's worth thinking about."

By now, many in the audience are wide-eyed and open-mouthed.

"Augustine, Jerome, Benedict, and later Gregory, were so threatened by women's power they didn't know what to do other than to condemn them. This set the stage for how women were viewed from that moment forward right up until today and isn't a surprising outcome in a Church governed by men who find women totally bewildering, therefore very frightening.

"The second thing to note is that the Church eventually declared all these guys, as well as Mary Magdalene, saints, which is the equivalent of being voted into the Catholic Church Hall of Fame. This is absolute proof of something, but I'm not sure what."

By now the audience is finding the professor's presentation quite enlightening; some are smiling, others are taking notes, and many are frowning.

"Centuries later, John Calvin, who was married twice, including once to his step-daughter, weighed in on the meaning of sex. John probably discovered that few things are more pleasurable than sex and then, perhaps overtaken by guilt, concluded few things are more sinful. Despite his slanderous personal behavior, his ideas caught hold and formed the foundation for much of what is considered morally acceptable and unacceptable human behavior in Christian life. Calvinists presumably engaged in sex yet believed that anything pleasurable was sinful—a viewpoint that would create deep psychological conflicts it would be impossible to resolve."

Many, including Professor Delavan herself, those seated, and those standing in the back of the room, chuckle. One woman raises her hand and asks if the sinful pleasures scale includes chocolate.

"More to the point, what is a psychologically healthy person to do regarding this natural human urge that religion, with the generous assistance of some articulate, yet certifiably mentally unbalanced men, has somehow twisted into an act overloaded with meanings far beyond its simple reproductive function?"

No one volunteers an answer.

"You are correct—there are no easy answers to these questions, and perhaps it is not important to try. Instead, tonight, in the spirit of knowing your enemy, I want to try to enlighten you about the Church's current thinking on sex and birth control, in hopes this will help you figure out how to go about dismantling it, which is easier than you might imagine."

Professor Delavan's audience suddenly goes quiet and, once again, begins paying close attention.

"First, the Catholic Church remains steadfast in its belief that the only true, Christian, and nonsinful purpose of sex is procreation. Everything else is against God's will and therefore wrong. Other religions used to share this perspective, but most have modified their views over time to better accommodate changing social norms, many of which articulate feminists spearheaded.

"For Catholics, the sex conversation remained stuck in the fourth century until the birth control pill became widely available in the early 1960s, allowing women to much more easily enjoy sex without fear of pregnancy. The Church realized this was a game-changer and spent the next eight years studying the issue. And before you ask, I can only speculate on the absurdity of celibate men talking about the birth control pill for eight years, because I have no idea why they thought they knew what they were talking about."

Professor Delavan smiles and the audience laughs out loud.

"In the meantime, millions of women began taking the pill and found they had never been happier. Their husbands, who were no longer being denied sex because of fear of pregnancy, were pretty happy too."

Again, her audience laughs.

"When the Church fathers finally decided against allowing women to use the pill or other artificial means of preventing conception, not surprisingly, very few were willing to give it up and go back to practicing the officially recognized, highly unreliable rhythm method, coitus interruptus, abstinence, or some other creatively undependable technique to avoid an unwanted pregnancy. In my mind, the bigger question, however, is why celibate men with no family responsibilities and no credibility regarding the birth control issue believed women would listen to them about this issue? I don't know about you, but no woman I know seeks medical advice from her priest, and I can't rationally imagine why the Church thinks its priests are qualified to hand it out or are even entitled to an opinion on a health-related matter between a woman and her physician."

Many nod in agreement.

"However, the really big problem arose when the advent of the birth control pill forced Pope Paul VI to enter the conversation. In his 1968 encyclical, *Humanae Vitae*, the pope argued against birth control for the following reasons, some of which are, quite honestly, valid ones. Others, not so much.

"First, His Holiness claimed the Church was steadfastly opposed to birth control for two thousand years, which isn't precisely true, because it was never seriously discussed until 1930. Nevertheless, this is what the pontiff claimed, insisting that God specifically desires that the purpose of sex is to conceive children and man should not second-guess God and interfere with His will for us. It hasn't escaped my notice that the pope referred to men as if they had the last word on this, entirely ignoring women's involvement in the sex question—and this might be a point to work with. While the patriarchal Church claims God agrees with its view of sex, and is unlikely to be open to alternative views, there's no reason women can't adopt their own views of sex.

"Second, Paul VI pointed out that if religion, as society's moral compass, says that birth control is acceptable, this opens the door to governments forcing mentally or otherwise compromised individuals to be sterilized, something Sweden, a heavily Protestant nation, had already done. This begs several complex moral questions: Who is fit to be a parent? Should any individuals, such as the mentally or physically impaired, be judged unfit to reproduce? And, regardless of cognitive or physical ability, should everyone who can bear children be allowed to do so?"

Professor Delavan pauses several seconds to let these questions sink in before adding that if the group wants the Church to change its position on birth control, they must confront these issues.

"Finally, if the purpose of sex is not to produce children in a loving family setting, then the only other reason to have sex is for personal pleasure, and a man who seeks out a woman for this purpose turns her into an object valued only as a source for his own gratification. This inevitably leads to emotional and physical abuse and rape, not to mention the loss of all respect for women as thinking, feeling human beings."

"Men are already objectifying women regardless. Husbands come home drunk and insist on sex with their wives regardless of the consequences," a voice in the back of the room points out.

Professor Delavan nods in agreement.

"Men also force women into sex as a way to exert power over them," another audience member offers.

"These are both excellent points. We can't fix all the things that contribute to this problem, but we can explore ways to help women protect themselves from the unwanted consequences of sex.

"Meanwhile, back to the supposedly celibate men who spent eight long years thinking about the birth control pill and came up with the following, ridiculously uninspired answer: natural family planning, otherwise known as the infamous rhythm method. This is basically the crapshoot version of birth control—guessing when a woman is fertile and avoiding sex during that time. What is important, however, is that there are priests—none of whom are family men themselves and, supposedly, do not have to confront the meaning of sex in their own lives—who believe even the rhythm method is a grave sin against God's law and that every sexual act should occur with the expectation that conception will result.

"This viewpoint, if taken seriously, would result in an epic disaster in terms of available planetary resources and the number of mouths to feed. When someone pointed this out to the pope, his answer was to grow more food. I do not know about the rest of you, but I find this particularly insulting evidence of how far-removed Church leadership is from the realities of everyday life for everyone but themselves. It is also a compelling argument for change."

Several in the audience applaud.

"When Pope Paul VI died in 1978, Pope John Paul I succeeded him. One of the new pontiff's very first declarations was that he was going to permit Catholic women to use birth control. Thirty-three days later John Paul I was dead, under circumstances that remain a mystery. As a result, and not too surprisingly, no pope since has been willing to touch this issue.

"Where does this leave us? For one thing, we now know the birth control edict can be reversed, because John Paul I was going to do it. But that aside, this is where I believe it gets very interesting, and provides you with some very valuable ammunition," Professor Delavan says, pausing to take a deep breath and a drink of water before continuing.

"Research tells us that approximately ninety-six percent of Catholic women have used contraception at some point in their lives. It is safe to assume that these women do not believe that ignoring the Church's ban on birth control makes them bad Catholics, but these numbers strongly support the argument that many Catholic women are using birth control regardless of the Church's opposition.

"Equally important, I believe, is that while the United States is only about twenty-four percent Catholic, forty percent of women who obtain abortions are Catholic. To repeat: four out of every ten women who seek abortions are Catholic. The remaining six women are spread across several protestant and non-Christian belief systems. Collectively, Catholic women are much more likely to seek pregnancy termination than women of other faiths, because other faiths allow women to prevent pregnancies in the first place.

"This is the strongest imaginable argument in favor of birth control because, by failing to allow women to practice it, the Catholic Church causes more fetal deaths by abortion than any other religion, government, or institution in the world."

Another collective gasp echoes through the room.

"If one believes, as the Church does, that life begins at conception, it follows that the Church's position against artificial contraception is responsible for murdering a lot of children. There is not a stronger pro-life argument in favor of birth control than the one these data provide."

Hearing these words, Professor Delavan's audience sits in stunned silence. One person at a time, they begin to applaud, then stand up. Maggie allows this to continue for several minutes before asking for quiet.

"Before opening this up for questions, two other, very important points need to be made," Maggie says. "One point I think we can all agree on is that no woman wants an abortion—ever. This is her very last choice for controlling her reproductive life. Every woman who finds herself in the position of seeking an abortion would far, far prefer to have avoided that pregnancy in the first place. By forbidding the practice of birth control, the Church is forcing women to seek abortions and then condemning them for doing it. I imagine most of you agree that this sounds like a massive catch twenty-two manipulation of women.

"The other point is that the ban on birth control disproportionately affects poor women. It's partly an access and affordability issue, but it's also fear. The hope their faith offers them is often the only thing sustaining them, and if they are repeatedly told birth control is a sin, they won't use it. They need to believe in something outside themselves, which the Church represents, more than they want to believe they can think for themselves."

The audience murmurs and a well-dressed young woman in the back of the room stands, asking to speak.

"I am not a Catholic, but I am engaged to a Catholic man I love very much, so this topic is very important to me—to us," she begins. "I have two questions."

Maggie gestures for the woman to continue.

"First, how do the men who run the Catholic Church know the mind of God so well they can speak for Him on this issue? And second, why does the Catholic Church feel such a strong need to control women?"

Professor Delavan asks Maggie to address the first question and says she'll try to answer the second one.

"I don't believe the Church hierarchy knows the mind of God any better than the rest of us do. But Catholicism is a powerful, controlling culture, and its leaders think if they claim they have a direct line to God, people will view this as a very attractive trait and want to sign on. It's a tradition dating back to the Middle Ages when nearly everyone was illiterate and clergy were the only educated members of society, thus were able to tell people anything, and the people believed them.

"Later, it came about that, regarding matters of faith and morals, the pope speaks *ex-cathedra*, meaning his word is infallible and cannot be doubted. Not everyone believes this doctrine, but lazy Catholics—and there are a lot of them—find it easier to accept what the pope says rather than do the hard work of discerning the truth for themselves. These folks will surrender to whatever the Church claims because it is much easier to be a follower than to be an independent thinker. For the most part, this has worked well...for the Church."

Maggie gestures for Professor Delavan to speak.

"You are asking an extremely important question," the professor tells the young woman, clearing her throat and smoothing down her wrinkled shirt at the same time. "It is my carefully considered opinion—and believe me, I've thought about this a lot—that the chief reason men in general, and the male patriarchy that is the Catholic Church in particular, feel the need to control women is that men deeply fear women, and wanting to control that which you fear is a natural reaction. The problem is women don't realize how powerful they are because our male-dominated society conspires in a million ways to be sure they never find out. Consequently, across history, women have failed to exercise their power in their own best interests and, instead, have allowed men dominion over them, which suits men just fine." She takes a deep breath before continuing.

"It may never be possible to convince the Roman Catholic Church to change its position on birth control, but it is definitely possible to convince women that they have the power and the ability to take control of their own lives and ignore the Church on this issue...and there is overwhelmingly solid evidence that a lot of Catholic women are already doing this. Sooner or later, the men in their lives will have no choice except to follow along. But this said, no one gives up power willingly, so achieving this goal won't be easy."

"One other thing," the young woman continues.

Millicent nods, encouraging her to continue.

"I've heard no mention of the relationship between sex and love. The Catholic Church appears to view the sex act as a mechanical, biologically driven behavior necessary for reproduction, and the notion of sex as an expression of love between two people seems to have escaped notice, which I find very distressing. As a condition of marrying my fiancé, I'm expected to raise our children Catholic, and I don't want to raise children in a religion that ignores love as a primary reason for sex between two people who care deeply about each other.... Can either of you help me understand this?"

The room is dead silent as Maggie and Professor Delavan, neither of whom have had any experience with love of the sort the young woman is referring to, look to each other for help answering the question.

Finally, Millicent speaks. "You make an excellent point and raise a question I don't have an answer to, but perhaps Sister Corrigan has a comment."

Maggie steps forward. "Your concern is valid but one I've not thought about before and feel unable to comment on. My only advice is that you do not look to the priest who is giving you and your fiancé instruction in the principles of Catholic marriage for the answer. I can assure you he knows even less about marriage and loving relationships than I do, and I don't know squat about either one. This issue is best worked out between your soon-to-be husband and yourself, without any outside interference."

The young woman thanks them both and sits down.

Seeing there are no more questions, Maggie tells the group that it appears the first goal of their action plan is to help women recognize their power to make their own decisions. She calls for a fifteen-minute break to allow everyone to begin digesting this concept and explains that afterwards, they will divide into working groups and start brainstorming ideas.

Maggie is gratified by the turnout for this meeting, but realizes that, going forward, she needs to find a larger meeting space—and the money to pay for it. If the group continues expanding, and all indications are that it will, she will need to solve this problem before the next meeting, scheduled for one month from now.

After the meeting is over, Maggie tells Bridget Mary she needs to speak with her about the space issue as soon as possible.

"I was wondering about that when I saw the turnout tonight," Bridget Mary remarks. "Thankfully the fire marshal didn't show up."

•••

Early the next morning, Maggie is sitting in Bridget Mary's airless office, coffee mug in hand, discussing the previous night's meeting and trying to figure out a plan going forward.

"First is finding a larger meeting space, hopefully for free," Bridget Mary points out. "It appears that this is a convenient location, so first is to determine what options are available close by. You can't select someplace too far from where most people are coming from, so you should pay attention to the zip codes on our mailing list," Bridget Mary directs.

Maggie knows there are several Catholic Churches within about five miles in all directions from the shelter. Since most make their basements available for outside meetings, she decides to begin her search by contacting them.

After four churches turn her down—for vague reasons that somehow pertain to disallowing Catholic groups the archdiocese does not officially recognize to use their space—Maggie is both suspicious and stymied. She conveys her concern to Bridget Mary who promises to get to the bottom of the refusals.

•••

Two days later, Bridget Mary comes into her office and takes a seat.

"I have our answer," she says, frowning.

"Answer to what?" Maggie asks, looking up from the pile of papers strewn about her desk.

"Why you can't rent space in any of the churches. Apparently, Cardinal O'Grady got wind of the meeting the other night and put out the word that no parishes were to recognize CWDC, which includes providing meeting space."

"How the hell could O'Grady have found out so soon when we haven't done anything yet?" Maggie asks.

"We may never figure that out, but my guess is it has something to do with the Mary Beth Dolan case."

"How is that possible?"

"The district attorney is a devout Catholic, and when he found out you were willing to drag the Church into the case by claiming a priest gave bad advice that led to a death, he arranged to have a drink with O'Grady and give him a heads up. O'Grady wouldn't let something like that go. He sent someone to find out more about you, which, armed with the information the DA provided, wouldn't be difficult, and then waited for an opportunity to squash you. I'm sure someone from O'Grady's office came to last week's meeting and reported back. Based on what he heard, O'Grady decided to squash the effort ASAP."

"I can't believe this. He really is a vindictive bastard!"

"If you don't believe this is possible, you aren't paying attention. The bottom line is there's an informant. But it was never going to be possible to keep CWDC under the radar forever anyway, so no point in wasting a lot of time being upset about it. Now we know, so we deal with it. Enthusiasm for taking action is growing much stronger as people realize the promised Vatican II reforms have either fallen on their collective face or are meaningless in the everyday lives of Catholics. We have to capture this passion for change and run with it, and maybe an opportunity will arise when we can use the communication channel between CWDC and the cardinal to our advantage."

"You really think this has something to do with my involvement in the Mary Beth Dolan case. That was years ago," Maggie exclaims.

"The cardinal has a memory like an elephant—he never forgets a damned thing, especially if it's something he doesn't like. My gut feeling is that the cardinal's directive against CWDC is somehow connected to that case," Bridget Mary answers.

"I suppose it could be. I probably never mentioned it, but I didn't want to let the final disposition rest in the case rest and volunteered to be charged under the child abuse mandatory reporting law, so I could introduce the idea that priests are giving women bad advice about remaining in abusive marriages. I had several discussions with someone on the DA's office about it. If the cardinal heard about that, it probably pissed him off," Maggie confesses.

"What the fuck? Why in the hell, in the name of all that is holy, did you do something as goddamned stupid as that?" Bridget Mary explodes, jumping to her feet. "You'd have gone to jail, the CWDC initiative would've crashed, we would have lost a grant writer, and been forced to report every abuse case that comes through our door, which gets Chicago social services involved. That is exactly what abused women fear most because they're terrified of having their children taken from them. Word gets out you did this, and women would stop coming to the shelters, and you'd be labeled a nutcase who belongs in a padded cell. You might as well burn down every woman's shelter, legal assistance program, and women's health clinic in the entire city of Chicago, because the effect would be the same."

By this time, the red-faced shelter director is pacing the floor, angrier than Maggie has ever seen her.

"I wouldn't have necessarily gone to jail, I could've gotten probation and a fine," Maggie points out.

"You'd get slapped with a several thousand dollar fine, which you can't pay, so you'd end up in jail anyway. And because you work for us, the shelter would've gotten dragged into the mess and run up a boatload of legal bills we don't have the money to pay for."

"It would've been a powerful statement," Maggie contends, not backing down.

"A powerful statement nobody would remember two days later, and only happened in the first place because you're pissed off at your brother."

Maggie winces.

"That was you being selfish, and your selfishness could've brought everything we've worked so hard to build crashing into the goddamned ground to be buried hundreds of feet under a pile of rubble that was formerly every woman's shelter in Chicago. It would take a generation to rebuild the trust we would lose, and that's assuming it would be possible to get funding for shelter programs ever again. Meanwhile, women would continue being abused and wouldn't have anywhere to turn...and it would've been all your fault, Maggie...every last goddamned bit of it would've been on you." Bridget Mary pounds on her desk for emphasis.

"Maybe it was stupid, but I don't think so. Regardless, I don't care. Somebody has to bring this situation to light somehow, and it might as well be me...but it doesn't matter. Marcia said the DA would've never pressed charges against a nun and doesn't have the time, interest, or resources to pursue Mickey Mouse cases like this anyway. To tell you the truth, I was disappointed," Maggie explains, showing no remorse.

"I should fire you for this...I want to fire you for this...I'm biting my tongue bloody to stop myself from firing you this instant," the shelter director shouts before taking in several deep breaths to calm herself. She paces for nearly five minutes trying to calm herself before continuing, perspiration glistening on her forehead as the heat from her fiery red face fills her small office space.

Maggie watches this, reluctant to say anything further.

"We have to pick our battles, Maggie. And this one would've been a waste of time and money we don't have and caused a massive shitload of damage. Nothing good would have come from it."

"Don't misunderstand me," Bridget Mary continues, as her breathing normalizes. "I agree with you that the Church has its head so far up its ass on this issue it can't see daylight, but dragging the archdiocese into a legal mess will only make the Church dig in further. Our best bet is a counter offensive: we use CWDC to get behind the notion of showing women how to advocate for themselves to give them the confidence to take what they want from the Church and blow off the rest—especially anything that is not in their own best interest."

Staring at the wall behind Bridget Mary's desk, Maggie doesn't respond.

"I appreciate your passion and zeal, Maggie, really I do. But you have to use your head, and if you ever do something like this again, I'll fire you on the spot. You're not a one-woman show around here, and if you get any more creative ideas, talk to me first," Bridget Mary instructs, finally sitting down behind her desk.

"One other thing, Maggie. Don't take this wrong, but you better be damned sure your zeal for going after priests advising women against leaving marriages isn't just about getting back at your brother. You have every right to be blind furious as hell at him, but you can't let your anger drag everybody around you into your hot-tempered family disagreements and hurt a lot of people—most of all, you. You've got too much talent to waste it on some misdirected personal vendetta."

"What do you suggest I do about meeting space?" Maggie calls out as the director stomps away, hiking up her pants and pulling down her sweater.

"Try the Protestants."

•••

After several days of trying, Maggie is surprised at how difficult it is to find a Protestant church willing to agree to rent space for CWDC meetings. For one thing, there aren't nearly as many of them as there are Catholic churches, and especially not in the raunchier neighborhoods surrounding the shelter. Each one she approaches asks why she can't use a Catholic church, and when she explains that the Catholic churches won't rent to her, the Protestants claim they don't want to become involved in any situation that would risk alienating the cardinal, with whom they have a good working relationship they don't want to jeopardize.

"O'Grady's like the stink from the Yards—hanging all over every damned thing for as far as the eye can see," Maggie tells Bridget Mary when she reports the results of her search.

"You don't have to be so honest when you explain why you want to use their space," Bridget Mary advises. "Just say their church is in a better location."

Maggie soon discovers no one believes that explanation and admits she's stymied.

A few days later, she is walking from the L station back to the shelter, through a neighborhood that is equal parts abandoned and barely inhabitable houses shedding paint and anything that isn't nailed down tight. Passing by empty storefronts and a bar on every block, she notices a hand-painted sign—*Our Daily Bread – All Are Welcome*—propped in a storefront window. A hand-written note on the door lists the days and times for daily Alcoholic Anonymous meetings; the hours when free lunches are served on Mondays, Wednesdays, and Fridays; and an invitation to a Sunday gathering in what appears to be an informal, street-corner church.

Looking through the window, she sees a large, mostly empty room containing several rows of folding chairs facing what looks like a card table that doubles as a makeshift altar. The walls are industrial gray, windowless, and empty except for a plain wooden cross hanging behind the table, next to the popular, sepia-toned portrait of Jesus that has been reproduced millions of times. The most impressive feature is the large, ornately carved, dark mahogany John Wing and Son upright piano placed within Jesus' view.

Maggie doesn't recall seeing the sign in the window on her previous trips back-and-forth to the L stop and guesses the large room must be recently gutted former retail space. She knocks on the door, and no one answers. After the second try, she pushes the door and, finding it unlocked, steps inside.

"Whoever runs this church can't possibly give a shit what the cardinal thinks," she whispers just as a trim, olive-skinned man walks into the room from a downstairs area.

"I'm Ben," he says, smiling broadly as he extends a strong hand. "Is there something I can help you with?"

Maggie is immediately aware that in all of her nearly forty-seven years she has never met a man quite as effortlessly handsome as the one standing before her. Awestruck, she does not answer his question. Instead, she notices his curly black hair has a few gray threads running through it, his even teeth reveal a lifetime of good dental care, and his gentle, deep blue eyes invite anyone he meets to reveal their deepest secrets.

After waiting a full minute, Ben repeats his question.

"I'm Sister Maggie Corrigan," she finally stammers, behaving as though she just met Jesus in person and has discovered he's an ordinary guy. For the first time in her life, she wishes she wasn't wearing used, mismatched thrift store clothing—a realization that causes her to blush furiously.

"Nice to meet you, Sister Corrigan. I'm Ben Cabrera."

"Please, call me Maggie," she says, gathering herself together enough to attempt to return the handshake. But since the gesture was already withdrawn, she reaches down and takes the hand hanging at the side of the tall man standing before her, embarrassing herself further.

"Only if you call me Ben," he smiles, gesturing toward the chairs. "Would you like to sit down and tell me what I can do for you?"

"Yes, that would be nice...I'm looking for meeting space."

"For what kind of meeting?"

"A Catholic women's group that the Catholic churches won't allow their space to be used for," Maggie blurts out, not meaning to reveal so much.

"What is this group doing that has it on the wrong side of the Catholic Church?" Ben asks, looking directly into Maggie's eyes, smiling slightly.

She has never experienced a man looking at her this way before, and stares at the floor in order to avoid looking directly at Ben. "We want to force the Church to change its position on birth control—allow women the reproductive choices and freedom they deserve."

"I can see how that might not go down too well. Do you mind telling me how you got involved in this?"

"That's a very long story...."

"I have the time if you do."

Without hesitating, Maggie explains her history with the issue, beginning with her mother's death up through her work at the shelter, helping abused women forced into being responsible for many more children than they can possibly care for. She finishes by recounting the Mary Beth Dolan story and her anger over priests advising abused women to remain in violent, dangerous marriages.

"You have a lot of passion for your cause...I really admire that," Ben says.

Hearing this, Maggie blushes again while continuing to twist the edge of her faded red, lint-covered sweater, which clashes badly with her hair.

"Not surprisingly, there is a lot of enthusiasm among Catholic women to take up this issue. Just by word-of-mouth, more than one hundred women and several men came to our last meeting, which drastically violated the fire code in our building. We can't risk that again, so need to find another place to meet. We were hoping to convince a slightly deaf

Catholic Church somewhere nearby to allow us to use its space, but the cardinal got there first—put out a directive saying parishes are not to host Catholic groups the archdiocese doesn't officially recognize, which obviously includes us. The Protestant churches we asked didn't want to risk alienating the cardinal, who has the reach of an octopus."

"And you would like to use this space?"

"If something could be arranged. I think it would be very suitable."

"One problem is that we don't have enough chairs for one hundred people. We don't generally get that many, even for lunches...although I expect that number will increase eventually."

"We could bring our chairs over and leave them here in case you need them. We can't pay much, and the chairs could be part of a deal that helps you and helps us."

"How much can you pay?" Ben asks.

"I'm not sure...maybe twenty dollars per meeting? Although we could start passing the hat and maybe collect more. I understand that it won't cover the electrical and heat, but we're operating without a budget right now, and have no fundraising strategy in place. I've been donating my salary from the shelter as seed money for mailings, coffee, and a few other expenses."

"Well, twenty dollars and loose change for a Tuesday night meeting is twenty dollars more than I will have had the day before. That and a few chairs will work, at least in the short run. What is your long-term financial plan, if I may ask?"

"We don't have one. I haven't had time to think that through," Maggie admits sheepishly.

"Have you put together an organizational plan?" Ben asks.

"Not really...I've submitted some successful grant applications for the shelter, but that's as far as my experience in this area goes, unfortunately. This is not a job I applied for—the shelter director, whose idea it was originally, handed it over to me a couple months ago."

"I have some experience with community organizing and could help you figure some of these things out—if you want any help, that is."

"Are you kidding? I need all the help I can get! I'd love it if you would be willing to do that, but again, there's no money to pay you." Maggie blushes for the third time in less than fifteen minutes.

"Not everything needs to be about money, Maggie. Sometimes just doing the right thing is enough. You seem to deeply believe in what you're trying to do, and I'm willing to help as much as I can. I suggest you come back Friday afternoon, if you're free, and we'll get started. In the meantime, jot down some ideas to help clarify your vision for what you want to accomplish."

"Thanks very much," Maggie says, resisting a never before felt impulse to hug the gorgeous man who has just offered her a lifeline.

"I'll look forward to it. Perhaps we should exchange phone numbers, in case something unforeseen arises."

Maggie nods and each of them scribbles their contact information on a scrap of paper, before proceeding toward the front door, where they shake hands again.

Holy shit—maybe there is a God after all, and He just sent me a savior, Maggie thinks, smiling broadly while walking the rest of the way back to the shelter. She can't help thinking about what she should wear on Friday—a puzzling question that has never before, in her entire life, entered her mind.

XIV.

God works in mysterious ways....

WILLIAM COWPER

"You have beautiful hair—you can't get your shade of red from a bottle," the bubble-gum-chewing hairstylist with bleached hair accented by several inches of dark roots, Purple Ruby fingernail polish, and thick, charcoal eyeliner tells Maggie as she fastens a plastic cape around the nun's shoulders and asks whether she wants a shampoo included—for a dollar extra.

Maggie shakes her head no, instructing the enthusiastic beautician hovering over her head with sharp scissors to stick with whatever's cheapest.

"If you quit messing with your hair yourself and let it grow a few inches, you'll turn heads wherever you go," the stylist says, snipping away while cracking her gum.

Maggie knows this isn't true but can't help blushing. That what she is wearing, or how her hair looks, matters to her at all is mystifying and disorienting. The ground beneath her feet is shifting, like sand washed back out to sea after a wave strikes the shore. She doesn't understand what is happening to her or why she feels compelled to make the first visit of her entire life to a beauty salon ahead of her Friday meeting with Ben Cabrera.

"Oh dear—I see a few grays starting to show. We can fix that by adding in a some blond streaks," the stylist says, still snipping.

Maggie starts to shake her head.

"Hold still, honey, otherwise you'll walk outta here looking as bad as you did when you walked in, and that'd be real disastrous for my professional reputation...you know what I'm sayin'? No offense."

Maggie remains silent, magnifying the sound of popping gum.

"How's that look?" the stylist asks a few minutes later, handing her a mirror and twirling the chair around the mass of red curls surrounding her head.

Maggie shrugs and says it looks fine.

"Come back in six weeks for another shape up," the stylist tells her as she finishes. "Ask for Suzi, and I'll make you into a movie star," she giggles. "Well, maybe me and someone to help with your wardrobe choices...that purple outfit you're wearing? Definitely not your color. It makes your freckles pop like polka dots on a clown."

It's my only matching outfit, Maggie thinks.

"And your footwear? Old ladies with flat feet wear those boxes you got on...and you ain't no old lady yet."

"These shoes are comfortable for walking," Maggie explains.

"You can't have beauty without pain, sweetie. Ditch the shoes."

Maggie starts to say that she can't afford to throw away her shoes just because they aren't the latest style, but her self-appointed beauty consultant is continuing to offer free advice without giving her an opening to curtail the conversation.

"You also need to work on a little make-up—a nice shade of lipstick that doesn't draw too much attention to your teeth, which need a little polishing up as soon as you can get an appointment. And get rid of those stray eyebrow hairs. We do plucking, manicures, and pedicures right here. I'll give you a coupon before you leave."

Maggie politely thanks her. *I've got to get out of here and end this torturous personal assessment,* she thinks.

"You know what you could do? Go to a department store make-up counter and ask for some advice. They'll want to sell you stuff, but they also help with selecting just the right shade of lip color, liner, and foundation. It's a fun way to spend an afternoon...gives your self-esteem a real boost, and you can go buy whatever they recommend cheaper at a drug store. You could be a real knock-out with the right clothes and accessories—maybe some earrings. The glasses on a chain thing, though? Definitely not a flattering look," Suzi instructs. "People will think you just got out of a nunnery."

Maggie cringes, nearly admitting to the nunnery connection and knowing the last place in the world she would ever go to is a department store, especially after a half-hour haircut that felt like a visit to another planet. The personal critique she has just received has shaken her so much she nearly forgets to put fifty cents in the tip jar on the way out the door to her meeting with Ben.

•••

"I'm glad you could make it," Ben says, again offering Maggie his hand as he stills the bell hanging from the opened front door with the other one.

Wild horses couldn't have kept me away, Maggie thinks.

"Since you're considering renting space from us, we should probably begin by me showing you around," Ben says.

Maggie nods her approval.

"The upstairs is just as you see it: one big room with my makeshift office in the corner. If you take the stairs to the right, they lead to the basement. That's where the restrooms, kitchen, eating area, and storage area are all located. Follow me and I'll show you."

Ben flips on a light, illuminating the stairwell. "As you can see, the basement is another large, nearly empty space. The large cafeteria tables with attached benches seat about seventy-two total. I just finished renovating the kitchen to add pass-through counter space. Two bathrooms are located near the stairs and the door next to the kitchen leads to the storage room."

The basement walls are the same dull gray as the upstairs and the only natural light is from small basement window wells. The rest comes from fluorescent ceiling lights identical to those upstairs.

"At some point, I might renovate part of the storage area into a small apartment for myself, but that's sometime in the future," Ben tells her.

"You must own this building," Maggie realizes, looking around.

"That's right. For nearly six months. It was a retail store—discount shoes, I think—and had been vacant a long time when I bought it. Before I could do anything, I had to get rid of the rats and a couple of raccoons making their home in the attic, plus relocate the vagrants who were living upstairs. That took a month. Then I gutted the place...did most of the work myself, I'm proud to say."

"You must've gotten a good deal on the paint," Maggie remarks.

"Yeah...the color is a mistake I need to fix," he admits, "but the walls need a second coat of paint anyway."

"Is this part of an organized religion?" Maggie asks.

"No, it's not. Actually, it's only generically religious—a hospitality house in the 'give shelter to the stranger' tradition. Nothing specific and no pray-to-eat requirements, which makes naming the place a little dicey. I want something unique, just not sure what, so Our Daily Bread will probably stick…it sends the right message."

"You don't have to answer this, but without organizational backing, how are you financing this effort?" Maggie asks.

Ben hesitates before answering. "A benefactor…it's kind of a long story."

"I'm in no hurry."

"Then I'll make us some coffee," Ben says, inviting her to sit at one of the cafeteria tables. "Give me a few minutes while the water heats. I might be able to scare up some cookies left from Wednesday lunch."

A few minutes later, he places a plastic tray with two mugs of steaming coffee, two paper napkins, and a saucer containing four cookies on the table. He tells Maggie he's expecting the piano tuner sometime this afternoon, so it might be better to work downstairs where they won't be distracted. After taking a sip of his coffee, he proceeds to answer her question.

"The benefactor is my father, but that isn't as simple as it sounds."

"It never is when family and money mix," Maggie acknowledges, wondering about the real story behind a Black man coming from a family with enough money to bankroll a social welfare initiative in one of Chicago's worst slum neighborhoods.

"He belongs to a prominent Winnetka family, where my grandmother, who immigrated from the Dominican Republic, worked as a domestic. She brought my mother, Angelina, as a playmate for the family's only child—a boy named Benjie. The two grew up together—Angelina became a beautiful young woman, but Benjie never outgrew his geeky awkwardness and didn't have much in common with the Winnetka tennis and sailing set, if you know what I mean."

"Not really, I've never been to the North Shore."

"It picks up where the Gold Coast leaves off…no homes under a million, minimum."

"A foreign land to me," Maggie says, stirring her coffee.

"Anyway, Angelina was Benjie's best friend, and not surprisingly, they fell in love—a secret they somehow managed to keep from their parents. She got pregnant while Benjie was in law school, and there was no way a White boy from generations of wealth could marry a Caribbean immigrant's illegitimate daughter with just a high school education, whose most promising future depended on the tips she received waiting tables. The family wasn't interested in a dark-skinned daughter-in-law, or a mixed-race grandchild either, but to their credit, they insisted Benjie step up and act responsibly toward the child."

"Don't very often hear that story," Maggie observes.

"It gets better," Ben smiles. "I was born the month Benjie, now Ben, graduated law school. He had a well-paying job lined up with an investment bank and was able to pay all our expenses, including daycare for me and tuition for my mother to go to secretarial school. When she finished, he pulled some strings to get her a job in admissions at Loyola University and moved us into a modest, but very adequate co-op apartment a few blocks away. It was a diverse neighborhood where she felt comfortable living and raising a son on her own."

"She was one lucky woman is all I can say," Maggie offers, breaking off a piece of cookie.

"And she's never, ever forgotten that. Her salary, plus Ben's dependable generosity, allowed us a safe, secure life—adequate health care, braces for my teeth, and so on. And one benefit of working at Loyola is that the children of faculty and staff receive generously discounted college tuition if they meet the admission requirements. I took advantage of that, and my father saw to the rest of my expenses. I lived in a dorm and had a regular college experience...and here's where it gets interesting...." Ben pauses to take a drink of his coffee.

"It's already pretty interesting," Maggie says, staring toward a far window well that has recently been cleaned out.

"I was raised in the Black church and loved it, but while at Loyola, I fell in love with Catholicism and converted—much to my mother's chagrin. It's a Jesuit school, and I decided I wanted to enter the Jesuits and become a priest. To her everlasting credit, my mother didn't throw a hissy fit, but she cried continuously for three weeks. Her only chance for grandchildren was gone, she was losing me to an institution and would never see me again, and so on. She even asked my father to intervene and try to talk some sense into me. He didn't do that, but he did try to reassure my mother I'd always be her son and that my decision wasn't the end of the world."

"Is he Catholic, your father?"

"Episcopalian—the church of rich Anglo-Saxon Protestants. He is a deeply spiritual man and, to his credit, seemed to grasp what was driving me to seek vowed religious life. The only thing he said was to take my time making the decision, to be sure it was what I wanted."

"What did your dad's wife think of her husband being so involved with you and your mother?"

"He never married. Neither did my mother. They never said this, but it's pretty clear they love each other too much to make a lifetime commitment to anyone else. The only thing my dad ever said about it was that he was pretty sure most people thought he was homosexual. He always laughed when he said it, so he probably didn't care.

"Anyway, after graduation I was accepted into the Jesuit novitiate in Saint Louis, and then delayed entering for a year to catch up with myself, so to speak. I wanted to work a regular job, and there weren't any for a philosophy major, so I drove a cab until I got tired of rich drunks throwing up in my back seat after a late night drinking themselves so stupid they couldn't find their flashy sports cars or insanely expensive, Gold Coast apartments. Eventually, I had enough and left for Saint Louis and began studying for the priesthood."

"After putting up with all that, it's no wonder the priesthood was attractive!" Maggie teases.

"Five years later, about three months before ordination, doubts about committing myself to celibacy reared their head and wouldn't go away."

"You're lucky the doubts came to you before ordination—that's not always the case," Maggie offers, looking down at the table.

"I'd had five years to observe the priesthood up close and concluded that it was a fundamentally dishonest way of life that denied a core aspect of human nature, which is to love and be loved by another human being, and I couldn't reconcile that realization with the priesthood as a lifestyle. It raised too many questions in my mind, and I started drinking, which began worrying me a lot, and concerned my spiritual advisor even more."

"I think alcoholism is pretty common among priests."

"So do I, and when my spiritual advisor wisely suggested I delay ordination for a year and take a position as a community resource development planner with the Jesuit mission on the Pine Ridge Indian Reservation in South Dakota, I jumped at the chance. He said it would be an opportunity for me to sort myself out away from all the temptations of modern life. It turned out that I loved Pine Ridge so much I stayed nearly ten years without ever getting around to being ordained. They were very important years. I learned a lot about myself that I couldn't have learned any other way."

"Like what?"

"Like how easy it would be for me to become an alcoholic...how much I prefer working alone rather than for somebody else...that I'm not a great team player, which makes me poor husband material according to the two girlfriends I had during this time, both of whom broke up with me. More importantly, I realized how gratifying it is to help others discover their best selves. Thankfully, the Jesuits trusted me enough to allow me a great deal of freedom and autonomy. They gave me a roof over my head and told me to go forth and do good works, and that's what I tried to do."

"How?" Maggie asks, paying close attention as she realizes he is talking about efforts similar to those the shelter is trying to organize.

"I began by establishing several Alcoholics Anonymous groups—alcoholism is a big problem among Native Americans. This led to becoming support staff at the free medical clinic—checking blood pressures, doing a lot of listening, and offering a lot of informal, practical advice, even when I wasn't asked! I also helped with after-school programs aimed at keeping teens occupied and out of trouble. I coached basketball and substitute taught in the school when they couldn't find anybody else. And I wrote grants to help support our efforts."

Ben stops to take a bite of cookie and drink of coffee before continuing.

"I loved it. I was happy and probably would've stayed forever, but one day I received a letter from my father, asking me to call him. When we finally connected, he told me my mother had been diagnosed with a debilitating neuro-muscular disease a few months previously, after several years of problems she did not want me to know about and that had been easy to hide. After all, I had only been back to Chicago twice since going to Pine Ridge. He felt I would want to know and perhaps consider coming back to be with her because her condition was only going to worsen. What he didn't say, but I could hear in his voice, was how much this was tearing him up, and that he needed me to come back, perhaps more than she did."

Ben hesitates again, then asks if Maggie wants more coffee. She shakes her head no.

"My father sent me the money to make a trip back, and my mother's condition, which was rapidly deteriorating, shocked me."

"Do you mind telling me what it was?" Maggie asks.

"ALS, Lou Gehrig's Disease...maybe you've heard of it?"

"I've heard of it, but don't know much about it," Maggie answers.

"Neither did I, and after seeing her, I've not wanted to learn more," Ben admits. "Eventually, muscles stop working. It's always fatal, and not a pretty death, if there is such a thing." The pain of revealing this shows on his face.

"My mother strongly resisted me giving up something I loved so much—insisted she could manage, and so on—and I knew my father would see to it she was well cared for, so I was torn. I loved what I was doing at Pine Ridge. I was good at it and didn't want to stop. While I was still struggling with the decision, my dad took me out to lunch and offered an idea: if I came back, he would front the money for me to set up something like the community organizing efforts I was spearheading at Pine Ridge but do it in a Chicago neighborhood. He said he'd carry it financially until I figured out how to make it self-supporting. It was the hardest decision I've ever had to make, but in the end, I decided to return. And now here I am, nearly forty years old and back home living with my mother!"

"How is she doing?" Maggie asks.

"The disease seems to have slowed some. She uses a walker but falls easily and has trouble feeding herself. Her speech is getting slurred, but it's still understandable. Someone comes in during the day to help her with personal care and prepares easy-to-swallow meals. My father comes every evening after work and stays until we put her to bed, which is usually around nine. I'm with her nights, and a cleaning person comes in once a week and also does the grocery shopping. We're making it work, for now. The tipping point will be when she can't get herself to the bathroom anymore. Then we'll have to find someone to come in full-time around the clock...at least that's the current plan."

"I'm sure she's glad to have you home. Probably makes her feel much better."

"She's glad I didn't go to the priesthood because it renewed her hope for grandchildren. Some days that's all she talks about...says she wants me to find someone and start a family of my own."

"Have you? Found someone?" Maggie asks, gripping her coffee mug.

"Someday I hope I do, when the time is right...or maybe someone will find me while I'm busy doing something else. It's hard to know how it will all work out, but right now I'm obligated to my mother and not spending much time thinking about it."

"You do realize you've just told me an incredible love story," Maggie says, stopping herself just as she reaches for his hand, a gesture she has never felt the urge to make toward anyone, especially not a man, ever before.

"I realize it now, but I didn't always," Ben answers.

"Where do your grandparents fit into this?"

"My mother's mother helped out with me as I was growing up and lived with us the last year of her life when she was dying of cancer, which was just after I started college. My father's parents are an entirely different story. I don't know either of them."

"Not at all?" Maggie asks. "You're their only grandchild."

"My grandmother wears a thousand dollar's worth of jewelry and carefully applied make-up to bed every night, in case there's a fire. She is far too concerned about social status to acknowledge an illegitimate grandson and I don't think having grandchildren was ever high on her list of things that define a successful life anyway. My grandfather, on the other hand, would've liked some sort of relationship, I think, if he could've figured out a way around my grandmother. When I was in third grade, he enrolled me in a monthly book club for kids to encourage me to read, and when I entered high school, he bought me two season tickets to Cubs games every year—for me and a friend. This went on until I went to Saint Louis. But there were no family Thanksgivings or Christmases, and he died when I was in the seminary."

"Why did you decide to start your own social welfare project?" Maggie asks, changing the subject. "Surely you could have worked within the existing Catholic structure."

"I don't think so. Here in Chicago, the most likely place for me would be within a parish, and I'm not interested in some kind of pseudo-ministerial role. The last thing I'm interested in doing is assuming I know what God wants and using that infomation as an excuse to tell other people what to do. Don't get me wrong—I love the Catholic Church, but I've outgrown the naïve faith I once had and so far, haven't been able to figure out a new version more suitable for a grownup."

"If you are going off on your own with this effort, why make it religious at all?"

"Simple answer: faith is the core of the Black church I grew up in. Believing in God and Jesus gives people hope, and the folks I've always worked with—including the ones who wander in here—need hope anywhere they can find it. I can provide that in a generic sort of way, without preaching about it."

"Do you believe in God?" Maggie asks, looking straight into Ben's soulful eyes.

"I do. I'm not so sure about Jesus Christ being the son of God, which is a little too contrived for me. But Jesus had a good social message, so I don't have a serious problem with Him, and He's a visual image folks can grab onto. It's not that easy with God—or the Holy Spirit, for that matter. Nobody knows what they look like. But why are you asking?"

"Just curious," Maggie shrugs, studying her cookie.

"I've never been able to entirely escape the Black church. I love the simple message and the lively gospel music, which is what I want to offer here—something far less formal and much more welcoming than the Catholic ritual. I hope to create opportunities to develop a community that comes together Sunday mornings to reflect a little, drink coffee, eat cookies, and enjoy a gospel music sing-along, which the Catholic hymns don't lend themselves to all that well."

"No, they don't," Maggie agrees.

"That's what I did with the AA groups, and we all had a lot of fun. As an added benefit, attendance at meetings increased and people tended to stay with the program, which is a forgiving social experience whose only requirement is staying sober."

"Is this the reason for starting the AA meetings right away?"

"It is. I don't need to tell you what a horrible problem alcoholism is in neighborhoods like this—although it's also just as big a problem for rich folks. But people around here don't have access to resources that could help them, and I hope to change that. Starting next week, I'll find out whether I'm right."

"And the piano—with all the carving, that's quite an instrument!"

"She's a grand old gal, which, believe it or not, I found at a Saint Vincent de Paul thrift store over toward Oak Park. I can't wait to play her, which will happen just as soon as the piano tuner does his magic, hopefully today. I've cleaned out the mouse turds and repaired some of the other effects of many years of neglect. Now she's badly in need of some TLC, which will probably cost me a lot more than what I paid for her, but she's worth every cent. I'm thinking I'll name her Mahalia, after one of the great gospel singers of our lifetime."

"So you play and, I assume, sing?"

"I had piano lessons as a kid and can read music, but I still need a day job," Ben laughs. "I can carry a tune, but I try to drown myself out banging on the keyboard."

His voice is too deep to not sing well, Maggie thinks.

Just then the bell hanging on the back of the upstairs door jingles.

"That must be the piano tuner," Ben says. "I'll get him started. If you don't mind, could you rinse out our mugs and wipe down the table? Mice are still a problem. I'll be back in a few minutes, and we can get going on what you came to do over an hour ago."

Not sure how to respond to the confidences Ben has shared with her, Maggie wordlessly clears the table and heads for the kitchen.

When Ben returns, he gets right down to business by asking Maggie to tell him about CWDC's goals.

"Right now they're pretty vague but center around doing something about Catholic women's lack of reproductive rights. We've formed three committees—fundraising, action, and publicity—but that's about as far as we've gotten."

"How did you get going in the first place?"

Maggie explains that it was Sister Bridget Mary's idea to do something to help Catholic women gain agency over their own lives, and as the director talked it up until eventually a lot of support for getting organized began to emerge.

"It took a while, but all of a sudden it's about to take off like a rocket, and we're not sure where we're going, but regardless, we're on our way now," she says.

"You do know it would be easier to infiltrate the Kremlin than to penetrate deeply enough into the institutional Catholic Church to affect the kind of change you're talking about," Ben says.

"I know that," she bristles. "But it doesn't mean it's not worth trying."

"Then let me suggest some ideas for moving forward...if you're willing to hear them."

"I'll listen to any ideas, believe me. It's not like I've ever done something like this before."

"One is to hook your star onto an existing organization with similar goals. The Women's National Alliance is the one that comes immediately to mind. Your group could follow the WNA lead, at least in the beginning. Have a conversation with the person in charge of the Chicago branch and explore how you can help each other in mutually beneficial ways. Or, if not them, then another, similar group might work."

Maggie writes this down, underlining it twice.

"Also, I wouldn't waste my time trying to reason with the patriarchy if I were you. That's beating your head against a cement wall, which will kill you and won't affect the wall at all. Instead, work with the staff at women's shelters and women's health clinics to get out the message that Catholic women have the right to make their own reproductive choices. Give the front-line folks working in the trenches the tools they need to carry this message forward effectively. My guess is they agree with what you're trying to do but don't know how to go about doing it."

"How do we get that message across?"

"Written materials, workshops, in-service programs, protest activities, and so on. These things will be enough to get you started and won't cost an arm and a leg...maybe ten or fifteen grand to get going."

"That's fourteen grand more than we have right now," Maggie groans.

"Then your top priority is identifying funding sources willing to bankroll something like this, and getting busy on applications. And you have to get a fundraising strategy in place. That might be a little tricky, given your goals, but I'm happy to brainstorm further, if you're interested."

"Thanks, I really appreciate anything you can do," Maggie says, standing up to leave.

XV.

"For I know the plans I have for you," declares the LORD,
"plans to prosper and not to harm you,
plans to give you hope and a future."

JEREMIAH 29:11

Over the next few days, Maggie can't get Ben Cabrera out of her mind. Before she left their meeting, she arranged for the next CWDC meeting to be held at Our Daily Bread in a month, but they made no definite plans to meet again before then.

She can't get her conversation with Suzi, who appointed herself Maggie's fashion consultant, out of her head either. As a result, she is restless and poorly focused. After wasting two days staring out her office window, daydreaming, Maggie calls Mary Pat and asks to meet for lunch.

"I can't do lunch but could meet you at the Morty's a couple blocks over from Cabrini tomorrow after school...I'll drop the little kids off at the apartment and meet you about four," her friend says.

"Nice haircut—you must've sprung some bucks for a professional," Mary Pat says when she arrives and finds Maggie waiting for her.

Hearing this, Maggie blushes bright red.

"Oops, touched a nerve," Mary Pat teases.

"I need some help with my clothes," Maggie blurts out.

"You've needed help with your clothes since you were born, and you've never given a damn what you looked like before—ever. Why now?"

"Because I'll be out there more...."

"Out where? Maggie, what are you talking about?"

"You know...more professionally involved..."

"Who are you going to be professionally involved with that gives a rat's ass what you look like? You're hiding something."

"Nothing to hide...honest," Maggie replies, a little too forcefully.

"One nice thing about living in an all-woman household is nobody cares how you look, so this is not something I've recently given any thought to myself. Why are you asking me for help?"

"Who else would I ask? You always looked put together in high school, and that ability doesn't just disappear," Maggie fires back.

"For starters, stop combining flowered shirts and plaid pants in one outfit. If you wear a print shirt, wear solid pants in a color that doesn't clash," Mary Pat offers.

"How do I know whether something clashes or not?"

"Whether it looks good with whatever else you're wearing...it's not rocket science, Maggie. Just common-sense stuff most girls figure out by third grade."

"We wore uniforms in third grade, and I've worn hand-me-downs and throw-aways my entire life. We were too damned poor for me to have any choices. After high school uniforms came the convent. I never saw a fashion magazine until I got my haircut last week. I just want something nicer than thrift store bargains, and better shoes, but I don't have money to pay for any of it." Frustration leaks from her voice.

"Do you want to tell me what this is really about?"

"I might, if I could, but I don't know myself. All I know is I want to look better."

"To go with your better haircut? You're practically menopausal, Maggie, and..."

"I am not," Maggie interrupts. "Not that it matters, but that's years away."

"Not as many years as you think. I had a hot flash just last week," Mary Pat shares. "Regardless, my point is all your life, you've gotten by fine not giving a shit about how you look. What happened to make you start caring now—you going nuts or something?"

"Can't you just stop with the questions like you're a homicide detective investigating a mob hit and help me figure this out?" Maggie pleads.

Mary Pat waits a while before answering. "I sew stuff for the kids and a few things for my sister and me—saves a lot of money. I suppose I could make you some things if you'll pay for the material."

"I'll also pay you to do it. It won't be as much as someone else could pay, but I don't expect you to do it for nothing." Maggie quickly adds.

"Any particular color?" Mary Pat asks.

"You decide," Maggie answers. "I don't know what the hell I'm doing... but something you think would look good on me and isn't purple."

"What's wrong with purple? I kind of like it."

"It might work for you. I was told it's not a good color for me—makes my freckles stand out like polka dots."

"Who told you that?"

"Suzi, who cut my hair."

"And is now your professional image consultant?"

Maggie ignores the dig and asks about shoes.

"Shoes are a personal decision. You'll have to figure that out yourself."

"Where can I get cheap ones that are more stylish?"

"Thrift stores are always the cheapest. Check every couple days and something will turn up eventually," Mary Pat advises. "The key to shopping at stores that specialize in used anything is you have to go every day if you want to get the good stuff before it disappears."

"Like I have time to do that? Why is finding a decent pair of shoes so damned complicated?" Maggie bristles.

"It isn't when you can pay for them. It's when you can't that everything gets more challenging," her friend reminds her.

They sit in silence for a few minutes, staring into their coffee cups and looking out the dirt-smeared window next to their table. Finally, Mary Pat asks Maggie if she's fallen in love.

"No way in hell," Maggie proclaims, blushing. "All I know about falling in love I've learned from listening to you carry on about Tommy, watching TV, and reading romance novels laying around the shelter, which are all pretty stupid. It's not something I'm interested in."

"That's what I thought...but stranger things have happened."

"Here's some money for some material," Maggie says, handing over twenty dollars.

"Thanks. I'll call you when I have something for you to try on, maybe in a couple of weeks."

"I need it by the next CWDC meeting," Maggie tells her friend.

"Why?" Mary Pat asks.

"I just do."

On her way back to the shelter, Maggie decides to take a detour into the downtown Loop and check out the make-up counter at Marshall Field's department store. Looking around after walking in the door, she realizes that, in comparison to the other shoppers, she would be all too easily mistaken for a homeless person. Fearing she'll be asked to leave, she quickly turns around and walks back out the door toward the nearest L that will take her back to more familiar surroundings.

•••

Less than two weeks later, Bridget Mary walks into Maggie's office, clears the papers off the vacant chair, and sits down.

"Didn't you get my note about stopping in to see me?" she asks.

"I did, and it completely slipped my mind," Maggie says. "I'm sorry. I hope it wasn't too important."

"It's very important. But you've been distracted for what seems like forever, and rather than insisting we talk, I thought it better to wait until you came to me. But this can't wait any longer."

"Whatever it is doesn't sound good."

"I don't know whether it's good or bad, but it's a potential problem for you. The Order is transferring me back to Omaha to head up a transitional housing program we established a few years ago that is expanding. It's an exciting opportunity in many ways, but I'm not keen on leaving and did try to talk my superior out of this...said I was needed here."

"And they turned you down," Maggie says, finishing the sentence because she sees her mentor's lower lip begin to quiver.

Bridget Mary takes a minute to compose herself before continuing. "My superior pointed out that I've been in Chicago nearly fifteen years, which is more than twice as long as we are supposed to stay anywhere, and she feels it is important to my spiritual life to move on to something else...to detach from work I've most likely become too attached to so I can refocus on my relationship with God. And she is right about that part—I'm very attached to what's happening here, and rarely, if ever, think about God."

"I'm really sorry...and I'm more than a little worried about how I'll manage without you," Maggie says.

"I thought about leaving the Order, but that wouldn't solve anything because I'd still have to leave the shelter, so there are no good options. My replacement will be arriving in less than a month. I'll stay to orient her to our operation, then will be on my way back to Omaha."

"Is Catherine staying? Hopefully?" Maggie asks.

"Catherine is coming with me. We're a team, and she goes where I go—no questions asked. I fought that battle a long time ago. I thought you knew."

"I suppose I did, but I was hoping she might be staying because someone has to run the educational programs, and her leaving means two new people coming in at the same time—a lot of change all at once."

"I doubt they'll send someone to replace Catherine. In fact, I'm sure they won't."

"Who are they sending to take over your position?"

"Someone you won't like and will find difficult to work with."

"You sound very sure about that," Maggie grimaces.

"I am. Sister Lillian Meyer's very experienced in organizational administration, but she's not from Chicago, she's not Irish, and she's not a weepy sentimentalist or an especially compassionate, empathetic person. She's a control freak who always thinks she's right and everyone else is wrong. She'll want to cultivate a relationship with the archdiocese, which for obvious reasons, I have avoided doing, and that will change things. She's one of the more humorless women I've ever met—all business and very little personal warmth. I can't see that she'll be a good fit here, but there's nothing I can do about it."

"Sounds like a laugh a minute! I can't wait to meet her," Maggie scowls, before asking about the future of the wide array of educational and skill-building programs they currently offer.

"You're not going to like this, but I'm going to recommend you take over the educational piece, in addition to pursuing funding sources."

"So...two full-time jobs?" Maggie asks.

"Basically, yes. At least for a while."

"What about the CWDC effort?" Maggie asks.

"Lillian's a stick-in-the-mud traditionalist, especially where the Church is concerned, and won't embrace it. The more important question is how much she will resist it, and I think she will, which brings me to discussing where this change leaves you."

"Obviously, I'd like to stay on and keep working on funding."

"I hoped you'd say that. But Lillian will never agree to the arrangement we currently have, with you living here for free and putting your salary into backing CWDC efforts. She'll ask for room and board, and certainly won't agree to any CWDC work happening on her watch. She's a bean counter, so no using our telephone, address, copy paper, et cetera—and certainly no work time spent on CWDC. She might go as far as to object to shelter staff—meaning you—being part of the effort."

"But she'd have to find out first," Maggie points out.

"That's true...and sooner or later, she will. My suggestion is that if you want to continue the CWDC initiative..."

"Of course I do," Maggie interrupts. "It's the reason I get out of bed in the morning."

"Then I suggest you find somewhere else to live and figure out some other way to fund CWDC. If you're not living here, Lillian will have much less opportunity to pay attention to what you're doing. You can treat this as a nine-to-five and use the rest of your time for your own interests."

"Will that work?"

"For a while. She needs you too much to raise a big fuss about anything, at least in the beginning, so you'll have some time to figure out how to get around her."

Maggie grins at this idea.

"Your immediate problem, as I see it," Bridget Mary continues, "is finding an apartment you can afford on your salary."

Frowning, Maggie nods.

"I want to talk about CWDC a little more," Bridget Mary says.

Maggie takes out a pencil and paper, then gestures for her to continue.

"It's pretty obvious the idea has legs, so you should put an organizational structure in place as soon as possible. Discuss this at the next meeting and set a date to elect officers and a founding board of directors whose primary goal is to raise money and focus the effort. Make it a 'Be the Change You Want to See Happen' initiative that teaches not just Catholic women to be change agents in their own lives, but also models it. Be as strong and aggressive as necessary to get what you want. And apply for tax-exempt status as soon as possible, so donations are tax-deductible."

"Do you know how to do that?" Maggie asks.

"Not really, but you can figure it out. You should expect the archdiocese won't like it, but you can cross that bridge later."

"Or sooner, if our spy, whoever it is, reports this back to the cardinal."

"I've been thinking about that," Bridget Mary smiles, "and my guess is whoever this person is might be more sympathetic to what we're trying to do than she, or he, would openly admit, and might be fairly selective about what information gets passed along."

"I hope you're right," Maggie says, looking doubtful.

"The other thing to do immediately is get a post office box for the CWDC mail. We don't get much yet, but that's bound to change, and no point in just handing Sister Lillian information she isn't looking for the minute she steps in as new director."

Maggie agrees and writes herself a note to take care of this immediately. She asks about telephone calls.

"You'll have to put the word out to call you evenings at your apartment phone number," Bridget Mary instructs.

"I'll start working on all this right away...I guess the good news is we're meeting somewhere else now, which makes staying under the radar easier," Maggie assures her.

"Now that these details are settled, I want to ask you why you've been so distracted recently, and why the new haircut and daily trip to Saint Vinnie's?"

"How do you know I go to Saint Vinnie's every day?" Maggie asks, trying not to look shocked that this is common knowledge.

"Because Catherine goes nearly every day searching for bargains for our women, and more often than not, she sees you there."

Seeing no point in denying this, Maggie remains silent.

"If I didn't know better, I'd say you're acting like a lovesick teenager... but you're not a teenager, and I don't know who the hell you'd fall in love with around here. Still, if you want to talk about it, you know where to find me," Bridget Mary smiles, standing to leave.

As she walks away, tears come to Maggie's eyes. "I'm really going to miss you," she whispers, not yet realizing the enormity of the changes that are about to occur.

•••

Finding a furnished apartment she can afford proves far more difficult than Maggie imagined. While the Back of the Yards isn't somewhere she wants to return to, her finances force her to consider the possibility, and she places a call to her cousin, Bridie, who still lives in the area, to ask about options. She knows she needs a quick explanation for why she is looking for an apartment, and that the fact that she is doing it will get back to Tommy and her sisters.

"What happen? They kick you outta that shelter you was living in?" Bridie asks.

"This is only temporary while the shelter gets some badly needed repairs," Maggie lies.

Bridie says she knows of a couple of possibilities. After looking at two dismal basement options Bridie suggests and she can't afford, Maggie rents the two rooms above the bar Bridie's husband, Kevin, owns.

Located on the corner of west 47th and South Princeton, which parallels the Dan Ryan expressway, Kevin's bar is within walking distance of Chicago's Robert Taylor housing project, which is the source of most of its regular clientele. It's a dangerous neighborhood, and Maggie hopes Kevin, a typical local Irish thug who, in addition to owning the building and the business, tends bar and flips burgers six nights a week, will put the word out not to bother the nun living upstairs.

Bridie insists the apartment meets code, but Maggie doesn't believe her. The bottom half of the fire escape is missing, and her only emergency exit is down the back stairs through the bar and out the side door opening into the alley, which is also the apartment entrance. She makes a mental note to ask for a dead-bolt lock on the downstairs door that leads directly into the bar.

The smaller of the two rooms contains a single metal-frame bed with a thin, stained mattress, a nightstand, and a wardrobe that only opens halfway before hitting the foot of the bed. A threadbare couch with grimy cushions splitting at the seams, and a cracked Formica kitchen table with two chairs occupy the other room. A hot plate sits on a small countertop, and a refrigerator stands in the corner across from the bathroom, which lacks a door. The smell from the rust-streaked toilet, moldy shower, and the only sink in the apartment, floats into the kitchen and living area. A decaying mouse is caught in a trap beside the toilet, and Maggie sees abundant evidence of several more, with plenty of cockroaches to keep them company. The water stains on the ceiling indicate the roof leaks, and the walls still have their original coat of dusty pink paint.

Bridie says the apartment has towels, bedsheets, cooking utensils, and dishes. She agrees to have Kevin pry open the windows and air the place out before Maggie moves in. Seeing that the screens are ripped, which accounts for the hundreds of dead flies on the floor, Maggie wonders which is the lesser evil: the flies or the greasy fried food and stale alcohol smells drifting up from the bar below.

"Who lived here last?" Maggie asks, wondering whether it doubles as a flophouse for drunks evicted from Robert Taylor.

"Nobody who paid rent. Kevin uses it when we have a fight and I kick him out," Bridie explains unapologetically.

Maggie starts to ask where Kevin will go if Bridie kicks him out while she's living in the apartment. But since she can't afford anyplace else and still have money left to seed CWDC, she decides not to raise the issue.

Standing in the nearly empty front room, Bridie offers to find a couple of rugs, and maybe a lamp. Maggie tells her that what she needs most is a desk, and a small table will do fine. Bridie assures her that there are some extra tables and chairs in the basement, and she'll tell Kevin to bring up one of each.

If nothing else, Maggie decides, her new apartment is strong motivation to find some way to increase her salary enough to move out as soon as possible. Meanwhile, she'll bring her clothes and a few books over and have a telephone installed. Before leaving, Bridie tells her to help herself to the cleaning supplies in the janitor's closet beside the men's bathroom downstairs in the back of the bar.

After spending a couple of hours cleaning her new apartment with a rank-smelling mop and dirty rags, Maggie looks around, takes a deep breath, and decides it's as good as it's going to get. She puts on her coat, locks the door, and starts walking toward the L station. With the wind at her back, she wraps her coat tightly around herself and pulls her cap down over her ears, trying to hide from the unhappiness she feels over her new situation. She has been forced into coming full circle—back to the kind of neighborhood she came from and resolved never to return to. She is once again trapped in living conditions at least as bad as the ones she left to enter the convent thirty years ago.

This is nothing I haven't experienced before, but its damned sad that, other than a convent, the nicest place I've ever lived in my life is an unfinished apartment in a homeless women's shelter, she thinks.

•••

A few days later, Maggie picks up two new dresses and a blazer Mary Pat has sewn for her. After trying them on and profusely thanking Mary Pat for her efforts, she tells her about her new apartment.

"Sounds worse than this," Mary Pat comments, gesturing toward the messy, overcrowded apartment in Cabrini Green.

"This is a luxury hotel by comparison," Maggie says.

"Why are you doing it, Maggie? Living in a rotten neighborhood, in two stinking rooms that aren't fit for human habitation. You could go to a convent someplace. I'm sure there are several in the city that would agree to have you."

"I wouldn't be able to maintain my CWDC efforts unnoticed, and I can't give that up—plain and simple. I'd leave the Order before I'd abandon that effort."

"CWDC means so much to you that you're willing to live in a hell-hole in one of the most dangerous neighborhoods in the city, with as many knives and guns as people and half a block from the busiest expressway in Illinois?"

"It definitely means that much to me."

"Does your Order know about this?"

"I doubt it. Mother Marie William rules with a much lighter hand than Mother Michael Joan did. I haven't been back to the motherhouse for the annual retreat since coming to Chicago over twenty years ago, and she's never said anything about it. As long as I submit my expense sheet every month, no one asks any questions. And I can keep getting Order mail at the shelter, so I don't see any need for them to know I'm moving."

"You've got enough experience under your belt that you could probably support yourself outside religious life. Do you ever think about leaving it behind?"

"Never," Maggie answers.

Mary Pat looks at her quizzically.

"I don't lead a religious life...I'm not even sure how worthwhile a religious life is. I don't pray regularly or go to Mass, because I can't stand watching some prissy priest prancing around the altar acting like he's God's personal mouthpiece, which grants him the right to tell everyone what God wants them to do. And the body and blood of Christ served up as Holy Communion is a cannibalistic ritual I can't bring myself to participate in any more. Whoever thought that up should've been shot. Offering the bread of life and wine of salvation would be so much gentler and more meaningful, but I'm sure gentle isn't in the patriarchal vocabulary. Every time I go to Mass, I leave angry because the whole experience is an exercise in unchecked male power, and I don't see any point in reminding myself of that."

"If that's how you feel, staying in the Church is disingenuous," Mary Pat points out.

"My vows give me credibility—power of my own. If Sister Maggie Corrigan tells a Catholic woman at the shelter that she can make her own decisions about practicing birth control, that woman is much more likely to listen, and perhaps follow the advice, than she would be if she hears from a once-a-week volunteer she rarely sees. That alone makes the vows very important to me. They are the key to my efforts to make change happen. Besides, they're not a big deal. I've been poor all my life, chastity isn't a problem, and obedience, at least so far, hasn't been difficult to manage."

"I think chastity is a very big deal," Mary Pat reflects.

"As concerns relationships with men, maybe, but the sisterhood is full of women who have 'forbidden friendships' with each other, which in reality are impossible to forbid, so nobody says anything. Technically, you and I shouldn't be friends—it takes me away from focusing on my relationship with God, whatever that's supposed to mean."

"You sound so cynical, Maggie, like you don't believe in anything anymore."

"I don't know what I believe...but whatever it is, it has relatively little to do with God—whoever He, or She is—and everything to do with trying to make people's lives better. And I know I have a better chance at doing that by remaining a nun."

"There's also the safety net, which is what I miss most of all," says Mary Pat. "As long as I was in the Order, I knew that one way or another, I'd be taken care of. Now things are fine as long as I'm here with my sister, but if something happens, she can't take care of me. My parents disowned me for leaving and are mad at Sheilah for helping me out. I have no resources to take care of myself, which is a little frightening."

"It's true that I'm probably getting more from religious life than I'm giving to it," Maggie admits. "But nothing has come along to seriously tempt me to break my vows or leave the Order."

"Nothing?"

"Why are you asking?"

"Just wondering," the former nun replies, "because you've started plucking your eyebrows."

XVI.

I'm no longer accepting the things I cannot change—I'm changing the things I cannot accept.

Angela Davis

Six weeks later, two hundred women, and a few more men than previously, fill Our Daily Bread's upstairs meeting space on the bitterly cold night of the first CWDC meeting at the new location. The heavy wind whipping sleet off Lake Michigan is rarely sufficient to keep Chicagoans home when they want to go somewhere, and tonight is no exception.

"These folks must be pretty serious about this issue to be here on a night like this," Ben remarks to Maggie as the hall nears capacity.

She smiles and tells him she hopes he's correct; otherwise, the cardinal has sent a lot of spies.

"Signal when you want me to plug in the coffee pot downstairs," he tells her. Wearing a black turtleneck sweater that emphasizes his broad shoulders, and tight, well-worn Levi's that give him a slightly rakish appearance, he's too handsome for Maggie to look at without risking a bright-red blush.

"You're staying?" she asks, staring at the floor.

"Well, you don't have a key to lock up, so yes, I'm staying. Truthfully, I'm curious about what you're trying to pull off here and want to hear what you have to say about how you're going to force change down the steel reinforced, concrete throat of Holy Mother Church. I hope you don't mind." He smiles.

"Of course not." Maggie answers, feeling herself grow warm.

A few minutes later, Maggie calls the meeting to order. The announcements include Sister Bridget Mary's departure, their new mailing address and phone number, and the reminder that they will be meeting at this location for the foreseeable future. The agenda focuses on the need to establish an organizational structure and deal with financial concerns.

After assuring the group she is remaining as "executive director," Maggie asks for volunteers to serve as officers and for three people willing to lead fundraising, action, and publicity committees. These individuals, in addition to the officers, will comprise the advisory board. Maggie is surprised that several of the volunteers are women identifying themselves as belonging to various religious orders serving Chicago, and isn't sure whether this is good or bad, but assumes they can't all be archdiocesan informants. She is thrilled Mary Pat is among those who step up to lead.

"Our first organizational task is to file our bylaws as a nonprofit, including the names of our officers, with the state of Illinois. This allows us to obtain tax-exempt status, which will make fundraising much easier because donations will be tax-deductible," Maggie explains, adding that this also means she needs a committee to draft a governing document.

"We're in dire financial straits, so my suggestion is we draft some simple, generic bylaws and file them, so we can become tax-exempt and start soliciting donations as soon as possible. We can hammer out the details later. If anyone disagrees, please speak up now. If there are no objections that can't be settled tonight, I'll move ahead with this."

One person in the back of the room asks about whether the archdiocese will object to formalizing the organization and raising money.

"I'm sure it will," Maggie says. "But we knew the cardinal would blow a strong headwind our way as soon as he figured out how serious we are about what we are trying to do. We can't let this stop us—we'll just deal with it when it happens."

Hearing no other concerns, she explains that she's going to pass around a sign-up sheet for individuals to indicate which of the three committees they'd like to join and would welcome help in drafting the temporary bylaws if anyone has any experience with this. No one raises their hand, so Maggie indicates she'll figure it out herself.

"There's one final matter before we break for coffee, then reconvene in working groups for a few minutes," Maggie announces, nodding toward Ben.

He smiles and signals he's already taken care of the coffee.

"I would like to open a bank account for the organization, so in a few minutes, I'm going to pass the hat. I realize we haven't done this previously, but a lot has changed in the past month, and we need to formalize the finances starting now, so I'm asking that you contribute as much as you can. After we cover the rent for tonight's meeting, the rest will go into the account, which will require two signatures for withdrawals, and the board will review monthly. Meanwhile, grab some coffee while our new leadership team sets up smaller circles for the individual groups. Fundraising will be in the front, publicity in the middle, and action in the back."

Maggie is very gratified when, twenty minutes later, she sees that by far the largest group is the action committee—individuals willing to put themselves on the line for the change they want to see happen. She notes that Mary Pat has chosen this group, and toward the end of the half-hour set aside for the group meetings, Mary Pat signals she wants to speak with Maggie. The two walk over to a corner of the room.

"Nice jacket. Fits you well and looks good with that shirt," Mary Pat smiles.

"That's not why you want to talk to me," Maggie whispers, feeling like she's been busted for something.

"I want to give you a heads up that the overwhelming consensus of the action group is to hit the ground running by acting as safety partners at women's health clinics that perform abortions and where anti-abortion protesters often show up to try to block the entrances. The group feels that being the change they want to see means putting themselves out on the front lines and showing women what bravery and standing up to opposition means."

Hearing this, Maggie smiles broadly and asks whether any are vowed religious.

"I'm pretty sure there are, but without habits, it's hard to tell. I might figure it out eventually, but I'm not intending to ask. What we would like to do is meet again in two weeks and bring a list of all the clinics in Chicago and surrounding areas. Once we have that information, we'll decide who goes where. Can we use this space again?"

"It's probably okay, but I need to check, which I'll do right now."

Maggie finds Ben in the kitchen, sleeves pushed up to reveal muscular forearms while he washes out the coffee pots.

"Any chance one of the working groups can meet here again in two weeks?" she asks.

He nods.

"I'm sure there was enough in tonight's collection to pay, but if not, can we run a tab?"

"Of course," he smiles. "And if you have a few minutes after the meeting breaks up, I have a couple of things I'd like to talk with you about."

Maggie says this is fine, and feels herself blush bright red. She stops by the restroom to splash water on her face before going back upstairs to tell Mary Pat that meeting in two weeks is fine.

"Why are you looking like that?" Mary Pat asks

"Like what?"

"I don't know...like you're happy or something? It just isn't you."

Maggie walks away without comment.

After chatting briefly with the leaders of the fundraising and publicity groups, Maggie finds Ben in his office. He gestures for her to sit down.

"I guess a lot of things have changed since we last talked," he begins.

Maggie nods her head.

"Are you upset about it?"

"About Bridget Mary leaving and me moving out of the shelter? I'm not happy about it, but I don't have much choice if I'm going to keep doing what I'm doing."

"Where are you going to live?"

Maggie tells him.

"That's a bad area. Are you sure you can't do better?"

"It's just like where I grew up—I can handle it," she answers.

"I'm sure you can, but since I know nothing about your early life, I would have no way of knowing that," he continues.

"It's not something I like talking about," she says, feeling a familiar anger rise in her. *How the hell can I explain that the illegitimate, biracial son of an immigrant from the Dominican Republic had it a whole lot better than a shanty Irish-Catholic girl from South Side Chicago?* she wonders. Then she remembers Ben had a loving mother who could care for one child and didn't die in childbirth, leaving five younger siblings to steal his childhood from him. His father wasn't an angry drunk who couldn't provide for his family, and he wasn't trapped in a Catholic culture that told its followers to go forth and multiply, no matter the personal and family cost. Compared to hers, Ben's childhood was the stuff of dreams.

"You did a great job with the meeting, and if you need help drafting the bylaws, you know where to find me," Ben says, changing the subject after sensing Maggie's not going to tell him more.

"Thanks. I better get going." She stands to leave.

"It's late, and you don't live in the safest neighborhood," Ben tells her. "Let me give you a ride back to your apartment."

Maggie refuses.

"Then at least let me give you a can of pepper spray. I keep a couple in my desk that, fortunately so far, I've not had to use," he says, as he opens a drawer and hands her a small aerosol can.

"Thanks...but it's really not necessary. I can take care of myself."

"No doubt about that, but you're afraid of something. I hope it's not me, because I'm not going to hurt you."

"It's not you...."

•••

A few days later, Maggie is struggling with a shelter funding application deadline when her phone rings. The caller identifies herself as Marcia Morgan in the Cook County District Attorney's office, adding that it's been a long time and she hopes Maggie remembers her.

Maggie says she does, and that this can't be a good news call.

"Do you remember a shelter client, Eulalia Banks?" Marcia asks.

"I never forget any of my failures. She was making good progress then decided to leave us when she learned her ex was being released from prison and she thought the kids needed their father. There was no talking her out of it, and I never heard from her again."

"She's facing murder charges."

"What the hell?"

"She allowed Jamal back into her life, and they ended up in East Moline," Marcia explains. "Jamal signed on with a barge company that hauls up and down the Mississippi River. Eulalia got work in one of the chemical manufacturing plants nearby. Then she got pregnant and had an abortion without telling Jamal. When he found out, he went berserk and started beating on her. The oldest daughter, Jada, saw what was happening and shot him."

"Seriously, Jada shot him? How the hell...?"

"It seems that a few days earlier, Eulalia became suspicious Jamal was having his way with Jada, or about to try, and gave her a loaded gun. Told her to shoot him if he ever came near her. When he took off on Eulalia, the girl didn't know how else to stop him and went for the gun."

"Did she kill him?"

"Almost. Got him in the crotch."

Maggie laughs out loud.

"I know—it seems like poetic justice, but it's still illegal. Due to her age, Jada's case went to juvenile, and with no priors and decent grades in school, she was given probation without jumping through a lot of legal hoops. Eulalia's situation is different. The pro-life Rock Island County DA, who's being influenced by an anti-abortion group that is a significant voting bloc in his area, had to charge her with something so he could hold her and settled on accessory to unintentional attempted homocide."

"That sounds like something he made up. How can somebody be an accessory to something somebody else didn't intend to do?"

"You're right. It's a stretch, but he's under stiff pressure to charge her with murder because she had an abortion, even though abortion is legal. Right now, he's just throwing pots of spaghetti at the wall and waiting to see what sticks."

"All this for trying to protect her daughter?"

"Basically. I think it'll be pretty hard to make serious charges against Eulalia stick, but she can't make bail so will remain in jail until a trial, where she'll probably be found guilty on a lesser charge. The bigger issue is that Jamal's suing to terminate her parental rights because getting an abortion means she murdered one of their children. He's calling her a baby killer and an unfit mother."

"Fuck—you've got to be kidding me," Maggie yells into the phone.

"You know I'd never kid about something like this."

"I can understand Jamal being pissed off about getting shot in the balls, but where the hell did he get the money to hire a lawyer to do something like this?"

"He didn't. He's the front man for a test case being brought by some anti-abortion, pro-life Bible-thumpers out of Arkansas. They're footing the bill."

"Where did you say this happened?"

"East Moline—a small town located along the Mississippi River across from Iowa—no place I've ever heard of."

"Wow," Maggie exclaims, then asks about the other kids.

"They're in temporary foster care, so everybody has a roof over their heads at the moment," Marcia explains.

"Does she need bail money?"

"I'm sure she does, but it would be more than you can scratch up. Since abortion is legal, the local district attorney, who is sympathetic to the abortion is murder argument, is still trying to sort it all out. Eventually, he'll realize being an accessory to an unpremeditated act is too weak to fly legally, so he'll have to come up with something else."

"If juvenile determined it was a self-defense case and didn't push it with Jada, I don't see how he has any case at all," Maggie offers.

"Eulalia could probably be charged with child endangerment for giving a thirteen-year-old a gun, but she was also a victim in this situation, so that could be a tough sell. She doesn't have any priors, so my guess is she'll get probation eventually, but it's in the DA and the abortion-rights folks' best interest to drag out a decision as long as possible and drum up all the publicity they can. Regardless, the criminal outcome won't take away the termination case, which the folks who are funding it are determined to push forward. Look, I know this stinks worse than dead fish on a hot summer beach, but nevertheless, Eulalia has to deal with it."

"It's a trumped-up legal move to frighten women into believing if they get an abortion, they risk losing the children they already have."

"That's exactly what it is, and all it takes is one successful case to set legal precedence. I'm sure the pro-lifers have been looking for one for quite a while, and this is perfect because Eulalia is too poor to put up a fight."

"They have to be paying Jamal," Maggie says. "There's nothing in it for him otherwise."

"I'm sure they are, probably several thousand dollars."

"Termination of parental rights is what? Can't be a criminal matter."

"No, it's a civil case governed by state child protection laws. There's a hearing, and Jamal will have to prove it's in the children's best interests to be removed from Eulalia's care and remanded to his. Eulalia will have to counter that argument."

"That shouldn't be hard. Jamal's rap sheet could wallpaper the DA's office. He'd have to look pretty hard to find someone less fit to raise kids than Jamal Jones is."

"True. Jamal hasn't exactly been an exemplary father, and I'm sure he doesn't want custody of six daughters, but he's getting paid a lot of money to say he does. No question he'll very willingly send them right back to Eulalia and hightail it down the river on the next barge out of town as soon as he can walk."

"He can't walk?"

"Not very well. Apparently gunshot-inflicted testicular injuries are quite painful and take a long time to resolve," Marcia deadpans, stifling a giggle. "The other side's only goal is to get a legal decision on the books, so pro-life groups can use it as an abortion deterrent. They'll keep the sun shining on this case for as long as they can."

"And victimizing a mother and her children is immaterial," Maggie sighs, before asking how Marcia became involved in the case.

"Susan Ross, the Rock Island County Victim Services Coordinator, contacted me because Eulalia has been asking for you to help her out, and the request was forwarded to her office. We met previously at the Midwest Legal Services Conference. A nice person. She feels, and I agree, that pursuing this case is wrong and would like to see Eulalia fight it but realizes there are no resources available to her and asked for suggestions."

"Do you seriously think this will amount to something?" Maggie asks.

"It's hard for me to imagine it will, but I'm not familiar with the family court judges in Rock Island County, where this will play out, so I don't think it's a good idea to assume anything."

"What did you tell Ms. Ross?"

"This is why I'm calling—I want to run something past you. Do you have a few more minutes?"

Grabbing a pencil and paper, Maggie says she has plenty of time for a situation like this.

"My thought is that Eulalia is a victim of her life circumstances—poverty and all that entails—and she has always had her daughters' best interests at heart, which is why she gave Jada the gun and why she decided on an abortion. She did the only thing she knew how to do to protect the children already in her care, which included not increasing that burden by adding another child there was no money to provide for. This makes Eulalia a good mother. If a judge can be made to understand this, he—or she—might be more sympathetic toward her and less inclined to grant the termination. I know it's a stretch, but it might work."

"When's the termination hearing?" Maggie asks.

"Right now, it's in two weeks, but Eulalia has the right to ask for more time, which I have advised. A public defender is assigned to the case, and that office doesn't have the time or resources to mount a strong defense against charges like this, so she's definitely at the mercy of the court. The other issue is, not too surprisingly, the case has generated a lot of publicity, thanks to the group bankrolling Jamal."

"So they're trying to terminate her parental rights before she's been convicted of anything?"

"Not exactly. Legally, both things are moving forward at once, so—"

"Sneaky bastards," Maggie interrupts.

"True, but smart legal strategy. Termination is a complex process. First the case goes to an Illinois Department of Child Protective Services officer who looks at the evidence and makes a recommendation. Then the case goes before a judge and three-person panel who review the evidence and recommendations, hear from witnesses, then make their own recommendations. Ultimately, the judge has the final say. Some judges rubber-stamp the panel recommendations more often than others. It depends on the case, and there's no predicting the outcome. I've not been involved in a parental rights termination case for several years but I can say that most states take parental rights very seriously, and decisions either for or against are not made lightly."

"Eulalia is a decent person who never got any breaks in life. I'm sure she's beside herself," Maggie says.

"No question about that. And unfortunately, I can't be directly involved in this case, since it's outside Cook County. But I told the county victim services coordinator, who has only been in her position a couple of months, I'd be in touch with you to let you know what has happened. I also volunteered to help her find people who could get this figured out—which is where you come in."

"I'm listening...."

"As I see it, two things need to happen: Eulalia needs to be represented by someone other than a public defender—a lawyer with more experience. I'm not sure how to find that person, but I'm working on it—"

"Willie Preston who runs our legal services clinic would do it pro-bono. I can ask him," Maggie interrupts.

"He's on my list. Go ahead and approach him, and if he refuses to take the case, let me know."

"He won't."

"If you say so," Marcia chuckles.

"What's the other thing?"

"An expert witness who can educate the judge about what life in poverty means for a woman. This testimony would be very helpful in building the case I described, and—"

"There are a lot of people who know more about living in poverty than there is time left on the planet to describe it," Maggie interrupts, "but none of them are experts in the sense of being able to explain it in a courtroom. They're too busy struggling to survive for another day."

"Actually, I have someone in mind," Marcia says. "But I think it would be best if you make the contact."

"Why not have the person in East Moline make the contact?" Maggie asks.

"From what I know of this person, she would be more likely to listen to a request from someone like you—who wades into the muck of women's lives and tries to help them—than to pay attention to someone who dots 'i's and crosses 't's for the legal system."

"What do you want me to say to her?"

"Explain the situation and ask if she's willing to become involved as Eulalia's advocate—and do it for nothing. There's no money to pay her."

"Where did you find this person?"

"She was a speaker at a Southern Poverty Law Center seminar I attended a couple years ago in Atlanta. She sees poverty as a social justice issue...believes it's a political problem, not a personal failing, and that the whole sorry mess is the fault of a competitive, profit-motive economy that needs to maintain a poverty class to ensure the rich keep getting richer. In her mind, competitive, free-enterprise capitalism is the culprit...the big kahuna responsible for most of what's wrong with our society. She made a very compelling case, and I liked her."

"How do I find this person?"

"Her name is Dr. Gillian Spencer—Professor Spencer—and she directs a poverty initiative at Virginia Southern University near Richmond."

"Can't you suggest someone a little closer?"

"To qualify as an expert, you have to come from at least fifty miles away," Marcia retorts. "I'm sure there are others who are closer, but they'll cost money we don't have. I have a feeling Dr. Spencer might do this gratis because, after hearing what you have to say, she'll decide she believes in the case, especially if the explanation comes from you. Besides, she's familiar with the Midwest—she went to graduate school here."

"And if she won't do it?" Maggie asks.

"Then we'll figure something else out, but I'm not ready to cross that bridge yet. If you have a pencil handy, I'll give you her phone number."

"I haven't said I'll do it yet," Maggie points out.

"Then why have you been wasting my time?" Marcia asks.

•••

The next day, Maggie calls Dr. Spencer's office and leaves a message for her to return the call, hopefully that afternoon. While waiting, she sorts through a week's worth of mail scattered across her office desk and comes across a letter whose return address is Queen of Heaven, Tommy's parish.

Recently, she has had two messages to call him, and has ignored them. She debates whether to throw the letter away unopened and finally sets it aside to read later. She figures it has something to do with their father's death several weeks ago, which she learned about when her cousin, Bridie, came by to collect the apartment rent. Since she can't remember the last time she heard from, or talked to, anyone in her family, and no one bothered to let her know her father had died, Maggie decided this was a nonevent in her life best ignored and didn't attend the funeral Mass. *If they wanted me to be there, they would've called me,* she told herself.

Later that evening, while sitting at the kitchen table in her apartment, she takes Tommy's letter out of the envelope just as a cockroach skitters across the floor, which she finds ironic, given her feelings toward her twin brother.

Dear Maggie,

I wish you'd returned my phone calls so I could tell you this in person. I have been diagnosed with advanced liver disease and am told I don't have long to live. This problem usually takes longer to appear than it has in my case, which is probably due to the curse of the Irish alcoholism gene running through the family, and my failure to adopt a habit of moderation at a young age.

There are some financial matters I need to discuss with you sooner rather than later. I'm still able to drive, so could meet you somewhere for lunch. Whatever works for you is fine.

Please be in touch soon. You have my phone number.

Your brother, Tommy

•••

After reading the letter, Maggie folds it back into the envelope, raises her fist toward the ceiling, and curses at God, the universe, every saint she can think of, and her Irish heritage. She has always suspected Tommy drank in high school, but didn't know how much, and was unaware he had developed a severe drinking problem, which he has obviously had for a long time, and is common among priests. Nevertheless, the news surprises her. But what surprises her more is her reaction: it's as if she cares, which if asked, she would strongly deny.

"So goddamned much suffering...even I could have planned things better," Maggie concludes several minutes later, after shouting into the emptiness all around her, trying to drown out the noise from the bar below.

XVII.

Rules are made to be broken...or to hide behind.
Douglas MacArthur

"Holy Christ, Bridget Mary. That woman is going to demolish everything we've tried to accomplish. She's ruinous," Maggie hollers into the telephone.

The former shelter director, who has been in Omaha for nearly a month, has finally returned Maggie's call, which she placed several days ago, immediately following her first official meeting with Sister Lillian, Bridget Mary's successor at Holy Mother of Consolation Women's Shelter.

A tall, angular woman, Sister Lillian wears the modified habit of the Sisters of God's Mercy, which includes a partial head covering with a short veil covering most of her steel-gray hair, pulled tightly back from her pinched, bird-like face. A thin, black belt cinches the waist of the formless, mid-calf length, long-sleeved black dress with a detachable white collar. Low-heeled black shoes and a silver cross hanging midway between her neck and her waist, complete the look.

All business and no playful humor, Sister Lillian took over her responsibilities at the shelter the day Maggie received Tommy's letter. Intent on hitting the ground running, the new director immediately began meeting with staff to discuss the shelter operations and what she plans to change. The consensus of everyone who has met with her is that she might have adequate administrative skills, but is intolerant of weakness, has little patience with the women who come to the shelter desperate for help, and is poorly suited to the kind of work they are trying to do, which requires copious amounts of the open-hearted compassion she clearly lacks.

Her contentious meeting with Maggie began on a sour note after Maggie called her by her first name and Sister Lillian insisted on being addressed formally. The tension between the two strong personalities held firm for the next two hours—ninety minutes longer than any of the other meetings with staff. They clashed continuously.

"She wants to hold fundraisers the women can organize and participate in—like bake sales, and holiday fairs, for God's sake. Says they would be esteem-building activities for the women, which might be true, but you tell me who the hell is going to come to a bake sale in this neighborhood, because I sure as shit can't think of anybody. We can't even get city sanitation workers to haul the trash away. And forget calling the cops for anything," Maggie fumes. "And you know what's the worst?"

"I'm sure you'll tell me," Bridget Mary answers, rolling her eyes at the thought of holding a bake sale in one of Chicago's most dangerous neighborhoods.

"She wants to establish a relationship with the archdiocese to open up a funding stream. Says she will assure the cardinal and head of Catholic Charities that the shelter's goal is to help women come to their senses and return to their husbands—keep the family together. This is exactly what we don't want to be doing, for Christ's sake. If we accept money from the archdiocese, we'll have to accept the strings that are attached, and we won't like them. You have to help me figure out how to stop this reign of terror."

"That won't be easy, Maggie. The Order decides who works where, and absent something egregious, like Lillian stealing money or becoming a raging alcoholic, there isn't much you can do about her. As I see it, you have two choices: figure out how to work around her or look for another job. And honestly, another job is probably the best option."

"I love it here," Maggie wails. "I've been here nearly twenty years and feel like this is where I belong, and I'll be damned if I let some holier-than-thou nun with the flexibility of a concrete bridge abutment run me off."

"That's the Maggie I know and love," Bridget Mary responds. "And I'm here any time you want to vent...I told you this wasn't going to be easy."

•••

A month later, partly out of defiance, and partly because she really doesn't want to do it, Maggie declines Sister Lillian's request to accompany her to a meeting with archdiocesan officials, including Monsignor Seamus O'Connor, the head of Chicago Catholic Charities.

"I'm sorry, Sister. I have a prior commitment I can't reschedule," Maggie lies. "But I'm looking forward to hearing about the meeting."

"That's very unfortunate, Sister. I'm sure Monsignor O'Connor would be quite interested in your insights regarding the challenges we face, as well as exploring possibilities for working with Catholic Charities in mutually beneficial ways."

He wouldn't want to hear one damned word I have to say, Maggie chuckles to herself.

Nearly three hours later, just as she has begun wondering why Sister Lillian has not returned, Maggie receives a phone call from Monsignor O'Connor's office, explaining that Sister Lillian failed to arrive for the meeting and asking if it needs to be rescheduled.

"I'm not sure what happened and will have to get back to you," Maggie says.

Another two hours pass before she receives a call from a clerk in the Cook County Hospital emergency department asking if she knows a Sister Lillian Meyer.

"She is the director of this women's shelter," Maggie tells the caller.

"Sister has had an accident and is being admitted to the hospital intensive care unit. Someone who can make decisions for her needs to come down here as soon as possible."

"I don't know who can make decisions on Sister Lillian's behalf, but I'll be right there," Maggie tells the clerk.

"Maybe you should bring a priest," the clerk says.

"What happened?" Maggie asks.

"My understanding is she slipped on the stairs at an L station and has a head injury."

"How bad?"

"I'm not supposed to give out those details, but last I heard, she's unresponsive at this time."

After Maggie arrives at the Cook County Hospital, she spends more than an hour wandering through the gigantic, rundown facility filled with frantic people chaotically rushing in all directions. Eventually, she locates a doctor she can discuss Sister Lillian's condition with and learns that there is concern about brain damage and paralysis.

"That's assuming she ever wakes up," the doctor says.

Hearing this, Maggie thanks the doctor and looks for a pay phone to place a collect call to Sister Lillian's superior at her Order's motherhouse in Omaha and inform her of the situation.

"Handle this however you feel appropriate, and keep me apprised of Sister's condition, but it sounds like the most important thing to do right now is to call a priest," Mother Francis, Sister Lillian's superior, instructs.

If she's as bad as it sounds, fat lot of good that will do, Maggie thinks, after hanging up the phone. She wanders the halls, looking for the nurses' station next to the ICU to request that the hospital's Catholic chaplain be called to administer the last rites to Sister Lillian.

Eventually, Maggie returns to the shelter, exhausted and unsure what she should do next. She begins rummaging around in her desk, looking for the phone number of the chair of the shelter board, who she reaches at home. After Maggie apologizes for the late hour and explains what has happened, the board chair tells her that she'll have to take over as temporary acting director immediately.

"I'll call an emergency meeting of the board to sort out how to proceed, but based upon what you've told me, Sister Lillian's recovery is unknown, so you should plan on assuming the directorship for the foreseeable future."

Maggie reluctantly agrees.

Several days later, Sister Lillian gradually begins to wake up. She is partially paralyzed and mentally confused. When a month goes by and there is no improvement, her doctor tells Maggie that she needs to arrange for placement in an extended care facility that works with brain-injured patients.

"I'm not sure how we can afford that," Mother Francis says when Maggie calls with the latest update.

"The sisters make their own health insurance arrangements through their employment, and we don't carry extended care health insurance for them."

"What have you done in the past when something like this has happened?" Maggie asks.

"The incapacitated sister lives here at the motherhouse and we care for her ourselves, but it sounds like Sister Lillian needs more than we can provide."

"You'll have to think of something, because the hospital wants to discharge her and I can't bring her back to the shelter."

"Not even temporarily, until we can get this sorted out?"

"She can't walk and doesn't know who she is, Mother. We can't handle a situation like that for five minutes, let alone days."

"Then I'll send a sister to Chicago to bring her back to Omaha."

"You better send at least three."

"Dear God!" the mother superior exclaims, hanging up the phone.

Meanwhile, the shelter board decides to request the Sisters of God's Mercy to appoint Maggie interim director for at least one year, until a suitable permanent director is identified. Maggie agrees to this plan and suggests the board, which includes several substantial shelter donors, take the unusual step of requesting input into the decision on the new director.

"I'm not sure that person should be me, but whoever it is should be familiar with how things work in Chicago," Maggie advises.

The next day she moves out of her apartment and back into the shelter's upstairs living quarters. *Sometimes God really does work in mysterious ways,* she thinks as she packs up Sister Lillian's personal effects.

•••

In her sixth week as interim shelter director, just as she is getting used to the abrupt change in her life, Maggie receives a call from Sister Margaret, the nursing director at Sacred Heart Hospital in Bridgeport, telling her that her brother, Monsignor Thomas Corrigan, is a patient there and is asking to see her. She had ignored her brother's letter, then decided that was too harsh, even toward Tommy, and she should listen to what he had to say. But with all that has been happening, she has been too busy to follow through. Aware that she can't put off seeing him any longer, Maggie agrees to come to the hospital right after lunch. Until Sister Margaret referred to her brother as Monsignor, she was not aware that he had been promoted. *A promotion of evil,* she thinks, slamming down the phone.

"I'm glad you finally decided to come," a jaundiced, emaciated Tommy Corrigan tells his sister when she arrives at his bedside in a sunny corner room at the end of a hallway reserved for patients who can afford to pay for private rooms. With a bloated abdomen, sunken eyes, and a jaundiced complexion resembling a ripe pumpkin, the priest is clearly very ill. His appearance shocks Maggie, but she does not reach out toward him. Instead, she pulls a chair closer to the bed and sits down.

"I'm sorry you're sick," she finally says, frowning at him.

"So am I, believe me."

"What do you want to talk to me about?"

"I'm leaving you my car and some money—enough money that, if you're careful, it'll last you."

"Where, exactly, did this money come from—the collection plate?"

"No, Maggie, I didn't steal it. The parish has always covered my living expenses, so a few years ago, I started investing part of my salary, plus the stipends people give me for weddings and funerals, and have done all right. If you don't go on a spending spree, you should be okay for the rest of your life."

"Our sisters need money more than I do, Tommy. Why not give it to them?"

"They have husbands and kids to look out for them, and you have nobody. Money can't fix that, but can help a lot, especially if you part ways with the Order at some point."

"Why would I do that?"

"Maybe you wouldn't go voluntarily, but given your views on the Church and the things you're involved in, you might be forced to leave."

"That's never seriously occurred to me," Maggie admits.

"Well, maybe it should," Tommy advises. "You're not supposed to accumulate property, and you vowed to give any inheritance or money you receive, to the Order. If they find out about this, they'll insist you turn it over, and you'll never see it again. You need to figure out some way to avoid that."

"I forgot about the inheritance rule. But I don't think keeping it a secret will be too hard. I'm rarely in touch with the motherhouse and don't live with other sisters in the Order."

"When I die, my obituary will appear in the paper, and my estate will be probated. I don't think you can assume no one will notice."

"They won't be expecting you to leave me money, Tommy. Priests aren't supposed to have enough of it to spread around. If any questions arise, I'm sure I'll figure something out. I'm more worried that Fiona and the others will ask questions—not that it matters. I can't remember the last time I spoke with any of them."

"Refer them to the lawyer who will be handling everything. He can deal with it. Just be sure you set it up with him so that when something eventually happens to you, it goes to them."

"How much are we talking about, Tommy?"

"A couple hundred grand—give or take. Not a fortune, but not chump change, either. And if you manage it right, it'll keep growing."

Exhausted from talking, Tommy falls silent, his eyes closed for several minutes, leaving Maggie to wonder where all this money he's talking about has really come from, because she is sure he's lying about how he accumulated it. Thinking he has fallen asleep, Maggie prepares to leave. Then her brother opens his eyes.

"One other thing, Maggie."

Hoping he wants to apologize to her for all that occurred in their family while they were growing up—things their drunken father should never have done to her, things Tommy could have protected her from when she was powerless to protect herself, and things *Tommy* should not have done to her either—she sits back down.

"I've had a lot of time to think since I found out my days are numbered, and I'd like you to ask Mary Pat to come to see me."

Maggie is taken aback by this request, and in an instant both anger and disappointment overtake her.

"How the hell should I know where Mary Pat is?"

"Don't give me that bullshit, Maggie. You could find her if you wanted to."

"You're right, Tommy, I could find her, but she might not want to be found by you."

"She deserves to make her own choice."

"What she deserves is for you to apologize for treating her like shit. If you're not prepared to do that, then you have no right to see her, and I'm not helping you do it. She doesn't owe you anything."

"When will you get over being angry at men, Maggie? We're not your enemy."

"Maybe not, Tommy, but in my experience, men think having a penis gives them complete dominion over women—to do with whatever they wish until they don't wish it anymore. It doesn't matter if that woman is their daughter, their sister, their high school girlfriend, or their wife—she's theirs to play with, regardless of how she feels about it...and sometimes it takes years for her to figure that out." Maggie begins choking up, which she does not want her brother to have the satisfaction of seeing, so she turns to leave.

"The money you're leaving me is payment for all you took from me, Tommy. Nothing more. I don't owe you anything. If you want to see Mary Pat, you'll have to find someone else to do your bidding," she says, rushing out of her brother's hospital room before he can see the tears running down her face.

Maggie rushes several blocks to the L, takes the first train that arrives, and rides it all the way to the end of the line before turning around and heading back in the other direction, toward the shelter. Using the long ride to gather herself together, she decides not to tell Mary Pat about Tommy's request. His former girlfriend is not that hard to find, and if he's serious about wanting to see her, he'll find a way to do it on his own. If, as Maggie strongly suspects, he wants to see her for the wrong reasons—reasons that would further hurt her best friend, who her brother has already hurt very badly—then she wants no part of it.

The other thing she thinks about is her views toward men. She wonders whether there is some truth to the notion of forgiveness, which she has never been a big fan of, because she feels unforgiveness is a protective shield for a woman who has been badly hurt. She knows the Church claims forgiveness is something victims do for themselves—an unburdening so they can move on with their lives—and has nothing to do with the person who has harmed them, but Maggie doesn't see it that way. To her, forgiving someone relieves the person who has inflicted the harm of the burden of guilt, and sometimes that's the only power a victim has over her abuser. She sees no reason she should forgive Tommy, because doing so would involve letting go of the anger that fuels her passion for change. This could allow him to conclude that what he did to her was acceptable because, like all sins, it is forgivable.

"Why am I even thinking about this? It's not like Tommy or my father ever asked for forgiveness nor can they hurt me anymore. One is already dead, and the other one will be dead soon enough, so it's not a conversation that is going to happen anyway," she mumbles to herself as she watches the city skyline fly by through the years of grime covering the commuter train window.

An hour later, on the way back to the shelter from the L station, Maggie is suddenly feeling more lighthearted than she has in a very long time. She decides to stop in at Our Daily Bread to see if Ben is around, so she can fill him in on all that has transpired recently. She finds him in his office, feet on his desk, reading last Sunday's *Chicago Tribune*.

"This is a pleasant surprise," Ben says, standing up and smiling. He's wearing the same black turtleneck he was wearing the last time she saw him, which further encourages his strong resemblance to Harry Belafonte.

"If you're not busy, I have a couple of things to fill you in on," Maggie smiles back, happier to see him than she expected to be, and very slightly less self-conscious.

"Let's go downstairs and talk over coffee and cookies. We have some homemade ones left from last night's AA meeting—they're very good."

Maggie stands in the kitchen, watching Ben make a fresh pot of coffee. He hands her a tin and tells her to put some cookies on a plate and take two napkins out of the drawer. She follows him into the eating area and sits down across from him as he puts a mug of steaming coffee in front of her.

"Black, if I remember correctly."

She nods, suddenly tongue-tied.

"It's been what—a month or more since I've seen you? Why the unexpected visit?" Ben asks.

"I hardly know where to begin...I guess the biggest news is that I'm now the interim shelter director, so I've moved out of that hell-hole apartment back into the shelter living quarters."

Ben asks what changed so fast, and she explains about Sister Lillian's accident.

"Honestly, she was a nightmare at every turn, Ben. I didn't know what to do. I feel like her misfortune is God's way of solving the problem and opening the door for me—telling me that I'm on the right path."

"One thing I learned in AA is to never assume we know the mind of God," Ben replies evenly. "The best we can do is merely our very best. Sometimes things break our way, and sometimes they don't. Neither situation is necessarily the hand of God—it's just as likely to be a result of the accidental universe at work."

Holding her coffee mug in both hands, Maggie doesn't respond.

"I don't mean to deflate you, Maggie, honestly. The important thing is to keep trying and not to give up...focus on what we can do ourselves and not spend a lot of time trying to figure out where God fits into anything, because even He can't micromanage several billion people's lives every day. It's mostly a shit-happens world, and you just have to hope you can deal with the mess when it lands on you."

Maggie remains quiet.

"Sorry, I didn't mean to preach or to take away from what you're feeling. It's just that you should take credit for the good things that come your way. Isn't that the core CWDC message—women are worthy of good things and capable of making good decisions?"

"In other words, take my own advice?" Maggie says, biting into a large chocolate chip cookie.

"Wouldn't hurt," Ben smiles, pouring them each more coffee.

"This change will be a big help with the CWDC efforts. If we can keep meeting here, I can use the shelter attic for extras—workspace for programming materials and smaller meetings. It just makes everything much simpler."

"How likely will it be that you become the permanent shelter director?"

"I have no idea and haven't even thought about it, because the final decision is up to the Sisters of God's Mercy. I expect they'll want one of their own in charge since it's their outreach effort, and they've always provided resources to help support it."

"Would you take it if it was offered to you?"

"Offhand, I think I would. I love it there, and the work means a lot to me."

"Then if I were you, I'd let that be known. Otherwise, they might not think you're interested."

"I hadn't considered that, but thanks," Maggie smiles.

"There's something else I want to say," Maggie continues. "I really appreciate everything you've done to help during all the upheaval. I'll never be able to repay you for all the good advice you've offered and want you to know it has meant a lot."

"If you seriously want to repay me, how about agreeing to help me repaint this place, beginning with picking out a more suitable color?"

"You've got to be joking. You want me to help select a good wall color when most days I can't even match up my clothes? No one in the world is worse at decorating decisions than I am. If you'd ever seen my office, you'd know that."

"I admit that when we first met your wardrobe choices were a little... unusual, I guess is the best description. But since then, you've definitely improved." Ben smiles. "And it's just a wall color. I'm not asking you to pick out my neckties."

Maggie blushes. "I guess I can try...and I'll definitely help paint. It can't be that hard."

"It's actually kind of soothing," Ben says. "How about we go paint shopping next Saturday afternoon if you have some time. We can do lunch and then choose a few paint samples to slop on the walls before making our final decision."

"It'll be a new experience," Maggie laughs.

"This is the first time I've ever heard you laugh, Maggie. You're much more light-hearted than I've ever seen you. It can't all be what's happened with the shelter. Something deep within you has shifted."

"Perhaps...but I better get back to the shelter before they fire me. Unless something comes up, I'll be here just before noon Saturday."

"I'm looking forward to it," Ben smiles, reaching for Maggie's hand then quickly pulling back.

"So am I...."

Walking back to the shelter, Maggie reflects on Ben's remark that something deep inside her has shifted. *Perhaps this is true,* she thinks. *The shelter is back on the right track, CWDC is moving forward, and this money I'm inheriting is going to open doors in my life that have always been nailed shut. Maybe it won't be all drudgery and struggling to survive...maybe there will finally be space in my life to actually be happy about something.*

•••

"For God's sake, Maggie—why the hell are you asking me what someone wears to go pick out paint? It's a shopping trip to a hardware store, not the Christmas Ball at the Palmer House," Mary Pat bellows when Maggie calls for another round of fashion advice. "Wear work clothes—jeans and a sweatshirt."

"But we're having lunch first."

"Who's having lunch first?"

"Just me...and a friend of mine, sort of."

"Must be a damned important friend if you're worried about what to wear. I hope someday you'll tell me the truth about what's going on with you, because you're acting like you've had a brain transplant or something."

"Here's a truth you'll be interested in: Silvia Bernstein, the Chicago coordinator of the Women's National Alliance, returned my call, saying she's very interested in exploring possibilities for teaming up with CWDC. She sounded quite enthusiastic. We're going to stay in touch and follow up."

"Nice change of subject, Maggie. The WNA is a nationwide group, and connecting with them does sound promising. It's good you decided to pursue it. I'd love to discuss all this more, but that screaming you hear is the kids fighting, and I have to break it up before somebody gets thrown out a window. Good luck with the paint. If it's a room you'll be spending a lot of time in, avoid purple—it looks good on a sample but doesn't flatter your freckles."

XVIII.

Poor women rarely succeed at finding good legal or other options available to them. In some states they do not receive very good legal representation and present themselves as a big risk for reoffending.
Retired Wisconsin Supreme Court Justice Janine Geske

When I answer my office phone, identifying myself as Professor Gillian Spencer, a loud, raspy voice lambasts me for not returning her calls, saying she has been trying to reach me about a legal case in Illinois she needs my help with. I ask who is calling.

"Sister Maggie Corrigan, from Chicago. Who else would it be?" the voice bellows back at me.

"If I knew who was calling, I wouldn't have asked, Sister. I always want to know who I am speaking with before continuing a conversation..." She interrupts to tell me to call her Maggie. I don't respond to that invitation or tell her the reason I haven't returned her calls is because, although her name is familiar, I can't remember where I've heard it or in what context, and I wanted to figure that out before talking with her. But before I can apologize for not getting back to her, she skips over the ordinary social niceties—how am I, how glad she is to finally reach me, or whether I have the time to talk—and starts right in with explaining her reason for calling.

"The problem is that since Eulalia is in jail and has no resources, she can't advocate for herself. So we have to find someone to do that for her, and your name came up," Maggie concludes five minutes later.

When I ask who referred her to me, she claims she can't remember. We're not off to a good start.

"The other problem is we can't pay you. You'll have to agree to do this because you believe in the case," Maggie continues, sounding precisely like every other nun I've known who plays the "it's the right thing to do" card when they want something from you and don't want to pay for it.

When I don't respond, she dangles the "this case has already received a lot of publicity, so you'll get some notoriety out of it," carrot in front of me. I explain that I'm an academic poverty researcher and don't seek notoriety. Plus, my university frowns on faculty getting involved in high-profile legal cases.

"I admit Eulalia's situation intrigues me," I say, "but I have several questions, beginning with why anyone thinks Jamal Jones is capable of being a good father and could win a termination battle against what sounds like a sincere, capable mother."

"Who knows...he has a longer rap sheet than the sports section of the Sunday *Chicago Tribune*, but none are for domestics—"

"Because Eulalia was ashamed, afraid to report him and risk retaliation, and she knew law enforcement wouldn't back her anyway," I interrupt.

"Exactly," Maggie affirms. "Eulalia's a good mother and has a lot of common sense. Her blind spot is Jamal. She can't seem to extricate herself from that relationship, even though she knows it's bad for her. It's like she's addicted to him."

"She probably is," I explain. "Whatever it is she gets from the relationship, which is hard for us to imagine, outweighs the bad which, to us, is enormous. I expect she sincerely believes he loves her and excuses everything else, which is pretty typical of emotionally worn down, generationally poor women. It's an 'any port in a storm' situation, because they don't believe they have other options."

"We're thinking that if you can explain to the judge and hearing panel that Eulalia and her children are victims of lifetime poverty, and she sought an abortion because she knew she couldn't care for another child without further jeopardizing the futures of the children she is already responsible for, she has a much better chance of things going her way. Because he's done it before, she knew Jamal would beat the crap out of her if he found out she was pregnant. She knew she needed her job because Jamal only works when he feels like it, which isn't very often, so hers is the only steady income they have. And she knew she was stiffing the welfare system by letting Jamal live with her, and if welfare found out, her benefits would have been cut, and she'd have been charged with fraud. She was in a no-win situation from all sides. The solution she figured out was based upon trying to care for and protect her existing children, which is what a good mother does, and she doesn't deserve to lose them because of it. This is a moral travesty, not to mention a massive miscarriage of justice." Maggie finally stops to take a breath. "And it's all Jamal's doing—"

"Another example of the all-too-common bad-man syndrome that plagues poor women," I interject.

"Do you know something, Dr. Spencer? If I had just a penny for every woman who got involved with a bad man, I'd be on a world cruise right now instead of sitting in the middle of a late spring Chicago blizzard."

"Do you know who is going to support the case for termination?" I ask.

"Some child psychiatrist from the University of Illinois, I think. The Illinois Department of Child Protective Services makes those decisions."

"I can't believe they honestly think they'll win this case."

"I doubt it too, but the law is biased against the Eulalias of the world, and the publicity this case is generating is enough for Bible-thumping anti-abortionists to believe they've won, regardless of the eventual decision. The fact a mother can be sued for termination of parental rights because she has an abortion scares the shit out of women."

"It's a clever strategy to push forth a wrong-headed idea, but honestly, I think you could find someone better suited to advocate for Eulalia."

"The Director of the Center for the Study of Poverty at Virginia Southern University isn't fried baloney. If someone with your credentials is willing to come here and testify for Eulalia on your own dime, it sends a strong message."

"A support letter wouldn't be enough?"

"A letter can't respond to questions. You have to show up in person."

Suddenly I remember where I've heard the name Sister Maggie Corrigan and a shiver travels down my spine. If she's who I think she is, I would love to meet her. Switching the conversation, I ask whether she's involved in some Catholic women's action initiative in Chicago. She says she is and asks how I know. I tell her I can't remember where I first heard her name, which isn't true, but two can play the secrecy game.

"I'll have to discuss the case with the university attorney before agreeing to this. Give me a week or ten days, and I should have an answer for you," I tell her.

She agrees to this and says that since she insists on being called Maggie, she would like to call me Gillian. "We're all sisters, and titles just get in the way of remembering that about each other," she points out, adding that she's looking forward to a positive response to her request for help.

"If the university says you can't do this on their time, you could always do it on your own," she reminds me, in a voice that says she has no intention of taking no for an answer.

Then, just as we are about to end the call, Maggie asks whether I am Catholic.

"Sometimes...but only on my terms, never on the Church's," I reply.

"Then I think we'll understand each other just fine," she replies, hanging up the phone.

•••

It takes several days to get an appointment with the university's legal counsel, whose office is in the tall, ivy-covered Stonewall Jackson administration building overlooking a central campus quadrangle surrounded by even more ivy-covered buildings named for revered Confederate war heroes.

John Wesley Adams III, Esq., stylishly attired in a dark grey suit, sparkling white shirt, maroon silk tie, and shoes so shiny they reflect his sculpted face, keeps me waiting in his book-filled office for ten minutes before making his entrance from a side door. The time allowed me to figure out that his desk is so large I could sit on it and float all the way down the James River to the Chesapeake Bay.

"Gillian, my dear—how wonderful to see you," Attorney Adams says enthusiastically while grasping my right hand in both of his in a non-handshake designed to remind me that I am the subordinate in the room. "I trust everything is well, and you aren't here to see me about anything that is going to cause us unnecessary upset or embarrassment."

I assure him I'm not involved in something as untoward as plotting the overthrow of the federal government, but my question does involve a legal case, which I explain in as much detail as I can. He claims to have read something about it in a law journal that reported it as "a case to watch."

"Which means the local DA is gaining widespread professional notoriety from this," I add.

The university attorney stares out of one of his tall office windows for at least a minute before speaking. "Here's the thing, my dear—"

"Jack," I interrupt, using the name I know everyone calls him. "Here *is* the thing: don't call me 'dear'. I thought we settled that issue a long time ago...Gillian is fine, Dr. Spencer is fine, and Professor Spencer is fine, too, but 'my dear' is not fine. Use that term of endearment with your wife, your girlfriend, your daughter, or the waitress you hit on when you buy your coffee in the morning, but don't use it with me."

After smiling at me indulgently, the university attorney begs my forgiveness, claims our earlier conversation regarding this issue entirely slipped his mind, and thanks me for reminding him. He then uses his perfectly manicured hand to smooth down his carefully styled hair and continues. "As I see it, legally speaking, of course, chances are good that the men on the hearing panel are probably doing, have done, or are thinking about doing the same thing to their daughters that Eulalia Banks thought Jamal Jones was doing to his. They don't want to set a precedent that encourages the mothers of these young girls to give their daughters loaded guns to shoot the bastards and will not be kindly disposed toward this woman."

"Eulalia is from Illinois, not some backwater swamp or mountain holler no one's ever heard of where God knows what goes on and is never discovered. I seriously doubt what you are saying is true."

"I fervently hope it isn't, Dr. Spencer, but I am not aware of any evidence suggesting incest or child sexual assault by adult males is a geographic phenomenon confined to any particular region of the country."

"You're right—it's not. Point well taken. Do you have any objection to my providing expert testimony in the case?"

"I'd prefer you didn't," Attorney Adams says, showing me his bright, white-capped teeth. "It might send the wrong message about how faculty are choosing to spend their professional time."

"Then I'll do it on my own time," I tell him.

"That, of course, is your decision. Just be sure no university resources are involved." He stands and prepares to leave.

"Preferences aside, there's no reason, from the university's perspective, that I can't do this, is there," I state as a fact, also standing.

"Not really," he agrees. "Most people around here have barely heard of Illinois and care not at all what happens there. They think of the area as an outpost on the American frontier where Abraham Lincoln had the misfortune to be born, and then somehow became president of the United States and freed all their slaves, which created a substantial economic inconvenience many still grapple with."

"Actually, Lincoln was born in Kentucky," I smile as I exit the room, closing the door behind me.

Seething at the attitude I've just encountered, as soon as I return to my office, I place a call to Sister Maggie Corrigan and tell her she can count on me to do what I can to help with Eulalia's case. She tells me to plan on coming to Chicago sometime in the next month or two and will let me know an exact date as soon as she does.

"We're doing some security updates and remodeling just ahead of the city condemning us and ordering the building torn down, which is a long story. I've got a lot on my mind right now, so if you don't hear from me again in a couple weeks, call." She hangs up the phone without saying goodbye.

•••

Eulalia's parental rights termination hearing is postponed several times and nearly three months pass before I make travel plans. In the meantime, from several conversations we had in the interim, I figure out that an organization Maggie runs, CWDC, got crossways with the archdiocese, and some very disagreeable people were picketing in front of the shelter, accusing her of being a fire-breathing feminist baby killer, which created a serious security problem.

"CWDC applied for tax-exempt status, and the archdiocese got its collective shorts in a knot and sent me a cease and desist letter, which I ignored, because tax exemption is a federal designation that has nothing to do with the archdiocese, and they have no say over who gets it, so couldn't stop us. Once we had the designation, we started raising money, mostly by soliciting private donations, which further upset the cardinal, who published a letter in all the parish bulletins saying we were not an officially recognized Catholic organization and contributing to our efforts was a grave sin. We ran ads in the Chicago newspapers refuting this, and the next thing we knew, the picketing started and the city was threatening to condemn our building. A lawyer friend of mine got it straightened out with the city before the Sisters of God's Mercy, who technically are responsible for the shelter operations, got wind of what was going on and took it as a reason to close us down entirely due to bad publicity, which I was getting worried about."

"What happened to the picketers?" I ask.

"They're still here, but not like before. It started fizzling out when the weather got bad and didn't pick up again, probably because we've had a cold, rainy spring."

When I finally arrive at the shelter to meet Maggie in person, I am surprised by how abandoned the overall area is. The immediate vicinity is mostly empty warehouse-sized buildings with broken windows and no doors, surrounded by cracked sidewalks sprouting weeds and scattered with broken bottles and other threatening objects. I see several underfed cats scrounging through trash and two dogs wandering loose. Since the area is too desolate for panhandling, I assume the people walking around live in the empty buildings and are wandering the streets looking to make drug deals. I don't like the odds that my rental car, once parked, will still be here—with all four tires still attached—when I return.

The three-story, brown brick building stands alone on the block. Chipping white paint surrounds windows that haven't been washed since the Eisenhower administration—and those are the ones that aren't cracked or broken out and boarded over with plywood. The roof is missing half its shingles, and six feet of loose downspout is swinging from a gutter formerly attached to the overhang near the front door.

A severely dented four-door sedan missing its hubcaps, and a rusted van with a cracked windshield occupy the asphalt and dirt driveway. Each vehicle has a thick chain running across its dashboard, through two open front windows, across the windshield, then bolted to a post cemented into the ground next to the building. This creative attempt at automobile security seems unlikely to deter even an amateur car thief in possession of a half-way decent bolt cutter.

A large, empty lot where the adjacent church must have once stood occupies the other side of the driveway. This once-sacred space is now weed-filled and littered with plastic trash bags, broken bottles, empty cans, and dirty diapers someone has been throwing out an upper floor window, completely missing the overflowing dumpsters below. The entire area is thick with flies, and the closer I get, the more pungent the smell from rotting garbage, animal, and probably human waste. Only a saint could live in a place like this, trying to help impoverished, mentally ill, abused, and otherwise downtrodden women barely surviving a life surrounded by endless miles of bad road.

At the top of the broken front steps, I'm greeted by a solid steel door—proof that the neighborhood is far from safe. This effort at security seems a little silly, since the average five-year-old could easily access the building by climbing through any of the ground floor or basement windows. I push the buzzer, which activates an intercom. After explaining who I am and why I am here, a hard click unlocks the door, allowing me to enter a small foyer where there is another steel door and what looks like a bullet-proof glass panel, behind which sits an older, stern-faced nun in a traditional habit. She looks me over very carefully, without smiling, before releasing the second door. When I am finally inside the building, she motions me to sit down and says she'll let Sister Corrigan know I've arrived. My guess is the nun who greeted me keeps a gun in her desk drawer, although it might not be loaded.

Looking around the small reception area, I see threadbare rugs scattered over badly scuffed wooden floors and mismatched chairs haphazardly arranged next to dirty windows. A large, velvet painting of a horse, a paint-by-numbers landscape, and a slightly crooked portrait of Jesus as a young man hangs on one dirty, chipped plaster wall. A life-sized picture of the Sacred Heart hangs on the opposite wall, staring at the horse.

"You've arrived!" says a voice that sounds much larger than the woman standing before me. Wearing paint-splattered pants and a tattered Chicago Bulls sweatshirt, she looks like one of the homeless women the shelter serves. Assuming I know who she is, without introducing herself, she explains she has spent the morning helping a friend paint his building in exchange for using the space for meetings and what, she hopes, will eventually be an offer to return the favor and help her repaint the interior of this building.

"You must be Maggie," I finally say.

"I see you've met Sister Mathilde," she responds. "She's a retired sister and one of our most faithful volunteers. When she's not greeting those seeking our services, she's playing grandmother to the children in the shelter and mother to their mothers. Since she's been here with us, she's read bedtime stories to at least one hundred and fifty grandchildren and guided more than forty daughters into responsible motherhood."

I detect a slight smile on Sister Mathilde's wrinkled face as Maggie describes her contribution to the work they are doing.

Maggie asks where I parked my car. When I tell her it's about half a block away, she says that might be a problem. "I should've remembered to tell you to park in a downtown ramp and take a taxi here—"

"If she could've found one willing to come into this neighborhood," Sister Mathilde interjects.

I ask how likely it is the car will still be here when I'm ready to leave, and neither nun answers. Instead, Maggie tells Sister Mathilde to find a couple of kids and tell them to watch my car. When I ask where she's going to find these kids, she doesn't answer that question either.

After motioning me to follow her up two full flights of stairs to the top floor, Maggie invites me into her cluttered workspace, which is a Class A fire hazard. She moves a pile of papers onto the floor to make room for me to sit. The streaks of sun pushing through the window accentuate years of crusted dirt and brown water stains streaking the yellowed ceiling tile. A faint smell of stale cigarette smoke hangs in the air.

"It's probably a little early for a drink," Maggie chuckles, gesturing toward her desk drawer. "I keep cheap bourbon on hand for emergencies and other special occasions," she says, not expanding on what sorts of emergencies she's referring to. She hands me a bottle of water, explaining that in this part of town the water isn't safe to drink. "God only knows what shits in the water supply, which is then delivered to us through 100-year-old lead pipes...it's a wonder we're haven't all dropped dead."

She ignores the ringing phone on her desk and looks at me. "I probably know a lot more about you than you do about me," she remarks, inviting me to begin the conversation.

I turn the question back onto her.

"I'm Irish-Catholic, South Side Chicago born and bred. Everything I know I learned growing up in one of the toughest neighborhoods in the city. In my world, if you don't develop street smarts by the time you can walk, you'll never survive," she says. Then she asks me how well I know Chicago.

"I've spent some time here, am a Cubs baseball fan, and during graduate school went to Soldiers Field a few times with my dad and a friend of mine to watch the Bears play football. And I've been an amused follower of Chicago's notoriously corrupt politics for years."

"The reason Chicago politics are what they are is because the ethnic Irish own the city and love a good fight. It's in our blood—hence the legendary political battles. Truthfully, they're fun, and sometimes somebody picks a fight just for the hell of it—I've done it myself."

"Given your love of a good argument, what could've possibly been the appeal of vowed religious life?"

"There weren't many options for a poor Irish girl from an immigrant family of stockyard workers. The convent was the best opportunity I had that wouldn't have ended up on the dole or in public housing with a gaggle of runny-nose kids and a husband who drinks his paycheck every Friday night. I figured I was gaining more than I was giving up, and the social justice aspect of religious life called to me. Being a nun opens those doors, which might otherwise have been closed."

The honestly of her answer surprises me, and I assure her I'm impressed she was willing to give up a more conventional life to work for greater justice for women, and she says not to be.

"I'm not brave enough to fall in love...and marriage, which is the expected result, has too many expectations I could never fulfill. It would bore me to tears eventually. And since I am severely deficient in motherly instincts, ending up pregnant would've been disastrous—I'm sure I would've had an abortion."

My eyes widen, revealing my surprise.

"Don't look so shocked, Gillian. My mother died because her uterus ruptured after seven kids in as many years. As the oldest, I ended up responsible for raising them practically by myself. Life turned even uglier than it already was, and all I could think of then—still think about now—is how things would've been different if she'd had birth control and if my dad didn't believe he could have his way with her whenever he felt like it. Compared to that, religious life is a picnic in a sunny meadow on a warm spring day. Best of all about this life, though, is that nobody gets in my face with a lot of emotional crap about sharing feelings."

I don't know how to respond, so we sit silently while Maggie stares out her dirty window and I stare at the floor, wondering why she's revealing this.

"I'm telling you this so you'll understand where I'm coming from, and why I advocate for women's reproductive rights from within the Church. The men who make the rules have to understand what they're doing to us. Women like you, with education and life options—you'll make your own decisions regardless of what the Church says. But poor women are too afraid to stand up for themselves and won't risk what they believe is their eternal salvation, which has to be better than what they're living through now, by doing anything the patriarchy says is wrong. It's frustrating as all hell."

Nodding my head in agreement, I ask if she thinks she'll be successful in changing the Church's vehement opposition to birth control.

"I can't not try," she shrugs.

Next, I raise the issue of what the next four days before Eulalia's hearing on Friday morning will bring.

"We'll meet with the lawyer late this afternoon. He'll lay out his plan then. Tomorrow I'll take you to meet Eulalia, to give you a feel for the person you are supporting in this awful fight. Wednesday and Thursday are to rehearse our testimony."

I ask what, besides contacting me, her role is in the case.

"I worked with Eulalia for a long time while she was here at the shelter, so I'll be testifying that she was sincerely trying to better her life, that her children were her number one priority, and that I saw, firsthand, what a good mother she is...and that getting an abortion made sense under her circumstances."

"What does your Order have to say about your involvement in an abortion case? Your superiors can't possibly think your position on this is okay."

"I've tried to stay under the radar and avoid the publicity...and we are allowed considerable latitude in what we think and do, so I doubt they know about it."

"Isn't that a little naïve? A Catholic nun testifying in favor of a woman getting an abortion is a headline. You won't be able to stay invisible very long once the hearing begins. It seems to me it'll only be a matter of time until your Order is made aware of it."

"The hearing is supposed to be closed, so I guess I'll cross that bridge if, or when, I come to it. In the meantime, worrying about it only distracts me from rescuing Eulalia from these anti-abortion thugs hell-bent on destroying her."

Since I tend toward trying to foresee problems and avoid them whenever possible, understanding Maggie's cavalier attitude about something she knows could have serious repercussions isn't easy. At the same time, I can't help admiring her for the courage of her convictions and her strong, brave-hearted determination to remain true to what she believes, and then act on that belief, even if doing so places her in opposition to the most powerful religious institution in the world.

Changing the subject, I ask her to tell me about her current operation and say that I would prefer to eat lunch downstairs with the residents, if she doesn't mind. She assures me that's a fine idea.

"Our focus is on women with children, and nearly all are fleeing some kind of domestic violence situation. A few others are here for other reasons—job loss, eviction, and sex abuse being the most common ones. Often, they have alcohol problems, and many have done time for soft crimes—forgery, welfare fraud, and so on. Residents are allowed to stay for up to sixty days, as long as they remain sober and participate in programs designed to help them find permanent housing, employment, and childcare. But we don't kick them to the curb if they're trying and haven't been able to put everything they need in place by the time sixty days are up. They also receive counseling and legal assistance with filing restraining orders, debt issues, and other problems. Those who need it are strongly encouraged to attend twelve-step meetings to deal with their addictions. Frankly, our biggest problem is the crowded conditions that come with communal living," Maggie explains.

"Being unable to get away from each other—plus crying babies and whining older children, and a tendency to steal anything that isn't nailed down—leads to fistfights. And if someone catches a cold or gets diarrhea, in the blink of an eye, everybody is sick. It's better than the situation they came from, but nothing about life here is easy. We try to help them, and the success stories are mostly a result of the tireless efforts of the retired sisters who volunteer to befriend the women, many of whom have never had a consistently positive, steadying influence in their lives before. After the women leave us, we try to stay in touch with those we can, encouraging them to continue making sound decisions. It works long-term less than fifteen percent of the time, but when it does, the difference is miraculous."

"My experience researching these programs is that they're endless, intense hours of hard, often thankless work resulting in a lot of recidivism and flat-out failures. It takes a very special person to carry out this kind of ministry," I acknowledge.

"That's one way to look at it," she responds, walking over to check on a toddler who found his way upstairs and is sleeping on the floor. "But we prefer to think of helping people as its own reward, regardless of the eventual outcome. Not to sound too corny about it, but the official line is that this is what Jesus would do. I don't know whether that's true or not, but it's an effective fund-raising ploy."

And I don't imagine Jesus would mind at all that you keep a bottle of whiskey in your desk drawer, smoke an occasional cigarette, and probably keep a gun in the reception desk, I think, smiling to myself.

"One of the things I'm most proud of is the medical clinic specifically for women's health concerns. I gave up the original director's office space to expand it into another examining room."

I ask how the women's health clinic differs from the regular health clinic, and Maggie gives me an incredulous, *surely you can figure that out* look.

"You dispense birth control?" I ask.

"Of course we do—and we refer for abortions. In my view, it would be immoral not to accommodate whatever choices the women make, and most want birth control, or an abortion if their situation calls for it and they can get one."

"Seriously?"

"Yes, Gillian, seriously. We have a reliable abortion referral network we utilize when necessary, which is more often than we'd like, believe me. Dispensing birth control is the far preferable option."

"I don't disagree with any of this, Maggie, but I still wonder how you're getting away with it?"

"It's an open secret among the sisters who volunteer here, many of whom have been doing so since before I became involved a good many years ago, but I've not heard any official objections, so far. It's not something I worry much about because any nun who has worked with women in chronic poverty strongly disagrees with the Church's position on birth control. And, except in extreme circumstances, my current superior avoids invoking our vow of obedience."

"This seems to me to be pushing pretty hard against those extreme circumstances. You don't worry about the threat of scandal, which the Church hates and will force the cardinal to act?"

"I'm not afraid of the cardinal, or of scandal, and meanwhile, I'm pretty busy—I just got appointed permanent shelter director yesterday."

"Congratulations. Your extraordinary energy is amazing," I say." Looking at her watch, Maggie says it's time to eat and motions me to follow her down to the cafeteria-style dining room. Today's lunch menu is beef stew, white bread, milk, an apple, and a cookie. After going through the food line, we carry our trays over to a table in the corner and sit down across from a tired, vacant-eyed woman surrounded by four school-age children.

"Mind if we join you, Joanne?" Maggie asks.

The woman nods her head while staring at me.

I introduce myself, and Maggie interrupts me to explain that I'm helping her with a project and that Joanne, and four of her children, have been with them for nearly a month while she gets some things sorted out.

Joanne tucks her dandruff-encrusted, stringy brown hair behind her ears and resumes eating. I ask the oldest child her name, and she says it's Mickey, adding that she's ten years old and is learning to read. I ask if she is from Chicago and her mother steps into the conversation.

"We're from downstate, not that it's any of your business. My husband lost his job and got depressed, so I quit my job to stay home with him because I was scared he'd suicide himself. Then we lost our house and decided to come to Chicago, to look for work, but he was still too depressed to hold down a steady job."

She stops to take a spoonful of stew. When it appears she doesn't intend to continue the conversation, I ask her what happened next.

"We were living in our van in some strip mall parking lot and got reported for vagrancy. Instead of being arrested I got sent here with my girls. My husband and our three sons are someplace else. We haven't seen them for a month and don't have no idea where the van is...somebody probably stole it by now. Anything else you want to know?" Joanne says, making no attempt to hide the bitterness in her voice.

I apologize, saying I didn't mean to intrude, and that I hope things start to turn around for her family soon. She tells the children to hurry up and finish their lunches and doesn't make eye contact with me again.

"A classic example of bad decision-making," Maggie says as we walk back to her office after lunch. "You tell me how the hell quitting your job after your husband just lost his is a good idea? It makes about as much sense as the women who come in after their husbands have beat them bloody again, and again, and again, and again, yet they still decide to go back to the bastard because their children need a father. Sometimes I don't understand these women at all."

Her attitude surprises me, but maybe it shouldn't. What she describes is the most common recurring story among abused women, which I'm sure she hears constantly. She continually fights the life-threatening battles in the war on poverty, such that it is, and comes face to face with its heartbreaking effects every day. Without some outlet for the frustrations, eventually getting out of bed in the morning would become nearly impossible.

As we walk past the reception desk, Sister Mathilde motions me over. "Some boys have been eyeing your car for the last hour or so. They're probably getting ready to steal it."

XIX.

Justice will not be served until those who are unaffected are as outraged as those who are.
BENJAMIN FRANKLIN

"You have to drive, because I don't have a license," Maggie tells me as we prepare to leave for the lawyer's office.

"Fine. Where are we going?"

"LaSalle. It's at the crossroads of two interstates, about seventy-five miles down Interstate Eighty from where we are now."

"Then, obviously, I'll drive," I respond.

"But I don't think we should take your rental car—we'll be putting on a lot of miles you'll end up paying for."

"I don't think leaving it here is a good idea. I'd rather pay for the miles."

"Here's what we'll do," Maggie says. "We'll chain up your rental and take the shelter car, and you can drive."

The dented rust bucket she calls the shelter car appears as roadworthy as four wheels held together with duct tape and chewing gum. It's a rolling death trap on the Chicago freeways and on fast, narrow I-80. Unwilling to consider an alternative, Maggie instructs me to back the crumpled mess out of the driveway and drive my rental car into the empty parking space where she'll chain it to the post. I repeat that leaving the rental car here is a stupid idea. Accustomed to getting her own way, she is unwilling to discuss the issue further, and also has me right where she wants me—a submissive Catholic school girl willing to do whatever Sister says.

I point out that it looks like rain—a good reason not to leave the rental car windows rolled down to accommodate the chain, which wouldn't matter anyway if someone really wanted to steal the car.

"You have to make choices in life, Gillian," Maggie says. "In this situation, your choice is between a wet car seat and a guarantee the car will be gone when you get back."

"I'm betting on the car being gone when I get back regardless."

Maggie ignores me and says to start rearranging vehicles.

During the drive out of the neighborhood toward the expressway, I see that the number of empty storefront buildings and open bars is about equal. Morty's coffee and donut places must be very popular because there is one every few blocks, usually right next to a payday loan company that allows someone to borrow on their next paycheck, at a 20 or 25 percent interest rate that begins compounding daily if the loan is not repaid within the agreed-upon timeframe—usually two weeks. This scheme exploits the poor as much as buying lottery tickets does, which the payday loan companies receive a commission from the state of Illinois for selling.

A walk-in medical clinic, several used car lots, and three used clothing and two used furniture stores—all single-story buildings—make up the bulk of the commercial enterprises in the area. The best-maintained building on our route out of the city belongs to the Benevolent Protective Order of Elks, a fraternity open only to men.

Along the way, when she isn't switching radio stations between country-western music and call-in talk shows, Maggie fills me in on what to expect when we meet with the lawyer. She explains that he was a professional basketball player until a few years ago, when he blew out his knee. He'd already begun law school during the off-season so quit playing to finish his law degree. Because he made enough money playing basketball that he doesn't need to earn a living, he decided to do pro-bono criminal defense work on cases sent to him through a wide referral network of agencies that deal with the poor who are in legal trouble.

"He didn't want to raise a family in Chicago proper, so he settled on a crossroads town between here and Iowa, wherever the hell that is, because most rural people are too poor to come to the city looking for legal help, and he can still get to Chicago when necessary. Seems like a dumb decision to me," Maggie says, again flipping the radio station, which is getting a little irritating. "Willie strongly believes that if he'd been involved in Eulalia's case from the beginning, she never would have gotten into this mess, and he intends to see it through to the end. We'd be damned far up shit creek without him."

I ask why, if money is not a concern for him, he didn't seek a stronger expert witness.

"It's a calculation on his part. He believes the best defense is a straightforward one based on Eulalia's life history and experience. He intends to make the case that the charges are without merit, which they are, and that the state is running roughshod over a poor inner-city Black woman just because it can, which is also true. In his view, the most effective way to handle this is to present testimony from someone who can objectively present scientific research data about the trials of a life in poverty, rather than involving some high-paid, so-called expert who makes a living as a professional witness and may not necessarily believe in our case. He feels confident about the decision."

"Even against a child psychiatrist from the University of Illinois School of Medicine? That sounds a little overconfident to me."

"The psychiatrist's expertise is the effects of parent-child separation and childhood instability on adult mental health. He'll probably say that the kids need the stability of an adoptive family, and my guess is he can sling bullshit medical jargon all the way to South Alabama, but is light in his loafers when it comes to the realities of daily life for poor people struggling to raise their kids as best they can, under circumstances he can't even begin to imagine. You can counter all his crap with hard facts."

"So my argument, which I believe to be true, is that Eulalia is a good mother and by giving her daughter a gun, she was doing what any good mother would do, which is to protect her child from a sexual predator. Do I have the basic idea?"

"Sounds like it to me," Maggie answers, as I pull the car into a strip mall.

We park in front of a storefront with a payday loan office that also sells lottery tickets; a chiropractor's office; and William G. Preston, Attorney and Counselor at Law all listed on a thick glass door that has been generously smeared with a wide variety of thriving germs. This is when she drops the bomb that she's arranged for us to stay at a convent attached to a school somewhere between here and East Moline for the next few days.

"The price was right," she smiles.

The front door opens into a dark hallway. The loan office is on one side, and another door through which the other two offices are located is straight ahead. Opening the second door, we walk into a reception area that is only a slight improvement over the hallway. A twenty-something, gum-chewing receptionist with a backcombed beehive hairdo and a smiley-face nameplate identifying her as Rochelle cheerfully asks how she can help us. Maggie explains we are here to see Attorney Preston. Rochelle invites us to "take a seat over there," pointing to a row of metal folding chairs lining two walls, and says she will let Mr. Preston know we are here.

"Help yourself to the coffee—it's free," she smiles, nodding in the direction of a table in the corner.

Less than a minute later, Willie Preston, standing nearly seven feet tall, sleeves rolled partway up muscular forearms, the top button on his shirt undone, and his tie loosened, walks through the door marked with his name and greets Maggie with a hug she pushes off. "Sorry, I forgot," he apologizes, then turns to me.

"You must be Professor Spencer," he smiles, shaking my hand. "I'm Willie Preston, and very, very happy to meet you. You're going to be a big help to us." As he steps aside to guide us into his office, I ask him to please call me Gillian. We walk down the linoleum-covered hall toward a windowless conference room furnished with a large, outdated dining room table, eight chairs, and matching credenza he probably picked up at an auction somewhere. Yellow legal pads and pencils are placed in front of two of the seats and a stack of files is in front of a third. A pitcher of water and glasses sit on a metal tray in the middle of the table.

"Make yourselves comfortable, and we'll chat for a few minutes," Willie says, lowering his still trim, athletic body into the chair at the head of the table. "Alisha—my wife and legal assistant—will be here in a few minutes to take notes."

He asks about my work and reminisces about playing basketball against my university when he was a starter on a championship University of North Carolina team. "I'm a Chicago boy and wasn't nuts about the South," he confesses.

"Having grown up on the Southern California beaches, I've had major adjustment problems too, but Richmond has its charms, and I like my job—most of the time. That helps," I explain just as a tall, elegant, olive-skinned woman with French bobbed hair loose around her face, enters the room. Willie stands to welcome her.

"This is my wife, Alisha. She's been helping with the legal research for this case and will be taking notes for us."

I reach out to shake her hand, and she winks at me.

"I guess great minds think alike," she says, smiling broadly and referring to the fact that we are both wearing Levi's, white shirts, and navy-blue blazers, and our hair is cut in exactly the same style. The big difference is that hers is a deep black and mine is dark auburn, and even without make-up, she could be on the cover of *Vogue*.

"I suggest the twins sit down, and we'll get started," Willie chuckles.

He proceeds to summarize the case and then breaks the news that the judge has had a family emergency, which probably involves a three-day fishing weekend with his buddies, and has moved the hearing up twenty-four hours, so we will be in court Thursday morning at nine o'clock. This gives me a chill because I don't see how just one day spent preparing me to testify can possibly work in our favor, and say so. Willie says he doesn't see this as a problem.

"I want you to be well-prepared but not overprepared, and there is a difference," he explains. "You firmly believe what you are saying, and you know what you're talking about, and that's enough. Anything more risks sounding contrived, and I want to leave those theatrics to the other side. Hopefully, they'll hang themselves with it."

I find this reassuring, since anything I know about what I'm about to do comes from television and crime novels.

"Eulalia will be brought from Joliet to the Rock Island County Jail Wednesday sometime. She'll appear in court but won't testify on her own behalf," Willie begins.

Hearing this, I hold up my hand to stop the conversation. "Isn't the fact she's in jail pending the outcome of criminal charges complicating her case?" I ask.

"Yes and no...regardless of what happens, the worst-case scenario is she'll be eligible for parole at some point, well before the younger kids are too old to need a mother."

"No child is ever too old to need a mother," Alisha points out.

Willie smiles at her and continues. "If she ends up doing jail time on the criminal charges—and I'm going to fight hard against that—there are good programs to keep incarcerated mothers and their children connected, and Eulalia is a great candidate to participate in one. I'm viewing the criminal case as so weak it's just a minor irritant in our effort to secure Eulalia's parental rights."

"But Eulalia won't be testifying," Alisha repeats.

I ask why not.

"She's afraid she might say something wrong, or the prosecution will twist her words into something she didn't mean to say and trap her in some way she won't know how to escape from, which is what she feels has happened so far."

I ask whether this is good or bad and Willie says he agrees that she was manipulated both before and during her earlier court appearances, so understands her fear, and will point this out in court. He would prefer she testify, but since she won't, he'll be using me as her mouthpiece.

"This is considerable added pressure on you, Gillian, but together, *we will* make it work," he assures me, with a strong emphasis on the "we will."

"You have to remember that she is a poor, basically illiterate inner-city woman the legal system is trying to charge with a crime she didn't commit. She's being railroaded because they want to use her as an example of what not to do."

"Can you please explain this further?" I ask.

"She didn't pull the trigger. At worst she can be accused of being a party to a crime since she gave her thirteen-year-old daughter a gun to defend herself against a likely sexual assault, which everyone involved in this case has somehow forgotten is against the law. Pursuing any kind of attempted murder charge based on those facts is a goddamned travesty right out of the gate. Confounding it all by calling a legal abortion murder just further confuses the issue," Willie says, his voice rising with each word.

Just then, a light bulb goes off in my head. "This is going to sound off the wall, but I'm going to say it anyway. Is everyone involved in prosecuting the case, including the judge, a man?"

Willie nods, a small smile breaking at the corner of his mouth. "There were nine men and three women on the grand jury that handed down the indictment, which was accessory to attempted murder and child endangerment because she gave Jada the gun. Legally, they couldn't do anything with an abortion charge because abortion isn't against the law. But including it in the beginning made it an issue and sensationalized the case, which is exactly what the anti-abortion folks want, because it opens the door to charges that Eulalia is an unfit mother."

"So the judge, whoever prosecuted the case out of the DA's office, the public defender, *and* most of the grand jurors were men?"

Willie nods again, Alisha's eyes widen, and Maggie inhales sharply.

"Is the reason she was charged at all because law enforcement, the prosecutor, and maybe even the judge didn't want it out there that mothers could do what Eulalia did and get away with it? Maybe getting a conviction on this case was personal for them because they didn't want any of the women in their lives getting ideas, and charging a destitute woman off the streets who is dependent upon some rookie public defender with a night-school law degree, and case files stacked so high in his office there's no room for him to sit down, is a slam-dunk conviction." I hear myself speaking more loudly than I intended. "It's an ugly thought, but life gets ugly sometimes."

Willie smiles knowingly and asks me where I got this idea.

"The university attorney suggested it. I admit that I was appalled that justice could be so easily manipulated, but after thinking about it, can't reconcile what's going on any other way."

"That was the first thing I thought of when I heard about the case, and I'd bet serious money that's exactly what happened," Willie says. "The problem is that, absent hard evidence, a hunch, no matter how strong, and mine's pretty strong, isn't grounds to argue for a dismissal."

I shake my head, thinking that sometimes it's very hard not to hate men in powerful positions.

Maggie, apparently harboring similar thoughts she does not want to keep to herself, clears her throat. "If this appalls you, Gillian, then you're pretty damned naïve. The scales of justice have never balanced for women. Powerful men have always been able to tip them whichever way they wanted—and always to their advantage. Surely you know that...or maybe you don't, being of the privileged rich class, and all that."

"Hey—she's on our side and doing it for free. Hold off on the insults," Willie cautions, staring Maggie down.

"When you see Eulalia tomorrow, be sure to give her my love," Alisha instructs, breaking the tension in the room.

Willie says we've covered all the preliminaries and suggests we all get a good night's sleep because the next three days are going to be long and hard.

Without responding, Maggie gathers her things and prepares to leave. She says little and does not attempt an apology as we drive west out of LaSalle toward the convent where we'll be staying. I am deeply regretting not insisting on taking my rental car on this trip because, besides worrying about it, the rust bucket is not useful transportation. At forty-five miles per hour, which is as fast as it goes and is suicidal on the eighty-miles-per-hour interstate highway system, the car shakes worse than a bunch of high school cheerleaders and drinks gasoline faster than a thirsty desert camel, and the squealing brakes draw unwanted attention every time we stop. Keeping it running so far has cost one hundred twenty-five dollars for three quarts of oil, brake fluid, and four tanks of gas, all on my dime—and the trip is less than half over.

Because the Rock Island County Jail is overcrowded and not equipped to house long-term female prisoners, Eulalia is in a holding facility at the Illinois State Penitentiary at Joliet. Located on the outskirts of a large metropolitan area bumping up against the Illinois flatlands, it would be very difficult for a prisoner to escape from Joliet and get very far unseen. The view from the prison tower is unobstructed for endless miles, except in summer, when the cornfields provide some cover. Nevertheless, the prisoner would have to scale a sixteen-foot electric chain-link fence topped with rolling barbed wire. Nearly all the guards are local boys with high school educations and thug mentalities that involve shooting first and worrying about the consequences later, so very few detainees even try to escape.

At this time, Eulalia is among the overflow of women prisoners temporarily housed at the facility. Most are chronic drug offenders or thieves, or have been charged with welfare fraud. Nearly all suffer from addictions, substance abuse, and other mental health issues complicated by well-documented statistics indicating most are also childhood-incest and sexual-assault victims. But the stronger bond among the women is that nearly all are mothers who, almost without exception, find themselves in prison as a result of relationships with men who manipulated and exploited them. An undisputed reality of these women's lives is that if they had made better choices about the company they keep—a lesson many have found very difficult to learn—their lives would be immeasurably improved. But most don't see it that way, because they believe life "happens" to them and they've never had choices about anything.

Maggie tells me that on her previous visit, Eulalia told her the inmates sleep two to a cinder block cubicle containing a bunk bed, a toilet without a seat or lid, and a sink. Bars, rather than a solid door, hold the two women occupants inside. Personal items are kept in a small box under the bottom bunk. Communal showers, which the women are allowed to visit once per week, are at each end of the long hallway.

"She said the entire place, including where they eat, smells like a mixture of strong disinfectant, mold, and urine."

Although the prison claims to operate on a rehabilitative rather than a punitive model, incarceration is a regimented life that follows a strict, inflexible schedule. Visitors must preregister and are only permitted on Saturdays, between nine and eleven thirty in the morning and one to three o'clock in the afternoon. Willie had to petition the court to allow Maggie and me to visit Eulalia on a Tuesday.

I'm not six feet into the main entrance when my underwire bra sets off the metal detector, which adds fifteen minutes to our check-in time.

"I forgot to warn you about that," Maggie whispers, while we are both subjected to the indignity of being thoroughly patted down before being led into a large room containing several cubicles separated by thick plexiglass. We are instructed to sit in cubicle B and wait for Eulalia.

Nearly a half hour passes before the door opens, and a short, squat prison guard, wearing a uniform stretched tightly across a substantial beer belly and thick biceps, leads a woman with frightened brown eyes, short, knotted hair, and a deep scar across her forehead into the room. Her olive-drab prison scrubs hang on her thin frame, and her scuffed, white sneakers, holding sockless feet, are missing shoelaces. Her hands, with fingernails bitten until they bleed, are free, but her bare ankles are shackled.

The guard tells us we have forty-five minutes and he'll be waiting outside the windowed door, watching.

Eulalia sits down without making eye contact.

Maggie introduces me and explains the purpose of the visit.

"Hi, Eulalia," I say, smiling slightly. "I've heard some nice things about you and am very glad to meet you"

"You're lying," she bristles.

"I'm not lying. Maggie tells me you are a very devoted mother. That counts for a lot."

This elicits a small smile, and I see that Eulalia's front tooth is chipped.

I explain that I will be trying my best to convince the judge and three-person hearing panel not to take her children away, and it would be helpful to me to know a little more about her, if she's willing to tell me.

She stares at the floor thinking about this for several minutes before speaking.

"I lived in Chicago all my life. We was a buncha poor kids, and I never got to school much. My mama—she depend on us to hustle for money. But when I grow up and had babies, I took real good care of 'em, even in the shelter. Them's all real good girls...never a speck of trouble and pay attention in school, just like they're 'posed to do."

I smile again and tell her it's obvious to me that she cares a lot about her children and has been a very good mother. Then I ask her to tell me about the shooting.

"I knowed Jamal Jones a real long time. He the daddy for my littlest girls. When he got outta prison, he wanted to come back to be a family, and I was too dumb to turn him down...just couldn't do it, even though I knowed he was trouble—always has been, always will be." She sighs deeply, and tears begin to form, which she wipes away with her fist. "Weren't no time at all after he got outta prison he was back repeating his bad ways. Trouble was, he kept sayin' he loved us—loved his daughters, and I didn't know enough not to believe him...or maybe I knowed but didn't want to know. And he were tryin' to be good—babysittin', when I was workin', and fixin' what broke saved us havin' to pay for what the no-good landlord ignored. I appreciated that about him. But I knew trouble was comin' eventually. When I got pregnant, I took care of it... and knowed then I'd have to get away from Jamal for good."

Maggie and I both affirm that everything Eulalia is saying makes sense.

"My sister in East Moline said there was factory work around there, so I took the girls and moved in with her for a while—thought it was a good opportunity to ditch Jamal. I got me a job scrubbin' out bathrooms in the factory nights and found a cheap place to live on the Illinois side of the river, near my sister...made enough money to keep the roof over our heads. A few weeks later, my sister in Chicago wrote sayin' she heard Jamal was askin' after us, and she figured it was only a matter of time until he found out where we was. That's when, Jada, my oldest, told me Jamal already done found us and had been comin' around nights when I was at work. I asked her 'bout him botherin' her, and she wouldn't talk about it but kept saying she hoped Jamal would go away. Weren't hard to know what she was tryin' to tell her mama, and that's when I got us a gun and gave it to her...told her to put it under her pillow."

"Where did you get the gun?" I ask.

Eulalia doesn't answer, and I finally say I suppose it doesn't matter but am just curious.

"On the streets, you can get anything you want," she finally tells me. "Police, they shoot Black folks all the time—just for being Black—so guns ain't the stupidest idea, you know what I'm sayin'? They ain't hard to get. Nobody wants to use 'em, but not havin' one is stupid. You can't expect the police or nobody to help. You only got yourself, is all. Ain't nobody else 'cept you and God, and I don't see God hangin' around, no matter what them preachers say. It's just me, myself, and I against a real dangerous world. I been thinkin' 'bout this a whole lot while I'm in here with nothin' to do but think, and that's my conclusion. I ain't got nobody but myself to blame for my troubles, and nobody but myself to rely upon. Heavy burden that is...real heavy."

Maggie and I both encourage her not to be too hard on herself for doing the best she could at the time, under very difficult circumstances.

"I admit I gave Jada the gun...and you know what? I'm not sorry I did," she tells me, eyes wide and fierce. "I was willin' to do whatever it took to stop my girls' daddy doin' to them what my daddy done to me. I knowed shootin' somebody's wrong, but so's messin' with little girls' privates, and I woulda said that in court, but the lawyer wouldn't let me say nothin' to defend myself. I don't think he wanted to win my case."

"I don't think he did either," I tell Eulalia. "You're a very good mother, and you deserve to keep your kids. I promise I'll do everything I possibly can to help you." I stop speaking because seeing tears in Eulalia's eyes again causes me to choke up.

Maggie asks Eulalia if she has clothes to wear to court on Thursday or wants us to pick something up, and she says that her sister came to visiting hours last weekend and brought her an outfit.

"My kids is all I got to live for. You've got to help me," Eulalia implores, grabbing my arm.

This causes the guard to burst into the room yelling, "NO TOUCHING," and reacting as if she's trying to assault me. I tell him he's mistaken and there isn't any problem, which he takes as an insult.

"I don't make mistakes," he says, grabbing Eulalia's arm and escorting her out.

At the same time, Maggie pulls me toward the opposite door. Walking out of the prison a few minutes later, she is fuming and says she needs a drink, which I suggest isn't a good idea. Nevertheless, she insists we find a bar with a payphone so she can call Willie. As I open the car door, she begins rummaging around in her purse, looking for what turns out to be a pack of cigarettes.

"We have to tell Willie what just happened in case that asshole guard decides to make something of it and reports Eulalia—really screw things up for her," Maggie insists.

"I don't think he can prevent her from appearing in court if that's what you're worried about."

"Sometimes you're so goddamned naïve you really get on my nerves," Maggie says, rolling down the car window to blow smoke out. "He could hurt her if he wanted to."

It's hard for me to disagree with a cigarette-smoking, bourbon-drinking, tough-talking nun; nevertheless, I want to believe she's overreacting. Pulling into the nearest convenience store, I tell her I'll wait in the car while she makes the call. She says I have to come in with her because she's not in the mood for some half-drunk jackass to make advances.

"He'd be a damned fool to try that," I whisper under my breath.

Maggie glares at me and tells me to bring my purse.

•••

At precisely nine o'clock the next morning, Willie walks into his conference room, carrying three paper cups of coffee and a newspaper. Alisha follows right behind him with a box of fresh-smelling donuts. Telling me the creamer and sugar are in the top drawer of the credenza, Willie announces that we have a lot to do today and best get started. I explain that I left Maggie on the telephone back at the convent where we spent the night, putting out fires of undetermined origin at her office, and she will call me to pick her up later. I thank them for the coffee, adding that I didn't sleep well with a life-sized crucified Christ hanging over a single bed with a lumpy mattress.

"Are you Catholic?" Alisha asks me.

"Christmas, Easter, weddings, and funerals. Anymore, I'm not observant beyond that...too many problems with its patriarchal culture and its morally obscene view of women."

"Are all nuns like Maggie?"

"She's definitely unusual, but most believe what they believe and aren't inclined to entertain alternatives. They can be intimidating that way, especially if they play the 'God's way or the highway' game, which Maggie doesn't. The Catholic sisterhood is God's army of angels on Earth, and I admire them tremendously—and whenever possible, avoid crossing them," I smile.

"She scares me a little," Alisha confesses.

"As a general rule, nuns scare me too," I admit. "The thing about Maggie is that she's exceptionally intelligent and tough-minded, and has an unwavering belief that she's always right but lacks most common social skills. I wouldn't want her on the other side of any issue I cared about."

"How do you think she'll be on the stand?" Willie asks.

"If you're thinking she's a loose cannon, I'd have to agree. This said, given a free reign, she'll scare the living shit out of the opposition."

Willie laughs. "And that is my concern," he says. "I'd like to have two supporting testimonies to counter the two on the other side, but placing an unpredictable witness on the stand violates rule number one in the *How to Win a Trial* handbook, which says don't put a witness you can't control on the stand. And I'm not sure I can control Maggie. In fact, I'm pretty sure I can't. But I also agree with you that she could bury the opposition."

"Maybe you could talk to her about this...try to tone her down a little," Alicia suggests.

"Not me," Willie answers. "I've known Maggie a long time, and I'm not going there. You're the Catholic—you talk to her," he says, nodding in my direction.

"Not me. I won't take on somebody a lawyer can't handle."

"I guess that settles that," Alicia says.

Leaving open the question of allowing Maggie to testify, Willie says he'll start by explaining tomorrow's procedure. "This is the hearing phase of a termination case, meaning the three people on the hearing panel are merely advisory, not decision-makers. They listen to both sides and then advise the judge on what they think the decision should be, and why. Unlike a jury trial where the jury has the final word, in this situation, the judge makes the final decision about whether Eulalia can keep her kids. The law is generally muddy about what constitutes valid reasons to terminate parental rights, or what constitutes the best interests of the child—not that anybody really cares—so there's plenty of flexibility to build a case for or against."

"What do you mean by the law not caring about the best interests of the child?" I ask.

"Think about it this way, Gillian: if the law cared about Eulalia's children, she'd never have been charged with crimes she didn't commit," Alisha answers. "Not only did the law, meaning the person charged with upholding the law, not care about those kids, he used the legal system to steamroll their mother, who, by all accounts, is a good mother and is now in jail. Everybody ignored the life-changing effect all this has on her children."

I sip my coffee and pick at the donut while thinking that failing Eulalia in court tomorrow, it will be a failure I'll never forget. After a minute, Willie asks if I have any questions, and I raise the accusation of abortion being murder as a psychological strike against her.

"Abortion is legal in Illinois," he says, "so that is an empty threat by publicity hounds. But to your point, this hearing focuses on the question of parental rights regarding currently living children, and the abortion issue is irrelevant."

"Surely the other side will bring it up, though," I say.

"If they do, I'll move to strike, and the judge will have to uphold the motion."

"You're sure?"

"Only a fool is sure, and the panel will have already heard it, but there's nothing I can do about that part. I'm confident I can argue a motion to strike to the point the judge will look stupid not doing it, and one thing judges hate is appearing stupid."

"What about the other children's father—or fathers?"

Willie says that is only relevant if the birth certificate names a father, which none of the children's birth certificates do, not even the ones for those Eulalia claims are Jamal's—and he has never denied. "Right now, he's claiming they're all his," he adds.

"My guess is the father issue is probably some combination of incest, Jamal, rape, and maybe someone else Eulalia cared about at some point in her life," Alicia says.

Willie doesn't disagree.

"It seems that the other side could portray Eulalia as morally loose—willing to sleep with anybody without regard to the consequences," I offer.

"Don't worry about it. I can shut down that conversation before it gets very far."

"But even introducing the issue will raise doubts in the judge and panel members' minds," I counter.

"Not likely," Willie answers. "A lot of people, especially in transient places like East Moline, have at least one, maybe more, close female relatives who don't know who the fathers of their kids are."

After shuffling papers around, Willie explains that he will be on defense, meaning that the attorney representing the state welfare department will present the argument for termination first and Willie will follow, presenting the argument for allowing Eulalia to maintain her parental rights. Next comes the state's supporting witnesses—the child psychiatrist and the child welfare caseworker assigned to Eulalia's children. Willie will be allowed to question them, but because this is not a trial, per se, he's been unable to get much information about the state's case ahead of time, so isn't sure what he will ask until he hears what they say. I point out the unfairness of this procedure, and he counters that it works both ways; the other side doesn't know what he's planning either. He adds that the hearing panel members can submit questions for the witnesses to the judge, and the judge can ask his own questions and follow whatever line of inquiry happens to interest him.

Willie hands me a list of the probable questions he will ask me tomorrow, and another list of over one hundred possible questions the state, Jamal's lawyers, the judge, and panel members could ask. He says to take the rest of the morning to read them carefully and make notes of any I want to discuss.

At this point, Willie unfolds the newspaper he carried in with the coffee and donuts and points to the front-page article on the pending hearing.

"This case has generated considerable publicity and there's a lot of interest in tomorrow's hearing," he says. "By law, hearings involving children are closed to the public, but expect a large media presence jamming the hallways outside the courtroom. There'll also be anti-abortion picketers outside the courthouse. They'll loudly accuse Eulalia of being a baby murderer and could get rowdy and obnoxious."

I grimace, saying I hope we can keep Maggie out of that argument.

Maggie calls me to pick her up at lunchtime, cheerfully assuring me that my car is still at the shelter and appears undamaged. When we return to the office, Willie says he's just received a call from Joliet that since court convenes at nine tomorrow morning, they'll be bringing Eulalia to the Rock Island County jail later this afternoon. He plans on meeting with her this evening and suggests we get busy preparing my testimony.

Willie sits me in a chair in the middle of the room and proceeds to fire questions at me. He tells Maggie to listen carefully because he'll be handling her testimony the same way—if he decides to put her on the stand, which he won't decide about until after he hears what the other side says. Our instructions are to answer in as few words as possible and not offer additional information. For the rest of the day Willie, and then Alisha, throw questions—first at me, then at Maggie. Some are straightforward, but more are designed to trick us into saying something we don't mean. This goes on for several hours after Willie leaves to meet with Eulalia.

•••

A few minutes before nine the next morning, a thick line of shouting abortion protestors and a large group of reporters holding microphones greet Willie, Alisha, Maggie, and me as we enter the Rock Island County courthouse.

"How does it feel to defend a baby killer?" someone holding an *Abortion Is Murder* sign shouts.

"Eternal damnation to all of you," someone else shouts.

"Do you expect to win this case?" an eager young reporter asks, shoving a microphone in Willie's face.

"Who are your witnesses?" another reporter asks.

Sandwiching Maggie between himself and Alisha, Willie tells us to keep our heads down, not to respond to questions, and to follow closely behind him. Within minutes of getting settled in the courtroom, a guard escorts Eulalia, who is pale, obviously frightened, and has a bruise on the side of her face that wasn't there when we saw her two days ago, into the small courtroom and seats her at a table in front of the witness stand, next to Willie and Alisha. Except for a spotlight directed toward the judge and another one directed toward the witness stand, the dark, wood-paneled courtroom is poorly lit. I lean forward and whisper to Eulalia that I'm ready to do all I can to be sure she wins this case. Her eyes are riveted on the hearing officers sitting at a table in front of the jury box, and on the Illinois Child Protective Services representatives, who have just entered the courtroom, and she doesn't acknowledge me.

Less than a minute later, the bailiff announces the judge, who swaggers into the courtroom, looking like a card-carrying good ol' boy, except this one is wearing a long, black robe. He takes his seat, gavels the court to order, and announces that the charges of unfit parenting sufficient to terminate parental rights brought by the Illinois Department of Child Protective Services against Eulalia Tonisha Banks have been dropped, and the case is dismissed. He bangs his gavel again and walks back through the door he entered less than a minute earlier.

Eulalia, looking like a deer caught in the headlights, is led out of the courtroom to return to Joliet and await the outcome of her criminal case. Not sure she fully understands that the parental rights case is over and her children have not been taken from her, I step toward her, but the bailiff shoves a beefy restraining arm in my direction.

As we leave the courtroom, the gaggle of reporters awaiting the outcome of the case want to know why we are now exiting the same courtroom we entered less than five minutes earlier. They are shouting random questions at Willie, at each other, and at everybody else within hearing distance. Grabbing onto Maggie's hand, Willie tells us to ignore them and keep walking.

As we prepare to walk out of the courthouse, word that the case has been dismissed has reached the abortion protestors, sending them into an angry frenzy. Seeing this, Willie drops his briefcase and uses both hands to stop us, saying we should stand back and wait for a while before leaving the building. Maggie strongly disagrees, arguing that we should all stand on the courthouse steps and make a statement that justice for Eulalia, and for women's reproductive rights, has finally been served. She and Willie, who is nearly two feet taller than she is, go toe-to-toe for several minutes, arguing over what to do next. When I can finally get a word in, I point out that, as a nun, she might not want the publicity associated with an abortion case raining down on her head. This gives her pause, and she finally agrees to wait inside for a while and then exit through a side door. For the next hour she paces around the courthouse, grumbling about what she calls "a missed opportunity to speak up for justice for women."

Later that morning, over coffee in a local diner, Maggie and I both press Willie for an explanation of what just happened. He claims he doesn't have one, but as Maggie and I discuss this further on the drive back to Chicago, we decide neither of us believe him.

PART FOUR

1984 – 2019

...and live on to inspire others.

XX.

The Women's National Alliance, like other women's organizations, is a feminist, multi-issue, multi-strategy organization that takes a holistic approach to women's rights. Priorities include winning economic equality with an amendment to the US Constitution that will guarantee equal rights and equal pay for women; championing abortion rights, reproductive freedom, and other women's health issues...and ending all forms of violence against women.

Women's National Alliance Mission Statement

On the Monday morning after Eulalia's hearing is dismissed, Maggie returns what she knows is an important phone call from Sylvia Bernstein, the Chicago Women's National Alliance Coordinator. She begins by apologizing for not getting back to her sooner. "I've been tied up in a legal wrangle," she says.

"I'm following up on our earlier conversation," Sylvia begins after exchanging pleasantries. "It seems that a significant number of our members are disenfranchised Catholic women who are very interested in CWDC, and it seems to me there is enough crossover purpose around the reproductive rights issue to work together more directly on this than we originally discussed."

"That would be wonderful, but right now CWDC is a fledgling group with nothing more than a lot of enthusiasm and energy. We're operating out of a coffee can full of loose change in terms of funding, and the organizational structure is pretty flimsy. Unfortunately, I haven't made a great deal of headway on either issue since we last spoke. This is my fault, Sylvia...I was pulled in too many directions at once."

"NWA is very committed to working with other groups of women who share our basic mission because we'll get more done that way. Let's worry about details later and talk about what might be possible first," Sylvia suggests.

"Sounds good to me," Maggie says.

"Every year we do something to mark the anniversary of the *Roe v. Wade* decision granting women the legal right to an abortion, and the thought for this year is to take out a full-page ad in the Sunday editions of both Chicago newspapers affirming the importance of this landmark decision. For this to be effective, there needs to be as many supporting signatures as possible. Depending on how many we get, it could be a two-page or even a three-page spread. Is this something CWDC would be interested in?"

"Offhand, I'd say yes, very definitely interested," Maggie responds, feeling her excitement at the idea building. "It might be most effective if the supporting organizations are identified, either by listing all the organizations together, followed by all the signatures, or separating the signatures according to organizational affiliation, which is what I think CWDC would prefer."

"Great idea, I'm sure listing individual organizations, followed by their members, would be fine. The only thing I'm not sure about is whether the group of Catholic women I mentioned would prefer being included in your group or as part of ours. Does that matter to you?"

"Not at all," Maggie answers, "but the cost might. Are you going to split that equally among the organizations or pro-rate it by the number of signatures each provides?"

"I don't know...and we are aware this won't be cheap. The national organization is taking the lead, and I think they plan on taking out an ad in *The New York Times*, where our headquarters are located, and listing all the member organizations, and individual signatures from around the country, in that one. That's really going to cost, but it will be a very powerful statement. In addition to here in Chicago, ads will also appear in several other major cities."

"Count us in. I'll figure out how to pay for it later."

"One other thing, Maggie...I want to give you a heads up that the subgroup of Catholic women in WNA is talking about organizing a boycott. I'm not sure on the details, but it sounds like they want women to boycott Mass on the first Sunday of every month, withholding whatever their financial contribution for that Sunday would be, until the Church changes its position on birth control."

"Holy shit!" Maggie yells into the phone. "That's a fantastic idea!"

"Is it fantastic, or is it asking for trouble?"

"It's both—definitely both—but if we wanted to avoid trouble, we'd never have gotten involved in this issue. ASAP, we need to set up a joint meeting with your group and CWDC to discuss this further. I'll ask the action committee chair, Mary Pat Donovan, to be in touch with you right away about a date and time. I'll also let our publicity chair know about the ad. "This is so, so exciting, Sylvia," Maggie exclaims. "I'm all in and will do everything I possibly can to help, I promise. And I can't thank you enough for wanting to include us."

Maggie's next call is to Mary Pat, who answers just as she is walking in the door after her school job. Her nieces and nephews are arguing in the background, and she tells Maggie to hang on while she takes off her coat and drags the phone into the bathroom so she can hear. Maggie tells her about her conversation with Sylvia Bernstein.

"Jesus, Maggie—you're talking serious social action that the cardinal won't take sitting down. Do you think the group will go for it?"

"Why not?" Maggie asks. "Hitting the archdiocese in the pocketbook is the perfect way to force change. It's bound to work."

"Not if the cardinal threatens excommunication."

"He can threaten all he wants, but I seriously doubt he'd excommunicate a thousand or more Catholic women. The Church would be committing political suicide."

"I disagree, Maggie. I think he'd do exactly that to remind women who's in charge—in case it accidentally slipped our minds."

"Call Ben at Our Daily Bread and get some available meeting dates as soon as possible. Then call Sylvia and decide on one that works."

"Okay, but I sure hope you know what you're doing because this is taking protest to a whole new level. The consequences could get ugly."

"You know what, Mary Pat? Ugly is forcing women to have more children than they can care for, and really ugly is dying in childbirth... resisting all that is beautiful."

XXI.

Cursed is the man who dies, but the evil done by him survives.

Abu Bakr

Maggie is still sorting through her backlog of mail and messages that accumulated while she was dealing with Eulalia's situation, when Mary Pat calls back to tell her the meeting with WNA is set for Thursday evening and will include Sylvia, WNA's Catholic splinter group, and CWDC's publicity and action groups.

"Wow—you got right on it!" Maggie exclaims.

"There seems to be a lot of momentum building. This boycott thing could swing out of control very quickly."

"There's no downside to us if that happens. I hope it does take on a life of its own. That way we're not entirely responsible for whatever outcome results, which limits the cardinal's ability to step in to stop it. Come to think of it, I seriously doubt most people in WNA even know who Cardinal O'Grady is."

"I'm sure they know who Cardinal O'Grady is. They just don't care."

"Whatever…this is sounding pretty exciting regardless. Good job on getting it organized quickly. I'll see you Thursday."

Hanging up the phone, Maggie spots three urgent messages from her sister, Coleen. Just as she prepares to pick up the phone to call her back, it rings.

"This is Maggie Corrigan."

"Christ, Maggie. Why the hell haven't you called me back?"

"Colleen?"

"Goddamned right, Maggie. It's your sister Colleen, who apparently you either can't remember or can't be bothered to talk to."

"I've been out of town and very busy. I just found your message a few minutes ago. What's wrong?"

"Tommy died! That's what's wrong," Colleen wails.

"This can't be a surprise, Colleen. He was very sick."

"Fiona and I were there a few hours before. He talked to us and asked after you. We told him we couldn't remember the last time we heard from you. You should've been there with us, Maggie. It ain't right you weren't."

Maggie doesn't point out that no one informed her that her brother's death was imminent, not that it would've mattered to her. Her priority during the last several days was Eulalia, and she would not have let anything, and especially not Tommy, interfere with that commitment.

"Then this afternoon Fiona calls and says Tommy left everything to you. Every goddamned thing—his car, his money—it's all yours now."

"How does Fiona know this?"

"She was next of kin on the hospital forms, and some lawyer called her looking for you. Is it true what he said, Maggie?"

"I'm not sure. Last time I saw Tommy that's what he said. I didn't know whether it was a done deal or just something he was thinking about."

"Why you? He had to know Fiona, Annie, and me coulda used that money and his car. We ain't got a pot to piss in—none of us. You and Mary, you both got God and your Order to look after you. I told Fiona I was sure you'd give the money to us. Ain't that right, Maggie?"

"I haven't thought about it, to be perfectly honest."

"I don't believe you. Somebody tells me I'm inheriting a car and a shitload of money, it's all I'm thinkin' about."

"I guess that's where we're different, Colleen."

"We ain't different, Maggie, except you think by goin' to the convent you're better than us. You took the easy way and turned your back on the real responsibility of Christian life: making a good Catholic family. Your Order takes care of you—we don't got nothin' 'cept drunken husbands, a buncha screaming kids, and a lotta huge bills we got no hope in hell of ever payin'."

"Knock it off, Colleen. I did my family duty from the time you were in diapers and won't apologize to you or anybody for making different choices when I had the chance. And it's good I did because you're all such ingrates. With Corrigan blood in their veins, God only knows what little shits my own kids would've turned out to be. The world doesn't need any more of the likes of us."

"Say the truth, Maggie. Why did Tommy leave you everything?" Colleen asks, calmer now.

"To buy my silence."

"I don't understand...silence about what?"

"Think about it, Colleen. You're smart enough to figure it out. If not, ask Fiona."

"You're making this up is what you're doing...trying to justify your good fortune at our expense."

"Think what you want, Colleen. You asked me a question and I answered it."

"Will you at least be at the funeral?"

"I don't know, to be honest...maybe."

"You weren't at Pa's funeral either. Why, Maggie? What did we ever do to you?"

"You don't know the half of it, Colleen. I'm sure it'll be a lovely funeral, with the cardinal at his finest as he sends the immortal soul of one of his brother priests onward to glory before God. It'll be a fine send-off."

"Fiona heard the cardinal might not say the Mass. Said it might be one of the assistant bishops. I suppose shanty-Irish Corrigans aren't good enough to deserve the cardinal himself."

Really? No cardinal at a priest's funeral? What's going on? Maggie silently wonders.

"I have to go now, Colleen. Thanks for letting me know about Tommy. I'm sorry you're so upset—honestly."

Maggie hangs up and tries to remember whether Tommy gave her the name of his lawyer. While she is rummaging through her purse, Sister Mathilde brings her a message from William Walker, along with a phone number.

"He said he's your brother's lawyer."

Fifteen minutes later, Maggie learns she now owns a three-year-old shiny, standard-issue black sedan priests either receive as outright gifts from parishioners or purchase at a very steep discount. It is not car Maggie would ever drive, even if she knew how, and she has no idea what to do with it. She also owns over $200,000 in stocks, bonds, and cash, which will be handed over to her as soon as she signs the papers waiting for her in Mr. Walker's office.

"Your brother left everything in very good shape for you," the lawyer tells her.

And I now know how to fund the newspaper ad…and it's even sweeter that Tommy's money is paying for it, Maggie thinks, smiling broadly.

After saying she will arrange to sign the papers within a week, Maggie spends the next half hour trying to decide whether to call Mary Pat with the news about Tommy. Her best friend still has family in Back of the Yards, and news of Tommy's death will travel fast through his old neighborhood, so she is bound to hear about it sooner rather than later. Realizing she will wonder why Maggie didn't tell her, she dials the phone.

Mary Pat's sister, Sheilah, answers. "Fiona told me about Tommy…I'm so sorry," she says after Maggie identifies herself and asks to talk to Mary Pat. "She's a little upset right now, Maggie. She might not want to come to the phone. Hang on a minute."

Maggie hears the receiver bang against the wall as Sheilah yells at one of the kids to stop hitting his sister.

Several minutes pass before Mary Pat picks up the phone.

"Why didn't you tell me?" she asks Maggie.

"I just found out an hour ago."

"You didn't know he was sick?"

"Yes, I knew."

"And you didn't tell me because…?"

"I wasn't sure what to tell you, Mary Pat."

"How about 'Tommy's dying, and if you want to see him, you better make it quick.'"

Shit, Maggie thinks. *I probably should have told her Tommy wanted to see her.* Then she remembers her earlier conclusion that if her brother really wanted to see Mary Pat, he'd have found a way regardless of what she did or didn't do.

"I'm sorry, Mary Pat—really I am."

"I always held out hope he'd come around…say he still cared. I know I sound like the stupidest woman alive, but I still love him, Maggie."

"It was liver cancer. The drink caught up with him," Maggie offers in an attempt to shift the conversation away from Mary Pat's feelings about her twin brother.

"No surprise that. He was hitting it hard in high school, and I don't imagine he ever stopped."

"So he did drink in high school. I wondered about it."

"Of course he did. He ran with a bunch of hooligans. They all guzzled whatever they could find. How could you not know that?"

"I was a little busy playing mother to five kids, Mary Pat. Tommy could've robbed the Chicago National Bank, and I wouldn't have noticed."

"Well, he drank a lot of whatever rock-gut hooch he could get his hands on. Surprising he ever got through seminary. And if he kept it up, which he must've, he was probably a functional alcoholic most, if not all, of his priesthood. A lot of them are, you know."

"I'm not surprised," Maggie comments.

"Are you going to the funeral?"

"Colleen said something strange about that. Fiona told her the cardinal might not say the Mass. That's hard to believe. That old fart loves nothing more than a funeral pageant where all eyes are on him, because the only other choice is the dead guy."

"I guess you haven't heard the rumor. The cardinal is supposedly lying low out of sight because the FBI is investigating something about stealing money and a relationship he has with some woman. How did you not know this?"

"I've heard rumors, but I've also been pretty busy and blew them off because I can't imagine the FBI giving a shit about whether Cardinal O'Grady has a girlfriend."

"It does if he's been dipping into the archdiocesan coffers to pay for her upkeep, which is what people are saying. He bought her a condo someplace on the Gold Coast, which isn't cheap living."

Maggie remains silent, thinking about what she's just been told.

"Can I ask you something else, Maggie?"

"Sure—anything...."

"Sheilah said Fiona told her Tommy left you a car and a lot of money and didn't leave them anything. Is that true?"

I forgot that gossip travels through the old neighborhood faster than the speed of light, Maggie thinks, sighing.

"There is some money, yes. I don't know the details yet."

"Where'd it come from?"

"He said he lived off the Church dole and invested his salary."

"And you believed him?" Mary Pat asks.

"I doubted he was telling me the whole story, but I can see how he could've done that. Besides, where else would he get the money?"

"Gambling. He bet the horses."

"How do you know that?"

"In high school we used to go to Arlington Park to bet on the horses. Tommy studied racing forms like they were the Bible and got pretty good at winning on one- and two-dollar bets. It made him a little crazy...like nothing else mattered except winning. He was addicted to the highs and the excitement too much to ever give it up. I'm sure the same was probably true with the booze."

"Jesus Christ, Mary Pat. How could I not know all this about my own brother?"

"Because you never wanted to know him, Maggie. All you ever wanted was to get the hell away from the Yards—and the Corrigans—as fast as you could. You hated everything and everybody there—even your own family. Maybe your own family most of all. Tommy was a deeply flawed man, but he wasn't all bad like you want to believe."

"You forgive him after the way he treated you?"

"I can't hate him. I told you before—he was the love of my life. There's no point ruining that by hating him. So yes, of course I forgave him...a long time ago."

"Would you have gone to see him if he'd asked to see you?" Maggie asks, hesitantly.

"I'm sure I would've." Mary Pat sobs quietly.

"I'm so sorry, Mary Pat, I really am," Maggie says, without revealing that she came between her brother's dying wish and her best friend's desire to say goodbye to the love of her life.

Maybe I'm as horrible as Tommy was, just in a different way, Maggie thinks as she hangs up the phone and pushes her office door shut a little too hard.

Reaching into the bottom drawer of her desk, Maggie extracts the bottle of cheap bourbon, then decides against the idea of a drink before noon and puts it back into the drawer. She sits with her hands in her lap, staring out her tiny office window. *If I tell Mary Pat that Tommy wanted to see her and I didn't pass along his request, I'll hurt her worse than she's hurting now and lose my best friend—only friend, really. If she asks me, and I don't tell her the truth, then I'm lying to my best friend, which also hurts her. Will she believe the reason I didn't tell her was that I was afraid Tommy would hurt her again? Or will she think I was taking one last jab at Tommy? She deserves to know he asked to see her...and I was wrong to not pass that message along,* she ruminates, in a rare admission of wrongdoing

After a few minutes, Maggie decides she will tell Mary Pat the truth about Tommy's request if she asks, but won't volunteer the information.

What is bothering her more, Maggie determines a few minutes later, is that she doesn't understand how any woman can claim a man who has hurt her as badly as Tommy hurt Mary Pat "is the love of my life." *It doesn't make any sense...although admittedly, I know next to nothing about love in any form. Any love I ever felt is a distant memory that died with my mother,* she thinks, with surprising sadness.

Worse, what Mary Pat is saying about forgiveness parrots exactly what Maggie hears from the abused women in the shelter who ultimately return to their abusers and is precisely what she hopes CWDC will be able to change. *Maybe by helping women to feel good enough about themselves that they aren't compelled to forgive abusive men, we can help them understand there's forgiveness and there's Forgiveness, and the concept doesn't mean forgetting or continuing on like before, as if nothing happened,* she wonders to herself.

Then it occurs to Maggie that perhaps the problem isn't just the Catholic Church; perhaps it is Christianity itself. *Jesus says to turn the other cheek. Saint Paul says women should be submissive to their husbands. The wider society says to forgive and forget, and women who listen to those messages always end up getting hurt—sometimes killed—for doing what they've been taught to believe is the right thing to do. Ungodly rage is the only thing that will save them, and they aren't brave enough to allow it to surface and then use it to save themselves. It's no wonder this issue is so difficult for women—everything and everyone conspires against them. Maybe forgiveness isn't such a great idea.... What if whoever has hurt you doesn't see anything wrong with what they have done and doesn't ask to be forgiven? Maybe the Jews have it right: an eye for an eye...and come to think of it, maybe that's why I've never seen a Jewish woman come through our shelter doors.*

•••

A few days later, on the morning of the joint WNA and CWDC meeting, Maggie quietly enters Queen of Heaven Church and slips into a seat near the back. She sees her brother's casket resting at the head of the aisle, and someone who is not Cardinal O'Grady is swinging an ornate thurible filled with incense in a wide arc around the body. Her sisters are sitting in the front pew. Several rows behind them, Mary Pat, dressed in black, is sitting alone. Various clergy, and people she assumes are members of the congregation Tommy served, are scattered throughout the cavernous old church, which is only about half full. Maggie expected to see many more.

The celebrant offers prayers for the repose of Monsignor Thomas Corrigan's immortal soul, and the homilist heaps praise on her brother as a "good priest." Maggie does not join the congregation in singing several hymns praising God, does not take Communion, and leaves before the funeral Mass is over, having no desire to accompany her sisters and Mary Pat to her brother's final resting place. Walking toward the L station, she is neither glad nor sorry she made the effort to attend Tommy's funeral but hopes no one saw her there.

XXII.

Never underestimate the power of a small group of women to change the world...it's the only thing that ever has.

Margaret Mead

Hoping to catch Ben for a few minutes, Maggie arrives early at Our Daily Bread for the combined WNA and CWDC meeting on the evening after Tommy's funeral. Earlier in the day, she'd spent a torturous hour trying to decide what to wear, finally settling on navy blue pants, a plain white blouse, a yellow cardigan to ward off the chill of the early summer evening, and tennis shoes. She finds the handsome director of the neighborhood outreach effort in his cluttered office, shuffling papers. He looks up and smiles broadly when he hears her familiar knock on the wall.

"Haven't seen you in a while," Ben says, walking around his desk and pulling up two chairs facing each other. "You never call—you never write," he teases.

"I've been busy the last few weeks. I was tied up with a legal issue involving one of our former shelter residents, got behind on my grant application due next week, and had a bunch of other things happen."

"Good things, I hope."

"Good and bad...or maybe not bad so much as what seems bad hasn't turned into good yet. I don't really know."

"You look—and sound—awfully tired, Maggie, so I won't complain that I'm behind on the painting because my helper isn't showing up. Now that it's dry, it's pretty obvious the color she and I chose, warm cream I think it's called, will require two coats to cover the industrial gray that's there now."

Maggie looks at the wall behind Ben's desk and smiles weakly. "It's going to look nice when it's finished," she says. "And I think a little paint therapy would do me good. But first, there are a few things I want to run past you if you don't mind."

"Depends on whether you can paint and talk at the same time."

"Let me get past tonight, then we can set something up."

"Works for me. Changing the subject, I'd like to sit in on the meeting, if you don't mind. When Mary Pat Donovan set it up, it sounded like a lively one," he smiles.

Maggie says she appreciates his taking an interest in CWDC and is always welcome, then turns toward the room where the meeting will be held. "It's good to see you again, Ben," She says as she leaves the small office.

Maggie estimates eighty-five or ninety people fill Our Daily Bread's upstairs meeting space. Sylvia Bernstein is standing in the back of the room talking to two women Maggie doesn't recognize, and she doesn't see Mary Pat anywhere. *Hopefully, she was just held up,* Maggie thinks.

Sylvia walks over, remarks that the turnout is terrific, and suggests Maggie open the meeting by summarizing the reason they are there, then invite discussion. She assures Maggie she will answer any questions Maggie can't, then indicates they should get started.

After a brief update, Maggie explains the ad idea and is surprised by the level of enthusiasm for moving ahead with it. She expected more discussion and greater hesitation from CWDC and the other Catholic women about going public in support of abortion rights as a key component of reproductive justice for all women, but the only question raised concerns finding the money to pay for the ad.

Sylvia steps up to answer. "National is running these ads in several cities and will negotiate a price with the largest newspapers in each area. Right now, the plan is to assign cost proportionate to participation. Here in Chicago, if more WNA women sign on than, for example, CWDC women, then WNA will pay a greater portion of the cost. Overall, cost will become proportionately less as more groups are included, and I don't have a feel for that yet. I've reached out to several organizations who might be interested, and my best guess is a few more will join in." Sylvia stops to acknowledge a hand in the back of the room.

"The subgroup of Catholic WNA members have been wondering whether we can be included with CWDC for purposes of this ad?" a grandmotherly woman asks.

Sylvia defers to Maggie to weigh in on this.

"CWDC does not have an organizational structure that includes dues-paying members yet and welcomes anyone who wishes to participate. So I don't see a problem with including your names with ours. We're grateful for every name we can add."

"Even if it costs CWDC more?" the woman asks.

"That's a good point," Maggie agrees, "but I think I've found a way to pay for our share of the ad, so the number of names won't be a cost issue for us. However, we do have to consider how WNA feels about losing names to us."

"WNA is more concerned with the total number of supporters than with what organization they belong to, so there's no issue for us if some of you want to identify with CWDC. Personally, I think it's wonderfully brave of Catholic women to sign on at all, and strongly believe that the more there are, the better they'll be able to support each other if trouble arises for them as a result," Sylvia responds.

"I'd like to speak to that issue," Maggie says.

Sylvia steps aside and hands her the microphone.

"A persistent rumor concerning the federal government pursuing an investigation of Cardinal O'Grady for, among other things, using archdiocesan funds is floating around out there. My unofficial understanding is that there is some truth to these rumors and to the concerns the FBI is investigating, which, if founded, are quite serious. I think it is entirely possible that under these circumstances this ad will escape the cardinal's notice. But if not, he has much more pressing things to worry about right now and still may ignore it," Maggie explains, trying not to smile too broadly.

Briefly, the meeting turns into a pseudo-news conference, with several women shouting out questions. Maggie raises her hand for quiet and explains she doesn't know any more than what she has just told them but feels strongly that they should view this upheaval in the archdiocese, which is likely to go on for a while, as an opportunity they would be foolish to ignore. Then, on the spur of the moment, she raises the issue of the proposed boycott.

"I didn't intend to talk about this tonight," she begins. "But since we are all together, and in the last few days have learned we are being provided with an extraordinary opening to take action, I'd like to discuss the financial boycott the Catholic WNA members are considering."

Maggie goes on to summarize her understanding of the WNA plan for the CWDC members who have not heard about a boycott until now, adding that since women are the largest weekly donor group in the Church, withholding their offering even one Sunday per month will be financially significant. "Supporting the boycott with women carrying *No Voice, No Money* signs while picketing outside the church makes a very powerful statement and will result in a great deal of publicity," she tells her audience.

The next question pertains to how the effort will be organized. Maggie explains that WNA and CWDC will spread the idea by word of mouth among its members, announcements in the WNA newsletter, and include it in the CWDC update at their next meeting. "My guess is news of this proposed action will travel so fast it breaks the sound barrier."

"So women would still go to Mass but would ignore the collection plate?" a voice in the back asks.

"Exactly," Maggie says. "Bear in mind that the Church doesn't tithe, and there is nothing in official Church doctrine about failing to give money being an occasion of sin. It's a practice the Church depends upon, and guilts people into, but the archdiocese can't do anything about how much money an individual does, or doesn't, contribute. This is the beauty of the idea: the archdiocese can't threaten anything to stop it."

"Could they have the picketers arrested?" someone else asks.

"They could try, I suppose," Sylvia answers. "But the right to protest is guaranteed under the United States Constitution. As long as the picketing is peaceful, and I see no reason why it wouldn't be, then I don't see a problem."

"I just thought of something," Maggie interjects. "The protestors will need a permit from the city, and given that Irish-Catholics run City Hall, that might be a problem."

"On what grounds would they deny?" Sylvia asks.

Maggie shrugs and says the Irish mafia running Chicago city government can do anything it damned well wants to do and should never be underestimated. "If they want to deny it, they'll find a reason."

"May I say something?" Ben asks, standing in the back of the room.

Maggie signals him to continue.

"First Amendment rights supersede local government regulations. So if the picketers stay on the public sidewalk, don't trespass onto Church property, obstruct traffic, or otherwise disturb the peace, they don't need a permit. As long as the picketing is orderly and nondisruptive, allows pedestrians to pass, and ensures entrances to surrounding buildings or the church itself are not blocked, there should be no problem. I don't see any need to involve City Hall at all."

Maggie mouths him a silent thank you and asks for any other comments or questions.

"I just want to be sure on this," another voice speaks out. "As long as we attend Mass, there is no sin involved in this action—right?"

Maggie nods her head yes, then asks if the group wants to vote on this. Seeing a mixed reaction, she asks for a show of hands among those who think the boycott is a good idea and is pleased when the majority of women indicate support for the idea. Maggie then asks for a volunteer to organize the effort for CWDC and coordinate with the WNA organizers.

"I'll do it," Mary Pat, who arrived after the meeting began, says, standing up. Relieved to see her friend, Maggie thanks her and suggests those who wish to work with the boycott stay to speak with Mary Pat for a few minutes after the meeting is adjourned, which unless there are further questions, is now. Maggie watches about fifty women walk toward the back of the room where Mary Pat is standing.

"Good job!" Sylvia exclaims. "This worked out really well."

"Thanks. I thought so. On another subject, do you have a minute to answer an unrelated question?"

"I'll be glad to try."

"First, are you Jewish...if you don't mind my asking?"

"I don't mind at all, and yes, I was raised in the reform Jewish tradition. As an adult, I've gotten a little lazy about it. Why do you ask?"

"One thing CWDC is trying to do is change the message Catholic women receive that tells them to forgive, forget, and go back to their abusers. As I was thinking about this recently, I realized we never see Jewish women in the shelter. I asked a few of the other shelter directors, and they said the same thing. Do you have any idea why this is?"

"I have a couple of thoughts," Sylvia says. "But first, let's sit down." She walks toward two chairs in the back corner of the room.

"Judaism is widely diverse, both culturally and as a religion, so I can only speak in sweeping generalities. In general, Jewish women in the US tend toward being well-educated and, in today's world, are rarely generationally as poor as, for example, Black or Hispanic women. If domestic difficulties do arise, they can usually manage the crisis without ending up homeless, so would not seek shelter services. But there is another reason that I think speaks to what you're really asking, which is how Jewish families are different from Christian ones—right?"

Maggie nods.

"After the Holocaust claimed six million Jewish lives, representing one-third of the world-wide Jewish population, Jews around the world realized they would have to replenish their numbers quickly or risk dying out. When the United Nations created the State of Israel, it was informally agreed upon that every Jewish family would have six children, one for every million Jews who perished in the war, so the country could grow quickly. Realizing that this was asking a lot of Jewish families, Judaism organized itself accordingly. Surviving Jews worldwide bought into this concept, and National Jewish federations assisted synagogues to develop communal, social, and other practical resources to support and encourage larger families and strong family life. But there are no penalties for deciding not to have lots of kids. You just do more volunteer work for Jewish Relief or Hadassah or some other Jewish social service organization instead...or engage in work that makes people's lives, and by extension, the world, better."

"This is so interesting, and makes so much sense," Maggie responds.

"But it's important to realize that, unlike Catholic and Protestant women, Jewish women are part of a religious culture that values them for who they are because it depends upon women to maintain Jewish family life and rituals," Sylvia continues. "As a result, women are respected and treated well. It's a separate and equal view of women embraced by both men and women. Of course, there are exceptions, and this delicate balance can falter, but as a general rule it holds: women are too important to the survival of Judaism to risk alienating them."

"Wow! That explains a lot, and it's very enviable."

"Don't misunderstand me—we have domestic problems, but assaulting women is rarely one of them."

"I wish there was some way that message could get across to Catholic women who believe their sole purpose in life is to have babies for the pope and his wife, Holy Mother Church."

"Until the last Jew who remembers the Holocaust is dead and there is enduring peace in the Middle East, Jews will continue to have generations of historical trauma binding them together," Sylvia explains. "Christian martyrdom is pretty much over now, so Catholics don't have immediate memories of a deeply horrific immediate past history hovering over them and are freer to fight among themselves. Women against the Church, women against the patriarchy, and so on....Judaism is about community and taking care of each other. Jews focus on what we call Tikkun Olam: repairing the broken world and doing mitzvahs, or individual acts of kindness toward others. Women tend to spend less time worrying about what the Torah says, or the Rabbi thinks, because that's for the men to debate—although this is changing. And issues like where to sit in synagogue don't matter much to women either, because who cares? We're just grateful we aren't suffering a pogrom and can sit someplace."

Sylvia's explanation leaves Maggie speechless.

"I think I would have been much happier being born a Jew," she finally says softly.

"Only if you're comfortable with half the world hating you," Sylvia points out.

"Half the world hates me now," Maggie counters.

"All any of us is asked to do is our part to make the world better, which you are trying to do. The rest is in Yahweh's hands," Sylvia smiles, patting her arm. "I'm really glad the CWDC group wants to join with us. I know it's not an easy decision for those women, and I admire their courage."

"So do I," Maggie says.

•••

"So tell me—what's the deal with the cardinal?" Ben asks Maggie as he is preparing to lock up the building after the meeting.

"I'm not sure. I think the old fart has a girlfriend he's supporting with archdiocesan funds," Maggie answers, then apologizes for being so crude and disrespectful.

"No surprise there," Ben says. "The best priests I knew all had girlfriends—or boyfriends. Made human beings out of them, and everybody was very much better for it...the same is probably true for nuns. The Church has this all wrong. Everybody needs somebody in their lives they love like no other, and who loves them back in the same way."

"I wouldn't know," Maggie says absently. "Before I forget, thanks for helping me out with the protest question. I learned something."

"My pleasure."

"Can I ask you something?"

"Sure...."

"I have a problem I need some help with, and I'm not sure who to ask."

"I'll do whatever I can."

"Well, for starters, I've just inherited a car I don't know how to drive and wouldn't be caught dead driving—even if I did know how. The lawyer gave me the keys a week ago and told me to pick it up, which I haven't done. I need to figure out what to do with it."

"How did this happen?"

"My brother died."

"I'm sorry, Maggie. I didn't know."

"It's no big deal to me personally, except he left me his car and a lot of money I don't know what to do with either—and by the way, this is a confidential conversation. I'm not supposed to own anything. Any monetary or other valuable inheritances the sisters receive are signed directly over to the Order."

"Anything you tell me is confidential, Maggie. Besides, I'm not sure who you think I would tell."

"I just want to be sure, because I'm staring at a big problem where that money is concerned. I've never had two nickels to rub together in my entire life and have no idea what to do."

"Let's deal with the car first," Ben suggests. "Where is it right now?"

"In the garage at the rectory where my brother lived. The lawyer said the insurance is paid for the next three months and to go get it as soon as possible. That was over a week ago."

"How about we get it, and I'll drive it back to my mother's place and park it in her extra parking space—at least temporarily, while you decide what you want to do."

"You would do that?" Maggie asks, surprised.

"Of course, no problem at all. You've really never driven before?"

"Nobody in my family could afford a car. If we couldn't get there on the L, we didn't go. If my dad needed a car for some reason, he must've borrowed one, although I doubt he had a driver's license. I have no idea how Tommy learned to drive—must've been a requirement of the priesthood."

"It probably was," Ben agrees. "I'm not sure about trying to teach you to drive myself. Your best bet is a driving school. I'll see what I can find out about that and let you know."

"I'm not sure I want to learn to drive."

"It's a handy skill, Maggie."

"That may be, but if I do ever drive, it won't be this car. I need to figure out how to get rid of it."

"The insurance is paid up for three months, so you have time to decide. Can we pick it up tomorrow?"

"I'll be here right after lunch...and thanks, Ben." Maggie starts to reach for him, then stops herself.

•••

Later that evening, while drinking a beer, Maggie plays reruns of Ben's offer to help her. Her feelings toward him are growing stronger, occupying more of her brain space and imagination. *He's taking up so much space in my head, he ought to be paying me rent,* she thinks, sitting in a chair, twisting a napkin into knots.

I think I might love him—God forbid, she finally admits to herself.

XXIII.

The evangelical counsel of obedience, undertaken in a spirit of faith and love in the following of Christ, who was obedient even unto death, requires a submission of the will to legitimate superiors, who stand in the place of God when they command according to the proper constitutions.

CANON 601; CODE OF CANON LAW

"Let me explain something to you, Bishop O'Hara," Maggie says, holding the telephone away from her head to reduce the impact of the voice screaming in her ear.

Bishop Michael O'Hara, one of ten auxiliary bishops in the Chicago Archdiocese, and one of the cardinal's strong-arm enforcers, is calling her to follow up on a letter she received from Cardinal O'Grady after the WNA ad recognizing the anniversary of *Roe v. Wade* appeared in the Sunday editions of Chicago's largest newspapers just over two weeks ago. In the letter, O'Grady expressed his extreme displeasure with CWDC and ordered Maggie to come to his office at two o'clock on the following Friday afternoon. She ignored the summons, which prompted Bishop O'Hara's follow-up phone call.

"I don't do command appearances, Bishop. I am not vowed to obey Cardinal O'Grady, and nothing binds me to follow his orders, bend to his wishes, or to consider what he thinks about anything," Maggie continues, her voice calm and free of emotion.

The increasingly frustrated bishop, who is under orders to present Maggie to the cardinal immediately, does not have the same level of self-control. "I beg to differ with you, Sister. Like every other Catholic in the archdiocese, you are obligated to honor the cardinal's directives, which include steadfastly avoiding participation in activities that reflect poorly on the Church. This includes public statements guaranteed to cause scandal. You're way the hell out of line here, Sister."

"I understand that the cardinal disapproves of CWDC and differs with us on the issue of women's reproductive rights, but nothing in his letter indicates he has any interest in bridging these differences. So I see no point in wasting either his time or my own."

"Sister Corrigan, I am sure you are aware it is customary for women religious working within the archdiocesan boundaries to meet with the cardinal when he requests it."

"I am aware of that, but customary and mandatory are not the same thing, and since he's not in my chain of command, I'm under no obligation to honor his requests," Maggie interrupts. "I am also quite sure the cardinal is preoccupied with other things right now. I certainly would be if the FBI was investigating me. I suggest we let this matter rest for the moment. Please give the cardinal my regards and assure him I am praying for him."

Hanging up the phone, Maggie laughs aloud as she realizes that CWDC is not only on the cardinal's radar but also has gotten under his skin. She was hoping for more time to organize the boycotts before the cardinal took notice, but now that he has, she has used the opportunity to set the terms of their conversation on the matter. Overall, she views this as an important first step toward their goal of giving women a voice in the Church, even if it has occurred sooner than she wanted. Maggie immediately places a call to Bridget Mary in Omaha, eager to share the good news.

After listing to Maggie's update, Bridget Mary shares her enthusiasm but dampens it with caution. "Don't underestimate O'Grady, Maggie. Even if he's out on his ear, he won't go quietly, and I'm sure whoever succeeds him will be a Church loyalist who is willing and eager to pick up right where O'Grady left off. What you have now is an early, relatively easy victory in a very long war."

A few days later, Maggie receives another phone call. This one is from her superior, Mother Marie William. She tells Maggie she is going to be in Chicago in a few days and would like to meet to discuss several things with her. Maggie has no choice but to agree and feels certain the timing of her Chicago visit is not a coincidence. They make plans to meet at Saint Alberta's convent attached to a parish by the same name located northwest of the Loop. Currently, three other Sisters of Charity and Justice assigned to Chicago are sharing the convent space with four vowed sisters from two other orders who also work in the city.

Mother Marie William, whose long history with Maggie goes back to Maggie's days as a postulant, came to religious life later than most. Originally from suburban Oak Park, she worked as an emergency room nursing supervisor in Chicago's Cook County Hospital before deciding to forgo secular life for a religious one. She is not the traditionalist her predecessor, Mother Michael Joan, was but is not as progressive as she could be either. She kept her religious name rather than reverting to her baptismal one when she had the chance, and she wears an updated version of the traditional habit rather than the ordinary street clothes many other members of the Order, including Maggie, have opted for.

Maggie has always considered her current superior approachable and has never forgotten Mother Marie William's patience and support during her early days in religious life. She finds her a good listener and appreciates that, for the last nearly ten years she has led the Order, she has adopted a hands-off approach to Maggie's life in Chicago. Nevertheless, she views their upcoming meeting with some concern and is surprised when Mother Marie William answers the convent's front door herself after Maggie knocks.

"Sister Maggie! It's wonderful to see you. It's been a long time," the mother superior says, reaching out to grab both of Maggie's hands in her own. Smiling warmly, Sister Marie William leads Maggie into the parlor, which like all convent parlors, is immaculate but not warmly welcoming. Furnished with mismatched chairs, a scattering of lamps, and worn rugs, it smells faintly of lemon furniture polish and beeswax candles. Maggie sees a pot of tea and a tray of cookies sitting on one of the end tables.

The two nuns spend a few minutes on pleasantries, and Mother Marie William stresses that she has heard good things about Maggie's work at the shelter. Maggie says she knows her superior didn't come all the way to Chicago merely to assure her she is doing a good job. After a moment's silence, the bomb drops.

"I received a call from Cardinal O'Grady a few days ago," the mother superior begins. "It seems he is concerned about several things you are involved with. Something about an organization you are starting and a large newspaper ad—I believe he said it was three full pages—in the first section of a recent edition of the Sunday newspapers. Are you aware of what he is referring to?"

Maggie indicates she is aware of the cardinal's concerns.

"The cardinal said he ordered you to disband the organization some time back, and you ignored him. He also requested a meeting with you after the ad appeared, and you refused. Is this true?"

Maggie indicates the information is correct.

"These are serious accusations, Maggie, and before responding to the cardinal, I'd like to hear your side."

Maggie takes a drink of tea and a deep breath before summarizing the CWDC brief history and planned efforts going forward.

"I can understand why this upsets Cardinal O'Grady—I'd be shocked if it didn't—but frankly, I don't care. I am surprised he has involved you because right now it appears he has far bigger things to worry about," Maggie says.

"First of all, Maggie, I don't disagree with you regarding the Church's positions regarding women, especially the birth control issue, and agree that things have to change. When I was working at Cook County Hospital, I saw what happened when Catholic women took the consequences of the Church's anti-birth control edict into their own hands and stood beside a good many as they died from botched abortions or the complications of too many pregnancies. I also saw a lot of battered and broken faces and other permanent injuries irate husbands inflicted, and even got to know some of the women by name, because I'd treated them so many times. It became so heart-wrenching for me, I had to leave emergency medicine and eventually leave nursing entirely. After seeing what drunk men are capable of doing to women, there was no way I could ever marry and raise a family. My only other options were the convent or secretarial school, and I can't type, so that's when I decided to commit my life to God."

Maggie nods at her superior's candor and does not interrupt her.

"Please understand that I'm not sorry I made that decision, and I don't want you to think for a moment that I come down on the side of the Church on this, because I don't. The problem is that as Catholic women religious, we are bound to uphold and honor the beliefs our faith rests upon, at least publicly, and the cardinal believes you have failed to do this, which has resulted in public scandal. Unfortunately, he is correct."

"You've got to be kidding me," Maggie explodes. "The cardinal, who is under investigation by the FBI for playing fast and loose with archdiocesan funds that he funneled to an offshore account in the Cayman Islands—where he has a condo he shares with a girlfriend he's had for decades and puts up in a penthouse on the Gold Coast...and he thinks what I'm doing is scandalous? He can't possibly be serious."

"I'm afraid he is, Maggie."

"Then he can go fuck himself."

Mother Marie William grimaces, and Maggie immediately apologizes for her choice of words.

"I understand your outrage, Maggie. I really do. All I promised the cardinal was that I would speak with you about this. I did not indicate I would order you to stop, and I won't. I've always believed in you, Maggie, even when Mother Michael Joan had grave reservations about admitting you as a postulant and later allowing you to take your final vows. I admire your spunk and resolve and won't issue a directive your vows obligate you to obey—mostly because I doubt you would do it, and that would force me into a position I'd rather not be in."

Maggie smiles gratefully, breathing a deep sigh of relief.

"However, I am also responsible for over one thousand other members of the Order. A good many of them are aware of your activities, do not agree with what you are doing, and have shared their displeasure with me. I am obligated to take their feelings on this matter seriously and am hoping we can find a compromise."

"How many are you referring to?" Maggie asks.

"Over three hundred at last count. It's not a small number, Maggie."

"Then what do you suggest I do?"

"Try harder to work behind the scenes rather than on the front lines. Keep your name and your face out of the news."

"I can do this on two conditions," Maggie tells her superior. "One is that this agreement stays between the two of us. You don't tell the cardinal or the other sisters that I've agreed to anything. Only say that you've spoken to me, and it was a mutually beneficial discussion."

"What's the other condition?"

"That you don't forbid me from accepting the position as executive director of the Chicago Chapter of WNA if it is offered to me. The current director is getting ready to retire sometime in the next six months and has asked me to consider taking over the position from her."

"They are a pro-choice group, am I right?" Mother Marie William asks.

"Yes. But the upside for the Order is that I'll be earning a much larger salary and will be sending much more money back to the motherhouse."

"If this would mean moving out of your current quarters, won't you have increased living expenses?"

"Perhaps. I don't have that figured out yet because we have only had a preliminary conversation."

"So it may not happen at all—is that right?"

"Yes."

"Then I'll agree to the first condition, and we'll decide not to worry about the second one right now."

Maggie smiles slightly and thanks her superior for being so reasonable.

"Two other things, Maggie—and the first is the most important. I want to know what is going on in your spiritual life. I'm told you are not in touch with our other sisters living and working in the Chicago area, do not attend their monthly Day of Reflection and Renewal, or participate in the other spiritual practices that are part of the Order's charism. These are the practices that keep the faith alive in us as individuals, and as a religious community, and mustn't be allowed to fade into the background of our lives."

Maggie takes another deep breath. "I don't know how to answer that question," she finally confesses. "I lead a very busy life and am always behind on something." She does not add that she has stopped going to Mass or attending other Church rituals because she can't abide male priests who think they know everything about what God wants for women's lives standing in a pulpit and issuing directives that induce nausea in her.

"Do you need to make an extended retreat to spiritually regroup and rediscover the core values of the faith?" her superior asks.

That is the last thing I need, Maggie thinks, panicked that her superior will order her to take a leave of absence and return to the motherhouse for spiritual counseling. "I don't think so," Maggie says softly.

"I'm concerned you are motivated more by a sense of self-defined, righteous anger than the conviction that you are doing God's work on Earth, as God desires, and as best we can discern God's will. If my perception is correct, you will burn out quickly, reaching a psychological and faith crisis you never saw coming, and I want to avoid this happening."

"I want to avoid it too, and I assure you I will pay more attention to the spiritual side of my life and to what I am trying to accomplish."

"Protesting is extremely seductive, Maggie. It is a very satisfying activity, regardless of whether it succeeds in bringing about the desired change. It is also a secular endeavor that often deeply bonds participants together into an 'us against them' community all its own. And the activity itself is frequently a lot of fun."

Maggie doesn't disagree.

"Anger can be a strong motivation that blinds one to the wider issues at play," the mother superior continues, "and often one has to search very hard to find a spiritual component to the sort of commitment to change you are undertaking. It is important to maintain an assuredness that you are doing God's will and not your own."

Maggie continues to listen carefully, hoping the sky isn't about to fall.

"Even if we find that answer, it's extremely difficult to continue keeping God first in our lives if we are not in continual contact with those who share the importance of maintaining this perspective. I don't get the sense you have tapped into what God desires as you pursue your efforts, and I strongly urge you to shift your focus in that direction. A good start is making a committed effort to reconnect with your fellow sisters here in Chicago and regularly participate in their spiritual exercises. Otherwise, you are protesting for its own sake, acting out of personal rage, and merely stirring up trouble because you can. Lasting change rarely occurs under those circumstances."

Maggie remains silent, afraid that if she comments on what has just been said, the words "strongly urge" will be transposed into a command she is obligated to obey. She feels sure her fellow sisters in the Chicago area, several of whom she knows from her years in the novitiate, do not share her enthusiasm for what she is doing and sees no value in what her superior is suggesting. What little connection with her religious community she may have felt in the past is gone, and she feels no need to reestablish it. She knows she won't follow through on Mother Marie William's suggestions because her primary emotional and personal support groups now are CWDC and WNA, and they are enough for her.

"Lastly, I've been told that there is a rumor floating around you have inherited money from your brother. Is this true?"

Aware that Irish-Catholic Chicago can be a very small town, Maggie doesn't bother to ask how her superior knows this. "My brother did leave some money. How it will be distributed among his surviving siblings has not been decided. There is wide variance in need among us."

"I'm sure you're aware of the regulation that all inheritances are signed over to the Order."

"I am aware of that, but as I said, no final decisions have been made."

XXIV.

In a time when many, Catholic and secular alike, would hail the disappearance of religious chastity as something worthy of rejoicing, as a sign of "modernization," I find it all the more necessary to openly proclaim the immense joy of living in chastity and the beautiful purpose it serves in the Body of Christ.

DOMINICAN FRIARS OF THE MOST HOLY NAME OF JESUS

"I feel like I'm being watched—spied upon," Maggie complains to Ben after describing her meeting with Mother Marie William, while painting the cafeteria in Our Daily Bread's basement.

"You're walking on the edge," Ben tells her. "I'd be very surprised if Church officials, and perhaps your Order, aren't keeping an eye on you—although I'm not sure how serious they might be about it."

"Serious enough to plant a spy in CWDC or WNA."

"You're sounding a little paranoid. Do you really think that's likely?"

"It's very difficult to know who everyone in either organization is, so it's definitely possible. I'm less sure about how probable it is, but I have to at least consider the possibility."

"How do you think your superior found out about the money?"

"My sister, Fiona. She has a mouth like a volcano and thinks she's been wronged. Colleen's just as mouthy but smarter, so it could've been her thinking if she makes sure the Order knows about the money, I'll be forced to give it to my biological sisters or risk expulsion from my religious community."

"They'd expel you over that?"

"They could, but whether they would is another question. The decision would depend upon my perceived value. If one of us is earning a large salary and contributing a significant amount back to the Order, which too few sisters are doing, then it's much more likely any transgressions would be overlooked. But I'm not in that category, so I don't know how they would handle it."

Maggie stops talking and walks over to the corner to refill her paint bucket.

"This color really looks nice—do you like it?" she asks Ben, intentionally changing the subject.

He agrees on the painting effort, then asks whether she has made any decisions about the money she inherited.

"I paid for the ad. The first financial contribution boycott is in two weeks. I'm on overload and can't deal with any more decisions."

"How about the car?"

"If you want it, you can have it. Otherwise, I'm getting rid of it as soon as I have time and figure out how to do it."

"That's very generous, Maggie, but I already have a car. You do know a low-mileage, one-owner Buick less than three years old is worth something, right?"

"I have no idea what it's worth. I just want to get rid of it."

"You have some time to think about it."

"I have thought about it, including giving it to my sisters, but they can't afford the insurance or the gas, and splitting a car three ways is a little difficult, so I'm getting rid of it. All ideas on how to do that are welcome."

"I can try to sell it for you, if you're absolutely sure that's what you want."

"I'm sure. If it's not too much trouble for you to sell it, that would be wonderful. We'll split the money."

"I don't need the money, Maggie. I'm happy to do it if it helps you out."

"Thanks...."

"Consider it done. Changing the subject again, did you apply for the WNA executive director position?"

"I did. I should hear in two, maybe three weeks."

"If that comes through, will you have to resign from the shelter and move out?"

"Yes—to both questions. I'll need to find a new place to live."

"Maybe you should use some of the money you just inherited to buy into a co-op like my mother lives in. I'm sure you could find one you can afford."

"Perhaps," Maggie replies, thinking that might not be a bad idea, but would clearly break the Order's rule against owning private property.

"Tell me the latest on the cardinal?" Ben asks.

"He hasn't resigned, but rumor is that he's on his way out, both physically and as head of the archdiocese. I heard he looked pretty rough at his annual Christmas Mass several weeks ago, which was the first time he'd appeared in public in months, and he hasn't been seen again since. He thinks he runs Chicago, which he basically does, and will fight to hang onto that power until death—or until the fat lady sings. It sounds like she might be warming up."

"My understanding is a federal grand jury is trying to subpoena financial records," Ben says. "Apparently, he dug in his heels and has refused to turn over anything, including his personal financial information. From what I've read in the ever-reliable newspapers, some people agree with O'Grady's claims that this is a direct assault on the Church, and on him personally, while others believe the cardinal is a crook."

"I come down on the side of 'O'Grady is a crook,'" Maggie says without hesitation. "Over a million bucks a year disappeared from the archdiocese, and nearly four million evaporated into thin air out of the Midwest Catholic Men's Club treasury during the years O'Grady was their chaplain. That was about the same time he was buying his girlfriend a lot of exotic real estate. I think much of this would be overlooked if he was personally popular, but he's a tyrannical leader who believes in centralized, hierarchical authority—namely his own—and thinks people come to his Masses to worship him instead of God. He goes full-boar ballistic when crossed, and my understanding is that several times during his career, various groups and organizations have sent recall petitions to Rome. A real charmer, that one."

"He probably has something on the Vatican that keeps it from acting," Ben offers.

"That's the general consensus, but it does appear the FBI investigation has brought his reign of terror in Chicago to a halt. It's been several months, and nothing further has come from the archdiocese regarding the *Roe v. Wade* ad, which surprises me. I'm sure the shit will hit the fan when the boycott begins, but we'll deal with that when it occurs."

"He has deep roots in Chicago going back years. I wonder why no one asked questions before?"

"Rumor is one of his priests got seriously ticked off and ratted him out to the FBI." Maggie unsuccessfully tries to hide the smirk on her face as she says this.

XXV.

Consistent, peaceful, nonviolent protest is the only thing that can change men's hearts and minds.

MAHATMA GANDHI

By the numbers, the first CWDC-WNA financial boycott is a huge success. More than one thousand Catholic women across twenty different parishes withheld their contributions to the Sunday collection at the eight and ten o'clock Masses on Palm Sunday. They picketed outside their churches, singing "Amazing Grace" and carrying signs that made a clear statement: *No Voice – No Money*; *We Will Listen to You When You Listen to Us*; *Our Mother Who Art in Heaven*; *Our Uteri – Our Ute-rights*; *My Uterus Belongs to Me, Not the Pope*; *Smash the Patriarchy*; and *A Woman's Place is Everywhere.* Maggie, carrying a sign that reads *Nobody Gives You Power – You Take It,* quietly joined the group gathered outside Saint Finnian's Cathedral, named for one of Ireland's three early patron saints.

But what normally would have been front-page news about Catholic women staging a well-organized protest that includes a financial boycott of their Church is lost, because Cardinal O'Grady dies on the morning of the first effort, capturing the news cycle for the next several days.

When Maggie hears about the cardinal's death on the morning news, she laughs out loud. *Guess we showed him,* she thinks. Later that evening, she tells Mary Pat she is still very pleased with their first effort. She estimates the parishes involved experienced about $5,000 each in lost revenue, and she intends to encourage the group to ramp up their efforts and expand to other parishes.

"It's going to take the archdiocese a while to try to do anything about this, so we might as well make hay while the sun shines," she says.

•••

The next day, Sylvia Bernstein calls Maggie to congratulate her on the boycott success and tells her that the WNA position is hers if she wants it, and she hopes she does. She promises to remain as long as necessary for Maggie to make the transition and explains that they need a definite answer by the end of the week.

Maggie's only hesitancy in saying yes to the offer immediately is whether to seek Mother Marie William's permission to lead the secular organization. She is leaning heavily toward an "ask forgiveness rather than ask permission" approach and not informing her superior that she has accepted the position. As the new executive director of the Chicago Chapter of the Women's National Alliance, along with her Catholic Women Demanding Change position, she will be managing two feminist organizations with several thousand members and be part of the nationwide WNA effort. This is so much more than she ever believed possible when she first began thinking about how to confront all the ways the Church—and the wider society—mistreat women, and she is too excited about being at the forefront of whatever happens next to risk being told she can't do it.

These are the thoughts floating through Maggie's mind when she receives a call from Sister John Martha at Saint Alberta's convent, where she met with their superior a few months previously. Despite Mother Marie William's suggestion that she reconnect with her fellow sisters, she has not made any effort to do it.

"Hello, Maggie," the voice on the other end says. "I thought you would want to know that we received a call this afternoon from the motherhouse, telling us that Mother Marie William has resigned, citing health problems. My understanding is that the leadership council will either jointly govern or appoint an interim until our annual meeting, when we will elect a new superior. I don't think all this has been decided yet. You are welcome to join us at that time."

Maggie expresses appropriate surprise and concern at the news, but turns down the accompanying offer to join the others for the trip back to the motherhouse in six months for the annual meeting and retreat.

While Maggie has always had fond feelings toward Mother Marie William, both as novice mistress and later as superior, she views this turn of events as another opportunity to move forward on her own. She has no idea who her next superior will be, but by the time that is decided, Maggie will be well-established in her new position as WNA executive director, most likely without anyone in the Order leadership noticing. She can't help smiling and, after calling Sylvia to accept the offer, decides to call Ben.

•••

Maggie is too busy planning her shift into the WNA directorship to pay other than scant attention to the copious speculation about who will succeed Cardinal O'Grady. She is arranging to move into a two-room walk-up apartment on the third floor of an older co-op building in Archer Heights that she hastily purchased with Ben's guidance. She deliberately chose the working-class neighborhood located southwest of the shelter because she can afford it and it seems reasonably safe. Polish and Russian Jews, Italians, and Czechs, most of whom either work in various manufacturing or City Hall patronage jobs, comprise the Archer Heights community, and she believes that if she keeps to herself and does not become involved in the local Catholic parish, her neighbors will take little notice of her. As an additional precaution, she decides to keep the post office box she opened for CWDC as her primary mailing address.

Faced with the dilemma of whether to tell Mary Pat about her move, which risks Fiona or one of her other sisters finding out, Maggie decides not to mention it for the time being. Instead, she turns to the challenge of furnishing her kitchenette apartment and invokes Ben's help in finding used furniture and kitchen equipment to furnish the two rooms that comprise her new home. After carrying the last box up the stairs on the sweltering day he helps her move in, he suggests something to eat.

"I'll wash up first, and then, if you can stand looking at me in a dirty Willie Nelson T-shirt while you eat, I'll go down the block and bring back a greasy, thick crust, extra cheesy pizza and some wine to celebrate your new digs."

I could look at you wearing anything, Maggie thinks, bone tired and grateful for the offer.

While Ben is gone, Maggie washes her face and rummages through unpacked boxes, looking for a clean shirt. She clears off the small table, which she pushes under the window. She pushes a half-used candle Ben found in a kitchen drawer into an empty soda bottle and unrolls paper towels for napkins.

"Not much of a dinner. The first meal here deserves something fancier," Ben says, walking in the door with a large pizza box, a bottle of red wine, and two paper cups he places on the table.

Maggie lights the candle off the gas burner on the stove and they both sit down. Ben pours the wine and dives into the pizza.

Maggie gulps her wine but doesn't touch the pizza.

"You're awfully quiet, and you're not eating. You feeling okay?" Ben finally says.

"I've got a lot on my mind."

"Care to share?"

"What do you know about love?" Maggie asks.

"Wow! For starters, I know I wasn't expecting that question."

"I wasn't expecting to ask it—it just blurted out…too much wine on an empty stomach. You don't have to answer." She takes another drink of wine, still ignoring the pizza.

"Are you referring to the 'Jesus says we should love everybody' kind of love, or something more specific, like romantic love?"

"Something more specific, I guess," Maggie answers, refilling her cup.

"I've fallen in love a couple times—or at least thought I'd fallen in love. It was a pretty intense experience full of emotions that sent me reeling into a world where I felt like I'd lost my mind and any control I thought I had over my life. It was the scariest, most wonderful thing that ever happened to me…and I wouldn't trade a moment of any of it, even if it didn't work out like I'd hoped."

"Did the other person love you back?"

"It seemed so. But it turned out a lot was just about the chemistry between us—and great sex. That blinded us to the deeper issues, and it took a while to figure out that we weren't compatible in the really important ways that hold a relationship together over time. We parted agreeably and respectfully—with a lot of sadness but without rancor. More to the point, why are you asking me?"

"I'm not sure."

"This is me, Maggie. Your friend, Ben. Don't lie to me."

"I think…"

"You think what…that you're in love?"

Maggie nods.

"Oh, my God! Seriously? Who with?"

Maggie stares at him, saying nothing.

After nearly a minute, Ben reacts. "Holy shit—not me?"

Maggie nods again.

Ben sets down his wine and drops his head into his hands, where it remains for what seems to Maggie like an eternity. Finally, he looks at her.

"I don't know what to say, Maggie. You're a wonderful friend...one of the best buddies I've ever had...but if I've somehow given you the impression there was something more, I profoundly apologize. I tried very hard not to say or do anything that would mislead you, and still I've hurt you...I don't know how I can ever forgive myself."

Maggie remains silent.

"You've got to say something, Maggie. We've got to talk this through."

"You never did anything to encourage me. Out of nowhere, I started having feelings I'd never felt before, every time I thought about you, and whenever I was with you. I decided it had to be love, because there wasn't any other explanation...and because you are so nice to me, I thought there was at least a remote chance you might feel the same way."

"How long have you been feeling like this?"

"Since pretty soon after I met you. A small, nagging feeling grew into something so much bigger, and there were times when I was so full of emotion I thought I might explode."

"And you carried these feelings around all this time? Jesus—we're talking about years. Why did you wait so long to say something?"

"A first I was confused. Then I began liking the way I felt toward you, but I didn't know how to start a conversation about it...or even if I should. It's not like I know what I'm talking about anyway. Everything about what I was—am—feeling scares the shit out of me."

"Here's what I know, Maggie: it's always been clear that you've never been in a loving relationship of any kind, which is the saddest thing imaginable to me. I saw many things in you that would need sanding down and smoothing over before you could handle the give and take of enduring intimacy—something that reaches far beyond sexual attraction. That kind of love requires keeping the other person's best interests always in your heart. My impression has always been that it is probably impossible for you to take that kind of risk because you've survived by building an impenetrable shell around yourself that doesn't let other people in. The thing about love is that it involves being vulnerable and not always in control of your life, and that would never work for you."

"You think I'm that damaged?"

"I'm sorry, Maggie, but that's exactly what I think. And that damage fuels the fire of your passion for justice...it's one of your strengths in a backward sort of way. You desperately need, and want, love and yet are so frightened by it that you take refuge in a religious commitment you don't really believe in but protects you from the messiness of real life—and enables you to do what you do. I don't see any way to change any of that, because then you wouldn't be Maggie anymore. You'd be someone who wasn't nearly as interesting, and I probably wouldn't like you as well," Ben says, in a weak attempt to put a positive spin on a very difficult conversation.

"You were so nice to me that I thought you might love me."

"I'm nice to you because I *like* you, Maggie, and because I try to be a kind and caring person. But there was never any spark to light the fire that would ignite into romance and lasting love. You've always been a warmly valued friend I care a great deal about—as a friend...nothing more."

"As simple as that?"

"I made sure it stayed as simple as that. The great temptation for me was to try to rescue you from all the hurt in your life, try to take away all that fear, pain, and anger you carry around, and use your vows to protect yourself from feeling. A real friend doesn't try to change someone...they accept the person as they are, and I wanted to be a real friend to you. Any attempt on my part to try to change who you are would've been me on a power trip, trying to fix you, and that would've led us both down an emotional rat hole."

"And I suppose there is the matter of my vows...."

"Honestly, Maggie, I don't think your vows are relevant. They're protective if you feel cornered, but with regard to honoring them, I doubt you ever give that serious thought. You've always looked for ways around them when it suited you."

"I don't know what you mean."

"Sure you do. Your religious vows give you an identity that says 'Hands off! My loyalties are elsewhere.' And you wear a ring to prove it. And let's face it, being married to Jesus is pretty easy in many respects. He isn't a dependent husband with a lot of ordinary needs and expectations that cut into your time, and you don't have to cook dinner for Him every night. Besides, people think vowed religious are a little closer to God than the average person, and who doesn't like that kind of power? Priests thrive on it too."

"My vows really aren't relevant at this point. You're telling me you don't feel the same way I do, so there's no place to go with this."

"Your vows, and your faith, are very relevant, because they're a huge part of who you are—at least who I think you are. I'm honestly curious how you reconcile your vows, and your Catholic faith, with some of the things you do, because a lot of the time I wonder how well you know yourself and what you actually believe."

"Most days I don't understand all this very well myself," Maggie finally admits. "I don't know what I think about God, or even whether I believe in Him...because if God truly is male, which no one knows, then I have real problems with Him running my life."

"That should be your first clue about what kind of girlfriend, or wife, you'd make," Ben smiles weakly.

"Even if God was female, I still don't know where the notion of God fits into my life. My entire existence has been going through the motions of being a believer because it's all I know how to do. When I was a child, believing God loved me despite everything else that was happening in my life, most of which was pretty ugly, comforted me. But eventually, I outgrew that childish notion, and now the grown-up me doesn't know how to believe in God, Jesus, the saints, or much else related to the Church, for that matter. I've not spent a lot of time thinking about it...and I don't want to. The Irish-Catholic Church is my cultural heritage, and there are things about it I love, and other things I hate. Either way, I can't deny that part of who I am...but that doesn't mean I believe everything the Church says or understand where I fit into any of it."

"What you're saying describes a lot of what was running through my mind as I got closer to ordination, and ultimately caused me to back away from it. You made a different choice. But that was a long time ago, and this is now. Why do you remain a nun?"

"I have no choice...." Maggie adds more wine to her glass while staring at the melting candle on the table as the sun sets outside the streaked kitchen window she hastily tried to clean.

"That's simply not true," Ben interrupts. "You own an apartment, have a nice nest egg, and have a good job. You could make it on your own financially and get along fine. You have plenty of choices."

"There's no nest egg. I own the apartment, but I used a lot of the other money to bankroll CWDC, and the money from the car to pay off some of my sisters' debts—and they had plenty."

"I'm sure they appreciated that."

"I doubt it. They wanted cash, which I knew their husbands would drink up, so I refused. My brother was wrong not to leave them something, and I feel like I did the right thing to help them out. Bottom line is: I need a job that pays enough to send money to the Order every month, which basically guarantees I'm left alone to do what I want."

"And what are you getting in return?"

"An identity. Without the Order, I'd be another sad-eyed girl from a crude, shanty-Irish family who couldn't get a husband or was married to a drunk who's just like her old man, and had kids until she was so exhausted she was nothing but an empty shell of the woman she could have been. Entering religious life and steadfastly claiming I wanted to dedicate my life to God, even if I didn't understand what that meant and wasn't one hundred percent true, was far preferable, and even with the nagging uncertainties, I came to believe it was what I was supposed to be doing with my life. So far, it has worked out for me."

"You're saying the Order protects you from real life, which is my point."

"I'm saying it saved me from the only other life I could've had, and never wanted. But regardless of what it is, or is not, I can't turn my back on the Order, at least not formally. I need the status that comes with being a vowed woman religious. Just plain Maggie Corrigan couldn't do what I want to do in terms of forcing the Church toward greater equality and justice for women, and Sister Maggie Corrigan might be able to."

"And you're not willing to give that up."

"It's not that I'm not willing to give it up so much as I *can't* give it up, Ben. The Order is the family I don't have and have never had. I admit I'm not a good family member, but in so many ways, they made me who I am, which is a hell of a lot better than who I would've been otherwise, and I'm not ungrateful for that."

"It's pretty clear taking your life in a different direction is not something you want to do, even if you think you love me and want something else, and I always sensed that about you. It's one reason I never allowed myself to think of you as anything other than a friend. But how do you reconcile all this with being in love with me?"

"I don't know. I haven't thought about anything other than how I feel about you."

"That's pretty naïve, Maggie. Falling in love always makes us think about future possibilities, because we never want those feelings to end and know it will be very painful if the reason for them doesn't work out."

"I told you...I haven't thought this through."

"Then let's do that now. The options are marriage, an affair, doing nothing and carrying on like we've never had this conversation—which is impossible—or acknowledging we want different things and going our separate ways."

"My impression is people have affairs all the time."

"Some people, maybe, but I'm not one of them. Affairs are just about sex, and I don't play those kinds of games. I've never had sex with a woman I didn't care deeply for and envision a committed future with, if things worked out. I have too much respect for women to use them as objects of raw, personal gratification without any emotional commitment, and I'm having a very hard time with the idea you respect me so little, you thought otherwise."

"It's not a question of respecting you, Ben. It's that, as you pointed out, I have no realistic idea about love relationships. The only thing I know for sure is that the Church is seriously screwed up when it comes to women, sex, and love. The only happy endings I know about are on TV and in romance novels. The real-life stories I hear from the women I work with, and my own family experience, would turn anybody off romance, marriage, and motherhood forever." Maggie sighs. "The truth is, I have no idea what real love is. All I know is that whenever I am near you, or just think about you, my emotions nearly overpower me. It's nothing I've ever experienced before, and it feels good."

"TV and books are fantasy and entertainment, Maggie, and usually bear little resemblance to real life. But you're dead right about the Church... it's worse than screwed up about sex and love—it's dangerously harmful."

"We at least agree on that," Maggie replies, looking out the window.

"Look, Maggie. I'm willing to give you the benefit of the doubt that you didn't mean to offend me, but you've come damned close anyway. Saddest of all is that you have so little respect for yourself that you would even consider becoming involved in a relationship that is nothing more than sex and has no future, so would end eventually. I would've thought you, of all people, would know better," Ben says, barely containing his anger.

"You're not exactly free either. You have a heavy obligation to your mother you can't turn your back on. What would've happened if you had fallen in love with me?"

"If you recall, when we first met, I told you that I wasn't looking for a relationship as long as my mother needed me. I said I wasn't going to make promises to someone that I wasn't free to make and, for that reason, wasn't going to become involved with anyone...and I haven't. Look, Maggie, I know that no one can help who they fall in love with, but we all have choices about how we react when that happens, and if I had fallen in love with you, I wouldn't have acted on it.

"What would you have done?"

"I would have very, very carefully, avoided any chance for intimacy to develop, and kept my distance as much as possible to remain in control of myself and the relationship. We wouldn't have painted walls, chatted over coffee, or done any of the other things we've done together. It would've remained a strictly business relationship."

"I didn't mean to offend you, Ben—honestly."

"The stars don't align for us, Maggie. I want a family with a couple of kids someday, and you've never indicated that life interests you at all. You're eight or nine years older than I am, and—"

"Even if you did love me back, and even if I wanted children, the motherhood ship has already sailed for me," Maggie interjects.

"That's true, but it doesn't matter. What's more important is understanding that this conversation was bound to happen eventually, because relationships aren't static. They're always evolving. And right now, things are changing for me, and I'd be telling you about them anyway," Ben finally says. "My mother doesn't want me to be alone and tied down to her any longer and is insisting on going into a care facility so I can be free to marry and give her grandchildren before she dies. She's made up her mind, and there's no talking her out of it. My dad has been searching out possibilities for nearly a month and thinks he's found one that will work. This will change my day-to-day life in some substantial ways and opens up possibilities for a new future."

"Like falling in love with someone," Maggie interrupts, shredding a piece of paper towel.

"Hopefully, yes. And given how you feel about me, that would hurt you deeply."

"Can we still be friends?" Maggie asks, staring at the candle, afraid to look Ben in the eye.

"We won't be enemies, if that's what you're asking, but friends in the same way we have been? Probably not. You would find it very difficult to stay friends with someone you are in love with who doesn't love you in the same way. I've been down that road a time or two, and believe me, it's a painful journey to nowhere that I wouldn't wish on anybody."

"So the answer is no?" Maggie asks, her eyes filling with tears as she stares at the pool of grease coagulating around the pizza they have barely touched.

"I couldn't handle it. I'd feel very guilty knowing that I can't, in good conscience, respond to how you feel toward me in the ways you want me to. I truly would feel your pain every time we were together, and I don't want that for either of us. I would start avoiding you and eventually tell you not to come around anymore."

"I want you in my life, Ben, and I'll take you any way I can."

"You don't know what you're saying, Maggie. I can't knowingly inflict that kind of emotional pain on you."

"On some level I've always known that I wasn't good enough for you and that thinking otherwise was a visit to fantasy land. But I couldn't stop myself from going there...the pull was a magnetic force more powerful than anything I've ever felt before in my entire life. I guess I owe you an apology for not being stronger. If I could've resisted, we wouldn't be having this conversation and could just carry on like always."

"You don't own me an apology for anything. People feel what they feel, and sometimes it all works out, and sometimes it doesn't. Love is very powerful and can't be forced into being what it isn't or stopped from being what it's meant to be.... It's not a question of good enough—it's that we're just not well-matched for romantic involvement, that's all. Relationships aren't a one-person show. They involve two people, and both need to be on the same page...and we just aren't, that's all."

"I should've known—probably did know—this would be your response, and I was wrong to bring it up. I'm really sorry. It was a bad mistake. Can't you forgive me and just forget about it?" Maggie says, looking at Ben through watery eyes.

"Nothing to forgive you for, Maggie. It took a boatload of courage for you to talk about this. I can't say I'm glad you did, because it has changed things between us, but they were going to change eventually anyway. I'm not upset with you, and I'll never stop caring about you, but the only cure for the pain you're about to experience is a lot of time and space between us. It's best if we don't see each other for a while."

"I think I understand," Maggie answers, biting her bottom lip and staring at the wall behind Ben's chair.

"I'm going to miss you, Maggie. I want you to know that."

"I'm going to miss you too...." She smiles, folding up the pizza box and pouring the last of the wine into her glass as she watches Ben walk out her door.

"Ben..." she calls after him.

He turns around.

"I know I've really screwed this up, but I've never trusted any man as much as I trust you. I want you to know that...I need you to know it...."

Ben remains silent.

"I don't let people touch me, but I'd like it if you hugged me goodbye. Could you at least do that?" Maggie asks, opening her arms as she moves toward him.

"I don't think so, Maggie." Eyes glistening, Ben closes the door very softly.

Maggie sits in the small kitchen for several minutes before taking her wine glass out onto the fire escape, where she stares off into the distance. With the noise of the city surrounding her, she begins sobbing.

"I've really fucked up and just made the worst mistake of my life. I should've just kept my goddamned mouth shut," she tells the sparrow who has landed on the fire escape railing and is staring at her.

XXVI.

The question isn't who is going to let me;
it's who is going to stop me.

AYN RAND

Over the next several weeks, Maggie dives into her new position with WNA, which includes moving nearly all of the CWDC meetings away from Our Daily Bread over to the WNA location.

"Why do that, Maggie? The price was right, the location is perfect, and it keeps the organizations separate, which is what everybody decided they want," Mary Pat wails when informed of the change.

"I just think it's better this way," Maggie answers.

"Well, I think you're wrong. It's a dumb idea."

"We won't know that until we try it...and I've got to go," Maggie says, hanging up the phone and swiveling her chair around to stare at the wall, silently admitting that she still finds herself thinking of Ben constantly. Honoring his request not to be in touch is more difficult than she imagined, and she has begun realizing that letting go of the closest thing she has ever felt to love for a man, even if it wasn't reciprocated, is impossible. She blames herself for imagined mistakes she thinks she can fix but doesn't know how to. The thought that, if she had handled things differently, there could have been a different outcome, haunts her.

At least once each day, she finds herself tempted to call Ben on some pretense or another, and more than once she has walked by Our Daily Bread, hoping to catch a glimpse of him, or that he will see her and wave at her to stop. At night she makes up reasons to get in touch with him, and the next morning remembers he asked her not to. She writes letters she never mails and drinks too much. Her old habits of not caring about her appearance have returned, and without Ben to notice, she doesn't care. She misses him more each day and hates herself because she can't get a grip on her emotions, which she perceives as a weakness she can't control. At night, over a bottle of bourbon, she tells herself that if this is what love means, she doesn't want any part of it, then becomes so upset and angry she can barely function the next day. She feels trapped in an intense cycle of unfamiliar emotions and all-too-familiar grief so intense that she is barely hanging on. Knowing Ben deserves more than she can give him does not help her to resolve the grinding emptiness she feels, and there is no one she can talk to about it. The only thing keeping her going is her new job and her passion for greater justice for Catholic women.

Partly for the chance at a change of scenery, and partly to get her mind off Ben, Maggie reconsiders her earlier decision not to return to the motherhouse for the annual meeting and election of a new superior. At the last minute, she calls Sister John Martha and says she would like to accept the offer of a ride to the meeting the next day and will take the L to Saint Alberta's.

"We can pick you up if that would be easier," her fellow sister offers.

"No need to bother," Maggie insists, not wanting them to know where she lives.

The nearly four-hour drive from Chicago to the motherhouse is relatively quiet. Beyond the initial pleasantries, Sisters John Martha, Matthew Mary, and Martha James chat comfortably among themselves but make little effort to converse with Maggie. Each answers her questions about their social work efforts among the city's African American community, but no one asks her anything until less than an hour from their destination.

"Is it true you are the Sister Maggie Corrigan who signed that Chicago newspaper ad?" Sister Martha James, the youngest among them, and the nun Maggie knows the least, asks.

"Yes," Maggie answers.

"Why did you do that?"

"I believe the Church is wrong on the birth control issue and felt saying that publicly was the right thing to do."

"But supporting abortion is not pro-life...."

"Neither is forcing women to have babies until they drop over dead."

"But our vows bind us to the Church's position on issues of faith and morals, and what you're saying flies in the face of that...makes it awkward for the rest of us who also have the SCJ initials behind our names."

"I don't mean to make it awkward for anyone, Sister. Nor do I believe our vows command us to surrender our ability to think for ourselves. And so there is no misunderstanding, the birth control issue is neither a question of our faith nor of our morals—it's merely an opinion rendered by the patriarchy and aimed at exploiting women. It can be easily argued that the Church's position is, in fact, immoral."

"Did you discuss this with Mother Marie William ahead of time?"

"I did not. It didn't occur to me."

"Weren't you concerned about scandal or controversy?"

"No, I wasn't."

"Well, perhaps you should be," Sister John Martha interjects.

The four ride the rest of the way in silence. Maggie recalls Mother Marie William mentioning that many of her fellow sisters disagree with her and begins wondering about how she will be received among them.

The answer comes soon after walking into the motherhouse entrance, where Maggie finds herself standing alone in the lobby, her suitcase at her feet. All around her, sisters are enthusiastically and joyfully greeting one another in the spirit of an eagerly anticipated family reunion. Several nod when they see her, but none come over to speak with her, nor do they respond warmly when she approaches them. She receives her room assignment and a packet of information from the reception desk and carries her suitcase up two flights of stairs to a room at the end of a long hallway in the old convent. The week's schedule indicates the community welcome Mass is at five o'clock today, followed by dinner and socializing.

Maggie doubts anyone will notice if she skips Mass and decides to rest before dinner. But instead of napping, she replays the conversation in the car several times, wondering whether she should have responded differently. Slowly, she begins to grasp just how intense her religious community's disagreement with her position on women's reproductive autonomy might be—something she has given no serious thought to until now. *I haven't been here an hour and am already sorry I came,* she thinks, frowning.

Just before six o'clock, she walks downstairs to the dining room and finds it empty, meaning Mass is not yet over. She sees an aide wheeling Sister Marie William down the hallway in a wheelchair.

"Maggie, I'm so glad you're here," she smiles weakly, extending her thin hand.

"I'm sorry you're so ill," Maggie says, trying not to reveal her shock at how frail her former superior has become in the months since she last saw her.

"Cancer is no one's friend, I'm afraid. I tried to make it mine so I could carry on with my duties, but it had other ideas, and I found it impossible for us to peacefully coexist. Perhaps this is God's way of saying someone else needs to step up to lead us through the difficult challenges ahead...although He certainly didn't need to send such a harsh message. Something a little kinder would have been appreciated," the former superior says, coughing into a handkerchief.

Maggie offers to help her settle in the dining room. Sister Marie William thanks her and says she prefers sitting off in a corner where, hopefully, she won't be noticed as the politicking over who will become the new superior begins in earnest.

As soon as the buffet line opens, Maggie brings a plate for each of them, then sits down and asks about who the new superior is likely to be.

"The front runner is Sister Stephen Elizabeth Conley. You may not know her because you haven't been back here since going to Chicago."

"Tell me about her," Maggie requests.

"She was a late vocation—spent several years as a foster care worker in Detroit before coming to us. More recently, she headed the social work department at a large Catholic hospital in Milwaukee. She's energetic, fair-minded, has management experience, and is more progressive than many are comfortable with, which is the barrier she must overcome if she is to be elected. The possibility that she is a radical reformer at heart, which I don't believe she is, concerns some of the older sisters who don't want change and don't understand that if we are to survive, several things must change dramatically. They automatically oppose every new idea and favor an older superior who will stay the course."

Hearing this, Maggie asks for more.

"We are facing major challenges you may not be aware of. The community is shrinking, which is a trend that began post-Vatican II. Older sisters are dying off, younger ones are leaving the Order to pursue secular opportunities, and fewer young women are interested in entering religious life because, more and more, they have options not available to earlier generations of women. There are over three hundred fewer vowed sisters in the Order today than there were just ten years ago, and the older, retired sisters outnumber the younger ones by nearly three-to-one. We have to find ways to support them and maintain our facilities at the same time—a massive financial challenge."

"I was not aware of that," Maggie admits.

"Financially, we are in very serious trouble. We have been forced to direct all the sisters who are able, up through age seventy-five, to seek paid employment, including those who may have already retired and preferred living here at the motherhouse and doing unpaid charity work in nearby areas. We expect them to support not only themselves, but also send money back to the community, which now includes many elderly and sick sisters like myself and, unfortunately, is a trend that will continue. After sending money to us, most are living hand-to-mouth and depend on the kindness of others to make ends meet. When you began working for a salary, we considered it an experiment we wanted to try—now it is an absolute necessity. But it is still unlikely to sustain us very far into the future. We're facing a very grim outlook."

Hearing this, Maggie realizes the Order might not oppose her job at WNA nearly as much as she thought. As long as she continues sending money, she now believes they are much less likely to interfere with her activities.

"I think Sister Stephen Elizabeth—she prefers being called Liz, by the way—wants to do more to encourage the sisters to find satisfying employment. This means we will have to rule with a much lighter hand, and the Order itself will have to carefully rethink the meaning of our vow of obedience—something I was wrestling with as I allowed more sisters to take secular social service jobs. This is fraught with potential difficulties that will not be easy to navigate."

Maggie nods in agreement but withholds an opinion.

"One of Liz's thoughts is to better connect with the sisters where they are living and working, stay in touch with what they are doing, and explore more effective ways the Order can support their efforts. The reality is that expecting the sisters to hold paying jobs outside of the Church changes our core mission of doing hands-on Catholic charity work for almost no pay, and we have to deal with that."

Maggie grimaces at the idea of her superior paying more attention to what she is doing and asks about the other possibilities being discussed.

"Something under serious consideration is requiring aspirants to have education beyond high school, which will allow them to get better jobs, but automatically reduces the pool of applicants considerably. Another idea is finding cost-effective ways for the sisters to become better-educated after entering the Order, so they can get higher-paying jobs that include health insurance and retirement benefits, or at least pay into Social Security. Eventually, this would be a big help to our budget but is also a substantial up-front cost we aren't sure how to cover."

"In other words, one way or another, we'll be expected to fully support ourselves going forward," Maggie asks.

"Basically, yes, but the Order will still be the sisters' spiritual home and primary commitment."

"Isn't there a concern that this makes religious life much less attractive because young women are giving up more than they are receiving in return?"

"Hopefully, young women who enter religious life don't do a cost-benefit analysis, Maggie. They do it because they love God, and the Church, and want to serve both—which is an issue you've always struggled with."

"That's true...sometimes that has been a struggle, but it's not one I've given up on yet."

"To your credit, I admit. But why did you come back now? I confess I never expected to see you here."

"I thought I should, considering the abrupt change in leadership."

"Then you should be forewarned that word has traveled since we last spoke, and now nearly all of your fellow sisters know about your signing on to the pro-choice newspaper ad. And not only do they strongly disagree with you, but also they seem disinclined toward forgiveness or letting it go and forgetting about it. They view your actions as a slap in the face to the Order, a direct assault on the Church, and a personal embarrassment to themselves. Many favor formally disciplining you."

"That explains the cool reception when I arrived. I guess it might be a very long, and very unpleasant week."

"Only if you let it be, Maggie. I suggest you attend the meetings, pray with us, and participate in the discussions in a straightforward manner that doesn't inflame anyone or any issue. I'm not suggesting this will be easy, and it won't make amends, but I haven't heard you say you want to do that—and until you do, reconciliation simply isn't in the cards. The most you can reasonably hope for is that the anger softens enough to allow some level of benign acceptance, but even that will be a heavy lift for many."

"I won't attend Mass when a male priest is saying it," Maggie tells her former superior.

"I am aware of your concerns about a male-only priesthood, but either you swallow your objections for the sake of being a team player, or live with the consequences of marching to your own drumbeat."

At that moment, the sisters begin entering the dining room, and seeing Sister Marie William, several walk over to her table to greet her. None acknowledge Maggie with more than a nod.

"It's been a while...maybe they didn't recognize me," Maggie says after the last one walks away.

"You're wearing a name tag," Sister Marie William reminds her.

•••

Four days later, Sister Stephen Elizabeth Conley is elected to a ten-year, renewable term as the Mother Superior of the Indiana, Illinois, and Michigan Province of the Pax Christi Sisters of Charity and Justice. At the celebratory Mass, most of the sisters renew their vows, emphasizing the one that promises obedience to the new superior. Maggie is not among them.

•••

Upon returning to Chicago, Maggie learns that Cardinal O'Grady's successor is an Italian, born and raised in the coal mining area of western Pennsylvania, and will be coming to Chicago in a month, after having served as Archbishop of Cleveland, Ohio. She's not sure what to make of this shift in the powerful relationship between the archdiocese and City Hall that, historically, has been based upon ethnic Irish heritage.

"Do you think he has mob connections?" Mary Pat asks Maggie when she calls to relay the news, which has not been publicly announced.

"Who knows? Mob connections are no different from the Irish genius for getting into bar fights—nothing more than a handy survival skill."

"So if he gets mad at somebody, he'll just order their kneecaps shot off?"

"He might," Maggie laughs. "But I think we need to get to know him before making any assumptions about his enforcement style."

That opportunity presents itself three months later, when Maggie, as director of CWDC, receives a nicely worded letter formally addressed to Sister Margaret Corrigan, inviting her to a get-acquainted meeting with the newly installed seventh Archbishop of Chicago. That he is the first archdiocesan leader not descended from Irish heritage has not gone unnoticed in the publicity surrounding his arrival. Nevertheless, everyone expects newly arrived Antonio Bonifacio Tetrone, who Chicago Italians are over the moon about, to be active in Chicago politics since he is now overseeing the wealthiest archdiocese in the Roman Catholic Church and has just been named America's newest—and youngest—cardinal. Many also believe that since the family's ancestral land produces wine, oil, and cheese, the new cardinal is undoubtedly politically well-connected, as well as independently wealthy.

Before responding to the letter, Maggie calls Mary Pat again to inquire about how the first Sunday boycotts are progressing.

"My best guess is we're involving at least fifty parishes now," Mary Pat says, "which isn't many, considering I'm pretty sure there are over five hundred parishes in the archdiocese. But the important point is that the effort is growing. My rough calculation is we're averaging a one thousand dollars in loss per parish—more in some parishes and less in others—so it's getting close to a fifty thousand dollar per Sunday impact now. It's not chump change, and the good thing is some of the women are giving the money they would've been giving to the Church to CWDC. It has to be helping our treasury significantly."

Maggie agrees that they are making more progress than she initially hoped for and decides it's time to meet the new leader of the Chicago Archdiocese.

The meeting takes place in the chancery offices, located a few short blocks west of the Lake Michigan shoreline. Monsignor Carlo Ancora greets Maggie at the entrance and escorts her into a sitting room where she and the cardinal will meet for the first time. He invites her to sit down beside a coffee table. A silver platter that includes an array of cookies, an English bone-china teapot, a silver coffee carafe, linen napkins, cups, saucers, and small plates has been placed in the center of the table. Monsignor Ancora assures her Cardinal Tetrone will be with her as soon as he finishes a phone call.

While she waits, Maggie takes in the opulent room that reminds her of what she has always imagined the inside of a palace might look like. Life-sized, color portraits of Chicago's previous archbishops and cardinals, dressed in ecclesiastical finery and looking seriously solemn, hang in ornate gold frames that present an elegant addition to the dark, wood-paneled walls. Heavy green-velvet draperies fringed in gold are tied back to reveal ten-foot windows, and well-cared-for Persian rugs cover highly polished floors. The antique furnishings have been selected for elegance rather than comfort. Italian Renaissance art, probably original and including several sculptures, and a large map of Sicily further adorn the room. *It looks like some Italian mafia boss lives here,* Maggie thinks.

Lost in the awareness that she has never been in a room like this in her life, Maggie startles when a side door opens. In stark contrast to the larger-than-life Cardinal O'Grady, who stood several inches over six feet tall, weighed more than three hundred and fifty pounds, and boomed out every sentence he ever spoke, an average-sized, unremarkable-looking man wearing a black cassock trimmed in red enters the room. He smiles as he walks toward Maggie with his hand extended. She knows he is expecting her to kiss his ring, but decides to shake his hand instead.

"I'm pleased to meet you, Cardinal Tetrone," Maggie begins.

"My friends call me Tony, and I'm very pleased to meet you, Sister Margaret," the soft-spoken cardinal responds.

"My friends call me Maggie, but I'm not sure we're going to be friends, so maybe we shouldn't jump to that conclusion just yet."

Looking surprised, the cardinal clears his throat, then continues.

"I see Carlo got you settled, but it doesn't look as though he offered you tea or coffee. May I?"

Maggie thanks him and says tea will be fine. He hands her a cup, offers milk and sugar, and then places two cookies on a small plate, which he sets on the corner of the table nearest her.

"I pride myself on getting along with the religious and the lay faithful in my pastoral care and must confess that your doubts about our ability to be friends caught me off guard, Sister. Would you care to enlighten me regarding the reasons behind your concerns?"

"Am I correct in assuming Cardinal O'Grady's auxiliary bishops have informed you about the various activities in the diocese?"

The cardinal nods.

"Then you are probably aware that I lead an organization called Catholic Women Demanding Change."

The cardinal nods again.

"And I assume you do not support our position on women's reproductive autonomy?" Maggie sips her tea and eats a cookie while she waits for the prelate to respond. He remains silent, waiting for Maggie to continue. Determined to outwait each other, eventually, the silence grows too heavy to uphold any longer and Maggie continues.

"I'm fairly certain you fail to see anything positive about our activities," she finally says.

"And I'm sure you are aware that I cannot singlehandedly amend the Church's position on family planning. You can protest here in Chicago until the Lord Jesus returns to walk on Earth among us once again, and nothing will change, because modifying this position can only come from Rome, and would only occur after lengthy, intense deliberation."

"I disagree," Maggie says evenly. "The Chicago Archdiocese is the largest, wealthiest diocese in the entire Church. If enough Catholic women here in Chicago register their dissatisfactions by withholding their financial support, sooner or later it will catch on in other dioceses, and Rome will be forced to listen. We realize change won't occur quickly and fully intend to remain in the fight for as long as it takes."

"Naturally, I'm sorry to hear that, but not surprised. I'm sure you understand I don't agree with your position or your methods, and I was hoping new archdiocesan leadership would open the door to a willingness to reconsider and perhaps suspend your activities as a good-faith gesture while we work toward some sort of reconciliation."

"I'm not sure how new leadership at the local level changes anything in terms of our intended outcome," Maggie says. "Am I missing something?"

"I am aware that Cardinal O'Grady could be very difficult to work with and created many hard feelings among his clergy and women religious. I am hoping they will not allow their negative experiences with him to spill over into their relationship with me. I prefer a congenial rather than an iron-fisted, authoritarian relationship with those I am shepherding, and am praying for the opportunity to prove this. I hope you will give me that chance."

The cardinal's words and demeanor catch Maggie by surprise. She came prepared for a fight, and as far as she can tell, she's not getting one—at least not immediately. As a result, she's not sure how to respond.

"Let me propose this," the cardinal finally says. "You believe very strongly in your cause, so go ahead and continue with your financial boycott activities for the time being. This will allow me to familiarize myself with the unique responsibilities associated with leading the Chicago Archdiocese and to learn more about the individualized traits that make up the Chicago Catholic Church. I propose we meet again in three months to discuss this further. By then, I'll have a better idea of how to respond. Is this agreeable?"

Too surprised to refuse, Maggie says that it is.

Hearing this, the cardinal stands and offers his hand. "Thank you for coming, Sister. It was a pleasure meeting you and learning about your efforts. Please don't hesitate to be in touch with me anytime. Father Carlo will show you out."

Maggie shakes the cardinal's hand just as Monsignor Ancora opens the door. *His hit man has been listening in the entire time,* Maggie realizes.

•••

As soon as Maggie returns home that evening, she calls Mary Pat to fill her in on the meeting.

"Are you sure you heard him correctly? He said to keep the boycott going?" Mary Pat asks.

"That's what he said...and that we'd talk again in three months. He didn't put up any kind of a fight, which is what I expected and was prepared for. I was so shocked I didn't know what else to do other than to agree. It's hard to have an argument when the other side isn't giving you one."

"What do you think it means?"

"I'm not sure. Either the archdiocesan coffers are so flush a few thousand dollars a month in lost parish revenue means nothing, he's setting a trap for me, or he sincerely wants to find some points of agreement and is buying time while he figures that out. I left the meeting feeling like I'll be spending the next three months waiting for the other shoe to drop. Bottom line, though, is that there's no way I believe he's that conciliatory."

"What was he like otherwise?"

"Nice—very polite, and very smooth. He projects genuine sincerity, which is a dangerous assumption to make that could lead to letting my guard down, especially since he almost seems likeable."

"Did you dress for the occasion?" Mary Pat teases.

"Nope."

"So what's your takeaway?"

"That it is very easy to be drawn in by him, but we'd be foolish to trust him. He's a company man, an Italian, and a loyal son of Rome. One way or another, I'm sure he has ways of getting what he wants."

XXVII.

May our adversaries make us strong.
May our victories make us wise.
May our actions make us proud.
H. Jackson Brown

After a long day spent working on a grant and conferencing with the New York headquarters of WNA about the next steps in the continuing abortion rights fight in the face of escalated threats to overturn *Roe v. Wade*, Maggie arrives home bone tired. She is halfway up the hallway stairs when she remembers to check her mailbox, which only happens once or twice a month. The only mail she receives at this address are her telephone and utility bills and notices about co-op meetings. She is surprised to find a personal letter with no return address.

After throwing her coat on the threadbare sofa and getting a beer out of the refrigerator, she sits down on the fire escape to open the envelope. Inside, she finds a handwritten note.

Dear Maggie,

I am writing to tell you that I am getting married in a few weeks, to the lovely young woman who was my mother's nurse through her final days. I truly believe Anna is my mother's final gift to me because were it not for her illness, we would never have found each other.

I wanted to tell you this myself rather than have you hear it from someone else, or somehow discover it on your own.

This doesn't mean you do not remain dear to my heart, because you are very definitely that. I think of you often, always with the hope you are well and happy.

I hope you won't hesitate to be in touch if there is ever any way I can be of assistance in your efforts to bring about needed change for Catholic women's lives and, by extension, for women in general. And I hope you wish me well in this new phase of my life.

Fondly, Ben

Maggie stares at the letter for a long time before carefully folding it and placing it back in the envelope. She finishes her beer and then takes a bottle of wine from the refrigerator. Rinsing out a glass, she wonders, as she often has, whether there could've been some way to hold their relationship together. She still believes she and Ben shared something worth preserving, and recognizes that all time has done is drive home how poorly she understands both herself and what a loving relationship between a man and a woman looks like. Nothing about the situation with Ben has gotten easier to bear, and in many ways, it's gotten worse. Letting go of the only good relationship she has ever experienced with a man has been excruciating, and even though she doesn't know what she could have done differently, she still believes she badly mishandled the situation, making it the worst mistake of her life. Her deep sadness over what she has lost remains with her, and she still thinks of him several times each day. As she sits down at the table to drink her wine, a single tear runs down her cheek, landing in her lap.

•••

A few days later, Mary Pat informs her that the first Sunday financial boycott efforts have nearly doubled in size and show no signs of letting up. Maggie is happy to hear this since she has received her second invitation to meet with Cardinal Tetrone, which is scheduled for the following week. She is also awaiting the final details for Mother Stephen Elizabeth's first Chicago visit since taking over leadership of the Order more than a year ago.

In the time since accepting the WNA position, Maggie has taken great care to file her financial reports with the Order on time and slowly amend her yearly budget to allow for a larger financial contribution to the motherhouse, which she hopes places her on secure footing regarding her WNA position. She's counting on not having to explain how she is able to be as generous toward the Order as she is, which is because she owns her co-op free and clear and isn't paying rent.

Maggie's second meeting with Cardinal Tetrone begins similarly to the first. Monsignor Ancora again escorts her into the chancery reception room, where the cardinal is waiting to greet her. He invites her to sit down and enjoy refreshments while they talk. After exchanging pleasantries, the cardinal's demeanor suddenly becomes serious.

"Since we last met, I have had the opportunity to learn a great deal more about Catholic Women Demanding Change, and about their boycott efforts," he begins. "My understanding is that this currently involves one hundred and two of our churches, and about twenty-five hundred women protestors. Is this also your understanding?"

Maggie assures him that, as far as she knows, his figures are correct.

"I also understand that, at this time, the overall estimated financial impact is approximating just over ten thousand dollars per Sunday or about five hundred twenty thousand dollars per year."

Again, Maggie agrees that this is a fair representation of the effort.

"Something that bothers me about this protest," the cardinal continues, "is that many of the churches being boycotted are in poor and working-class neighborhoods where the parishes are already struggling financially. The financial hit the boycott has brought on is particularly difficult for them because they depend upon every nickel in the collection plate to make ends meet. If those churches are forced to close because of financial shortfalls, parishioners and the wider community members who depend upon their food pantries, after-school programs, and spiritual comfort will be deeply hurt."

"The only reason those churches would close is if you would decide to close them, Eminence," Maggie answers, using the formal title to address a cardinal, and wishing she had known this information before the meeting. "I'm sure the archdiocese can afford to make up the difference, if it wants to."

"The archdiocese is already subsidizing several of these parishes, and we do not have a bottomless well of money for financial aid to assist struggling parishes. Each parish is expected to take ownership of their own finances and find creative ways to remain afloat."

"Has it ever occurred to you that these parishes would be much more financially solvent if the families weren't so large and supporting so many children wasn't such a huge financial drain on the parents?" Maggie asks.

Receiving no response, she continues.

"The reality is that birth control is an issue that affects poor women and poor families the most. We already know that wealthier Catholics practice birth control and can, and do, obtain abortions if they want them."

"Where did you hear that?" the cardinal challenges. "I find it very difficult to believe what you are claiming is true."

"The Women's National Alliance keeps those statistics. I believe they are reliable," Maggie answers, instantly sorry she brought up WNA.

"Does CWDC have any connection with this national women's organization?" the cardinal asks, looking directly at Maggie.

"My understanding is that some of our members belong to both organizations," Maggie sidesteps.

"Are you one of those women, Sister?"

Maggie acknowledges that she is.

"Then, please, tell me more about it," the cardinal requests, never looking away from Maggie's face.

"It is a nationwide feminist organization dedicated to bettering women's lives in both public and private spheres. This includes promoting women's equal employment and educational opportunities, equal pay for equal work, and reproductive autonomy, among other things...basically all issues that concern women directly."

"And tear at the fabric of Christian family life," the cardinal interrupts.

"With all due respect, Cardinal Tetrone, we were discussing the parish boycotts, not the full spectrum of women's rights or the rules governing Christian family life."

"These things are not unrelated. Surely you see that?"

"Of course, but the boycott is very specifically focused on giving women control over their reproductive lives—nothing more. What happens to Christian family life as a result is not something we've been concerned with—although, candidly, I can't see how it wouldn't improve it."

"When women have more choices, Sister, they will make decisions that are not necessarily in the best interests of holding the family unit together."

"You mean they will make decisions that are not necessarily in the best interests of men having their clothes washed, their meals cooked, their house cleaned, and sex whenever they want it," Maggie bristles, feeling herself getting much angrier now. "Any message in support of that position, which is what the Church's message is, enslaves women against their will and in the name of God, as determined through the eyes of a powerful patriarchal institution. We find this unacceptable."

"That is not a problem I can solve, but I cannot allow the boycotts to continue, either."

"How do you propose to stop them?" Maggie asks.

"There are ways."

"You would begin excommunication proceedings against more than twenty-five hundred Chicago Catholic women? It seems to me that action risks creating a massive public relations problem that you'd much rather avoid, especially so soon after arriving here."

The cardinal remains silent, and Maggie waits.

"Excommunication is not at the top of my list of options. I would begin with lighter sanctions—public condemnation and refusing Communion, for example."

"How will the women protestors be identified at the Communion rail?" Maggie asks.

"I'm sure the pastors know who they are."

"Again, this creates a significant public relations problem. All it would take is one call to the newspaper and a couple of television stations and things would get much more unpleasant for all concerned—but most of all, for you. The backlash would be huge and played out on a public stage. I don't quite see you coming out on the positive end of that."

"Backlash?"

"I'm sure the WNA organization would step up in support the women who are being singled out—'punished' might be a better word. For example, they would join the picket lines at the parishes, and while you now have fifteen to twenty-five women at each parish, you would suddenly have two or three hundred. A protest that has not received a lot of public attention so far would suddenly become newsworthy."

"Short of handing out birth control pills after every Mass, how do you propose stopping the boycott, Sister?"

"Put out a statement saying you understand the women's concerns and are creating an archdiocesan Commission on Women comprised of women religious and laity who will take a deep dive into the issues and make recommendations that you will forward to Rome—and that you are naming me to lead this commission."

"Out of the question. That would be political suicide for me," the cardinal exclaims.

"So would having this argument play out on the evening news channels. Were that to occur, you would lose control of your message, and we both know that is never good."

The cardinal grimaces but doesn't respond. Maggie waits a moment and then tells him he doesn't have to decide now but should let her know soon. In the meantime, he has her word that she won't leak anything discussed at this meeting to the press.

"I look forward to hearing from you soon," she smiles, holding out her hand, which the cardinal ignores. Instead, he stands and turns to exit the room, leaving Maggie on her own to find her way out.

"Permit me to ask you one more thing, your Eminence."

The prelate stops walking and turns around.

"Do you have sisters?"

"I have five, but I don't see how that is relevant to anything."

"And Monsignor Ancora?"

"I believe he has three. But I still don't understand the purpose of your question."

"Before we meet again, I suggest you both ask your sisters about their opinion of the Church's position on women and listen very carefully to what they tell you. I expect their answers will not only surprise you, but you will learn something."

Cardinal Tetrone leaves the room without commenting further.

That was interesting, Maggie thinks. *I'll give him two weeks, and if he hasn't said anything by then, the press may receive an anonymous tip about boycotts at several of Chicago's Catholic parishes.*

•••

Coincidentally, ten days later, the Sunday *Chicago Tribune* publishes a feature story by Chicago-based freelance writer Suzanne Carter, pointing out all the ways the Catholic Church exploits and, in some cases, outright abuses women. She quotes Sister Maggie Corrigan, currently executive director of the Chicago chapter of WNA, as saying that the Catholic Church has a lot to answer for where women are concerned, and WNA is committed to supporting their Catholic members in any actions they wish to take to advance their cause for justice and a greater voice within the Church. Carter concludes her article by again quoting Maggie: "I have personally met with Cardinal Tetrone and find him congenial and willing to listen to new ideas. I hope that, with time, my first impressions are not proven wrong."

"Shit—I forgot all about that interview," Maggie tells Mary Pat when her friend calls to tell her about the article.

"Well, I guess you're busted...and just in time for your meeting with your new superior," Mary Pat says, pointing out the obvious.

"I knew I couldn't stay under the radar forever, and I'm kind of relieved it's all out in the open now. I just wish I'd planned my debut a little better," Maggie says, taking a deep breath. "The possibility of being found out was always on my mind. The truth is, it's part of my job to be out there speaking up for women, and I wouldn't be serving women or WNA if I didn't do that."

"What do you think Mother Stephen Elizabeth will say?" Mary Pat asks.

"I have absolutely no idea. Frankly, I'm a little more concerned about what the cardinal will say when he discovers I wasn't entirely forthright with him about my connection to WNA."

She doesn't wait long to find out the answer. Less than twenty-four hours after the article appears in print, the cardinal calls her.

"I'm calling about the article in yesterday's newspaper," he begins, without preliminaries.

"I thought you might be reaching out regarding the conversation we had earlier," Maggie counters.

"I'd like to know why you didn't inform me you are the executive director of WNA?" the cardinal asks, a little too forcefully.

"It's a secular job, and I didn't think it was relevant to our conversation."

"Please explain how a Catholic nun running a secular organization that supports abortion rights is not extremely relevant to our conversation?"

"I wanted to remain focused on the issue we were discussing and not overwhelm you with the power of my position," Maggie explains, glad this is a telephone, rather than a face-to-face conversation where she would be unable to resist smiling deviously. She takes great satisfaction in realizing her efforts have the cardinal's attention.

"If it's not an organizational secret, please enlighten me about how powerful you think you are."

"Well, several thousand Chicago and Northern Illinois women pay dues to the local WNA chapter. Nationwide, there are hundreds of thousands of members, in all fifty states. Not all of them are Catholic, of course, but all of them consider themselves part of a large feminist sisterhood that stands together on issues that are important to them as women, regardless of religious beliefs. In terms of sheer numbers, we are not as large as the Church, but I do think it's safe to assume we are a force to be reconned with."

"Goddamned feminists...a man's worst nightmare," the cardinal mutters, ending the call.

A few minutes later, he calls back.

"One other thing, Sister: I want you to call off the boycotts."

"I am aware that you want me to do that, Eminence. But your wish is not necessarily my command, and my understanding is that we are negotiating a way to end the boycotts that will be acceptable to both sides."

"I don't negotiate, Sister. I am telling you to call it off."

"And I am under no obligation to do as you ask."

"Need I remind you that all religious in the archdiocese are under my jurisdiction?"

"My vow of obedience is to my religious superior, Eminence, not to you. To my knowledge, there has never been an agreement between the Pax Christi Sisters of Charity and Justice and the Chicago Archdiocese that states our sisters are formally obliged to follow your orders. If there is some confusion about this, I suggest you take it up with my superior, and if you'll hang on for a moment, I'll find that phone number for you. I'm sure I have it somewhere."

"So the only way you will call off the boycott is if I agree to form an archdiocesan commission on women?" the cardinal asks, suddenly taking on a more conciliatory tone.

"That is correct."

"And if I refuse, the boycotts continue?"

"Again, Eminence, you are correct."

"Fine. You'll have your commission, which will form as soon as the boycotts have stopped, and the collections are back to their former amounts."

"I'm sorry, Eminence, but those conditions don't work. I can stop the picketing and officially withdraw the boycott, but I cannot force the women involved to return to their previous levels of financial support. That is up to you."

"How is it up to me?"

"If you prove, by your actions, that you are making a good-faith effort to hear the voices of Catholic women and work with them to gain a seat at the table where decisions about their lives are made, the boycotters are much more likely to resume their previous level of support. If you fail to do this, I can't imagine why they would want to financially support the Church at all, and I expect monetary contributions would fall even further."

"I'll have Monsignor Ancora work on the details for this commission. Expect to hear from him soon."

"I look forward to it. As soon as you and I have signed a memorandum of agreement regarding the formation of a commission on women, I assure you that the official phase of the boycott will end forthwith."

"I hope so, Sister. Trust goes both ways, and I would hate to see you fail to uphold your end of this bargain."

"And I would hate to see you fail to uphold yours, Eminence."

The cardinal slams down the telephone.

XXVIII.

Life is what happens to you while you're busy making other plans.

John Lennon

"Good to see you again, Maggie," Mother Stephen Elizabeth says as she walks into Saint Alberta's well-worn parlor, where she is staying with the three Order sisters based in Chicago.

Maggie's nervousness about the meeting increases when she sees that her superior is carrying a copy of the recent newspaper feature article identifying her as the current executive director of WNA. Fearing this possibility, Maggie had already decided to wear the most professional thrift store outfit she owns, and at the last minute pulled her hair away from her face with a bobby pin on each side. Impeccably groomed, Mother Stephen Elizabeth is wearing a business suit and her hair is professionally cut. A three-inch silver cross hangs from a thin chain around her neck.

The two nuns sit down across from one another at a small round table where tea, finger sandwiches, and fruit have been set out between two place settings. The superior pours two cups of tea and pushes the plate of sandwiches in Maggie's direction, inviting her to help herself.

"Before we begin, tell me how you are doing, Maggie, given the controversy you've stirred up."

"I'm fine, thank you, and not at all upset about the controversy. I view it as significant progress."

"I had a call from the cardinal a few days ago, which I have put off returning until I had a chance to talk with you."

Maggie explains the boycott and pending formation of the commission on women, stressing how pleased she is about the accomplishment. Mother Stephen Elizabeth listens attentively and without expression.

"It sounds like you have achieved a lot, Maggie. However, I do wish you would have discussed the WNA position with me. Reading about it in the newspaper has been awkward."

Maggie acknowledges that telling her superior about the position would have been the proper thing to do, then proceeds to excuse herself by explaining that the opportunity arose during a transition period in Order leadership, and she assumed there were other, more pressing things to be concerned about.

"The position offered an extraordinary opportunity, which Mother Marie William and I had discussed previously, so I decided to accept it and deal with any fallout later. I probably should have sought permission, but I was right about one thing: it has been an extraordinary opportunity. I don't think the cardinal would have budged on the women's commission idea if I wasn't the executive director of WNA, with the energy of thousands of women behind me."

"Perhaps you are right, Maggie. But you are heading up an organization whose core values fly directly in the face of Church doctrine, and that is extremely problematic."

"There is a difference between promoting women's reproductive autonomy and promoting abortion. I stand for the former and have not spoken out publicly on the latter."

"But aren't you splitting hairs? There is a very fine distinction between those two concepts."

"No question it's walking a tightrope, but so far, I have been able to do that."

"I must caution you to proceed very carefully."

"An advantage of the position is that the salary has enabled me to increase my direct support for the Order significantly."

"This is true, and not irrelevant to my decision not to ask you to resign. You have been faithful to your monthly budget, which is very reasonable and allows for a substantial monthly payment to the Order. But this brings me to another question: I know you no longer live at Holy Mother of Consolation Women's Shelter, nor are you living in a convent, so I am wondering where, exactly, you are living that allows you to surrender nearly half your earned income?"

"I live in a co-op apartment in Archer Heights."

"How did this occur?"

"I inherited it when my brother died."

"Your brother the priest?"

Maggie nods.

"I'm surprised he could afford to own any Chicago real estate on a priest's salary. Regardless, you are aware that all inheritances go to the Order, correct?"

"I am, but technically, my sisters and I inherited it together. They agreed I could live there rent-free. I only pay utilities and the quarterly co-op dues."

"For me to allow this arrangement to continue, I must ask that you provide legal documentation indicating that you jointly inherited and now jointly own the property with your sisters and that, upon its sale, your portion will come to the Order. We've loosened our regulations on cars, and sisters who inherit motor vehicles are allowed to keep them if they need them for their work and can afford to maintain them, but we remain firm in our position against owning real estate."

Maggie realizes meeting these conditions will be complicated, but once again reminds the mother superior that the arrangement benefits the Order most of all.

"When I return the cardinal's phone call, I will explain that I have spoken to you about the WNA position and am assured you are acting in good conscience and being thoughtfully prudent in your words and actions. I want to assure him I understand his concerns but don't want him getting the idea that we tell our sisters what to do, or that he can try to pressure me into bending to his wishes." Mother Stephen Elizabeth smiles.

"I think the matter between the cardinal and me has been settled—at least for now." Maggie smiles back.

•••

Shortly after the Archdiocesan Commission on Women is officially launched, Maggie is sitting in a local doctor's office for the first time in her life. She had been aware of a lump in her breast for some time but paid little attention until it became too painful to ignore. Now she is being told she must undergo a biopsy procedure.

"I can schedule this for next week," the kindly doctor, who was recommended by her WNA secretary, tells her.

"I'm very busy right now. Maybe it will disappear eventually," Maggie says.

"You've said it's been there for a long time, so I'm afraid it's not going to disappear on its own, Sister. It could be nothing, or it could be something we need to treat, but either way, we need to find out what it is as soon as possible."

"I'd prefer to wait."

"That, of course, is your decision, but I think waiting would be a serious mistake."

"I've never been sick before...this is the first time I've ever been to a doctor."

"I'm sure it's very frightening, but I promise you this is something we can deal with, once we know what it is. And in situations like this, sooner is always better."

"You sound like you think it's serious."

"It definitely could be...but perhaps not. It's all speculation at this point. We won't know for certain until we perform a biopsy."

Maggie waits three months before finally agreeing to the biopsy, which only occurs because the lump is continuing to bother her. One week later, early on a sunny Wednesday afternoon, while sitting across from the doctor's desk in his modest office, she receives devastating news.

"I'm sorry, Sister, but you have breast cancer."

"What exactly does that mean?" Maggie asks, gripping the arms of her chair.

"Your breast will need to be completely removed. We won't have all the answers until we examine your lymph nodes after surgery, but since you waited a long time before pursuing a diagnosis, my educated guess is that there will be post-surgery follow-up recommendations."

"Like what?"

"About six weeks post-surgery, you will begin at least a year of chemotherapy, followed by several radiation treatments. Individual reactions vary, but once recovered from the surgery itself, most women carry on with their daily lives while undergoing additional treatment. Plan on being more tired than usual and losing your hair, but otherwise, the side-effects should be tolerable. In post-menopausal women like yourself, the long-term outlook is generally quite optimistic."

Maggie is too shocked to react and feels the room begin to spin.

"Let me get you some water while you take a few minutes to absorb this," the doctor says, seeing Maggie grow pale.

Twenty minutes pass before the conversation resumes.

"The sooner we deal with this, the better, so we'll need to schedule the surgery right away," the doctor explains. "My nurse will give you more information and instructions, but expect to go into the hospital by the end of next week, at the latest. In the meantime, try not to worry too much, Sister. It will be a little rough, but I think you'll come through this just fine and be as good as new."

After hearing this news, Maggie leaves the office. Numb, she aimlessly wanders the streets, wondering what to do next.

Until now, I've always been able to handle whatever's been thrown my way, she thinks, growing angry. *Who the hell would've guessed something like this would happen? Being machine-gunned* down *by one of Al Capone's or the Italian archbishop's hitmen wouldn't be any worse than having the fucking wrath of God rain down on me just because I'm trying to do good in the world,* she thinks, kicking at a telephone pole so hard she splits the sole on of one of the heavily worn wooden clogs from an Archer Heights thrift store.

It's a fucking lonely, empty life when there's nobody I can turn to for comfort, Maggie silently laments, barely resisting the impulse to look for a telephone and call Ben. Although CWDC no longer meets at Our Daily Bread, one of the committee chairs recently held an emergency meeting there and reported that after meeting Ben's little son, it's obvious the boy has a natural and adoring father. After nearly six years, she still thinks of him at least once each day. She knows she cannot step into the middle of his life with needs of her own, but she desperately craves his comforting presence and reassurance as decisions she doesn't know how to resolve race around in her head. How will she manage immediately after her surgery? How will she get through chemotherapy and radiation treatments? Will she be able to remain involved with WNA, CWDC, and the newly formed Archdiocesan Commission on Women she now chairs?

Continuing to wander the streets instead of returning to her office, she looks for the nearest L station and climbs aboard the next train, wherever it is going. By the time she finally returns to her apartment nearly four hours later, it's nearly dark outside.

After a sleepless night, Maggie knows she has to make some decisions, beginning with accepting the fact that she has no one who can step up to care for her in the immediate aftermath of the surgery. She can't recall the last time she spoke to her sisters but knows that because pleasant conversations between them are so rare, she would remember one if it had occurred. Mary Pat is still very much part of her own sister's household and would not be able to stay with Maggie when she comes home from the hospital. Her only option is moving into Saint Alberta's convent immediately post-surgery. However, when she calls to discuss this, Sister John Martha tells her they are sorry to hear she is ill and will pray for her, but the most they can manage is having her come for the first week after she is discharged from the hospital.

"I'm sorry, Maggie, but an extended stay is out of the question. We simply don't have space. You'll be sharing a room with Sister Martha James, and I can't inconvenience her for six weeks. Perhaps after your stitches are removed, you can go to the motherhouse until you are strong enough to be on your own again."

The motherhouse is the last place Maggie wants to spend a month, but she is slowly realizing she has no choice. She also has no idea how she will get there—a problem she dumps into Mary Pat's lap.

"I drive, but I don't have a license or a car," Mary Pat says. "It wouldn't be a good idea for me to drive all that way anyway. If something happened, it would be a mess. My nephew just got his license through driver's ed in high school and might be willing to drive you if you can find a car, but I doubt very many people are willing to loan you their car so a sixteen-year-old can drive you all the way to Indiana and then return whenever he feels like it."

Maggie eventually asks her WNA secretary to drive her to the motherhouse and return for her a month or so later. She informs the WNA Board of Directors of her situation and asks for a six-week leave of absence, which she knows might be pushing herself, but doesn't want to be away from the job she loves, and that sustains her, any longer. She makes similar arrangements for CWDC and the archdiocesan commission which, without Maggie spearheading it, is likely to be suspended in a holding pattern. After accomplishing these tasks, she feels so desolate, she decides she would rather die than be unable to carry on with the work that defines her.

•••

One month later, battered, sore, and exhausted from her surgery a few days earlier, Maggie is staying at Saint Alberta's until she can travel to the motherhouse. She finds not feeling well very challenging and is dismayed to learn the doctor's predictions were correct; she will need one year of chemotherapy followed by radiation, which will hopefully take care of any stray cancer cells. After that, she should be fine, and statistically, a recurrence is unlikely. Hearing this, she dismisses her previous thoughts about her illness being God's way of punishing her and refuses to view it as anything more than a minor inconvenience, a decision that improves her mood considerably.

The three sisters residing at Saint Alberta's are polite toward Maggie and careful to ensure her physical needs are met, but do not go out of their way to make her feel welcome. They speak over and around rather than with her at meals, and they do not invite her to join in board games after dinner, or watch television with them, nor does anyone offer to go with her to her post-surgery follow-up appointment. Her only phone calls are from Mary Pat and her WNA secretary. After her stitches are removed and the doctor says he won't need to see her for a month, she is more than ready to leave the convent, but has little hope the motherhouse will be much different.

Maggie's room assignment at the motherhouse is a windowless novice's cell—about seven feet square with a bed covered by a sheet, thin blanket, and one pillow. She finds a towel and washcloth in the cupboard. A kneeler is placed below an outsized crucifix hanging on the wall. "One thing I don't need is a crucified Christ staring down at me while I sleep," Maggie grouses, grabbing the bottom of the cross to see if there is any way to remove it. "I've never understood why the image of Christ crucified is everywhere... it's a barbaric symbol that is supposed to remind us of how awful we all are and make us feel guilty about it," she mumbles, as she pulls at the securely fastened image. "I guess the suffering Christ is screwed to the wall just like Catholic women are."

The bathroom and showers are down the hall. Maggie asks for an extra pillow to support her shoulder while she sleeps and is told there are none. When she wakes up in the middle of the first night to go to the bathroom, she painfully stubs her toe on the bed frame and hits herself in the face opening the door into the hallway, letting loose with several expletives never before heard in a convent.

The atmosphere at the motherhouse mirrors Maggie's experience at Saint Alberta's. The sisters are polite but make little effort to welcome or comfort her. She eats alone because no one joins her or invites her to sit with them. She is not included in the after-dinner bridge or Scrabble games, invited to watch the biweekly movie, or encouraged to join lingering after-dinner conversations over coffee. Other than Mother Stephen Elizabeth, no one asks how she is feeling, and her only support comes from afar, in the form of a few get-well cards from her colleagues at WNA and CWDC.

Over the years Maggie has never expected everyone to agree with her, but she did not expect to become an outcast either and is surprised by the depth and breadth of her fellow sisters' negative attitudes toward her. After four weeks of being socially ostracized, she is certain managing chemotherapy on her own will be far preferable to being shunned and ignored, which is what she is currently experiencing.

One evening, shortly before Maggie is to return to Chicago, Sister Helen Maria Smith, a young novice who is preparing to make her solemn profession within the next year, asks to join Maggie for lunch. She explains that she has a question she believes only Maggie can answer.

"I know many of the sisters are upset and deeply angered by your work for women's rights, and I'm wondering why you took the position you did on birth control and abortion, which is contrary to everything the Church and we, as Sisters of Charity and Justice, believe. How could you do that to us?"

Maggie continues chewing for a long time while considering her answer. "First of all, I didn't set out to do anything to the community, and I find it unfortunate that many feel I have embarrassed the Order, and them personally. I didn't intend nor did I expect that to occur. I thought most would understand that if the Church allowed birth control, abortion would become a moot point—there would rarely be a need for it. I truly believed almost everyone would personally agree with my position on reproductive autonomy and privately support it, even if they felt they could not do so publicly. And I felt certain that forcing the Chicago Archdiocese to create a commission on women would be widely celebrated."

"I've not heard anyone say they're excited about it. Most seem to feel it's wasting time and resources that could be better spent on direct aid to the poor."

"It's unfortunate that the distress the sisters feel I have caused has lasted so long. I expected it would blow over eventually and am surprised that it hasn't." Maggie takes a drink of water before continuing. "As to why I took up the issue at all, I felt then, and still feel, that it was the right thing to do. I believe institutionalized patriarchal dominion over women's lives is immoral no matter who is doing it, and it is especially egregious that the Church leads the way in continuing this practice, which has no basis in scripture, by the way. More to the point, I don't think the Church's views toward women, or its treatment of them, is what a loving God could possibly want for Catholic women's lives—it's what the patriarchy wants, but not what God wants—and I could not be more certain about this."

"If you can't accept the Church as it is, why don't you just leave?"

"Because I don't want to, and because I am forcing some positive change to an institution that no one seems to understand means a great deal to me. If I didn't care about the Church so much, I certainly wouldn't have spent my entire life trying to push it toward greater justice regarding women who, by the way, are half the world's population."

"But all you do is criticize, and you have never attended Mass or prayed with us the entire time you've been here. I don't think you're Catholic at all. I think you are using the Church to push your own personal agenda."

"It's truly unfortunate you feel that way, Sister Helen. My hope has always been that there was room for differences of opinion within the Order, and I accept full responsibility for my error in judgment."

"Do you intend to seek forgiveness?" the young novice asks.

"I don't see any reason to."

•••

Back in her co-op in Chicago two weeks later, Maggie finds she tires easily, and when she is told she must begin chemotherapy at the end of the month, she realizes she will have to step aside and let someone else take over the WNA leadership, at least temporarily. The decision is deeply painful, but she knows it is the right one for the organization and hopes to convince the board to allow her to stay on as coordinator of their reproductive rights campaign, which is a less demanding, less public position she thinks she can manage while undergoing cancer treatment. The board agrees, and assures Maggie the directorship remains hers just as soon as she is able to reassume it.

Next on Maggie's list is arranging for someone to drive her to and from the hospital each Monday and Thursday for the next twelve months, where she will spend entire afternoons submitting to chemical infusions designed to kill off the cancer cells that have invaded her body. Never having had ongoing medical care before, even as a child, she finds focusing on her body upsetting and disorienting. Her entire right side is painful, and being right-handed, finding she can barely lift her right arm makes everything worse. She is angry, frightened, upset by the restrictions that have been forced upon her, and is feeling sorry for herself.

"This cancer is totally controlling me. It decides my mood, my appetite, what I can and can't do, and even how I look...and I hate it. I don't understand why it had to happen to me now, when such exciting things were on the horizon. The timing has ruined my life, and it's not fair...it's not like I'm a bad person," she whines when Mary Pat calls.

"Cancer's not selective, Maggie. It's an equal opportunity stalker that attacks anybody, good, bad, or indifferent, and it's never at that person's convenience. You, above all people, should know life isn't fair and stop taking this so personally."

"I feel like God is punishing me."

"Well, He's not. And thinking that way is not helpful, so get over it," her friend instructs, hanging up the phone.

The day before Maggie is scheduled to undergo her first chemotherapy treatment, Mary Pat takes her to a store specializing in the needs of cancer patients to select a wig for the inevitable hair loss she will experience. The appointment does not go well.

"I'm not wearing any goddamned wig," Maggie yells at Mary Pat after trying one on. In a fit of frustration, she walks out the door.

"Fine," Mary Pat calls after her. "Wear a scarf or go bald, but either one is going to be damned cold in the winter."

Maggie ignores her best friend and keeps walking toward the L. She boards the first train, which happens not to be going to Archer Heights. When she finally arrives back at her apartment nearly three hours later, she finds Mary Pat sitting on the front step, waiting for her.

"How did you know where I live?" Maggie asks.

"Fiona told my sister—how else?"

Maggie briefly wonders how Fiona found out, then shrugs and fishes around for the key.

"I'm coming inside, and we're having a serious conversation, Maggie. Cancer or no cancer, I'm the best friend you'll ever have, and you treat me like dirt. I'm sick of it."

After they are both inside, Maggie goes to the refrigerator, takes out a bottle of cheap wine, and washes two glasses in the sink. Drying the first one, she hands it to Mary Pat.

"I thought you weren't supposed to drink alcohol," Mary Pat reminds her.

"There's a lot of things I'm not supposed to do."

"Have you ever considered that your anger is making your cancer worse?"

"I've never known you to blame the victim, Mary Pat. Why are you starting now?"

"I'm not blaming you, Maggie. But you act like you're the only person who's been dealt a bad hand. Shit happens. Don't you ever wonder how your mother would feel about seeing you so angry all the time?"

"No, I don't. I never think about her at all."

"Maybe you should. She loved you, and it wasn't her fault she died—"

"Maybe she got the better deal, given the life she was destined to lead."

"Death is never the better deal, Maggie."

"The goddamned Church was calling all the shots, and they were bad ones. What's good about that?" Maggie interrupts.

"Okay, fine. It was the Church's fault, but the Church doesn't give a damn that you're still pissed off. It couldn't care less how you feel about anything. I don't dispute that there's a lot in the world to be pissed off about, but stress and anger are very hard on a person, and you've carried around boatloads of both all your life. The only person you're hurting is yourself. All that pent-up energy has to go somewhere—"

"You think I gave myself cancer?" Maggie yells, throwing a nearby book on the floor.

"That's not what I'm saying. But being mad at the world and everybody in it, like you've been all your life, is very hard on your body, and one way or another, there's a price to pay for that. If you don't unload all that crap somehow, it's going to interfere with you getting healthy again. You need all your energy for healing, which begins by letting go of some of your anger."

Maggie remains silent for a long time.

"It's very hard for me to admit this, but without my anger, I don't exist," she finally says, her lower lip quivering. "Without something to fight against, my life is meaningless. This way, I'm doing something real and know I am still alive...otherwise, there's no point."

"But being so angry—it's hurting you. Can't you see that merely being alive and helping others is enough? That's all God asks of us."

"I don't know what God asks, or doesn't ask, and neither do you. I am who I am, and I'm not going to change, regardless of what God wants. My anger is too big a part of me—I can't let it go."

"Is it true that before Tommy died, he asked you to tell me he wanted to see me, and you refused?" Mary Pat asks, getting to the heart of why she wants to talk with Maggie.

"Who told you that?" Maggie feels her heart speed up.

"Fiona told my sister Tommy said he wanted to see me and had asked you to tell me, but he didn't think you did. He died a few hours later, before she could get word to me."

"It's true. I didn't tell you because I believed he was going to hurt you all over again, and I didn't want to give him the chance."

"No, you wanted to hurt him. Not telling me he wanted to see me was just another way for you to do it."

"I thought I was protecting you—"

"I'm a big girl, Maggie. I can take care of myself. I would've gone to see Tommy, and you knew it. You had no right to take that choice from me."

"No, I didn't...but there's nothing I can do about it now."

"How about saying you're sorry, for starters, and promising you'll never, ever do something like that again? Promise me you'll never be dishonest with me again."

"I wasn't being dishonest. It was a sin of omission."

"It was one hell of a big one, Maggie. I can't think of too many that are worse than not telling your best friend that the man she has loved all her life is dying and wants to see her."

"I was never sure whether not telling you was the right decision and finally decided it probably wasn't, but time passed, and it became a mistake I couldn't correct...."

"Until it was too late."

"Until it was too late. But I don't think I was being dishonest. I would've told you the truth if you had asked me."

"But since I didn't know Tommy was dying, there was no reason for me to ask, was there?"

"I didn't know whether you knew or not but figured Fiona would tell your sister at some point and you'd find out that way. Just because I didn't say anything doesn't make me a dishonest person."

"It doesn't make you a trustworthy one. Everything about you is dishonest, Maggie. Can't you understand that?"

"No, I can't, but I'm sure you're about to explain it to me."

"You aren't religious at all—you're lying about that, just pretending to be devout to get what you want, which is attention and protection. If you pretend to love God and believe in what the Church stands for, your Order will take care of you for the rest of your life. But you don't honestly believe any of it. You're using the Order to get what you want: security, recognition, and the respect wider society bestows on nuns because most people believe they live for God by always trying to do good in the world.

News flash, Maggie, that's exactly what they do—except for you. You live for Maggie Corrigan—nobody else. And for some reason, you chose to do battle with the Church over everything you hate in the world, because you think life cheated you out of what you deserved and it's the Church's fault. Well, guess what? Nobody deserves anything, Maggie. Life's a crapshoot, and it's all the luck of the draw...and some people are just plain luckier than others. That's the way life is, and what happened to you as a kid doesn't give you a right to be so damned selfish, angry, or self-righteous."

Maggie remains silent.

"You didn't tell me about Tommy because you didn't want him to see me and find out I still loved him...or talk about our son and hear things that would have made him happy and brought him peace—neither of which you have any of, because you're too selfish and love is a completely foreign concept to you."

Several minutes pass and Maggie still doesn't respond.

"Okay, I've had my say. It's over now," Mary Pat finally says.

"If you did something to me like what I did to you, I'd never forgive you," Maggie whispers.

"I guess that's where we're different, Maggie. I don't want to be angry and hate everybody, and you do. I believe people can protest injustice and work for change without hating the world at the same time. The world and everybody in it is flawed. Nobody is perfect. You can either accept that or spend your life being pissed off about it and die alone. If you're fine with that, so be it."

Hearing this, Maggie slumps in her chair, briefly closing her eyes.

"You're exhausted. I should leave you to get some rest," Mary Pat says, standing up.

"I do fine for a while and then suddenly am overwhelmed with fatigue so heavy I can barely move. Otherwise, I'd talk about this for as long as you want to talk about it."

"I don't ever want to talk about it again," Mary Pat tells her life-long friend.

They sit in deep silence for several minutes, until Mary Pat speaks again.

"Before I forget, I bought you a wig. You don't have to wear it if you don't want to, but you'll have it just in case. Also—the one-sided, flat chest thing: either stuff some socks in your bra or get whatever it is they give women who've had your surgery, because right now people are staring at you in places you don't want them looking."

Maggie chuckles for the first time all day.

"You need to eat, so I'll make you a sandwich before I leave," Mary Pat says, walking toward the kitchenette, where she continues the conversation. "One more thing: I've arranged to be available to take you to chemo tomorrow, and for a few times after that, until you see how it affects you. I'll be here first thing in the morning."

Hearing the kindness in her friend's voice, Maggie lets out a deep sob.

XXIX.

When the principles that run against your deepest convictions begin to win the day, then the battle is your calling, and peace has become sin. You must, at the price of dearest peace, lay your convictions bare before friend and enemy with all the fire of your faith.

Abraham Kuyper

"Is this Sister Maggie Corrigan?" a three-pack-per-day cigarette voice asks when Maggie answers the phone in her apartment late on a Sunday evening. She has just returned from a WNA committee meeting where she reported on the safety partnerships they are providing to patients at women's reproductive health clinics throughout the Northern Illinois region. Without answering the question, she asks who is calling.

"Is it true you are a patient advocate at an abortion clinic, Sister?" a man identifying himself as a news reporter wheezes into the telephone.

"I have no idea what you're talking about," she tells him.

"Well, Sister, we received a tip and photos several people have identified as you escorting women into a reproductive health clinic outside Peoria that performs abortions," he replies. "I thought you might want to comment on this before we run the story."

"Goddammit," Maggie exclaims, slamming down the phone. "How the hell did he get my phone number anyway?"

Two years ago, at Maggie's suggestion, the WNA reproductive rights group decided to become volunteer patient advocates and safety partners for women seeking abortions at various sites around the greater Chicago area. The effort quickly expanded to include Peoria, Rockford, DeKalb, and several other locations. Wanting to participate in the effort, yet stay under the radar, Maggie became a safety guide and advocate at a women's reproductive health clinic far outside Chicago. The clinic, in a semi-rural area, serves low-income women who often encounter angry, pro-life supporters trying to frighten them out of obtaining an abortion.

In the eighteen months since her cancer diagnosis, rather than slowing down, Maggie has become increasingly more involved in the reproductive rights issue. She tolerated chemotherapy better than she expected and has been able to resume her WNA director position and maintain her other commitments. But this phone call throws her a curveball. She takes off her wig, which scratches her scalp in the places where her hair has failed to grow back and pours herself two fingers of bourbon before climbing out the window onto the fire escape to think about what to do now that her advocacy activities on behalf of women's reproductive choice are about to be exposed, and likely force a showdown with her Order.

She's known for a long time that her in-your-face activism over the years has earned her some heavy-hitting enemies who have been waiting for just the right opportunity to make her life a living hell, and it looks like they are about to be handed that chance. But never one to back down from a fight, she has no intention of backing away from this one; she just has to figure out what her next move will be.

"I've survived worse," she whispers to the sparrow sitting on the fire escape railing staring at her.

In recent months, Maggie hasn't given a great deal of thought to being discovered because the archdiocese has, once again, been in upheaval. Shortly after her cancer diagnosis, it was announced that Cardinal Tetrone was suffering from a terminal illness. He died a few weeks later, and the Archdiocesan Commission on Women, which Maggie had struggled to get off the ground, died with him. Before Rome could name his successor, the archdiocese found itself mired in an epic pedophilia scandal that continues to occupy the news cycles. Maggie quickly realized that whatever she was doing paled by comparison and decided that she had been handed another opportunity to ramp up her efforts without much, if any, official archdiocesan objection.

The new archbishop, a native Chicagoan of Irish heritage, was named a month ago. George Michael "Mick" Sullivan was previously an auxiliary bishop under both Cardinals O'Grady and Tetrone, and the Vatican has already announced that he is being promoted to cardinal. She has known Mick Sullivan by reputation for several years, is aware that Tommy played poker with him fairly regularly, and believes it unlikely he will concern himself with what she is doing, even if her activities are exposed.

For the next two years, Maggie carries on with no intention of curtailing her efforts—until she receives a call from Mother Stephen Elizabeth, instructing her to return to the Pax Christi Sisters of Charity and Justice provincial headquarters at the motherhouse immediately.

XXX.

Strengthen the female mind, and there will be an end to blind obedience.
MARY WOLLSTONECRAFT

Resistance to tyranny is obedience to God.
SUSAN B. ANTHONY

Early on a Friday morning, four days after her summons to return to the motherhouse, Maggie leaves her Archer Heights apartment. Right after finishing cancer treatment, she finally obtained a driver's license and bought a cheap, second-hand car to travel back-and-forth to Peoria. She dislikes driving and breathes a sigh of relief when she finally turns off the perpetually congested Dan Ryan Expressway south onto Interstate 65 toward central Indiana.

Once the traffic thins out, Maggie begins thinking about possible reasons for this sudden command appearance and decides it most likely involves the recent newspaper headline identifying her as "Chicago's pro-abortion nun."

"I don't see how you're going to escape this one, Maggie. The wire services will pick up a sensationalist headline like that, and it'll be all over the news in several states. You might as well prepare for a rough ride because there's no way the Order won't find out about it," Mary Pat said with a sense of foreboding when she called Maggie after reading the article.

"We'll see...maybe you're overreacting. Besides, the article is incorrect—I'm not pro-abortion, I'm pro-choice," Maggie replied.

"I wouldn't bet on that hair-splitting point saving your ass. I'll be praying for you—even if you don't want me to."

As she is driving through Indiana, Maggie recalls that several times in the eight or nine years since she took over the leadership of the Chicago branch of the Women's National Alliance, she has received letters from her superior, reminding her to stay under the radar and avoid negative publicity, and she can't recall acknowledging any of them. About a year ago, after an interview on a national television network special regarding a women's right to choose, she was officially reprimanded, followed by an invitation to discuss the issue further, but she never responded.

I'm still sending half my monthly salary back to the Order, so they can't be that upset with me, Maggie thinks as she turns off the highway onto the flat, two-lane road leading to the provincial headquarters. *This scenery never gets any better,* she reminds herself.

Fifteen minutes later, she parks her car and takes her overnight bag up to the motherhouse entrance. Identifying herself to the sister at the reception desk, Maggie explains that she is expected and asks for a room assignment. She is handed a key and directed to the elevator at the end of the hallway, which she is to take to the second-floor guest quarters.

"There must be some mistake. I am one of the Order nuns, and normally I stay in the convent," she tells the novice sitting at the desk.

"I'm sorry, Sister. My instructions are to notify Mother Stephen Elizabeth when you arrive and to direct you to the guest rooms. I'll let her know you are here, and I'm sure she will be in touch soon."

Seeing no alternative, Maggie does as she is told. She exits the elevator on the second floor and finds her room midway down the hallway, past the communal bathroom. When she opens the door, she is surprised by how much it looks like the cells in the convent—a single bed, desk, chair, a wardrobe, and a large crucifix crowd into an eight-by-eight-foot space. She cracks open the window, then sits down on the single bed where she tossed her bag.

A few minutes later, there is a light knock on the door.

"Sister Maggie Corrigan?" the voice asks.

Maggie opens the door.

"I'm Sister Eileen, Mother Stephen Elizabeth's assistant. She has asked me to escort you to her office."

Sister Eileen is not someone Maggie has ever heard of, but notices that she is young enough to be her granddaughter, which suddenly makes her feel very old. *This is the second person here I don't recognize. Maybe my resolution for the new millennium should be to show up more often,* she thinks as they walk down the hall.

Exiting the elevator, she turns left. Sister Eileen stops her.

"The administrative offices have been moved, Sister. Please follow me this way."

By the time they reach Mother Stephen Elizabeth's office, Maggie's arthritic knees are seriously complaining.

"Please wait here, Sister. I'll let Mother know we have arrived."

Maggie gratefully sits in the nearest chair, and fifteen minutes pass before her superior, with neatly cut hair and wearing a business suit, opens her office door and invites her in.

I guess I should've dressed more formally, Maggie thinks, tucking her yellow-striped blouse into her red pants.

"Hello, Maggie," Mother Stephen Elizabeth says, offering her hand. "I trust you had an uneventful trip."

Accepting the handshake, Maggie remains silent as she looks around the room. She finds the office's sparse modesty striking. Except for a prominently displayed crucifix, the cream-colored walls are bare, and industrial-gray carpeting covers the floor. A large desk sits near an interior door, and a small, circular table is in the corner opposite two small, north-facing windows that do not allow enough natural light to brighten the room significantly. The superior motions Maggie toward the table.

"Two other sisters may join us later, so sitting here will be more comfortable," the mother superior says.

Hearing this, Maggie feels an unease settle into the pit of her stomach.

"You are probably wondering what this is all about?" Mother Stephen Elizabeth begins.

Maggie acknowledges that she is.

"I want to start by acknowledging that this is going to be a very difficult conversation. I expect you will be deeply upset by what I am about to tell you, and any time you wish to take a break, please say so."

Maggie suddenly feels as though she is either on trial for her life or is about to undergo a modern version of the Spanish Inquisition. Her heart is thumping in her chest.

"I am sure you are aware that your activism has been a source of concern to the Order for a very long time," Maggie's superior quietly continues.

"Yes, I am aware of this," Maggie admits, looking her superior in the eye.

"And you recall you have been cautioned several times about this before finally being officially reprimanded because of your support of women's reproductive rights?"

"My answer has always been that I have never sought publicity for myself or my positions and can't help that notoriety has, on occasion, found me. Surely you realize I have no control over that."

"I understand you have no control over the media, but you absolutely have control over your actions, and volunteering at an abortion clinic, apparently for several years, has crossed the line. A good many of your fellow sisters, and the Order's leadership team, find this unacceptable, and we can't ignore it any longer."

"How many is a good many?" Maggie asks.

"Nearly all. The leadership team and I have received several hundred communications from sisters throughout the province expressing their dismay—anger might be the better word—at your actions. As you know, despite the vow of obedience sisters take, my philosophy is to, whenever possible, avoid hovering over our sisters. Instead, I prefer trusting them not to engage in unacceptable activities. I've tried very hard to allow you the freedom to pursue the cause of women's reproductive autonomy because you are so passionate about it, but you've gone too far. The leadership team has met and carefully reviewed the situation, and we agree that the only recourse left to us is to formally censure you and set forth certain requirements you must agree to abide by if you are to remain in the Order."

Mother Stephen Elizabeth hands Maggie a sheet of paper containing a numbered list of items.

"While you look this over, I'll get us some water," the superior says.

"What the hell—I'm being kicked out?" Maggie asks, turning pale and suddenly feeling light-headed.

"That isn't what I said, Maggie. I said certain things will have to change if you wish to remain, which isn't the same thing. I'd like you to take a few minutes to look these over, and then we'll discuss them. Here is a pencil if you wish to make notes. I'll be right back with some water. The restroom is through the door behind my desk, if you need it."

The room begins spinning, and Maggie fears she may pass out.

Several minutes go by before Mother Stephen Elizabeth returns. Handing over a cold bottle of water, she asks if Maggie would like to discuss the items now or wait to discuss them with the entire leadership team tomorrow morning. "I've set aside the entire afternoon today, so we can talk now, or you can come back after Mass and breakfast in the morning, whatever you're most comfortable with."

"Why did you put me in the guest quarters instead of the convent?" Maggie asks, taking a deep breath.

"For your own good. Your fellow sisters are very angry with you right now, Maggie. I feel you, and they, would be better off if, on this visit, you do not stay in the convent, and take your meals in the guest dining room rather than in ours."

"What are you afraid of—a cat fight?"

"Of course not, but I did think that after hearing what I have to say, you might want to be alone with your thoughts."

"I'd rather get this over with now and not meet with the full leadership team tomorrow morning," Maggie says, going back to the original question while trying to maintain her composure.

"Very well. I'll go over these with you, and we can discuss them one at a time. Do you have any general questions before we begin?"

"What exactly does it mean to be officially censured?"

"The leadership, on behalf of the Order, will issue a formal, public condemnation of your actions, explaining that what you have said and done runs counter to the Order's beliefs and standards for acceptable behavior that we, as the solemnly vowed Pax Christi Sisters of Charity and Justice community of women religious baptized into the Roman Catholic Church, expect from our sisters in committed religious life."

Afraid she might begin hyperventilating, Maggie puts her hands over her nose and mouth and takes several deep breaths.

"Never in our history has this action been taken against one of our sisters, and believe me, we don't want to take it now, Maggie. But you have ignored our efforts to work with you, and we cannot allow you to continue as you have been, so we have no choice. But I also want you to know that we have also strongly resisted Bishop Werner's efforts to force us to expel you, so he can begin excommunication proceedings."

"Expel me? Would you do that?"

"We are the family you marry into when you forgo everything to become a bride of Christ, Maggie. We don't expel one of our family members merely because we disagree with them. The problem in your case is that you have pushed the boundaries of acceptable religious family behavior beyond their outermost limits, forcing us to act."

"I don't see how this is any of Bishop Werner's business."

"Frankly, neither do I. But Bishop Werner leads the Indiana diocese where we are located and, for years, has been threatening to begin excommunication proceedings against you if we didn't curtail your activities. In his mind, that includes expelling you from the Order. However, there is nothing in our charter that obligates us to obey the local bishop, and without our cooperation, taking any official action against you would be very difficult—but not impossible. He has, thus far, declined to push us harder. However, after this most recent newspaper article, I expect to be hearing from him again any day."

"What will you tell him?"

"That we aware of the situation and will handle it as an internal personnel matter."

"Surely I'm not the first sister to run afoul of the Order's expectations."

"Of course not. In previous cases, the sisters involved either expressed remorse and asked for forgiveness, promising not to repeat the offense, or voluntarily left the Order. You have not chosen either path. Instead, you have remained in religious life and ignored requests to bring your behavior into line with the expectations for women religious."

Seeing perspiration break out on Maggie's forehead, the superior asks if she wants to take a break.

"No. I want to get this over with as soon as possible."

"Very well. Let's go over the requirements together. The first one is that you resign your Women's National Alliance position immediately."

"Are you sure you want me to do that? It will cut off my monthly contribution to the Order, which isn't just pocket change."

"We are aware of this consequence, Maggie, but we are dealing with a grave moral concern. The finances are irrelevant."

"I beg to differ—you've been receiving a substantial amount of money from me for nearly ten years, and it hasn't been a moral problem. You also received somewhere around twenty thousand dollars a year from me for quite a long time before that. How is that money all of a sudden not relevant?"

"Perhaps the best answer is that your activities have now become a great embarrassment that flies in the face of all the Order, and our pro-life Church, stand for. You have claimed to be a Catholic nun in good standing while loudly and publicly supporting abortion rights, thus taking a public position on a moral issue that is in direct opposition to Catholic doctrine and Canon law. Rather than being in the state of grace Catholics at all times strive for, you are in a continuing state of mortal sin and cannot participate in the Eucharist, which is the core of Catholic sacramental life. In this context, the money involved is meaningless."

"I knew I was walking on the edge of a cliff, but the Order continued to accept the money I sent, knowing how I was earning it. That implied what I was doing was acceptable. I reasonably assumed everyone understood that pro-choice includes the abortion option but doesn't advocate for it. I also assumed the Order agreed that women having reproductive autonomy was morally correct, although it could never publicly admit that."

"That was magical thinking, Maggie, with no basis in reality."

"I can't quit. I need a paying job."

"If you wish to remain in the Order, you'll have to find a different one."

"I couldn't earn as much money."

"That relates to the second requirement. Since you never provided us with documentation that indicates otherwise, we believe you own your co-op apartment. Otherwise, your living expenses would be much higher, and you wouldn't have as much money available to send to us. As you know, the Order forbids private ownership of property and other material goods. You'll either have to provide legal proof that your sisters own the apartment you are living in and are allowing you to live in it rent free, as you have claimed, or you will have to sign it over to the Order. We aren't interested in being in the real estate business, so we would sell it immediately."

"And pocket the profits, since it's completely paid for," Maggie points out.

"You are allowed one month to either provide the documentation or to make this transition, no more," Mother Stephen Elizabeth says, ignoring Maggie's comment.

"That's not long enough. You're actually forcing me to return here."

"That is not an option for you at this time, Maggie. The Order expects all the sisters who are physically able to continue supporting themselves until at least age seventy-five, and longer, if possible, before retiring to the motherhouse. Barring something unforeseen, you have at least seven years to go before we can consider allowing you to return."

Maggie grimaces. "Third on this list is that I never speak publicly again on the issue of reproductive rights or oppose any other doctrines pertaining to the Catholic faith. Is that correct?"

"Yes, it is."

"What you are saying is that I'm being silenced."

"That is correct."

"Why don't you just expel me from the Order? Kicking me to the curb would be a clean break and make the problem disappear."

"You are sixty-eight years old, Maggie. Religious life is all you know, and we don't want to take that away from you. We just want you to stop publicly promoting beliefs that run counter to the faith and our pro-life moral framework...stop embarrassing the Order and the other sisters in the community who strongly disagree with you, for fully valid reasons, I might add."

"And if you did expel me, you would risk a very ugly public relations debacle. Sending an arthritic, sixty-eight-year-old nun out into the world alone, with no resources to care for herself, would reflect very poorly on the Order. An eager investigative reporter would love writing a story like that."

"We hope it doesn't come to that, Maggie. But whether or not it does is entirely up to you. We have prayed that you will agree to the requirements we've set forth, which we believe are fair, so we can put the matter behind us as quickly as possible and begin the healing process."

"I deeply believe in the positions I've taken on women's equality and women's reproductive rights, and I'm not sorry for any of it, so I don't think much forgiveness and healing is going to happen. The best to reasonably hope for is forgetting, and based upon what you've said, that's not happening soon either. In the meantime, I need to think about this."

"Of course you do. You're facing a major upset in your life, Maggie, and are welcome to remain here for as long as you need to as you discern your best future. If you decide to accept these requirements and remain in the Order, you'll be required to sign a document to that effect, witnessed by all members of the leadership team. If you leave here without doing this, we will assume your decision is to exit the Order and will proceed accordingly."

"I still need to think about it."

"I suggest we go over the last requirement and then end this afternoon's meeting to allow you some time alone. Try to get some rest before making any decisions."

"According to this list, the final requirement for me to remain in the Order is that I attend the annual retreat each year and renew my vows at that time, along with the others?"

"That is correct. However, for the coming retreat in June, we want you to renew your vows individually, standing before the entire congregation. It will symbolize your sincerity and commitment to the Order and to remaining in religious life, which is a very important aspect of the community's healing process. You've done a lot of damage, Maggie, and you must show, by your actions, that you are willing to help repair it."

"It will be very awkward for me to do this individually, before the entire community."

"It shouldn't be. Most sisters look forward to renewing their vows each year, and some ask to do it individually. I'm sorry you are finding it awkward, but we feel it is necessary for you to make a public statement of your commitment to us, especially since no one can remember the last time you participated along with the others in any aspect of community life. I meant to check on this earlier, but my guess is that it was the year I was first elected superior, and I am now in my second ten-year term. That's a long time to ignore this vital aspect of religious life."

"I'd like to return to my room now," Maggie says, taking several deep breaths.

"Of course, and I want you to know I am praying for you and am available any time you want to talk—even later this evening if you wish. I know this is a terrible blow, and with all my heart, I wish it hadn't come to this. But now that it has, I want to support you as much as I can."

Frowning, but saying nothing, Maggie returns to her room.

•••

After pacing around her bed until it seems the walls are collapsing in on her, Maggie decides to walk outside around the perimeter of the building, gathering her thoughts about what to do next. Eventually, she returns to Mother Stephen Elizabeth's office, where she finds Sister Eileen sitting at the outer desk.

"Can you tell me where I can find a telephone with an outside line? I need to make a phone call."

"I'll have to check with Mother Stephen Elizabeth. She should be back shortly. I suggest you come back in an hour."

"I'll wait," Maggie replies, sitting down. A half hour passes before she sees her superior walking down the hall. She stands and walks toward her.

"I'd like to use the telephone for an outside call," Maggie says.

"Of course. Use the one in our conference room. Sister Eileen will show you the way."

Hearing this, Sister Eileen rises from her desk and leads Maggie down the hall.

"Try to make it short—our telephone bills are too high already," the junior nun says.

As soon as Sister Eileen leaves, Maggie picks up the phone and dials Mary Pat's number. She breathes a massive sigh of relief when she answers on the first ring. "You won't believe what has just happened," Maggie begins.

"You got kicked out of the Order."

"Almost. They're publicly censuring me and laying out several conditions for me to remain. Otherwise, I'm sixty-eight years old and out on my ass."

"What are the conditions for staying?"

"Resign from WNA immediately, give up all my reproductive rights activism, and sign the co-op over to my sisters, with my share going to the Order when I finally die, or it's eventually sold. They will issue a statement saying that, as a condition of remaining a member of the Order in good standing, I have agreed to back away from my abortion rights activities, which fly in the face of the pro-life values the Order and the Church subscribe to—or something like that. I haven't seen the exact wording. On top of all this, I'm not allowed to stay in the convent while I'm here, ostensibly for my own protection because the others are so pissed off at me."

"You really are in deep shit. It sounds like they're trying to force you to resign."

"I can't. I don't have any retirement savings other than social security, and I didn't start paying into that until I took over as shelter director. The payout wouldn't be enough to cover the co-op taxes, fees, and utilities."

"What happened to the money you inherited?"

"I spent it on the co-op, paid off some of my sisters' bills, and used the rest to support CWDC efforts. There's hardly any left—a couple thousand at most."

"What if you sold the co-op? That would give you some cash."

"And live where? It wouldn't be enough cash to see me through retirement regardless. Basically, they've screwed me tight to the wall."

Realizing her voice is rising, Maggie quickly checks on whether Sister Eileen left the conference room door open and is horrified to see she has. She turns her swivel chair around and kicks it hard, causing it to slam shut.

"I see what you're saying, Maggie. So let's think this through rationally. I don't know about Mary, but I'm sure Fiona, Colleen, and Annie will agree to letting you live in the co-op free as long as you foot the bills and they inherit it eventually. How do you think Mary would feel?"

"I doubt she'd care. Last I heard, she was teaching sixth grade at a parish school in Yakima, Washington. We exchange Christmas cards, but that's all, and I don't think anybody else hears anything more than that from her. What if Fiona and the others want to sell the co-op for the money? They might do that."

"Then you'll have to be very nice to them and hope they don't, which I realize might be nearly impossible for you."

"What about supporting myself?"

"You have a ton of connections. You could freelance as a grant-writer for women's shelters in Chicago and make enough money to support yourself. It wouldn't be that hard to do."

"But without my activism, I'll be dead inside. I can't imagine that kind of life."

"Then you leave the Order and take your chances on the rest. Either way, bear in mind that at some point in the next two or three years, WNA is going to want to replace you with someone younger. You should've been thinking about your future before now anyway, so maybe this will turn out to be a good thing if it forces you to do that."

"What are you, Mary Pat, nuts? There's no way in hell this is a good thing. My two options are to remain in the Order and drop dead now or leave the Order and drop dead in the poorhouse sometime later."

"What was your plan before all this?"

"I didn't have one. The Order was my fallback. I figured by the time I got to the point where I couldn't take care of myself and had to return to the motherhouse, I wouldn't care anyway.... Since that appears to have fizzled, what would you do if you were me?"

"I'd have never gotten into the mess in the first place. You probably remember I left my Order when we got crossways."

"You left for entirely different reasons, Mary Pat. You could've stayed and worked it out pretty easily if you'd wanted to."

"That's true. But I was young enough I knew I could survive outside, so leaving wasn't that scary. I've never understood how you've bucked the system so hard and gotten away with what you've gotten away with for so long, and for years I've been waiting for it to catch up with you. I'm surprised you haven't felt the same way—like you were playing with fire and bound to get burned sooner or later."

"I did feel that way, but I loved the thrill of flirting with danger. I knew I was clever at it and facing the fear made me feel strong and competent...and worthy...like I was somebody important and my life meant something. And the longer I got away with it, the less the fear of getting caught mattered enough to make me want to stop."

"But you've been caught now, Maggie. If it were me, I think I'd be feeling a huge sense of relief."

"What kind of relief is there in having your life torn all to hell and being steamrolled into submission to something you don't want to do?"

"Relief that you don't have to keep looking over your shoulder, wondering when you'll be found out. I'd feel like a fraud living like you do, on the edge of an abyss and knowing I'm doing things I'm not supposed to be doing...and the fear of exposure would exhaust me. Even though things were really tough for a long time afterward, I was never sorry I left, because I wasn't pretending anymore. My life felt more honest...if that makes any sense."

"It doesn't...I've never felt what I was doing made me a dishonest person. And now, I feel like I've been busted for a crime I didn't commit and have to figure out how to stay out of jail anyway."

"And you have a big decision to make."

"The way it's been put to me, there really isn't much of a decision. Either mend my ways immediately and remain in the Order, which is a secure future, or leave and eventually end up right back to where I came from—on the dole."

"What do you think you'll do?"

"Isn't it pretty obvious?"

"What's always been pretty obvious to me, Maggie, is that you'll figure out something, because you always do. And somehow you always land on your feet. Call me when you get back to Chicago. In the meantime, I'll be praying for you."

"That's the second time I've heard that today," Maggie says, ending the call.

•••

Early the next morning, following a sleepless night, Maggie walks to the administrative offices and tells Sister Eileen that she wishes to see Mother Stephen Elizabeth as soon as possible.

"I'll pass the request along. Best you check back in an hour," Sister Eileen says.

Instead, Maggie sits down to wait. Ten minutes later, Mother Stephen Elizabeth enters the office complex and, seeing Maggie, motions her into her office.

"Give me a few minutes to rearrange some things, so I can give you my undivided attention," the superior says, pulling out a chair at the table for Maggie.

"I'm here to negotiate the terms of the criteria for remaining in the Order," Maggie begins.

"There's nothing to negotiate, Maggie. The leadership team spent a great deal of time in discussion and prayerful thought as we determined how to move forward, and the criteria set forth are cast in stone. If I gave a different impression, I apologize."

"You've just demolished my life, and you're expecting me to just roll over and then deal with all that implies in a month?" Maggie asks, her voice rising.

"That is correct. If your decision is to remain in the Order, I suggest you resign your WNA position immediately and make yourself available to assist with the transition to a new executive director. You'll also have to settle the matter of your property ownership to our satisfaction. We have already had our lawyers draw up the agreement you will be required to sign saying that you fully understand the requirements for remaining a member of the Order in good standing and intend to abide by them—if that is your decision."

"You got lawyers involved?"

"We felt it was prudent. They also drafted the official censure document and, assuming your decision is to remain, wrote the public statement we will make once this matter is concluded."

"You really don't trust me, do you?" Maggie says, feeling more defeated than she has ever felt in her life.

"I wish the answer were different, but unfortunately no, we don't trust you, Maggie. You must realize you brought this on yourself, over a very long period of time, and have put both yourself and the Order in an extremely difficult position."

"Draw up the paperwork. I'm staying," Maggie says, standing up.

"I would prefer you think this over for a while longer before making a final decision. I don't want you approaching this with the idea you'll do whatever is needed to get past the current crisis and then find ourselves revisiting the issue again in a year or so."

"There's nothing to think about. You've been very clear about what my options are, and I've made up my mind to remain. I'm just as anxious to get this settled as you are, so the sooner I can sign the documents, the better."

"I'll notify the leadership team and the attorneys. We should have everything ready for you by Monday afternoon."

"That's the day after tomorrow. Can't it be sooner?"

"I'm afraid not. I strongly suggest you take the time between now and then to reflect on your past actions and how those need to change going forward. If you wish to speak with one of our sisters skilled in spiritual direction, I'd be happy to arrange that for you…it might be very helpful."

"What would be more helpful is a telephone. I need to make some calls later this afternoon," Maggie answers, feeling that her back is firmly against the wall.

"Of course. And speaking personally, Maggie—I'm glad you're remaining in the Order. If we can help you find some way to rechannel your passion for justice into something more in line with the Order's mission and core values, we'll all be better for it. I hope you'll be willing to work with us on that."

Maggie leaves the office without responding. She walks toward the front entrance of the building and sits on an outside bench, overlooking the acres of rich farmland for more than an hour, thinking about how to resign from WNA without embarrassing herself too much. She decides to call her board chairperson and explain that, given her age, they need to be considering a new director soon anyway, and her Order wants her to work on something else—which is basically the truth.

"My bigger problem is talking to Fiona about the co-op. I really need to think about that—otherwise, my sisters will sell it right out from under me for the money," she mumbles to herself, fishing her car keys from her pocket. A few minutes later, she leaves the motherhouse grounds to drive into the nearest town in search of a fast-food drive through. On the way back, she looks for a place to buy a paperback novel to read while she awaits Monday afternoon.

Upon her return to the convent, Maggie decides to call Irene Meyer, the young woman lawyer who is the current Chicago chapter's WNA board chair. After several rings, Irene answers, out of breath. Maggie identifies herself and asks if Irene has a few minutes to talk.

"For you, always," Irene replies.

"I'm calling to give you a heads up that I have to resign my position, effective immediately," Maggie begins.

"Oh, no, Maggie. Please, please tell me it's not a health problem," Irene responds with more concern than Maggie knows she deserves under the circumstances.

"My Order wants me to channel my efforts in a different direction, and after thinking about it, I have agreed. I'm sixty-eight years old, and pretty soon you'll need to be looking for someone else to lead the organization anyway, so I decided there's no time like the present to begin the transition."

"Can you stay on until we find someone?"

"I'm afraid not. But I will assist with transitioning to an interim director."

"This is horrible news, Maggie. We'll never find anybody as feisty and energetic as you are. You're really good at making things go your way—our way—and nothing will be the same without you. Are you sure there's nothing we can do to keep you longer?"

Hearing this, Maggie chokes up and whispers a barely audible thank you. After a few deep breaths, she explains she has to vacate the position now.

"Tell me, what are you going to be doing next?"

"I'm not sure, but I think it will involve helping women's shelters with funding applications. That's a good fit with our charity mission, which the Order wants to reemphasize," Maggie answers, recalling Mary Pat's idea, which she'd given no thought to until this instant.

"Whatever you do, you'll be fantastic at it, and of course we'll give you a recommendation that will light up the sky like the Fourth of July fireworks off Navy Pier. And personally, I'm glad you're remaining in Chicago, so I can bend your ear occasionally."

"Leaving Chicago was never in question—it's where I was born and where I intend to die."

"I just thought of something that might be helpful," Irene exclaims. "I do pro bono legal work for the Chicago Women's Shelter Directors Association. As you know, they're a referral organization that helps connect shelter directors' needs with available resources. Shelters are always scrambling for money, and someone with grant-writing experience would be an answer to their prayers. I can give their executive director a call and tell her about you. My guess is within a month, you'll have more work than you can handle."

"Thanks, that would be great...very helpful to me in hitting the ground running. I appreciate it, Irene. A lot." Maggie says, exhaling a deep sigh of relief.

"No problem. We can't afford to waste a moment of talent like yours, Maggie. The needs are too great."

"Can I ask you a totally unrelated question that it has just occurred to me you might know the answer to?"

"Of course."

"I own a co-op apartment in Archer Heights that I want to keep living in but need to sign over to my sisters sooner rather than later. It's something that's been on my mind since I realized I'm going to be seventy pretty soon. Do you know how I do something like that?"

"I do, and it's easy, especially if you own the property free and clear."

"I own it, and there's no mortgage, if that's what you're asking."

"Then all you have to do is deed the property over to your sisters with the caveat that you can live in it as long as you want to. When you die, the title automatically transfers to your sisters, or whoever else you designate."

"But they can't sell it unless I die?"

"That's right. It's a nice thing to do for survivors because it makes sorting out inheritances much less complicated."

"How do I do this?"

"A title company can take care of it in a few minutes. You'll sign a form, and it'll cost you a few bucks, but not nearly as much as a lawyer would charge."

"Do I have to tell my sisters I've done this?"

"You don't have to, but there's no reason not to."

Oh, yes, there is, Maggie thinks, before thanking Irene profusely for the information.

"We need to get together next week and start planning the transition. There's no time for a going away party, but I'll treat you to a nice lunch. And now I better go before my son kills his sister," Irene says.

Hanging up, Maggie breathes another sigh of relief as she walks back to her room, where she plans to spend the weekend reading the legal thriller she found on the book rack at the interstate truck stop.

•••

A few minutes before the appointed hour on the following Monday afternoon, Maggie walks into in the austere conference room in the Order's office complex. Another crucified Christ, the outsized symbol of human cruelty and suffering, hangs below a series of small windows near the ceiling, breaking up the wide expanse of beige paint on the bare-walled, claustrophobic room. Shivering from the chill in the air, she wishes she had worn a sweater. *Jesus was crucified for his ideas too, so at least we have that in common,* she thinks in anticipation of a meeting she fervently wishes she wasn't being forced to attend.

At precisely two o'clock, Mother Stephen Elizabeth, accompanied by Sister Eileen and the Order's four-member leadership team, enters the room. A stately middle-aged man Maggie assumes is the lawyer follows them and takes the seat at the head of the table, with Maggie on his left and the other six members of her Order on his right. Mother Stephen Elizabeth begins by invoking the Holy Spirit to guide them through this difficult moment. After all the amens are uttered, the lawyer straightens his muted green tie, clears his throat, and hands the mother superior a stack of papers.

Maggie notices that while her superior is wearing a skirt, blouse, and jacket, two of the leadership team members are wearing modified habits that include shorter dresses, head coverings and crucifixes; another is bare-headed and wearing a plain dress and a crucifix around her neck, and the person she assumes is the mother general's representative wears the Order's full habit.

"I don't believe you know everyone, Maggie," says Mother Stephen Elizabeth. "To my immediate left is Sister Mary Carol Evans, representing our sisters in Illinois. On my right are Sisters Emily Anne Morgan, representing sisters ministering in Michigan, and Marjorie Jane Feeney, representing the sisters living and working here in Indiana. To Sister Mary Carol's left is Sister Judith Maria Garcia, representing the Superior General of the Order. Together with myself, these sisters form the Order's leadership team. Our attorney, John Dooley, has graciously agreed to join us, and I believe you've already met Sister Eileen, who will be taking notes in addition to recording the meeting. We all know why we are here today, so I think it best if we proceed without comment. Mr. Dooley, I understand you have the necessary documents needing signatures."

"I do, Mother. The first document lists the requirements Sister Corrigan must agree to if she wishes to remain a member of the Pax Christi Sisters of Charity and Justice. By signing this document, Sister Corrigan attests that she fully understands the requirements for continued membership in the Order and intends to honor them." The lawyer hands the documents to the mother superior, who hands them across the table to Maggie, along with a pen.

"Take all the time you need to read through it," Mr. Dooley advises.

Maggie affixes her signature immediately and slides the document back across the table. One by one, each leadership team member affixes their signature as witnesses. Mother Stephen Elizabeth signs last.

"The second document is your formal censure, which I have prepared under the guidance and approval of your mother superior and her leadership team. This does not require your signature, Sister, but we are required to provide you with a signed copy. We will wait until you have read it over before proceeding to sign it in your presence."

Maggie remains impassive as the lawyer hands her the heavy piece of paper, bearing the Order's insignia at the top.

Official Censure of Sister Margaret Corrigan, SCJ

Following a lengthy period of thoughtful discernment and prayer, the Leadership Team of the Midwest Province of the Christian religious Order of the Pax Christi Sisters of Charity and Justice, by unanimous consent, imposes the following censure upon Sister Margaret Corrigan, vowed into the novitiate in 1951 as Sister John Mary and solemnly vowed in 1955 as Sister Ellen Clare, before returning to her baptismal name:

- *Whereas Sister Margaret Corrigan has, by publicly advocating for abortion rights in word and action, willfully and knowingly failed to honor the scripturally mandated Christian values governing the Pax Christi Sisters of Charity and Justice; and*
- *Whereas Sister Margaret Corrigan has violated her vows, the covenants governing the Pax Christi Sisters of Charity and Justice, and the sacred doctrines of the Holy Roman Catholic Church; and*
- *Whereas Sister Margaret Corrigan has willfully and knowingly taken ownership of private property in direct violation of her vow of poverty and of obedience; and*
- *Whereas Sister Margaret Corrigan has ignored every directive to modify her words and actions to align more closely with the covenants, principles, and cherished values of the Pax Christi Sisters of Charity and Justice, and the doctrines of the Holy Roman Catholic Church.*

Be it therefore resolved that, Sister Margaret Corrigan is hereby formally and publicly censured and ordered to cease and desist all aforementioned, and unnamed related activities. She is further ordered to honor and obey, without exception, all of the requirements set forth as conditions for remaining a vowed member in good standing of the Pax Christi Sisters of Charity and Justice community.

Failure to comply with the aforementioned will result in immediate, permanent expulsion from the Pax Christi Sisters of Charity and Justice, forgoing any privileges associated with her membership in the Order, and any rights to financial or other compensation.

Signed:

Sister Mary Carol Evans, Member of the Illinois, Indiana, and Michigan Province of the Pax Christi Sisters of Charity and Justice Leadership Team representing Illinois;

Sister Emily Anne Morgan, Member of the Illinois, Indiana, and Michigan Province of the Pax Christi Sisters of Charity and Justice Leadership Team representing Michigan;

Sister Marjorie Jane Feeney, Member of the Illinois, Indiana, and Michigan Province of the Pax Christi Sisters of Charity and Justice Leadership Team representing Indiana;

Sister Judith Maria Garcia, Member of the Illinois, Indiana, and Michigan Province of the Pax Christi Sisters of Charity and Justice Leadership Team representing the Superior General of the Pax Christi Sisters of Charity and Justice; and

Mother Stephen Elizabeth Conley, Superior of the Illinois, Indiana, and Michigan Province of the Pax Christi Sisters of Charity and Justice.

Dated this 20th day of March, in the year of our Lord 2000.

Wordlessly, Maggie spends less than thirty seconds glancing at the censure before returning it to Mother Stephen Elizabeth, who hands it to Sister Mary Carol Evans for her signature. After all members of the leadership team have signed, Mother Stephen Elizabeth affixes her signature and hands it to Sister Eileen along with the signed agreement and asks her to make copies.

"The following public statement will be released as deemed appropriate," John Dooley says, handing Maggie another sheet of paper.

The Pax Christi Sisters of Charity and Justice are aware that Sister Margaret Corrigan has engaged in actions that are not in accord with the principals, covenants, values, and expectations of vowed members of the Order or in keeping with the doctrinal beliefs of the Roman Catholic Church. The leadership has discussed these issues with Sister Corrigan, and she has agreed that, in order to remain a vowed member of the Pax Christi Sisters of Charity and Justice religious community in good standing, she will cease all offending activities and permanently withdraw from public activism of any kind. Because of the gravity of her actions, Sister Corrigan has also been formally censured.

The Pax Christi Sisters of Charity and Justice prayerfully regret the distress this situation has caused, consider this matter resolved, and will have no further comment.

"Where do you intend to release this?" Maggie asks.

"That has not been fully decided," Mother Stephen Elizabeth answers. "Right now, besides the Order membership, it will go to several Catholic news outlets who have previously reported on your activities. It is impossible to know who else might pick it up, but hopefully no one does. Copies will also be sent to Bishop Werner, Cardinal Sullivan in Chicago, and Bishop Santora, who heads the diocese where your abortion-related advocacy activities occurred. I personally feel this is sufficient."

"I never, ever advocated for abortion. I advocated for a woman's right to control her reproductive life—and there is a difference. We would not be sitting here if you and others understood that," Maggie says.

"Isn't that playing with words, Sister?" Lawyer Dooley asks.

"With all due respect, Mr. Dooley, this is not a matter you are entitled to an opinion on."

"I want you to know, Maggie, that we are all glad you have made the decision to remain with us," Maggie's superior interjects in an attempt to diffuse the conversation. "We have prayed for a satisfactory outcome and believe we have achieved that and can put this behind us now."

The other leadership team members nod in agreement, while Maggie, in an effort to remain silent, tightly clenches her jaw.

Sister Eileen returns with document copies for everyone. Mother Stephen Elizabeth hands the originals to John Dooley and then asks Maggie if she has any questions.

"Just one: if Jesus Christ had been born a woman, would Christianity, which is the justification for these actions, even exist?"

Hearing these words, spoken without emotion, everyone in the room sits in stunned silence, staring at the table. Eventually, Sister Emily Anne says she thinks a prayer of thanksgiving is appropriate and proceeds to say one Maggie has never heard before.

Leaving the meeting, Mother Stephen Elizabeth asks Maggie to join her for supper.

"Thank you, but I'm going back to Chicago."

"It's a long drive, Maggie. Freezing rain is predicted, and it will be dark by the time you get home. Are you sure you don't want to stay until tomorrow?"

"I'm sure."

2019

I would like to be remembered as an intelligent woman,
a courageous woman, a loving woman who teaches by being.
Maya Angelou

The phone begins ringing just as I unlock my office door. I grab for the receiver while putting down my briefcase and juggling an armload of books.

"This is Gillian Spencer," I answer.

"Professor Gillian Spencer?" the caller asks.

I indicate that it is.

"This is Regina McDowell, the superior of the Midwest Province of the Pax Christi Sisters of Charity and Justice. Do you have a moment?"

"I will just as soon as I finish putting down an armload of books." I drop the books on my desk and sit down. "Sorry to keep you waiting. I was just coming back from the library."

"No problem, I'm just glad to reach you. The reason I'm calling is to tell you that Sister Maggie Corrigan died in her sleep last night."

Hearing this, a knot forms in my stomach, and I don't respond right away.

"I'm sure this is a surprise, and if you need a moment, I'll hang on," Mother Regina says.

"No, I'm fine—I think. I wasn't aware she was ill."

"She wasn't, so this is something of a shock to us too, although being in her late eighties, death is never really a surprise."

"No, I suppose it isn't, but somehow I didn't put the words Maggie and death in the same sentence—at least not yet. She was too..."

"Ornery?"

"Yes—that's a good word."

"When was the last time you spoke with her?"

"I called to wish her a happy new year, so several weeks ago."

"She had a stroke in late January, which it sounds like you didn't know about."

No surprise there, when you've been hoarding your blood pressure medication for the last couple years, I think to myself.

"She recovered well enough. The bigger problem, according to the staff, was that afterwards she was even more testy and cantankerous, if you can imagine—until two days ago, when she suddenly became much more compliant and polite. Staff described her as happy—or as happy as Maggie got—and then she died...."

"It sounds like she had a premonition and was ready to finally let go."

"That occurred to me too, and we'll never know. But the reason I am calling you is that she left several instructions, among them that she wants you to give the eulogy at a memorial service for her—and before you respond, let me explain, because it is a little challenging."

"I can only imagine," I reply, glad this is a telephone conversation, and the mother superior can't see me roll my eyes.

"Maggie wanted to be cremated, and we don't normally cremate deceased sisters. She also wanted her ashes spread over Dingle Bay—a request that is impossible for us to honor because of the expense, and because no one here has ever heard of Dingle Bay. The dilemma of what to do with her remains looms large, since she seemed adamant about not wanting to be buried in the cemetery on the motherhouse grounds. But this is only one problem."

"What's the other one?"

"She didn't want a male priest saying her funeral Mass, and since those are the only ones the Church officially recognizes, to honor this desire, we can't have the traditional funeral. The leadership team agrees that we want to do something to mark Maggie's passing and have settled on a simple remembrance service that the other sisters in the community can attend if they wish, along with anyone else who might want to remember her. We don't expect many, and the plan is to hold it in the small meditation chapel next to our dining room. It holds thirty at most."

"This seems appropriate. Do you mind telling me what her other instructions are? Did she ask for family members to be notified?"

"The only people she mentioned were you, the Chicago chapter of the Women's National Alliance, and a sister who is a member of a Franciscan Order in Los Angeles.. I called to speak to her earlier today and was told Sister Mary Corrigan is in ill health, but the superior assured me she will inform her of Maggie's death. We'll put a brief death notice in the Chicago newspapers, but at her age, I don't imagine many who knew her earlier are still alive or able to travel here."

"Anything else?"

"Only that the music selections include Frank Sinatra singing *My Kind of Town*, which apparently is about Chicago and definitely awkward in a convent prayer service. The Dingle Bay depository for her ashes request isn't an easy one either. I really don't know what to do about either of these."

"I doubt Maggie would seriously object to dropping her ashes into Lake Michigan somewhere along the Chicago shoreline, which might be a suitable alternative to Dingle Bay, which I think is in Ireland. I have no idea how difficult it would be to find the Frank Sinatra recording, but I can look."

"Thank you—but please don't look too hard. I have a feeling Ol' Blue Eyes singing his musical heart out about Chicago at a convent memorial service would be too much for our traditional sisters. Someone might faint."

"Do you have a timeline for all this?"

"Tomorrow is Ash Wednesday, which is the beginning of Lent, and I'd like to wait a few days before trying to pull together an unconventional remembrance service that will require some careful thought. I'm wondering about a week from Thursday, if you're willing to come and that date works into your schedule."

"Of course I'll come. I'm both humbled and honored."

"I suggest you plan on arriving the Wednesday before and staying in our guest quarters. I'll reserve a room for two nights in case the return flight or the weather are problems. Let me know when to expect you, and I'll handle everything on our end. I have a dinner meeting that evening, but after that, I'd like to get together for a few minutes and chat, if you won't be too tired."

"This all sounds very nice. Thank you very much, Sister—Mother—and I'll keep in touch regarding my travel plans and so on...."

"Please, call me Reggie—I'm not nuts about titles...."

Sounds just like Maggie, I think, smiling.

"One other thing—how does it happen you know Maggie?"

"I knew about her for a long time before I actually met her, which was a good many years ago. She asked for my help with a complicated parental rights case, but didn't keep in close touch after that until she contacted me because..." I stop speaking mid-sentence.

"Because she wanted you to help her escape from here?" Reggie chuckles.

"Because she wanted me to write a book about her."

"I think I heard something about that. Did you agree to do it?"

"Not at first, but Maggie convinced me her story was worth telling. I've been working on the book for a while."

"I was a young, recently-professed nun when most of the uproar she caused was happening and was too busy trying to figure myself out to pay a lot of attention. I became superior several years after the censure and didn't make any effort to find out the details—mostly because even though I knew she'd been a huge pain in the backside for my predecessor, I liked Maggie. I couldn't help admiring her zeal in believing what she believed regardless of what anybody else, including the Order or the institutional Church, thought. She was fun to talk to, and as far as I could tell, her biggest problem was that she was so far ahead of her time that her valiant efforts at justice left everybody else in our archaic Church in the dust. Maybe someday the world will catch up."

"She was definitely the most unique nun I ever met."

"You probably can't answer this now, but since she has died, do you think you'll finish the book?"

"I don't see any reason not to."

"I was hoping that would be your answer."

"Really? Maggie thought the Order would oppose it."

"I know some of the older sisters don't agree with me, but I don't necessarily view Maggie as a black mark on the Order or the Church. Let's face it—the Church has big problems where women are concerned, and somebody has to call them on it and force change, which is what Maggie tried to do. Otherwise, eventually the Church will become so irrelevant, it will die a natural death, and it does too much good in the world to allow that to happen. I realize she caused a lot of upset, but most people who try to move the status quo off dead center are very upsetting."

"That's true."

"It's been wonderful talking to you, Dr. Spencer, and I'm looking very forward to meeting you."

"Me, too—and call me Gillian...please."

"Got it. We'll keep in touch."

After the phone call ends, I sit in my chair, staring out my tall office window across the tops of trees gone bare for the winter. I can see all the way to the James River, and watching it flow toward the Atlantic Ocean, about one hundred miles from here, I begin wondering why Maggie wanted me to eulogize her to her fellow sisters. What did she think I could say that no one else would?

•••

Ten days later, I arrive at the motherhouse just after 5 p.m. the night before Maggie's remembrance service. The receptionist directs me to my room, tells me dinner is served buffet style in the guest dining room just around the corner until six o'clock, and hands me a handwritten note.

"Mother Regina dropped this off for you," she says.

My room is at the end of a long, third-floor hallway and has a private bath as well as a view stretching all the way to the Wabash River. It is a spartan accommodation that includes a single bed with a colorful bedspread, a desk with a small, fake, Tiffany-style lamp, and a closet that contains three hangers and two side drawers. Except for two large corner windows, the cream-colored walls are blank. I sit down in the desk chair and open the note.

Hi, Gillian –

Hope you had a pleasant trip and trust that you are settling in. Don't eat dessert because I'll be knocking on your door around eight, and we can go downstairs and visit for a little while. I'll also show you where Maggie's service will be tomorrow. See you shortly. – Reg.

At five minutes past eight, I hear a soft knock on my door. Opening it, I see a slim, middle-aged woman with soft features, bobbed naturally blond hair that's just beginning to gray, and bright eyes smiling broadly.

"I'm Reggie McDowell," the woman says. "I hope you're Gillian Spencer. Otherwise, I'm disturbing someone who has no idea why I'm standing here."

Smiling, I return the warm handshake.

"Let's look at where the service will be held and then raid the kitchen, shall we? Hope you don't mind taking the stairs. I don't have my 10,000 steps in today, and if I'm not religious about that, I can't fit into my pants," Reggie says, walking toward the stairwell and reaching the bottom floor in record time.

"I've really been looking forward to meeting you, Gillian. Sort of an 'any friend of Maggie's is a friend of mine' kind of thing, but my gut feeling is we might think alike about a lot of things," she tells me as we round a corner and come face to face with a wall of windows marking the entrance to a dining room.

"The meditation room is this way," she says, motioning me.

We walk through a curved doorway into a small, one-window space containing about thirty chairs in a horseshoe around a podium to the right of a small wooden altar containing a row of candles. A small spinet piano rests against a side wall.

"I think this will work fine," she says. "I can't imagine there will be more than twenty-five people at most...perhaps some of the staff who cared for Maggie and the core group of nuns living here who feel obligated to attend services for deceased sisters, whether or not they knew them. The service will be simple: I'll preside and offer prayers and a gospel reading. There will be some music, and your remarks. I found a picture of Maggie and had our IT people turn it into black-and-white to hide that hideous wig she insisted on wearing. It will be next to the urn. That's basically it."

"Sounds fine to me. Do you want to know I found a CD of Frank Sinatra singing *Chicago*?"

"I was afraid to ask."

"You'll need a CD player or a boom box or something to play it on."

"Hmmm—I'm not sure we have one of those. I'll try to remember to check tomorrow. Anything else you can think of?"

I shake my head no.

"Then let's go to the kitchen and see what we can find. I don't know about you, but I can't drink coffee after about 4 p.m., so there's milk, juice, water, and diet root beer—maybe some decaf instant coffee, which I don't recommend."

We walk through the dining room into a large, institutional kitchen where Reggie points to a small corner table.

"Sit over there while I find where they hid the cookies. What do you want to wash them down with?"

"Water's fine, thanks."

She sets a plate of homemade cookies, a can of root beer, and a bottle of water on the table.

"Tell me something I don't know about you," Reggie begins.

"I don't know what you already know," I shoot back.

"Hey, I know how to navigate the internet, so I know a lot about you—and was familiar with your research before I called you."

"How's that?"

"The short answer is until recently I worked for the US Bureau of Labor Statistics. The long answer is I have a PhD in economics from Notre Dame and headed up the BLS women's employment division until the sisters elected me superior and I left Washington to come back here."

"You're Regina McDowell the economist?" I exclaim.

"Right before your eyes."

"How did I not realize that?"

"Beats me—I know all about you!" Reggie teases.

"Just the other day I was reading something you wrote and wondering why I hadn't seen any recent publications from you in the professional literature. How did you end up going from an upper-level federal government job to running an Order of religious women?"

"I'm a nun. I'd hoped to keep professionally active for a while longer, but..."

"You didn't want to become superior?"

"Not really. I loved what I was doing, and there was no reason to stop. But the Order has been struggling for a long time and needed someone who understands what's at stake to guide us through the forthcoming challenges. I'm still not sure I'm the one to do that, but there wasn't anyone else—and I had thirty years with the government and could retire with a nice pension, which without my Washington, DC, living expenses, meant coming here was a significant net gain. So it was hard for me to mount a very strong argument against stepping up to answer the call... but I still miss my job and life in Washington."

"I don't recall ever hearing you were a nun, although maybe I should've guessed. One of the things I like about your work is that it reflects all that is good about Catholic social teaching—caring for the less advantaged and suffering poor. That isn't a common approach in government anymore and has been sadly eroding away since probably the Roosevelt administration."

"That was one of the hardest things about leaving government work when I did. I felt like I was abandoning a viewpoint that is desperately needed and someone had to defend, especially after a misogynist and narcissistic liar was elected president. I suppose I was being a little egocentric, but women's rights are in real trouble."

"Well, we fought for them once, and I guess we can do it again," I say. Finishing my cookie, I stifle a yawn.

"You've had a long day, and I'm keeping you up. Is there anything you need? You know the meal schedule?"

"I'm good, thanks. Do you want anything from me before tomorrow?"

"I don't think so. Maggie's ashes were delivered to me this morning, and since it's Lent, there won't be any flowers on the altar, so there isn't really any preparation."

"Except for finding a boom box, if those even exist anymore," I smile.

"Except for that. Go on upstairs, and I'll see you tomorrow. This should go very smoothly."

•••

Just after noon the next day, as I am walking from the elevator toward the large foyer and reception area inside the motherhouse entrance, Reggie comes running toward me.

"Thank God you're here—we've got a problem."

"What kind of problem?"

"One I never saw coming. There are a lot more than a hundred people in the foyer saying they're here for Maggie's funeral."

"Seriously?"

"I wouldn't make that up."

We walk toward the foyer and the gathering crowd.

"Do you think they're protestors?"

"Oh, my God—I never thought of that. But I don't think so. They're too well dressed."

"I don't think there's a dress code for protestors."

"You don't know that, but as near as I can tell, these are all people who want to pay their respects. See that handsome man standing by the door? His name is Ben Cabrera, and he said Maggie was an old friend. The tall man over there with the beautiful woman is Willie Preston and his wife, Alicia. The woman next to him said her name is Eulalia Banks, and that's her daughter, Jada, standing beside her. Do any of these names mean anything to you?"

Feeling myself about to choke up, my only response is a nod.

"The two priests are Archbishop Santora from Detroit and an auxiliary bishop from Chicago, who said he's representing Cardinal Sullivan, who is too old to travel. The cardinal sent a flower arrangement this morning that takes up six feet of space and needed two men to carry it into the meditation room."

"Guess he forgot it was Lent," I quip.

"He's pushing a hundred years old, Gillian—he forgets everything."

For several more minutes, we watch people continue filing into the reception area.

"FYI, Archbishop Santora has asked to give a benediction at the end. I started to say that Maggie didn't want priests involved in her funeral, but she's just going to have to eat this one, because I'm not saying no to an archbishop who's just traveled two hundred miles to be here."

"I wouldn't either."

"Glad you agree. See those two men over by the reception window?"

I nod.

"They said Maggie married them several years ago."

"Married them how?"

"They claim she became a strong supporter of gay marriage and got an officiant license off the internet and began performing ceremonies for gay and lesbian couples. Do you know anything about that?"

"She never mentioned it to me, but I'm not surprised...are you?"

"Ask me later. I've got all the surprises I can handle right now," Mother Regina says, taking a deep breath. "That really tall woman over there said she's from the Cook County District Attorney's office and worked with Maggie on a case...Marcia, I think she said her name is. Does Cook County include Chicago?"

"It does."

"I wonder how Maggie was involved with the DA's office. I suppose she could've ended up in jail, although I think I would remember something like that."

"It was a domestic violence case. Maggie wanted the priest who kept advising the woman to return to her abusive husband prosecuted as an accessory to her murder."

"No kidding?"

"Maggie wanted them all thrown in jail. Thankfully, stiffer mandatory abuse reporting laws are making it much more difficult for clergy to tell a woman to go back to her abuser for the sake of the family and get away with it."

"God bless her. And changing the subject, do you think the others are shelter directors and Women's National Alliance representatives from Chicago?"

"You haven't asked?" I tease.

"No, I haven't worked my way through a crowd I never expected, but give me a couple hours, and I'll be up to speed."

"Sorry...good point. These people have made quite an effort to be here, which says that people who knew Maggie really respected her."

"As soon as word gets back to the convent, which I'm sure it has by now, there'll be a lot more sisters coming too—maybe fifty or so. They're all retired and don't have anything else to do, and certainly won't want to miss something this big."

"By my count, we're talking upwards of one hundred fifty people—right?"

"In my wildest dreams, I never expected this, Gillian."

"Neither did I. But, honestly, I'm really glad it's happening."

"I'm not dressed for this. As superior, I should at least be wearing a cross. Do you have one on you?"

"You're kidding, right?"

"I wasn't, but I guess it is a pretty ridiculous question."

"Not to change the subject, but surely you're not planning on jamming all these people into the meditation room. Can you use the dining room?"

"It's not cleaned up from lunch. We'll have to go over to Saint Vincent de Paul Chapel. I asked maintenance staff to open it up while someone looks for a dolly that can move Cardinal Sullivan's flower arrangement that apparently weighs twice as much as I do. I can't remember the last time we used the chapel—the heat's turned off, and it's probably thick with dust. I put out the word to find a sister who can play the organ, but who knows how that will work out?"

"If it's an old pipe organ, I think someone needs to turn it on and warm it up—fill the pipes with air...."

"It's an old organ."

"Then we may have to sing acapella," I smile. "What about refreshments?"

"I sent staff on an emergency run to the truck stop to grab whatever they could find. I just can't believe this! I didn't even bother having a program printed up."

"It's almost one, Reg. We better get moving."

A few minutes later, Regina invites everyone to follow her through a long breezeway to the chapel. When we are about half-way there, she gasps.

"Shit—I forgot Maggie! Gillian, run back to my office and get her. While you're there, rummage around in my desk and see if you can find my cross—silver on a chain—and bring that too."

"I don't know where your office is."

"Then ask someone, for God's sake. You're smart—you can figure it out."

I grab someone from the back of the line who looks like she might be a nun and ask her to take me to Mother Regina's office and then back to the chapel. Fortunately, I guess correctly, and a sister who looks to be about eighty says to follow her. Regina's office is down several corridors, and the nun, wearing white sneakers, is moving along considerably faster than I am, wearing heels. When we arrive at the mother superior's office, I explain that I also have to look for a cross Mother Regina can wear.

"Give her mine and tell her to return it to Sister Sophia," the nun says, pressing a large silver cross in my hand. "She'll know where to find me."

I arrive back at the chapel out of breath, just as everyone is being seated. Lacking another option, I walk up the center aisle and place the urn on the altar, next to Cardinal Sullivan's gigantic flower arrangement. I'm not sure that's where Maggie's remains belong, but I don't know what else to do with them, then realize I forgot the picture. Reggie gestures a question about the cross, and I walk over to where she is seated behind three dozen gigantic peach gladiolas and hand Sister Sophia's heavy cross to her.

"Return this to Sister Sophia—she said you'll know where to find her," I whisper.

I hope you're enjoying this, I tell Maggie, looking skyward after I find a seat in the front of the chapel and catch my breath. With the late winter sun shining through the stained-glass windows, the chapel doesn't seem nearly as cold as I expected it to be.

Mother Regina steps out from behind the flowers and up to the pulpit. She introduces herself and graciously welcomes everyone, adding that she hopes they will remain for light refreshments following the service. She asks the group to stand and join in the opening hymn, which she will lead because no one remembered to turn on the organ in time to warm it up. She has a surprisingly lovely singing voice. After offering a brief biography stating the facts of Maggie's life, followed by a prayer and two scripture readings, she invites me to the podium to speak.

Suddenly, I have a lump in my throat, and need to clear it several times before I begin.

"When asked to eulogize Sister Maggie Corrigan, I was humbled, honored, and most of all, astonished. I wondered why she chose me as the person to remember her to those she leaves behind to mourn her passing. We weren't colleagues or lifelong friends. We were just two people who knew and liked each other—at least I liked her. I was never really sure how she felt about me."

Hearing this, several in the church chuckle.

"I couldn't help wondering what she wanted me to say, or thought I would say, to those gathered to remember her remarkable life. Was it something she believed no one else would say about a tough old broad with a garbage mouth who could swear like a sailor, tossed her whiskey back straight, never cared about what she looked like or what others thought of her, and was easy to get along with as long as you did everything her way? I never determined the answer to that question.

"What I do know is that Maggie was one of the saints who came marching in through the door the Vatican II revolution opened. She gathered a determined army around her, and together, they trooped straight into the heart of women's lives, fighting to free them from patriarchal oppression. She loved justice and mercy and believed in a ministry that was about inclusion, not exclusion. She was a good woman who had the misfortune to be born into a male-dominated religious culture at a time when God is male and the patriarchy rules. As a fire-breathing feminist with the courage of her convictions, Maggie realized this didn't work for women and was fearless in her determination to face it down and force a change.

"Maggie thought what she thought, was certain beyond even unreasonable doubt that she was right, and didn't care whether anyone, including her Order or her Church, agreed with her because if she did care, she would never be able to push her cause forward.

"'It's a luxury I can't afford,' she told me when I asked her why she never worried about offending others.

"What she did care about, above everything else, was the pursuit of justice, particularly for women and especially regarding their right to reproductive autonomy within the Roman Catholic Church, which is, for those of you who may not know, the largest, wealthiest, most powerful patriarchal institution in the world. Maggie believed with all her heart that women should have moral agency over their lives and that the patriarchal Church was profoundly and morally wrong to deny them this right.

"Maggie wasn't patient or emotionally expressive and most of the time, I didn't think she liked people much at all. Yet she spent her life in passionate pursuit of a better life for the poorest and most vulnerable women among us—those who need our caring compassion and empathy most. Somehow, she figured out she didn't have to like anybody, but still could honor that internal force driving her to fight with her own voice, on her own terms, for women's reproductive rights, by taking on the largest, most powerful, and most deeply entrenched political network in the world—the Roman Catholic Church. As you are driving away from here later this afternoon, think about what raw courage it took for her to make this controversial, emotionally volatile issue the cause of her lifetime.

"Maggie believed that the end she was seeking justified whatever means necessary to achieve it, including boycotts, public demonstrations, covert operations, and breaking Church law.

"'If the Church had jails, I'm sure I'd have ended up in one,' she'd chuckle when recounting her fearless and relentless campaign for women's reproductive autonomy.

"Because God is widely perceived as male, and Maggie wouldn't tolerate a man telling her what to do, I doubt believing she was doing God's work on Earth drove her passion to seek reproductive justice for women. But if it wasn't God, what, as a vowed woman religious, did drive her? She deflected the question whenever I asked it, and I finally concluded she may not have known or, if she did know, may not have given me a straight answer anyway.

"But this I do know: Maggie firmly believed the people's voice *was* God's voice, and that the Catholic patriarchy was deaf to that voice, and so badly mistaken about the full spectrum of women's equality that bringing that patriarchy to its knees by whatever means possible was right and just—because on their knees, begging for mercy, was where those power-hungry men belonged. That's how wrong she believed the Church is regarding women, how angry she was about that, and how determined she was to change it.

"'The sisterhood of Chicago's Catholic Women Demanding Change was a powerhouse. We faced down the institutionalized Catholic patriarchy, had a few small successes, and one hell of a lot of fun,'" she once told me.

"Not long ago I asked her if she had any regrets, and she said she only had one—and refused to tell me what it was.

"'It's personal,' she said, in such a wistful way that I doubt whatever it was had anything to do with her activism. I hope it was deeply personal—like falling in love. And if that is what happened, I hope that person loved her back, because everybody deserves love in their life—even if they are hard to get along with, which Maggie definitely was.

"Just this morning, I learned something I never knew about Maggie that revealed to me how much she understood love. Apparently, several years ago she downloaded a marriage officiant license off the internet and began performing marriages for gay and lesbian couples. Her Church—our Church—opposes these relationships, but Maggie viewed them as a loving, holy state of being worthy of recognition and lifetime commitment. In this, and many other ways, she was a loyal daughter of the wider human family and willingly did her part to make that family a better, more loving one. If doing this meant speaking harsh truths to the all-powerful Roman Catholic Church, so be it.

"This leaves me with one remaining question: what would Maggie say to you if she were standing here?

"She wouldn't say anything about herself, but she would take the opportunity to repeat what she has always claimed: that the Catholic Church, despite all the good it does, is dead wrong where women are concerned, and that expecting women to live their lives as servant wives and baby machines is institutionalized slavery and a violation of the most basic of all human rights.

"She would say that women's reproductive rights are neither a political issue nor the business of men or the wider society. She would say that unless men are willing to accept financial responsibility for the babies they insist on fathering, they are not entitled to a voice, or a vote, on the abortion or birth control question.

"She would say that no woman ever wants an abortion, but by opposing abortion and forbidding the use of birth control, the Catholic Church is trying to have it both ways—forcing women to seek abortions to end unwanted pregnancies that using birth control could have prevented in the first place.

"She would say that by failing to address this essential moral issue, the patriarchal Catholic Church loses all credibility where women are concerned. And she would find this tragic, because Maggie also saw the goodness in the Church and knew that nearly all of its greatness and holiness arises out of the tireless efforts of vowed nuns just like her who spend lifetimes toiling in the trenches of real life, teaching children to read, nursing the sick, and steadfastly caring for the abused, the struggling poor, the immigrant, and the most vulnerable among us whom no one else can be bothered to care about.

"She would say that all she ever wanted to do was force the Church she loved to reexamine itself and its role in society and then act justly toward women and other disenfranchised groups.

"In one of our last conversations, she asked me whether I ever wondered why God didn't send His daughter instead of His son to save the world.

"'Are you assuming God is a man?' I teased.

"'I'm not assuming anything, but a woman would never create a patriarchy,' Maggie shot back.

"I confessed that I hadn't given the son versus daughter question much thought. But after I learned Maggie had died, I did begin to think about it.

"Ultimately, I decided that eighty-seven years ago, God realized the patriarchy He'd had a hand in creating wasn't working for the half of the Church that is female. Knowing He had to fix this problem, in His infinite wisdom, God finally decided to send His daughter to straighten things out.

"Her name was Maggie Corrigan, and like others who have been maligned when they tried to change the world, the world wasn't ready for her either. But ready or not, Maggie arrived, rolled up her sleeves, and in her words, got to work smashing the patriarchy. I always thought this sounded a little harsh, but Maggie disagreed.

"'Sometimes smashing something as stubborn as the patriarchy is the only thing that gets its attention, and I did manage to do that,' she replied.

"Regardless of whether you believe she was a heretic or a heroic savior, I think everyone here would agree that Sister Maggie Corrigan was, above all else, fearless."

Acknowledgments

I discovered feminism and Chicago politics at about the same time. Simone de Beauvoir's riveting book, *The Second Sex* gave me my first documented glimpse of the profound impact patriarchy has on women's lives. Chicago mayor Richard J. Daley's nationally televised temper tantrum at the 1968 Democratic National Convention introduced me to Chicago politics. Simone profoundly changed my life, and Daley, who controlled everything but the wind in the Windy City, forced me to let go of my political naiveté. Both informed this book, as has the enormous amount of time I have spent in Chicago over the years. It's a great city unlike any other on the planet, and although I am not originally from there, or even from the Midwest, something about Chicago always feels like home, and I've always loved being there.

I am profoundly grateful to the hundreds of poor women who trusted me enough to share their stories with me during the years I was an academic poverty researcher. They were, in so many ways, smarter than I was regarding the difficult ways of the world, and from them I learned more about the daily struggles of life in poverty than any book taught me. They nailed my feet to the harsh ground of their reality and made me a much better researcher than I would have been otherwise—and I've never forgotten them.

I am very grateful to the many Catholic nuns I have known—those who taught me, who fought for justice, who worked with me on social welfare research initiatives, and who are my friends. These self-assured women would, with all-knowing smiles on their faces, stand down a raging bull to get what they wanted and have refused to back down from the fight to force the Catholic Church they love into greater equality and justice for women and other marginalized groups. They are the collective inspiration for the fictional character Sister Maggie Corrigan.

What differentiates the fictional Maggie from real-life women religious is that, among other things, rather than working for change from within the Church she deeply loved, she went public with her fight. And to some degree, the strategy worked. Even though progress has been by quarter inches, and still has a long way to go, today there are women in leadership positions within all Catholic dioceses, priests are no longer counseling women to remain in abusive marriages, and the astronomically high birth rate among Catholic women continues to decline. However, in the wider society, women's reproductive lives remain a political football, freely tossed about in male-dominated state legislatures throughout the country. As a result, the fight to secure women's reproductive autonomy rages on, with no visible end in sight.

Vowed religious women have made a much greater difference in Catholic women's lives than they realize because, if asked, they would say, "I was just doing my job." In reality, by teaching women that they have choices, that their birth isn't their destiny, and that they are not born women—they become women—the Catholic sisterhood has done much more. Every Catholic woman alive owes these freedom fighters sincere and everlasting gratitude.

Finally, I owe buckets of gratitude to my award-winning writer husband who thoroughly read and discussed several drafts of the manuscript that ultimately became this book, and is the greatest proofreader in the world. He is my severest, most trusted, most valuable critic, and even though I don't always take his advice, he makes me a much better writer. I try to return the favor whenever possible.

I am also deeply grateful to my all-woman publishing team at Warren Publishing, especially my editors, Karli Jackson and Amy Ashby, and my publicist, Lacey Cope. They both did a dynamite good job of pushing this story forward to be all it could be, and I can't thank them enough. This book deserves the kind of send-off only women can provide, and I am thrilled beyond words that all of us found each other.

Discussion Questions

1. While all cities have their own, unique personalities, Chicago surpasses them all. Native Chicagoans are tough, proud, bluecollar aristocrats who don't break. For these reasons, could this story have been set anywhere else? Could Maggie have accomplished what she did without the intuitive understanding that comes with being ethnic Irish and a native Chicagoan?
2. Why wasn't Maggie more afraid to take on the Chicago Catholic Church? Why was she so willing to disregard the rules governing her religious Order? Would she have been able to accomplish as much as she did if she fit the stereotypical notion of a nun?
3. In what ways is Maggie a sympathetic character? If you knew her personally, how would you feel toward her? Is having a difficult personality typical of someone who is a courageous risk-taker on the forefront of change?
4. Mary Pat Donovan was Maggie's closest personal and life-long friend, yet Maggie failed her badly by not honoring Tommy's request to see her before his death. Did Maggie deserve Mary Pat's forgiveness? Why did she receive it?
5. The concept of forgiveness is a complicated one. Does everyone deserve forgiveness? Does forgiveness allow the offender to continue the hurtful behavior? Is the notion that forgiveness is something we do for ourselves a valid one?
6. Given Maggie's attitude toward men, why did she allow herself to fall in love with Ben? Could they have had a future together under

different circumstances, or was she too emotionally damaged to ever heal enough to have an intimate relationship with anyone?

7. What part did Maggie's emotionally damaged, conflicted relationship with her family play in her resolve to take on the Catholic Church and her brother? Was everyone too angry with each other, and about the hand they'd been dealt, to ever reconcile? Would she have taken up the fight with the Church if she had grown up in a loving home?
8. Should the Sisters of Charity and Justice have forced Maggie to leave the Order? What does it say about the vowed sisterhood that, despite everything, the leadership wanted her to remain among them in their religious community?
9. Would Maggie have attempted to change the Church if Vatican II hadn't occurred, allowing her much more freedom in her religious life? Was she hiding behind her vows and using the title "Sister" as a means to her own ends, or did she honestly feel a religious calling that led her to take up the cause of women's equality and reproductive autonomy? Would she have taken up this fight if she had not entered religious life?
10. Should the Catholic Church have any say regarding reproductive rights at all? Should men have a voice or a vote in how women manage their reproductive lives, especially since women have no voice in how men manage theirs?
11. Should Catholic women become officially recognized, ordained priests? Should priests be allowed to marry? Should celibacy be optional for both priests and women religious?
12. Maggie's anger and emotionally damaged personal background played a big part in her unrelenting passion to take on the most powerful religion in the world and fight for change. Is it harder to garner the needed energy to take on powerful institutions and force change for purely altruistic, "it's the right thing to do" reasons, rather than for personal ones?
13. Could Maggie have ever found peace in her earthly life, or was she a natural-born fighter who was only happy when she was fighting for a cause?

CPSIA information can be obtained
at www.ICGtesting.com
Printed in the USA
BVHW040346070722
641540BV00006B/54/J